David Herter

Brian Stableford

This edition of

ONE WHO DISAPPEARED

is limited to 100 jacketed hardcovers signed by
David Herter and Brian Stableford, and 500 unsigned hardcovers.

This is copy

From David Herter, whose work *Kirkus Reviews* called "distinctive and imaginative, moving to its own disconcerting logic," comes a poignant and masterful novel about a group of artists from the hinterland of Europe between the World Wars, who clash with the clockwork of Time.

Hollywood, 1949. Czech composer Paul Haas lives comfortably at Universal Studios with his wife and family. But he's haunted by memories of the past, of home and of friends and loved ones lost in the recent war. When a telegram arrives, hinting at answers to mysteries that trouble him, it leads Paul to Brentwood Hills and a startling revelation. Driven by what he has learned, Paul feels compelled to journey to his homeland to perform a necessary act of devotion.

Prague, Czechoslovak Republic, 1929. In his beloved homeland at the zenith of her brief democratic flourishing, Paul is drawn into the orbit of Karel Capek, author of Rossum's Universal Robots, and his brother Josef, an avant-garde artist, both blissfully unaware of the shadow of impending war.

After an encounter with a young flautist, who alone spies his secret, Paul seeks out a mysterious village where his mentor, the eccentric composer Leoš J——, had snatched a melody from the air and disrupted the fabric of time. Now, in ruins far older than Christianity, Paul embarks on a temporal odyssey towards a great conflagration, where artists from his homeland, Europe and America will join to challenge the coming chaos.

With *On the Overgrown Path*, *The Luminous Depths* and now *One Who Disappeared*, David Herter has crafted a singular epic of time travel; a reverie on the World Wars; an explication of a near-forgotten strand of Eastern European science fiction, music, and painting; and a memorable evocation of those artists who, for a brief moment, changed the heartbeat of the world.

ONE WHO DISAPPEARED

BOOKS BY DAVID HERTER FROM PS PUBLISHING

The first two volumes of the Czech trilogy

On the Overgrown Path (2006)

"Just as there are touches of D.M. Thomas's *The White Hotel* in Herter's depiction through his beloved Janácek of the warp and weave of a civilization under stress, so there are suggestions of Algernon Blackwood's "The Willows" in the way he spells his great composer into tranced rapport with whatever breathes there and does not wish to be taken into music."

—John Clute

The Luminous Depths (2008)

"The Luminous Depths has a richness of prose and a density of allusion and ideas reminiscent of authors like Aldiss and Wolfe -- and, incidentally, it is a page-turning cracker of a horror story. Outside his homeland, Karel Capek may be remembered primarily through his legacy of the term "Robot." It is Herter's achievement in this novella to lead us through the narrow window of that single chthonic word to a rich evocation of a fragile, doomed period of Central European history."

—Stephen Baxter

OTHER BOOKS BY DAVID HERTER

Ceres Storm (2000)
Evening's Empire (2002)
October Dark (2010)
The Cold Heavens (forthcoming)

DAVID HERTER

ONE
WHO
DISAPPEARED

INTRODUCTION BY **BRIAN STABLEFORD**

2011

One Who Disappeared Copyright © 2011 David Herter

Introduction Copyright © 2011 Brian Stableford

Cover art and White Mountain poster Copyright © 2011 Vladimir Verano

The right of David Herter to be identified as Author of this Work has been asserted by him in accordance with the Copyright, Designs and Patents Act 1988.

Published in November 2011 by PS Publishing Ltd. by arrangement with the author. All rights reserved by the author.

FIRST EDITION

ISBN
978-1-848630-34-5 (Signed Edition)
978-1-848630-33-8

This book is a work of fiction. Names, characters, places and incidents either are products of the author's imagination or are used fictitiously. Any resemblance to actual events or locales or persons, living or dead, is entirely coincidental.

Design and layout by Alligator Tree Graphics.
Printed in England by the MPG Biddles Group.

PS Publishing Ltd / Grosvenor House / 1 New Road / Hornsea, HU18 1PG / England

e-mail: editor@pspublishing.co.uk • *Internet:* http://www.pspublishing.co.uk

INTRODUCTION

One Who Disappeared is the third volume of a trilogy, which began with *On the Overgrown Path* and continued in *The Luminous Depths*. There are, of course, numerous ways to concoct a trilogy; many are merely three-decker novels, others follow the N-shaped trajectory favored by scriptwriting theorists, in which a set-up phase is followed by a phase in which everything goes wrong, in order that the concluding phase can take the form of a soaring ascent. The most ambitious and most appropriate way to plan and build a trilogy, however, is the inverted pyramid.

The inverted pyramid begins with a phase that is economical, neat and self-contained; a perfectly-satisfactory work of art in its own right. On top of that is placed something much larger; not merely, or even necessarily, larger in terms of mere wordage, but something more substantial, with greater reach and grasp, which is, once again, whole in itself, perhaps to the extent of seeming conclusive. On top of that is then placed something so much larger, thematically and ambitiously, as to seem vast. The escalation of scale is, in itself, easy enough to contrive, but what is difficult is to keep the whole structure in balance, so that it stands up and does not wobble, in spite of its seeming defiance of safety. The third volume of such a trilogy must not only absorb its predecessors into a coherent whole but must demonstrate their perfect balance, prove that they function as a pivot and an intermediate support that are both essential and reliable. Without that, the whole edifice falls.

David Herter's trilogy, to which *One Who Disappeared* provides a spectacular and moving conclusion, does not fall; on the contrary, it remains perfectly suspended, sturdy and elegant—and by virtue of its topography, it does not, like more myopic literary projects, taper off into soothing closure, but opens wide to an even vaster and more glorious universe of possibility.

One Who Disappeared brings back the key characters carefully introduced in the earlier volumes, who include four individuals known to history—the composer Leoš Janácek (never named in full, and usually called the Maestro), his pupil Pavel Haas, the artist/writer Josef Capek and his younger brother, the writer Karel Capek—and one who never achieved fame in our world but is no less important to the world within the text, the flautist and sometime resistance leader Magdalena, who provides this volume with its title. Bringing these characters back is no trivial matter of dusting them off, winding them up and setting them going again, because the deaths of the four historical simulacra are a significant aspect of the earlier elements of the series and a vital aspect of the theme of the whole project. In order to extend their literary roles, time has to be unraveled and tied in knots—but such painful unwinding and awkward knotting is also an important component of the earlier elements of the series, and a vital aspect of the theme of the whole project.

In order to perform this narrative function, the author provides a "time machine", but it is no mere glorified bicycle; it is a machine partly intrinsic to the nature of the world, which participates in and draws energy from what the narrative calls *the Heartbeat of the World*, and partly manufactured by human creativity—specifically, by music, and by the technical evolution of music from its roots in folksong to its analysis and alchemical transmutation by such twentieth-century composers as Igor Stravinsky and Arnold Schoenberg. The activation of this kind of time machine is no mere matter of flicking a switch; it is a difficult, costly and not-overly-predictable business—as it ought to be, given the kind of narrative and historical labor that it is obliged to carry out. In the eventuality—which is an eventuality, and not an end—the device works all the more magnificently for working in mysterious ways, and so does the trilogy.

One of the seeming puzzles of modern aesthetics has been the divergent evolution of the visual arts, literature and music. The pioneering philosopher who reinvented the term "aesthetics" in the mid-eighteenth century, Alexander Baumgarten, belonged to the school of Christian Wolff, the most ardent follower of Gottfried Leibniz—who had argued in his Theodicy that because God was good, any flaws in Creation must be inherent in the creative process rather than the results of mistakes or malevolence on the part of the Creator: a position sometimes summed up, especially by its detractors, as the conviction that we live in "the best of all possible worlds". Baumgarten reiterated this conviction in his representation of art as "secondary creativity", in which the artist, struggling with inherently flawed and frustrating processes, ought to do his very best to mimic God and produce simulacra of the best possible world: that of experience. The production of images of other possible worlds—what he called "heterocosmic creativity"—was, in Baumgarten's view, inherently bad art.

The history of the visual arts since Baumgarten's day has, in large measure, been a heroic tale of the gradual, obstinate and triumphant evolution of heterocosmic creativity, from a boom in mythological painting through the advent of impressionism to the deconstructive endeavors of abstract expressionism. The history of literature has, meanwhile, been very largely a story of the meticulous development of a new naturalism in the novel, of which Baumgarten would have approved thoroughly, given that almost all the literature produced prior to his own era had been blatantly "heterocosmic". Most of the literature produced afterwards was heterocosmic too, but it was castigated more successfully by critics than the parallel trends in heterocosmic art. Music never fitted comfortably into Baumgarten's thesis, in that it was never apparent that music could be "naturalistic" in any meaningful sense, but he compensated for the difficulty with a theory of harmony that elevated the work of Johann Sebastian Bach and the more conservative works of Mozart to a pinnacle of unsurpassable achievement.

Heterocosmic literature—of which *One Who Disappeared* is not merely an example but an exceedingly self-conscious and philosophically-sophisticated example—has not yet quite recovered from Baumgartenian stigmatization in terms of critical evaluation, although it does seem to be en route. Even music, despite the essential dodginess of Baumgarten's fudge, still suffers to a not-inconsiderable extent, reflected in Herter's narrative by numerous acknowledgements of the fact that the innovations of composers like Stravinsky and Schoenberg attracted considerable and sustained animosity from many critics. The narrative also takes care to acknowledge the particular problems occasioned by hybrid art-forms, such as Josef Capek's book illustrations and stage sets, and—most especially—the awkwardly-knotty combination of narrative and music contained in operas. Such self-consciousness is not uncommon in contemporary fiction, and even philosophical sophistication is not so very rare, but where Herter's trilogy becomes truly exceptional is in tying an even-more-Gordian knot between this whole complex of aesthetic conundrums and the philosophical bedrock from which it sprung to begin with: theodicy—the problem of evil.

The period of time covered and re-covered by the trilogy, that of 1930's and 40's Europe, of which the particular biographies of the real individuals whose simulacra feature therein are tragically illustrative, represented something of a break in history, because it was an era in which the hollowness of the Leibnizian apology for the morality of Creation, long since mocked into near-oblivion by Voltaire, became not merely glaringly obvious but utterly, almost unspeakably, horrible. It was an era in which Creation screamed for heterocosmic reconstruction: a project impossible, of course, in terms of primary creation, but not in terms of secondary creation—which does, after all, have a reality of its own, as a forceful aspect of human experience.

Once the discovery has been reluctantly accepted, in the face of overwhelming evidence, that we not only live in a frankly malevolent universe but are inclined to participate in that malevolence if we are not extremely careful, the question becomes a matter of how best to do it, as carefully as possible—or, more specifically, what armaments are useful for the purpose of living well in hostile circumstances, and how to deploy them. The attempt to answer that question and its corollaries is not merely the best endeavor of ambitious works of art but the whole function of art, the medium and its messages alike. *One Who Disappeared* is heroic in confronting the matter directly, scientific in tackling it analytically, artistic in tackling it elegantly, brilliant in achieving such a marvelous equilibrium, and—neither last, save in the arbitrary ordering of this list, nor least—authentically inspirational in its heterocosmic obstinacy.

Brian Stableford
October 2011

ONE WHO DISAPPEARED

CONTENTS

BEFORE	9
THREE: CHARLATAN	19
TWO: THE LIMPING PILGRIM	107
ONE: WHITE MOUNTAIN	267
AFTER	363

For DM

" . . . *the sun a severed neck.*"

—*Zone* by Apollinaire,

A note on pronunciation:

Karel Čapek: KAH-rel CHOP-ek
Josef Čapek: YO-sef CHOP-ek
Leoš Janácek: LAY-osh YAHNA-check
sčasování: CHAZ-oh-VAHN-ee

BEFORE

"*F*ind your seats."
"*Le concert commencera bientôt.*"
"*Finden sie ihre sitze.*"

Whispers and murmurs—chaste, as though at worship. Clogs scrape the floor as latecomers gather on stools, on benches, in the corners, in the nooks and crannies of the oblong attic.

"*The concert will soon begin.*"

Kerosene lanterns gleam from angled rafters and cast wan shadows in every direction, and the voices, no louder than the clogs, rustle down from the tall gables like unseen birds.

"*Trouvez vos chaises.*"
"*Das konzert wird in kürze beginnen.*"

Wearing threadbare clothes they shuffle toward any mismatched stool or kindling chair or pile of loose excelsior that has not yet been taken, and there is always more room in the nooks of the Hannover Barracks's attic, which tonight is their Rudolfinum, their National Theater. How to count them all? They might slip into their own shadows. They clutch to their malnourished bodies the ghostly tatters of lost lives and professions: here a doctor, a chanteuse; there a cobbler, a maternity nurse, an engineer. In the dim high attic of plain, red-dotted tile and bare wood, in the deep shadows and wavering light they blend one into the next, from Prague,

Krakow, Vienna, Brno, Teplice, Kutna Hora. Jew, Gentile, Roma, most are clad in the same poor garments that they wore here, the only possessions they retained when they were lined up by fours in their towns of deportation. *Transports, transports.* The whispered anxieties of the old life have translated into the new, where the talk is always of *transports east*, always of the *black birds* of the Waffen SS arriving to demand another thousand victims. Most are *Unprotected* from these lotteries and the *forty-and-eight* freight cars, and spend their days striving—beyond the simple human needs, beyond food and clean water and medicine and cigarettes, beyond the illicit electrical lines for hot plates, beyond the right of cohabitation liaisons bought with a half loaf of bread or ten cigarettes—striving for that blessed role of *Protected*. Yet this evening, if only for a few hours, this anxious democracy, administered by the Council of Elders, supported by AK-1 and AK-2 and their Untouchables, surrenders here in the Hannover attic to the pleasant dictatorship of a single conductor over his musicians, though the conductor has not yet arrived.

"*Le concert commencera bientôt.*"

"*Find your seats.*"

The musicians begin to tune their instruments, in the Ghetto Theresienstadt, in December, in 1942.

Startled by the long low note of an oboe, heads turn toward the end of the oblong attic. On a raised plywood stage, five men in tuxedo coats and woolen pants seat themselves on fine oaken chairs. They call their group the Sudeten Wind Quintet—named for their barracks, not their political affiliation. Behind them a legless piano is propped on mismatched stools, unoccupied. To the oboe's melancholy glow is added a flute's silken fire. Smiles break out. Steaming cans of *wrucken*, a weak soup of broth and white turnips, are passed back and forth, as are cigarettes, though smoking is not allowed in the Ghetto.

"*Finden sie ihre stühle.*"

"Time to wait, nonetheless," remarks a young Turk with dark hair and a demonic profile. It is he who repaired and retuned the broken piano, and arranged for it to be propped on stools. Afterward in an impromptu recital, he dispatched his favorite Mozart, Brahms and J____. Now, arms folded, dressed in a twill and brash burgundy-collared suitcoat mended by his sister Eliska, he leans back in a fine Biedermeyer chair, happy to have other people making the music.

At twenty-three, Gideon Klein could pass for a decade older.

"Time to wait," mutters one of five young men who sit with Klein and borrow some of his attitude.

"Gideon, you look pleased with yourself, and before the performance even begins!" This from a wiry boy in threadbare tweed, presentable but for the lining that has been torn out of the sleeves and which he now cups in his hands.

Gideon smiles. "I sense Ančerl is wringing the suspense."

"From you?" asks another, stowing a cigarette just passed to him. "Gideon Israel Klein, you have an iron constitution."

"Egon Israel Kohn, if mine is iron, yours is steel."

Laughter from the other five who sit around in chairs and stools not as fine as Gideon's, but Gideon is the guest of honor tonight.

"Tell us what it feels like, Gideon." Egon scratches at a flea bite on his narrow wrist. "To be a famous composer about to attend a concert in his honor."

"Or to be sitting in such a fine chair," adds young Meyer. All five have an easy, insouciant air; all five were once part of the AK-2 *aufbaukommando*—the construction detail first deployed to the decommissioned Fortress, and therefore, *Protected*. They built these barracks, and five others, and watched as the Fortress intended to hold a thousand people slowly filled up with twenty-thousand men, women and children.

"He cannot speak, he is so happy." Egon shares a grin with Meyer.

"No. I am thrilled, Egon, to have an entire concert devoted to my music." He straightens his shoulders. He looks around for his sister Eliska but spies Irena, who sits with her mother under a kerosene lamp. Dark-haired with a pale oval face, she smiles at him from across the attic. Gideon recalls the mingling scents of excelsior, rose-water and sweat, the taste of her cherry-juice lips, the feel of her slender neck with its fine dark hair along the nape, and her nipples of velveteen purple. The fucking had been brief but passionate. He swallows against a pang in the back of his throat. Perhaps another encounter will be arranged.

"Yet you are not playing the piano?"

"*Hmmm?*"

"You are not playing the piano, or giving the audience a lecture before the music begins, as usual?"

"Gideon is daydreaming."

"Yes. A marvelous dream, I think."

He forces his eyes to the stage, sits up straighter and blows into his hands: hands which—for two short years of his young life—were famous throughout Prague; hands that dazzled Jew and Gentile alike with their prowess on the concert grand; in the National Theater, in the Rudolfinum, even in faraway Venice. "Tonight, I am being *serenaded*."

"Have you heard it played yet? Your *Divertimento*?"

"He heard it in Prague, in '38," says Egon.

"I meant *here*, idiot."

Gideon shakes his head. "I stayed away from rehearsals." He transcribed the piece from memory, writing it down onto coarse brown paper smuggled in by the Czech gendarmes—

A rustle, as the crowd looks over its collective shoulder. Gideon turns, hoping for Eliska, expecting Ančerl, but it's V. Ullmann, showing little obeisance in this church of music; he *clomps*. Taking up a stool that has been saved for him, he nods at Gideon. V. Israel Ullmann, the camp's published critic, is also the most senior composer in a Ghetto full of them.

"Viktor loves your music," remarks Egon.

"But will he love the performance?" mutters Meyer, who helps to print the newspaper. His hands are blackened with the ink, which he claims wards off the bedbugs.

To the oboe and flute, Zdenek adds his clarinet, fluttering up and down the scales, its wispy, lackadaisical tone contrasting against the brittle clacking of its keys.

Scratching an itch on the back of his hand, Gideon thinks of Prague in better days, before the paper summons was slipped under his door. The freedom that was not freedom, in the aftermath of Nuremberg, yet now seems like a gift from Heaven. Forbidden to play the piano in public or have his compositions performed, he used a pseudonym, appearing at concerts given by the Moravian-Silesian society, skulking through the streets of the Lesser Town to the apartment of Professor K. Wallerstein at U Pujeovny 5/III where, as though from a fairy tale, a crowd of Jews would melt out of the afternoon and assemble for several hours of music until the 5 p.m. curfew loomed. The most ardent of music lovers would stay the night, playing everything from Mozart to folk tunes until dawn made it safe to—

Among tuba, flute and clarinet, which have been tossing up portions of his *Divertimento*, the latter quotes lengthily of the Adagio. A melody that is not Gideon's but the *Maestro*'s, taken from his song cycle *Diary of One Who Disappeared*.

He smiles.

And, listening, he recalls that he did not always stay the entire night. Once, for a girl, he risked the curfew. A lonely walk down the cobblestone street, free, in the Prague dark; the early morning hours after a joyous night of performing.

"Tell us what you are thinking, Gideon Israel."

"Yes, Gideon Israel."

Knowing that he is being humored, Gideon says, "Egon Israel, Meyer Israel. I am reminded of the days of the occupation." Those days when the darkness was inching steadily across them all, unseen. He startles—the horn player has joined in, blurting out a serial variation on the Maestro's tune. The clarinet joins. They chase one another into the distance of the loft.

"Gideon, what are you thinking?" asks Egon.

"Once," he says, setting his bony elbows on his knees, "in the winter of '41, something miraculous happened to me." He adds, "I've never spoken of it before."

Except to Eliska, he thinks.

They stare. Egon, Meyer, Benedict, Gustav, Manfred. They are younger than he; two are amateur musicians, two are poets, one a painter.

"Tell us," says Gustav, the painter. "What was it, Gideon?"

"Did you meet Charles Chaplin?"

"Douglas Fairbanks?"

"Greta Garbo?"

Shaking his head, Gideon sees it then, spinning out of the dark sky.

"It happened after an evening concert, such as those at your uncle's house." He smiles. "I had another place to be," the others chuckle, "so I ventured out in the early morning hours."

"Curfew?" asks Egon, who has not heard the story but wishes to set it up properly for the others, no doubt.

"Yes. Curfew. Walking along the Ulice Heidelberg in Lesser Town."

They nod knowingly, even Manfred, a country boy from Olomouc who has never set foot in Prague.

"It was snowing, like it is snowing tonight. The street was white, glowing in the lamplight. The windows were dark. Every now and then a light peeked out from behind a blackout curtain, but otherwise you felt that Prague was asleep, in uneasy dreams."

"But not the *Naciste*, eh?" Egon jostles Gideon with his elbow.

Gideon ignores him. "The snow was falling out of the dark, materializing, as out of nothing." They nod, recalling nothing older than the huddle in the Brunnenpark yard that evening, when looking up into the darkness of the sky to escape the drudgery of Theresienstadt all around. "Millions upon millions of flakes settling down over the Old Town Square, into the black Vltava. Unending. And I stared up, blinking against those flakes as they kissed my eyelashes." He smiles, seeing it then. A single flake, spinning. "Spinning," he says, "from out of the dark. Not falling with the flakes, but appearing *amongst* them."

Meyer touches his forearm and gestures with his eyes. Eliska waves from across the room; Gideon feels a measure of ease he had not known he lacked. His shoulders relax; he thanks Meyer with a glance.

"What was it?" says Benedict, the writer.

"I thought, at first, it was another snowflake. Larger than the others. But a snowflake nonetheless. Pointed at the edges, and spinning as it fell ahead of me, thirty meters in the air."

"*Not a snowflake?*"

Gideon smiles. He has them. They are as rapt as the audience at his lecture the previous week, when he read from and discussed K. Čapek's translations of Apollinaire. "I knew it wasn't, almost immediately. It fell slightly slower than the snow. So that . . . so that, spinning, it seemed to be rising slowly upwards against the never-ending fall."

Silent, they stare upwards at the skylight, perhaps conjuring the brittle night sky above the snow-laden roof of the concert hall.

"Perhaps caught on some current of air?" says Egon.

"But the air," says Benedict. "It would have moved the snowflakes, too."

"I moved toward it and it descended, slowly, toward me. I felt dizzy, as though the sidewalk were heaving. I was happy from the night's playing, and filled with that adrenaline that we would feel when evading the curfew. Before the adrenaline became a permanent part of our lives."

The others laugh.

"I was stunned. Staring up. It was close enough I could discern the sharpness of its many wings."

"Wings?"

"Wings, Gideon?"

"I blinked, and blinked again. Yet there it remained. You remember those days. You remember. We felt always like a finger was pointed at us, even then. We lurked in the shadows. We avoided the eyes of the Gentiles. And here was this mystery, pointing its finger at me. Falling toward the cobbles ahead of me.

"I stopped. Afraid now. Though I could not have told you why. I was alone. The object was clearly light, of some sort of paper. Harmless. Yet there it fell, pointing its finger at *me*, Gideon Klein. And so I stopped. Stopped dead along the Ulice Heidelberg, wanting it to fall ahead of me. But some complex geometry seemed to take this into account, and it, falling slower than the snow—but naturally, not changing its course—came toward me even as the flakes drifted naturally along the street. Floating down directly to strike me, light as a feather, here." He touches his chest.

They stare at his finger.

The clarinetist has not stopped practicing the melody from the Adagio. Gideon is distracted. He recalls the lines in the Maestro's song cycle:

The sun rises
The shadows grow.
Oh, what shall I have lost?
Who will give it back to me?

The five pairs of eyes have returned to his face.

"And. . . ?"

"And." He smiles. "It bounced off my chest, and fluttered down to the ground."

"You picked it up?" asks Benedict.

He nods. "Nervously. Feeling the finger pointing at me. Feeling the tall dark buildings on either side of the street watching me. I picked it up. The pointed folds, like petals of a strange flower. The paper, glowing amidst the snowfall." He meets their eyes, and allows a dramatic pause.

"And?" presses Meyer, smiling.

"And behind me, a voice called out, '*Sie!*'"

"*Naciste,*" says Egon, satisfied at having predicted the course of the story.

"Yes. *Naciste.* I did not turn. I did not want to meet his eyes. '*Sie!*' he shouted again. I shoved my hands in my pockets and continued walking, fearful, any moment, of the crack of gunfire, and the bullet striking my back."

"And were you shot?"

Gideon ignores Egon. "I continued walking, and again he said, *Sie!* Not too loudly. His voice wavered a bit. Which caused me to stop and turn. A single soldier in black."

"*Waffen SS.*"

Almost imperceptibly, Gideon's hand clenches. He recalls the numbing fear, how his chest grew hollow and cold. He nods. "The louse was drunk. He carried no gun. Wandering out of a lady's apartment, perhaps. But now he staggered toward me. He tried to keep his bearing, but the snow made him dizzy. He stared down at the ground. And he walked, you see, toward what I had dropped."

"Did you run?"

"I stood still. I was perhaps a fifty meters ahead of him. I knew I could get away, in the state he was in. I figured that once he saw the object, its mystery would distract him. As he leaned—very awkwardly— over to pick it up, I could have run. But I remained.

"I too was curious, of course. He looked at it as I had. He turned it over and over in his hands, touching the pointed vanes." Again, Gideon pauses. This time it is to slurp from the can that Egon has passed him; *wrucken* full of turnips and bits of fat, recently cooked on an illicit hot plate. Uncharacteristically, the broth is hot and tremendously reviving.

"What happened, Gideon?" says Benedict, taking the can in turn.

"What happened?" Gideon's hot breath smokes fiercely in the air. "Why, he *unfolded it.*" A demonic smile.

Rustling. People glancing back. Murmurs rising to sporadic applause. Maestro Ančerl has appeared. He ducks his long frame under the lintel beam near the stairs, waving his cork baton—the same baton he once waved from the podium of the National Theater.

"And . . . !"

Gideon's smile gutters. He sees it again, that miraculous thing.

"And . . . the *Naciste . . . vanished.*"

If not for the applause, and for Ančerl now passing by, they might have peppered him with questions. Egon might have chided him for making up stories. But the musicians now have their conductor, and the concert is imminent. Only Benedict, sixteen years old, cannot let the story lie. Into Gideon's ear he shouts, "*Vanished into the snow, you mean!*"

Maestro Ančerl strides up behind the box that serves as podium. The five musicians settle their instruments on their laps.

"Vanished," says Gideon, with finality, folding his arms across his chest.

Gone from Prague, he tells himself.

"Good evening, friends," announces Ančerl, resonantly.

Applause. Some turn on their benches and stools to smile in Gideon's direction. His heart pounds.

Gone from Prague. Gone to hell.

He feels the music in the air—the Maestro's music.

He sits back in his chair. He glances over at Eliska, pleased to see her here, and safe. And seeing too the *Naciste* vanishing from the dark, snowy street.

"*And you never looked up, Gideon?*" she had whispered, when he told her. "*Never wished to see such snowflakes falling from the sky again?*"

Yes. During every snowfall . . . I hope to see them.

Even this evening.

The sky over Ghetto Terezin is ripe with such clouds.

THREE: CHARLATAN

"Gideon Klein could not reconcile himself to seeing an artist of Haas's caliber not participating in the musical activities. So, one day, to wake him from his lethargy, Klein put in front of him several sheets of manuscript paper, on which he himself drew the musical staff, and urged Haas to stop wasting time."

—*Music in Terezin* by Joža Karas

1. THE BROTHERS HAAS

He shifts his haunches on the wicker stool and leans farther over what Hugo calls his "desk", the flat panel of a 35mm movieola, in California, in 1949.

The stave paper is studio-issued, stamped at the corner *PROPERTY OF UNIVERSAL STUDIOS MUSIC DEPARTMENT*; it distracts him from row upon row of empty, linear stave lines and an idea hovering in the aftermath of the just-run scene—piano, clarinet and muted trumpet in slouching roundelay. With the curtains once more thrown open, sunlight hammers onto the paper, further heightening the crest in purple ink. *PROPERTY OF UNIVERSAL STUDIOS MUSIC DEPARTMENT.* Dust motes hover, as does a scent of hot plastic and steel. His ebon hair, graying at the temples, is combed high and away from his forehead,. His profile, though softened from his years in America, remains formidable. He wears a freshly-pressed black-striped cotton shirt, a black tie clipped at an angle with a silver-plated *Luxembourg Lines* crest. His sleeves are rolled up, his tie loosened. The clip—a gift from Sona on his fiftieth birthday—along with the silver-and-pearl plated Timex on his right wrist, from Hugo, are his most ostentatious possessions. Eraser shavings dapple his trousers.

Paul Haas sets down the pencil, spreads his fingers, then makes a fist, trying to rid the kinks from his knuckles.

The screenplay bound with brass clips, the timing sheets,

the mug of cold tea and several worn India rubber erasers clutter his desk along with the pristine stave paper, whose corner is anchored by a speckled black rock retrieved from the beach at Carmel, a rock his daughter Olga has insisted bears the likeness of Beethoven, and his son William that of Clara Bell.

The bungalow reigns in silence. No more noisy meetings between Hugo and his set designers, or Hugo and his editors, or Hugo and his directors of photography on the other, far-more-cluttered side of the office. The wicker chairs and plush couch are empty. Cigarette smoke has dispersed. He craves a cigarette, but makes no move toward the Chesterfield pack in his breast pocket. He pulls the spotting notes front-and-center. Typed out by Sal Kaplan, his music editor, all but three entries on the blue form are checked off.

12 seconds. Reel 2 scene 11B. Int. burlesque house. source music.
9 seconds. Reel 2 scene 13 Ext park. Harvey fighting Haas, dolly in to extreme close-up on fist.

And the one he's currently working on:

14 seconds. Reel 3 scene 15A Day from car to trees, Harvey leaps out onto curb, pans across with him as he strides into hotel entrance.

The idea occurred the fourth time he ran the scene on the movieola: a slow, tricked up bass line in the piano, with a lazy-eight quarrel by the clarinet and trumpet—a variation on the somber, jazz-infused passacaglia in the main titles. Just the sort of cliché Hugo's been pressuring him to include, complicated with a tricky change in meter as Laurence Harvey strolls through the revolving doors on his way to the fisticuffs scene.

Unaware he's doing so, Paul taps out the rhythm on the flat panel, his wedding ring of modest Bohemian gold now a castanet. He snatches up the pencil and draws a bar on the first two left-hand measures. As he sketches the notes with impatient flicks and dabs, his other hand pins the tricky rhythm, the heel of his right foot offering a straight beat. He nabs the bass line with little x's, picturing the scene run so many times it exists as a fourteen-second continuum: Laurence Harvey springing from his black Jaguar to the curb and strolling through the rain to the Luxor's revolving doors, into the lobby where Hugo—playing the older swain of Harvey's *ingénue* girlfriend—waits in shadow. The clarinet and trumpet shadowbox in the upper registers, growing more agitated as the camera whips past the revolving doors.

Paul feels a simple pleasure in the task. With the scene finished, marked with rough approximations of timings and action, he lays down the pencil nub and wipes the shavings from his trousers. He stretches. Sunlight flows like liquid over his sinewy forearms, drops his shadow to a carpet etched with cigarette butts, spotlights one of Hugo's blue slippers. An aureate glow strikes framed posters on the opposite wall—brother's bit parts—*The Fighting Kentuckians*, *A Bell for Adano*, and *The Princess and the Pirate*, as well as less ornate posters for Hugo's own films—*Pick-up* and *Shakedown*. And soon, *Edge of Hell*. His wristwatch says *11.05*, but it's stopped again. Winding it, he tries to find the Belmont clock. Hugo's always moving it, sometimes setting it on his desk to remind him of a deadline, other times burying it in a pile of clothes for the laundry department to cart away.

Paul combs back his hair. Tugs his tie into position with quick, sharp movements. Adjusts the tie clip, smiling down at the Luxembourg crest and its promise of a cruise around the world *one of these days*. Pats the cigarettes in his breast pocket then stretches again, extending his legs.

He steps down from the stool. *Time for a walk.*

Bob Hope, leering out from *The Princess and the Pirate*, seems to agree.

Studying the posters, Paul wonders how long before Hugo removes all reminders of his *bit-part acting* career. The serious Hugo, born out of the tragedy three months earlier, is enthralled in his new *important* show, rightly so, and looks forward to the day this last one—"*the last of my hackwork*"—is wrapped. On the new show he is once again writer and director, an extension of his successful efforts at Barrandov in

Prague before Paul, Sona and their daughter Olga, along with Hugo and his wife and daughter, emigrated.

The *new* Hugo.

He smiles.

As though to chastise him, a photo of six-year-old Zikmund—Hugo's son—watches from the bookcase, brown hair combed carefully across his pale, serious forehead, over eyes the same color as his father's; the corner of its dustless bronze frame bedecked with a black ribbon.

Tangerine sunlight, Hugo calls it.

As Paul steps from the air-conditioned bungalow onto the Fourth Alley, the sunlight hits him full force, the warm breeze ruffling his collar. He squints up past the water tower and its *UNIVERSAL* crest to the cloudless sky. Not quite *tangerine* today; perhaps luminous Czech-made *limonade*. Shadows fall sharp. The breeze is redolent of diesel and eucalyptus, with a hint of salty Pacific ocean.

He pulls the pack of Chesterfields from his shirt pocket, taps out a cigarette, lights it. He inhales deeply.

The alley, serving as a conduit between Studios A and C, is practically empty at this hour. Earlier, a mob of French Revolutionaries in powdered wigs tromped past the bungalow, much to Hugo's delight. Now the alley is occupied only by a few burly men lugging a palm tree. One of them, a negro gaffer on Hugo's *pick-up*, nods to Paul, cigar jutting up like the lifting of a hat. Paul nods in turn, and they, *citizens of the movies*, part ways as would Paul with a fellow soldier in the Emperor's army, on midnight watch in Brunn.

He chooses not to head all the way down Fourth, remembering that the way was blocked with free-standing sets for the new Tyrone Power film. He cuts down between Studios B-3 and B-4, hands in the pockets of his coat, head tipped back to receive the slices of sunlight.

How colossal the studios seemed in 1935, when the newly arrived Haas brothers toured Twentieth Century Fox, Metro-Goldwyn-Mayer,

Universal—each a miniature country with its own fenced borders, with its own police force and fire brigade, with simulacra of mountains, forests, cities, with suburbs and housing, with serfs and margraves. In Prague's Barrandov studios the president had carried the moniker *the Louis B. Mayer of Czech films* yet had been approachable, even ordinary. Approachable and ordinary in a way that the true Kings of Hollywood were not. Paul expected to glimpse them only from afar, yet within a month of his arrival found himself being introduced to the *real* Louis B. Mayer at *Madeleine's*. Not only cigar-chomping Mayer but gin-swilling Ronald Coleman and suave George Sanders, who had heard Paul's *The Insect Play* at the Metropolitan and was frighteningly effusive in his praise. Mayer, on the other hand, quipped, "Opera composer, eh? We've had trouble with *your sort*," and slowly waved a Cuban cigar in front of Paul's neck, as though beheading him with the ember.

"*Hey!*" Behind him a young American voice shouts, "Mr. Haas!" A gofer in a canary-blue suit runs toward him. "Glad I caught ya!" The kid waves a light blue envelope. "Telegram, sir."

He drops the cigarette butt, steps on it. "For Hugo?" he says, in careful English. "I am on my way to see him . . . "

"Nah. It's for you. Paul, right?"

After a pause, "Yes. I am Paul."

Out of breath, the boy hands it to him. "Thanks, Mr. Haas."

"Thank you."

Hugo would have tipped the boy; Paul reaches into his trouser pockets to fish for a quarter, but by then the boy is halfway down the alley. He starts walking again, rounding the corner.

WESTERN UNION LOS ANGELES, CA
To: Paul Haas
UNIVERSAL STUDIOS HOLLYWOOD
Bungalow 221

He runs his thumb under the flap, unfolds the paper.

Sunlight turns the paper transparent, outside bleeding through to the inside. He holds it at the proper angle to read the double-spaced typescript.

> TO PAUL HAAS. WE MUST MEET TO DISCUSS A PROJECT. 116 N. ROCKINGHAM AVE BRENTWOOD PARK. TODAY. MUST BE BETWEEN 3 AND 6 PM TODAY.

Erich Korngold lives in Brentwood. But Korngold wouldn't send a telegram. He'd telephone directly, asking to meet at Warner Brothers, or some lovely restaurant. And would sign his name, surely.

Today?

Between 3 p.m. and 6 p.m.

He senses something Imperial, as though this were a *summons*. Or is it the fault of the telegrammatic style? Therefore: a studio producer? A famous actor? A *margrave*? He feels the urge to dismiss it.

Too soon.

He'll respond: let's meet next week, I have a scene to complete. Yet the telegram promises a mystery. As well as an afternoon away from drudgery. He ponders the question until he reaches the doorway of Studio 3-C. CLOSED SET / DIRECTOR: HUGO HAAS, reads the placard. Tucking the telegram in his pocket, he pounds on the door. A moment later, it groans open. Walt Thomson, the lighting technician squints at the sunlight. "Hey, it's Paul."

He uses some slang taught him by Hugo. "*How do*, Walt." Grateful for the shadow, if not the cloud of stale effects smoke, Paul steps into the studio, past the baffles and rows of cabinets, onto the bustling stage.

Today, the set is fully assembled and lighted, and Paul stops, stunned.

For the past fifteen years *home* has faded into memories both fond and terrible. *Home* has been reduced to newspaper clippings, to letters, to photographs relegated to the closet in his study. Home is no longer the House of 9 Biskupska Street in Brno, capital of Moravia, of the Czechoslovak Republic: it's 4111 Delmonica Drive, Pasadena, California, USA, with Sona and Olga and little William. *Home*, that other home, is a dream they conjure amongst themselves in conversation—Brno cathedral, the Monkey Mountains, the Cabbage Market, Špilberk Hill and the old dragon at the Town Hall, as they once were or as they are, or as they can no longer be, now that the Soviets have forever severed them from that world.

Yet at this moment, spread across the far side of the studio, *Home* basks as a brilliant cyclorama vista of linden trees and bucolic green fields, of rolling pine hills and purpling skies. Moravia, lost forever—except for here, and now.

Driven by the dark tragedy of three months past, Hugo Haas has rekindled a dream of it, here, now, among the drab industry of Studio 3-C.

"The spiritual star, Fixtus, has detached itself from the cosmos and is speeding towards our earth. The resurrection of all the dead is at hand. The first harbingers are on their way already. The spirits of the departed will walk amongst us like living men, and the ravenous beasts will once more eat grass, as they did in the Garden of Eden."

—*The White Dominican* by Gustav Meyrink

2. THE THIRD PERSPECTIVE

A moment before he spots his brother beyond the bored extras and scurrying gaffers, Paul hears his voice.

"Yes. Good, Robert. Hang it for much light, eh? Tres bien."

Hugo Haas stands beside the bulky VistaVision camera in that newly quiescent way of his, now listening intently to his cameraman, now to his set designer as a scrim of luminous fabric is hoisted up to the lights.

"Perhaps a shade lower, then, and give a glow to the faces. A very slow pan?" His voice—dark, plangent—resonates amongst the American chatter. He wears a gray shirt with the sleeves rolled up, brown trousers with black suspenders; his heavy-set build gives an impression of power rather than corpulence. Thick salt-and-peppered hair remains mussed: Hugo is a director now, not an actor. His gentle chin is covered with a faint and somehow boyish growth of beard. "Maybe we shoot from both angles, Bob? And then, we follow them as they walk, yes? Oh, and what a lovely glow! Did the job."

Careful not to trip on the cables or strike his head on one of the boom arms, Paul approaches the dream of Moravia floating under 1500 watt tungsten.

Hugo breaks into a grin. "Like it, Pajo?" He gestures expansively.

"Marvelous."

"Took Bill Menzies five minutes to sketch it out, three

hours for the blueprints." Though Hugo trains with an American vocal coach, his voice is forever infected with Czech modulation: a distinctive accent that typecasts him in B-movies as portly nefarious European-types.

"The land looks like Strektot."

"Really?" Hugo studies the broad, glowing vision, as though from Paul's point of view, and runs his hand through his hair. "I didn't have any pictures of Olomouc to show him. So I described it from memory. Looks a bit small, maybe?"

"Like a dream."

Hugo grins and spreads his bear-like arms. "But on the big screen—huge!" He turns to the cameraman. "Right, Bob?"

"Diffuse and anamorphic to the nth degree, Mr. Haas." Surtees matches Hugo's smile.

Hugo ducks under the boom arm and joins Paul at the edge of the set. Clapping him on the shoulder, he says, "Hey, I got the part in the new *King Solomon's Mines*."

"That is *wonderful*, Hugo! Congratulations!"

"Small part. Most small. But it's the best in the show." He lifts his chin and scratches his beard, shutting his eyes briefly as an itch is dealt with, eyes of calm pale blue, so often remarked upon in the Czech press. "My character's a bastard of a guy, shows up halfway through, bumped-off ten minutes later. I'm Haggard's *Herr Kurtz*, the lone white man who's gone a little crazy amongst the natives, named Von Brun." He waits for Paul to catch the German homonym.

"*From Brno*." Paul grins.

"Who else could they have found, eh? I leave for Nairobi next month, which means my shooting schedule on this film is now cut by three days. Another reason why I cannot go to lunch."

Paul decides it's Providence: he'll have time for a snack, a shower and shave and a slow cab ride through the afternoon snarl. "I'm very happy for you, Hugo. I can't wait to tell Sona."

A Haas in Africa. No doubt Hugo's ego will rise to the occasion.

Hugo claps him on the shoulder. "How goes the music for my sleazy film?"

"On target. I should finish by the weekend." He nearly tells Hugo about the Brentwood summons, but there are too many unanswered questions; better to wait until afterward and give a cogent report on his good fortunes. "I finished 11 and 12. I'll have 13 done by evening, and—"

Hugo has returned to his cameraman, who holds up colored gels for the director's inspection. Once again, Paul is held rapt by the dreamlike set and, by extension, the entire production—the visuals, the talented crew and actors, the many *strangenesses* of Hugo's screenplay. He's thrilled at how Hugo has reinvented himself, retaking the ambition and drive that had made him a star at Barrandov. Certainly, Paul had been uneasy at the subject matter. The *Magdalena*, and her fate, comprise memories both sweet and profoundly sad.

In the corner, the radiant young star of the movie is watching him, amused. No older than nineteen, she's perched on a stool while a hairdresser grooms her long auburn hair. She holds a cigarette with wrist crooked above the white tissue paper that drapes her pleated green robes. Both white and green contrast against the beige of her slender neck and heart-shaped face. "He's not listening to you, is he?"

Approaching her, Paul shrugs broadly. Not for the first time he finds himself speechless at her beauty.

Jean Simmons borrows the brush from the hairdresser. Then, brushing her bangs low over her solemn yet smiling eyes, says, upward to him, "*Dobry den, Pani.*" And, working to stress the first syllable, "*Dobry den.* How's that?"

"Very good, Miss Simmons." She insists on learning some Czech, though the film is entirely in English, with the single exception of a drunken German actor employed as vivid background in the S.S. scenes. Paul has even given her a copy of Karel's famous children's book, *Dasenka: the Life of a Puppy*, in Czech with English translation.

"Paul, Hugo says that you once lived together next to a Gothic cathedral."

"We did, Miss Simmons. Brno Cathedral."

"And he says that one night, coming home from a tavern, you somehow nearly punched his lights out."

"Punched his . . . ?" Paul laughs. "Hugo's recollecting is not well." Adding, "He was quite drunk, you see. And *he* hit *his* head on the stairwell while I tried helping him up."

She smiles and begins combing her bangs again. "I rather believe it to be true."

"Believe what?"

"Wanting to punch Hugo's lights out now and then." They watch their director clap their cameraman on the back. "He says you were a champion Czech boxer in the 'twenties."

Paul laughs, and actually feels himself blush. "Now he is pulling your arm, Miss Simmons."

"My arm or my leg?"

"Both, I'm afraid."

"You have the air of a retired boxer, Paul."

"I've heard that before." Paul studies her face and finds Magdalena's lovely seriousness in its features. Beneath the tissue paper Miss Simmons' green pleated robes are derived not from the rare grainy newsreel footage of the *Sylvan Uprising* but from Soviet propaganda posters and earlier *Kameradschaftsbund* leaflets discovered in post-war Berlin. "Don't listen to Hugo. Truthfully, I had asthma as a child. And I have never been a boxer."

"What was the *White Mountain*, Paul?"

"*White Mountain?*" Surprised at the question, as much as by the intense sudden scrutiny of her violet eyes, he replies, "Why, the Battle of White Mountain, Miss Simmons, was the most famous battle in our history." He returns her smile. "Where did you hear of it?"

"Oh. Whenever something goes wrong on the set, say a light bulb explodes, or Dick Widmark bungles a line, your brother mutters, *Oh, hell, this will be my White Mountain.* I've asked him what he means but he simply won't tell me."

"The battle did not go well for us, Miss Simmons. We Czechs lost, in 1620, and were forever the property of another country after that." He adds, "Except for a brief twenty years between the wars."

"*Slečna Jean, prosím!*" Hugo beckons from the other side of the camera, and extends his hand.

Rising, she sighs. "And today is the unlucky day, Paul, isn't it?"

At first, he doesn't understand. Then, "Yes. That's the legend about such Fridays, Miss Simmons. Nonetheless, I wish you very good luck."

She stabs out the cigarette on a dessert plate. And, after exhaling upward, "*Dobry den*, Paul. Back into the battle."

Paul watches her stride onto the set, the lithe green robed beauty walking under luminous scrims to Hugo's side. Hugo, no longer smiling but gravely intoning direction, gesturing to the foreshortened cobblestone path and the field beyond. From this distance, she might *be* Magdalena.

Paul often recalls the tragic yet triumphant subject matter from two perspectives—from witnessing, first-hand, Magda's transformation in Brno in 1931, and much later from reading about her tragic end in the *Los Angeles Times* in 1944. Now, he tries to imagine the *third* perspective being cobbled together in front of him, in these long, somewhat dull hours spent under hot lights, to be captured, and kindled, on that very wide, very tall square of VistaVision celluloid.

Hugo has the touch. Hugo will make magic of this, as in his old days at Barrandov. Unlike the pair of lurid B-movies he's directed for Universal so far, *Blood of the Sylph* might earn him great acclaim, and forevermore define how Magdalena is remembered, correcting the myth of—as the news wires termed her, in a telling that merged close to quaint Eastern European folklore—the *Sylvan Jeanne D'Arc*.

But his certainty of Hugo's vision falters, as always, when confronted by the tedium of creation. Young Miss Simmons dutifully takes her mark under the lights. Gaffers and technicians murmur to one another in low voices. Tape is ratcheted from its reel and drawn out from camera to the tip of the actress's nose, which she greets with a smile. Behind her, a gaffer lugs in a linden tree. Hugo walks here and there, peering, gesturing, announcing. If nothing else, the pain of Zikmund's death, and of Lenka's abandonment with seventeen-year-old Mara, does not reach him here. He is in his element, and Paul can only hope that the shoot will not be rushed but allowed to go on for week after week.

Finally, recalling the telegram in his pocket, Paul departs the studio in search of a cab, eager to explore the mystery in Brentwood Hills.

California pine and eucalyptus engulf the sedan in shadow. *Can't Get Started Without You* plays on the radio. Paul gazes out at sculpted foliage and leaf-dappled drives under the brilliant sky. Black iron fences. Jacaranda arching overhead. A Packard parked along the road. Sunlight overtakes him again. A sudden break between the properties reveals Los Angeles spread out below and into the hazy distance. In moments like these, the landscape feels as large as when he first arrived—Paul, Sona and Olga; Hugo, Lenka and little Mara traveling out of New York, first the *20th Century Limited* to Chicago, then the *Chief* to Los Angeles, a journey of three days and three nights. In Europe, a journey of three *hours* can take you into another country, but here they found only small towns, large prairies, tremendous mountains, endless forests stretching to the horizon, and still, and always, they were in America, unending.

Hugo—by then the star of Barrandov studios—wrestled with that vastness during their trip, his personality growing larger with every mile chewed up by the locomotive. Sona and Paul were delighted at his expansiveness, though Lenka grew weary from it. By the time they reached the California border his legend was known by nearly all the passengers. On the third day, as they woke to palm trees and tangerine sunlight, the steward asked if he was getting out at Pasadena, which was where all the 'film folks' disembarked 'in order to avoid reporters.'

In Hollywood Paul found immediate fellowship in the expatriate community, especially among the *Mittel-European* composers: Korngold, a Brno native, Franz Waxman, Hugo Friedhofer, Bronislau Kaper, and that most gentle of gentlemen, Dr. Miklós Rózsa. Paul and Sona have attended a few of the *century parties*, usually at Hugo's behest, and some of the cultural soirees Hollywood adores to offer. They've heard W.H. Auden read at the Swinebuck club, and Aldous Huxley at the MGM Canteen, and—best of all—Igor Stravinsky conducting *Petroushka* and *Rite of Spring* at the Hollywood Bowl. But to a great extent their social life derives from Sona's orbit; other Doctors of Radiology, staff nurses, administrators and the like, and friends from the neighborhood, parents of Olga's schoolmates.

All of which returns him to the mystery of the summons. He touches the telegram in his pocket. Staring out the window, he recites to himself the stars who live in Brentwood. Gary Cooper. Tyrone Power. Clark Gable.

> TO PAUL HAAS. WE MUST MEET TO DISCUSS A PROJECT. 116 N. ROCKINGHAM AVE BRENTWOOD PARK. TODAY. MUST BE BETWEEN 3 AND 6 PM TODAY.

He wears his fine cashmere suit—drawn from the bungalow's closet, intended for sudden meetings with studio executives. It has grown uncomfortably snug since the last time he donned it. He taps the paper, idly. He checks his Timex: twenty past three. He stuffs the telegram back into his inner pocket, lifts the small satchel with its notepad and elegant pen, and relaxes his shoulders. He tells himself that the answer will soon be revealed. Nonetheless, his fingers continue tapping the leather, drumming the questions onward. As the taxicab follows the winding road farther and farther, past enshadowed estates, he nearly loosens the tie, nearly unbuttons the top button of his shirt.

But then the cab driver is slowing, pulling over to the curb. "Here you go, pal. 116 North Rockingham."

Palm boughs hover over a tennis court of red clay. The mansion, reminiscent of the French Riviera, perches on a hillside overlooking the valley. As Paul walks up the empty driveway he wonders if it, too, is empty. But as he reaches the path of flat rocks leading to the porch he hears a piano, faint, playing a single note, then another. Twelve in all, like a grandfather clock marking noon, or midnight, then repeating. Another twelve.

Paul stands before the double-doors. A brass knocker invites his hand, but so does a bell to his right. He rings it; hears, fainter than the piano, the dolorous toll within.

The twelve notes are sounded once more, then cease.

His imagination conjures up a roster of executives and producers—cigar-chomping, bellicose, demanding that Haas not waste their time. Or, given the mansion's size, perhaps a Czech margrave exiled to California?

He rings again, for less than a second, noting the *mezuzah* on the doorpost. Paul hears footsteps. Then, close by, loudly, the door's handle rattles then relents. A chain *swicks* in its track. A bolt clicks, and the door is pulled open on a wide Spanish-style entry. Standing before him, no taller than Paul's chin, is a sparrow-thin elderly man in a black suit, gazing up with large, haunted eyes.

Arnold Schoenberg, the *Prophet of Serialism*, the *Monster of Modern Music*, gestures him stiffly inside.

"Had times been normal, then the music of our time would have been very different."

—Arnold Schoenberg

3. HARMONIELEHRE

"*Meester Haas*," says the old man in a gray, grave voice. "*Welcomen.* Inside, please."

Stunned, Paul forces his shoes over the threshold. "Herr Schoenberg, this is a great surprise. I thank you."

"*Ja.*" Staring up, Arnold Schoenberg studies Paul's face, and gives a brisk nod. "Good. Herr Haas, we will speak in the tongue of my countrymen."

"It was once the tongue of my countrymen, too, Herr Schoenberg." After fifteen years in Hollywood, Paul considers himself blasé about celebrities, yet here is a man whose music he's worshipped since his student days, an Austrian who is now part of the expatriate community that includes such luminaries as Stravinsky, Huxley, Thomas Mann, Alma Mahler, Franz Werfel. He has often hoped to encounter Schoenberg at a dinner party and shake his hand. Now, he does so. "I am honored."

"And I am pleased the telegram found you, Herr Haas." Schoenberg shuts the door behind him. His black shoes are polished. His black tie is crisp and narrow. "I put the Americanized *Paul*, and not *Pavel*, and so I feared the paper would pass you by."

"It found me, Herr Professor."

A menorah presides over the brick fireplace next to a Tellihim. Many paintings—expressionist, vividly colorful—decorate the walls, along with the rare photograph. One, seemingly of a gravestone, beckons to Paul, but Schoenberg is moving further into the room.

"And you had no difficulty with the address?" His voice, of a high tessitura, is as stark as his suit.

"None, Herr." He follows. Two couches and three overstuffed chairs gather around a long, low table. The high ceiling only emphasizes the emptiness as the old man leads him to the grand piano in the corner. "I had an appointment today for lessons, with a young student from the neighborhood, which I have canceled."

Paul has heard rumors that the great man's finances are poor. *Arnold Schoenberg: piano teacher to local high school kids.*

"Do you wish a drink?"

"I would love one, Herr." He cannot help himself from adding, "It is truly a great pleasure to meet you, Herr Schoenberg. I have been an admirer since I first encountered *Gurrelieder*, in Brno. And later, *Transfigured Night*, and the *Serenade*."

Schoenberg might not have heard. He stares at the keyboard and, a moment later, this bird-like man in the stiff black suit perches on the bench. His gaunt hands lift over the keys: impressive hands, still, devilish hands. The fingers span nothing tonal. They descend to strike a chord—an augmented E-F, of nine notes. After allowing the chord to begin its dying fall, the fingers strike another, then another. Twelve chords in all. As the strangeness fades into the living room's Bauhaus air, Schoenberg lifts his head. "And so *thirteen*, Herr Haas, is left to vanish with it." He stares down at his hands. "If you had come within an hour of 1:30, I would not have answered the door. Yes, Herr, I am somewhat superstitious."

"It is 13 Friday after all." Paul offers a smile.

"Yet I have only had the greatest of luck to meet you today, Herr." He wants to ask if the rumor is true, that Schoenberg has titled his unfinished masterwork opera *Moses und Aron*—not *Moses und* Aaron—to avoid a title with that dread number of letters.

Schoenberg slowly stands up. "A drink." He passes vivid, expressionist self-portraits, akin in their burning-eyed intensity to Munch, though one—disconcertingly—is of a cowboy. Hopalong Cassidy tossing a lasso.

"I heard a radio transcription recently, Herr Haas. Of your *Insect Play*, when Morton Gould conducted it in New York." Reaching the wet-bar, Schoenberg exults, "Tremendously moving."

Amazed, Paul affects a bow. "You honor me, Herr Professor."

Schoenberg turns to the bottles. A wide window looks onto a backyard porch and palm trees. Sunlight casts his shadow sharply on the carpet. The hands that pounded the strange chords now brush past whiskey, vodka, and settle on port wine. "I am not a fan in general, Herr, of *pleasant* music," he continues, lifting the bottle and setting it down on the rubber mat. "Yours *cuts to the bone*."

"Herr Professor, that means much to me, thank you." He thinks then of Karel and Josef, and his pleasure is bittersweet.

"And now you work in cinema." Schoenberg pours the blood-red liquid into two snifters. "They asked me to write music for the movies. They begged and pleaded." A smile, as he turns. "And so I wrote for them a grand work for a huge orchestra, and to this, they blanched. Too expensive."

Paul sees Louis B. Mayer, gesturing with his cigar at Paul's throat.

"I took my piece and polished it, and now it is a concert suite." He beckons. "Let us sit on the porch, Herr Haas, in the brilliant American sunshine."

Paul follows the composer through the glass doors, onto a teakwood deck. A table sits with five high-backed chairs and a white umbrella above. Palm trees frame the valley in splendor. Schoenberg chooses the chair deepest in shade, beside a bowl of walnuts, and seats himself. "I commend you for the recording you have made of Terezin composers."

"You've heard it?" This two-year-old project, a limited pressing of 78s of works by Ullmann, Klein, Krasa, Schul—performed by a fix-up band of Korngold's favorite musicians—sold mostly to collectors in New York during *The Insect Play's* run. "That pleases me very much."

"The work of Gideon Klein, especially, was very moving. The *Divertimento*." His fingers rootle amongst the walnuts. "A great tribute."

41

"He was influenced, of course, by your system, Herr."

"And also your Maestro, yes?" Schoenberg squints. "Herr J⎯⎯, whom I met at the triumphant *Káťa Kabanová* in Berlin."

Hearing the twelve-tone variations on the great *Diary of One Who Disappeared,* Paul stares out at the valley. "Herr Klein was incredibly gifted, Herr Professor. And he drew from sources that were close to me."

Schoenberg turns his attention to the bowl of walnuts. He lifts a device which is like a nutcracker, but not quite. Instead of simple bars and a spring, the sides are flat, with teeth-like protuberances and, at the apex, a musical note. Herr Professor has a reputation for inventions almost as large as that for music, constructing items as varied as toys, a cardboard violin, tape dispensers, skirt hangers, and many other devices made solely for the creation of music in twelve tones—cylinder booklets, slide rules, and notation typewriters, not to mention his mysterious *tone-row generators.*

Exposing a withered wrist emerging from the stiffly ironed shirtsleeve, his fingers search among the walnuts—creating a faint, somehow pleasing wooden percussion in the bowl.

"Your own design, Herr Professor?" Paul points to the device.

The fingers search, discard, then choose a plump, deeply brown walnut. "It grips the nuts where others would allow them to fall from my feeble hand." The instrument is brought to bear.

Paul leans forward. "I am reminded of what Igor Stravinsky likes to say. *I am an inventor of music.*"

Schoenberg burps, a small eruption in his hollow chest that causes his eyes to widen, then his lips to grimace. The hand tightens. The walnut's shell, and the chambered meat inside, crack and crumble to the tabletop. "And *he* has called *me,* Herr Haas, a *chemist.*" Recovering, he sets the instrument beside the bowl, then begins to pick among the dregs. "We are . . . at odds with one another."

At a loss for any safe reply, Paul merely sips his wine, and stares out, far out, into the heat-hazed valley. In the lull, the question resurfaces: *Why have I been summoned?*

"I am an old man, Herr Haas. An old, frightened man. On this most cursed of days, my thoughts turn not to composers who are among us and productive, but those we have *lost*. Those whose music *was silenced*." He shifts in the chair; a bony shoulder lifts as he gestures to the tennis court. "Over there. Right over there, in the late thirties, I used to play tennis every day with Herr Gershwin." The hand lingers, then returns to rootle among the walnut chips. "You would think his music is not the stuff for Arnold Schoenberg. But I found it, and him, delightful." He lifts the meat to his mouth. "A great composer, a good tennis player, and dead, by the age of 31." The sound of his dry chewing, of the walnut pulverized further and further then finally swallowed, his only commentary.

"You have known many great men, Herr Professor," says Paul, after a pause. He feigns to sip his wine. Schoenberg's demeanor has changed, there in the umbrella's shadow. Sunken into his chair, he gazes with fierce intensity at his hand on the table's edge. "Too many lost," he says. Schoenberg's shoulders lift. He sits up further in the chair and raises his glass in a toast. Paul brings in his own, and the glasses faintly clink. Both sip deeply. "They tell a story in Vienna, of Anton Bruckner's devotion to his departed colleagues." Again, he lifts a bit of walnut and chews, this time speaking around it. "To Beethoven, most of all, of course. The *All-Highest* of departed colleagues. And who now possesses something very precious of Herr Maestro Bruckner's." Schoenberg's demeanor changes yet again: a smile. And the expectation that Paul ask him a question.

"How could that happen, Herr Professor?"

"In Wahring Cemetery, in 1888, Beethoven was exhumed by the scientific community, the casket was opened, so that they might perform all sorts of skeletal measurements of the timeless genius before the bones were reburied in a newer, larger, grave of honor. And midway through, Herr Bruckner barged in." Schoenberg pauses, as though watching the scene playing out in the begonia shadows. "When the scientists told him he was not to be there, he shouted obscenities and brushed them aside." Both of the bird-like hands come together, and lift from the table, trembling. "He grasped the skull. He raised it up to his eyes, saying, 'Isn't it true, Herr Beethoven? If you were alive, you would allow me to touch you? I, your spiritual heir? Yet even now they wish *to forbid me that?*'" Schoenberg smiles, and for an uncomfortable instant, Paul is aware of the skull beneath the skin. "The scientists grappled with him, this crazed composer. And somehow, during the melee, one of the lenses fell out of Herr Bruckner's *pince-nez*. He discovered this only afterward, Herr Haas, while outside, brushing himself off. And this so delighted him that he crowed like a cock. He was entirely *certain* that the lens had dropped into the casket and would now share *eternity* with Ludwig Von Beethoven."

Schoenberg drinks deeply of his wine, which gives his bloodless lips a bloom until he licks it away. The lips mutter. Numbers. *Ten, eleven, twelve.* "I have had nightmares lately, Herr."

Paul sits forward. "I . . . I'm sorry to hear of it."

"I dream of those now dead. Long dead. Not only friends and family, but the great talents that were lost to us from the horror of this century. They seem to have built to a crescendo, on this dread day . . . These past months, ever since my wife died . . ."

Suddenly, the old man's black suit, the scent of faded flowers in the house, the sight of bouquets tossed into the garbage: everything makes sense. "Herr Professor, I will stay with you tonight, if you wish. Once Saturday morning comes, you will be able to rest, and not have the nightmares."

The hand lifts and waves irritably. Then, mustering himself in the suit—or perhaps, it is the suit that musters him—Schoenberg rises to his feet. "*Remain*, please," he says, gesturing with a flat palm at Paul. He walks across the patio and into the house. And Paul is left to sip his wine, left to stare into the blue sky, aware of the emptiness of the house behind him and the silence of the red clay tennis court where Schoenberg once challenged George Gershwin to duels.

I dream of those now dead.

Paul straightens in the chair. The tie is tight around his throat and the cuffs bite into his wrists.

Not only friends, and family, but the great talents that were lost to us from the horror of this past century.

Magdalena, he thinks, and Karel and Josef. All victims of terrible violence. And the Maestro, lost to no *great horror* but to simple pneumonia, supposedly caught while searching for the son of his beloved Mrs. Kamila, lost in the woods of his native Hukvaldy, in 1928.

Hukvaldy, 1928. Los Angeles, 1949.

And the two connected, this instant in the sun struck Brentwood Hills, by such regret.

"*Herr Haas.*" The gray, grave voice.

Schoenberg stands at his shoulder, hollow eyes fixing soberly on Paul's. "Now is the time to show you this."

In both hands he lifts a large piece of laminate plastic. It quivers in the pounding sunlight, enclosing a shape of strange folds and pointed corners, a luminous parchment of strange silvery texture covered with microscopic staves and chords, in purple ink.

A stave flower.

"Where . . ." Paul sits upright, heart pounding. "But where did you find it?" He resists taking hold. "Herr Professor?"

"I *created* it, Herr Haas." The old man's shoulders sink. His arms drop to his sides. "I and the Devil incarnate. Created *it*. Created *them*. *All* of them."

"In Arnold Schoenberg's personality and art, we revere above all the unyielding search for the Absolute ... In his devotion to the unconditional, this master of music comes perhaps closest to the old masters of the cabbala."

—Franz Werfel, 1946

4. SATOR, AREPO, TENET, OPERA, ROTAS

As Paul steps into his home on Delmonica Drive and quietly shuts the door behind him, he forces his hands to relax, stifling their nervous taps. The emotions that overwhelmed him during the walk down Sunset and, eventually, during the cab ride home, have subsided. Memories of a stave flower floating down out of Brno's midnight sky, of the nightmarish journey into a future now past, of Josef's naked face blinking blearily covered with blood, of Magdalena screaming deep within writhing branches—they too subside to a familiar entryway with its clutter of shoes and children's toys, to a radio, a Naugahyde couch, an end table covered with copies of *Look* and *Life*, a Rockwell Kent linocut above the fireplace.

This, too, is yours, Herr Haas.

He grips the satchel to his chest, palm flat on the leather. He breathes deeply and wills his shoulders to relax.

Herr Haas, take it.

"*Manjel?*" Sona pokes her head out of the kitchen vestibule, then smiles and strides toward him in dark stockinged feet. "Sneaking in?"

Lowering the satchel to his side, but still gripping it tight, he holds her with his free arm, her warmth scented with nutmeg and something buttery. He leans in to kiss her hot neck, closing his eyes as her hair caresses his chin. When he pulls back, she lifts up a finger and taps his lips: cookie batter.

"Tough day?"

Tasting the batter, he glances down at his rumpled striped shirt, tie, and the tie clip she gave him for his birthday. He cannot recall changing out of the suit at the bungalow, yet he has. "As Hugo would say, I was *put through the wringer*."

"The new show? Is he having you work on both at the same time?" She's still wearing the dark and handsome dress of a consulting surgeon, with the identification badge clipped over her breast; she must have only recently gotten home. "What is it, Pajo?"

He shrugs. He struggles to recall the breakfast conversation. Today—today has been a big day for her. "But . . . but tell me, Sonicku, what about the meeting. The presentation?"

She's had a difficult day herself, he realizes. This is a good thing. She lets go of her concern for him and bites her lower lip, her eyes downcast. "Well . . . " She looks away—he studies her profile, the same one which he fell in love with twenty years ago, lips turning into a smile. She grins, licking the batter from her finger. "They're buying all the equipment I recommended."

"That's wonderful, *manželka*."

"Frannie had to leave early. Something about driving her mother to Burbank. So I'm concocting dinner and dessert with Willie."

"*Papa!*" William Michael Haas comes bounding in. Five years old, with striking facial resemblance to Paul's Uncle Michael. Paul summons the strength to lift the boy—ignoring Schoenberg's haunted eyes somewhere beyond the plaster wall—and kisses him on the cheek. "You been good for mama?"

"Yes!" The boy tugs on Paul's hand, leading him to the Indian head table, and exclaims, without a trace of Czech accent, "Look what I made!"

Sona nudges Paul. "He did a project with Frannie. Isn't it beautiful?"

On a piece of cardboard, green and yellow macaroni has been pasted into the shape of a leaning palm. "Well now, that's *wonderful*."

"It's a palm tree!"

"Yes." Paul tousles his hair. "A most fine palm tree!"

Sona says, over her shoulder, "We were going to *eat* that macaroni." The boy trails Sona back into the kitchen.

Paul picks up the satchel, and follows. Olga sits at the table. Studious, dark-haired like her mother, she's at work on algebra and barely looks up from her notebook. "Hi, Dad."

He smiles. "Are you swimming in numbers, Olinka?" Briefly he is standing in Mrs. Premyekova's apartment, in that other future. The future now past. Windows draped with blackout curtains, the air reeking of pig fat and iodine, and Mrs. Premyekova, threadbare, an Arcimboldo portrait of herself: *You divorced your wife, to save her, and your child.*

"I'm up to factors now," says Olga, with an index finger drawing back her long black bangs like a curtain away from her eye—a gesture that she learned from her mother. A moment later, she returns to her homework, the reticent young adult with little of the silly girl she once was. Yet the night before she entertained him and Sona by singing the Burma-Shave jingle while little William Michael scurried around on the kitchen tiles, acting the part of the shaver.

You made *her go away, Pavel, to her sister's in Olomouc. With little Olga.*

Sona takes a can of beer from the fridge. She cracks it with the can opener and hands it to him. "Your father's had a tough day."

He tells Sona, "I have some work to do."

"Before dinner?"

"Yes." He clutches the satchel in both hands. "I have work."

She follows him and brushes her hand between his broad shoulders, as she used to do so when he was running to catch the streetcar. "Just because he's your brother, you shouldn't let him run you into the ground."

Paul fumbles for the rheostat switch, turns it.

Three lamps brighten in the small study. Against the window sits an oak desk adorned with a vase of green glass—Bohemian mercury

49

glass—cluttered with scripts and score sheets, with pens, erasers, an empty pack of Sen-Sen, cigarettes, an ash tray, a lighter; a Wheeldex given him by Hugo, said to contain every worthwhile name in Hollywood. Though Paul rarely touches it, Hugo loves to flip through and recite names that would interest Paul. Heifetz is in there, as is Bruno Walter, Stokowski. Even Stravinsky. Beside the desk is the Naugahyde couch where Hugo loves to recline while waxing about future projects or lost days in Brno. The walls are adorned with photographs and paintings of the old country and new—and every item argues against what Arnold Schoenberg has said to him, and what Schoenberg has *given* to him.

I created it, Herr Haas. I and the Devil incarnate.

He pulls the drapes, drops the satchel on the desk, sets the can of beer beside it; then to the wetbar—one of Hugo's accoutrements—where he reaches past whiskey and gin for Hugo's seltzer bottle and a clean glass. He fills it, shakes out a few aspirin from the pillbox, and chases them with the fizzing water, then replaces the glass.

On the closet door hangs a small, framed linocut. Angular branches recall the monstrous tree looming over the tumbled columns of the Conservatory. The inscription, half-hidden by the gold frame, reads: *A reminder to Pavel, opera composer and future American, 1935, Josef.*

He takes it down, peering under the edge of the frame, both reassured to see the handwriting and feeling foolish to have been so. Tasting the sulfurous air of that other Brno; Brno, 1944.

A *reminder*.

Josef did not chastise him for leaving. In fact, both he and Karel implored him to go, saying that America, now, was the place of *greatest power*. That he would bring his *From the Life of Insects*, soon to be retitled *The Insect Play*, to the opera stage in New York and London, and continue developing his power as an artist in the spotlight of America. Karel assured him that he and Josef, Bohu, Max and the others would continue to educate and warn—however subtly—the populace of their country.

He pulls a Chesterfield from the pack, drops it next to the satchel, takes up the lighter. Thinking of Josef's silver phoenix, he lights it with a shaking hand.

"*Remember what Wells said,*" Karel told him, that last afternoon in Prague. "*To persuade the world, we must use the only weapon available to us.* Fear."

Paul sits down heavily in the chair. The springs squeak. He leans an elbow on the plush arm and cradles his forehead, rubbing at that headache, and smokes. As he rubs his eyes, Schoenberg hovers in the sparking darkness. Paul blinks him away. He takes up the satchel, unsnaps the clasp and opens it. *This is yours, Herr Haas.* Inside, the pages look drab, brown, utterly ordinary, the first batch held together with a rusty paper clip. Paul reaches for it, then relents. His hand becomes a fist.

He stares into the Bohemian glass for a long moment, then turns to the walls, to posters for *The Insect Play* at the Metropolitan Opera, to a framed rave by Olin Downes in the *New York Times*, to a photograph of Olga at her *bat mitzvah*, to another of a family vacation at Mt. Shasta. Unsure what he's looking for he stands up, moving from picture to picture until he finds it: a pencil drawing, a caricature, likewise framed. Pavel and Josef and Karel tower over the belvedere mansions of London. The technique lacks Josef's brilliance or Karel's refinement. After all, it's not theirs, it's not a drawing at all. It's a *picshua*, carrying him back two decades, to those strange months in 1931.

He seeks the inscription at the bottom. *H.G. W., 614, St. Ermins, Westminster SW1.*

At first, Mr. Herbert George Wells seemed to possess an open mind.

In his cozy study, with a fire crackling and hissing in the brick fireplace and rain falling beyond the tall windows, brandy was poured, cigars and a half-Gauloise lit and on sumptuous divans they sat with him and told their story, punctuated with Josef's nightmarish and detailed sketches.

With each further turn of the screw, Wells, clad in a royal blue smoking jacket torn at the collar and black slippers, became more quiet, merely grunting when Pavel handed him a sketch of a grim German corpse, its mouth stuffed full of flowers.

Finally, the verdict: "You wish to avoid, Čapek, most certainly avoid, *Cassandra's noose*." Paul can vividly recall his voice—its high tessitura muffled by that walrus mustache. "It is a noose that one can swing from only once. After that one does not lose one's life, but something worse—one's *credibility*."

The air, scented with tobacco and camphor.

And Karel, of course, exercised his famous pragmatism, tapping his lips with the cigarette holder and stepping around the subject to Wells' point of view. "Yes, you're right, of course."

"If you had proof, solid proof, and not something that could be easily manufactured, a tale told by artists." He held up the theater booklet reading *Brunn German City Theater, Protectorate of Bohemia and Moravia, May 1942*.

"Yes, yes."

"Even this feuilleton you say the Maestro fellow wrote—*Heartbeat of the World*. You failed to find it in the newspaper archives?"

"Yes, a disappointment."

"*Monsieurs*, I once wrote a book subtitled *An Experiment in Prophecy*." Setting aside the booklet, Wells took up his pencil and pad, and drew a picture—or as he termed it, a *picshua*—of his three solemn visitors from the Czechoslovak Republic. "Many of my works could be given that title, and many of yours, Čapek. I would submit that you proceed along the same lines, as prophecy, yes, but *via* fiction."

Josef, in an irritable tone, said, "But you see, *Monsieur*, it is hard to relate as *fiction* what one has encountered as *fact*."

Karel nodded, exhaling sharply. "My brother is right." Blinking up into the lowering smoke. "We are willing to risk looking like fools, *if* the nightmare could be changed."

52

"To persuade the world, we must use the only weapon available to us. *Fear.*" H.G. smiled over his sketchbook. "Only through personal disaster, or the manifest threat of personal disaster, can normal human beings be sufficiently stirred to attempt a revolutionary change of their conditions."

"But *Monsieur* Wells," said Pavel, "human beings can also be *inspired*, surely."

"Up to a point, *Monsieur* Haas. Of course." Then, to Karel, "You already have a pulpit to address your people. You are listened to, and respected. But you have many *snipers* to the right and left of you in the Czech press. As do I, in the British. They would make hash of such absurd notions of time travel, with . . . " He held up the booklet. "With stage props." And before the three could reply: "I speak from experience, of a sort. Daily, I wish I had not written in a certain notorious essay of a coming *war that will end War*. If, however, you had in your possession the *device* that you said transported you, this, this *flower* made up of musical staves and writing . . . "

"Yes." Karel stroked his lips with his first and second fingers. "*Had we only.*"

And Josef muttered to Pavel, "*Pity we didn't bring back a* Naciste *for Mr. Wells.*"

"Yet it should not be entirely discouraging. You must merely work by more *subtle* means. Continue educating people about the fascist threat, as I have been doing to the utmost. Tease them with the phantasm of a sinister *Lord Paramount*. As to some of it, *hold back.*" Wells set down his pencil and leaned back, fixing Paul with his basilisk stare. "The part about the *pogrom* . . . I would sit on that card. Some people are uneasy with the Jewish question, some are, quite frankly, bored. It would seem like—I apologize, Haas—like useless filigree on your nightmarish invention."

Useless filigree.

Paul stabs the dregs of his cigarette in the ash tray. He reaches for the satchel, hearing Schoenberg's gray, grave voice—*"This is yours, Herr Haas,"*—then relents.

<hr />

Inside the closet, half-hidden behind coats and jackets, stands a filing cabinet. He fishes out a key from the overhead shelf and unlocks it. Wrestling against the coats and jackets—the smell of mothballs making him queasy—he slides out the top drawer. Inside are several thick file folders and a hardcover book. He grabs them all. *The Labyrinth of the World and the Paradise of the Heart,* the 1923 Aventium edition—Josef's own—is graced with his hypnotic linocut of a six-pointed star that forms the outline of a city.

He sets everything on the desk. At the end of Hugo's sofa he lifts the lid on the phonograph, turns on the power, lowers the volume. Amongst the dozen or so 78s he finds one with a plain black and white wrapper. No striking linocuts; they could not be afforded. The project was financed mostly through donations, and the generous services of Alfred Newman, head of Fox's music department.

Music from Theresienstadt, 1941–1944

Paul Haas/Hollywood Symphony Orchestra, Ken Darby, Hollywood Bowl Chorale and Soloists.

The back of the jacket features photographs of Viktor Ullmann, Gideon Klein, Hans Krasa, Zikmund Schul. The portraits date variously from the early twenties—Ullmann's, the oldest—to just before the Nuremberg laws. Sardonic, handsome Gideon Klein, the youngest and perhaps most-talented of the group, is seated behind a concert grand.

While Paul was preparing the album, Mrs. Premyekova haunted his thoughts. Not the plump landlady who held back tears upon his emigration from Brno, in 1935, but the other, older, *starved* Mrs. Premyekova from that *other* Brno, in 1939. The one who spoke of the *other* Pavel Haas's fate: Theresienstadt, among those other composers. A death at Auschwitz, certainly. And now, a vestige of that other future sits on his desk. One that Schoenberg, and the other mysterious eight, carried with them into their *Caesura room*.

If Schoenberg is to be believed.

He slips the shellac disk from its sleeve and lays it on the spindle, then drops the needle on the first band: Gideon Klein's *Bachuri l'an tisa* for women's choir, composed in 1942. The voices—twelve of them, from the pickup choir conducted by Alfred Newman's assistant, Mr. Darby—begin to sing the gentle, sad lament.

Klein, he recalls, survived Theresienstadt as well as Auschwitz, dying at the hard labor camp at Furstengrubbe.

Paul sits down at the desk. He lifts *The Labyrinth of the World* while the choir sings with a lovely, lambent tone somehow akin to the green Mercury glass atop the desk. After many minutes leafing through the interior linocuts, he tips open to the title page, and Josef's inscription.

Good luck in America, Pavel, a Pilgrim in the land of great freedom and greatest power, Josef, Dec 18 1936.

A soft knock upon the door rouses him. Glancing at the clock—9:05—he says softly, "Yes?"

The door opens. Olga peeks in, wrinkles her nose at the smoke. "Are you hungry, Papa?" Her wondrously intelligent eyes take in the pages laid out on the desk, the satchel, the book.

Quietly, so as not to break the spell woven around these myriad pictures and memories, he says, "Olinka, I am like your uncle tonight. I am eating cigars and drinking seltzer."

She tips her head, drawing strands of hair away from her face. "You're playing the sad music again."

The chorus is singing Viktor Ullmann's *Hosana*, in slow 5/4 time. They listen to a few bars, the two of them, in the glow of the Bohemian glass. "It's not all sad, Olinka."

She offers up a sandwich wrapped in a napkin. "Here."

He rises and takes it from her, and kisses the top of her head. "And how goes your homework?"

"Done." She walks to the desk. "Willie's watching *Break the Bank*, and Mom's reading a textbook."

"And you?"

Another smile. "I have the radio." She looks past him at the spread of *picshuas* and folders. "At school today," she says, "my music professor, Mr. Stanton, spoke of you."

"Oh?"

Olga is always a mystery to him. He can never expect what she will say and do: this is the joy of seeing her every day. "Really, he did so? He spoke well, I hope."

She nods. "He told the class that you were a great modern composer, and compared you to Bartok and Kodaly." A thoughtful pause, as she turns to him. "Which isn't really right, is it?"

Paul smiles. "It is close enough."

She shrugs, staring down at the carpet. "I'll let you get back to work, Dad. But listen to some happy music, please?"

He gestures; the record player is hers to command. Smiling one of her mother's smiles, she lifts the needle arm, swings it back, carefully removes the record and tucks it in its sleeve. Then she chooses a Benny Goodman.

"Not too loud, dear."

She drops the needle, turns down the volume. Before departing, she kisses him on the cheek.

For a time he can only listen to the music and feel Olinka's warmth and comfort.

The first folder is marked *Evidence*. Within are newspaper clippings from the *Los Angeles Tribune*, the *New York Times*, the *Times* of London, *Punch*, and others: from 1937, articles tracking the *Anschluss* of Austria, and a wire service story from London about "a group calling themselves *Tvrdosinji*, or *The Obstinates*, in Prague, led by the world-famous robot-play author Karel Čapek, joining forces with their artistic foes the *9forces*, led by the collage-artist Karel Tiege." From 1938, reports about the Sudeten Crisis and its fomenter, Konrad Henlein. About *Kristallnacht*, and the invasion of Prague, and editorials from New York urging *hands-off, European war for Europeans only*. From 1940, a dispatch about Heydrich the Hangman and his tyranny over Prague; and a year later, of his assassination—the first major divergence from the events as Paul saw them in that other Brunn.

He flips through the brittle, yellowing pages, past Dec 7, 1941 and D-Day, until he comes to an etching of *The Sylvan Magdalena*. The resemblance isn't quite there, with her long hair threaded with leaves, and a face that is far too Romantic, in a *Kameradschaftsbund* style. "Hundreds of Nazis died at Strektot's fields and hills in Czechoslovakia at the hands of this lovely murderous maiden, according to reports from operatives in the S. S. A," reads the lead paragraph.

Strangely, it's the cartoon from *Punch* that captures her likeness the best. The wayward mass of hair, the slender neck, a hint of defiance in her eyes as she lifts the flute. In Grecian robes she looms over a miniature forest while a diminutive Nazi officer in the foreground shouts into a telephone, "*The Czech women are not to be fooled with, Mein Fuhrer!*"

The only photograph, from a 1944 London *Times* front page article (*Sylvan Uprising Results in Tremendous Toll*), shows her from a distance, clad not in fanciful robes but the uniform of the Czech legionnaire. She stands amid a horde of followers—men and women alike—in the *scasovani* foliage, a riot of wild twisting trees the article deems "*a forest out of Mr. Max Ernst, which, some say, actively slaughtered the Waffen S.S. forces fifty kilometers south of Prague.*"

Her death is reported in another front page article, with the familiar ikon rendering that would pop up in Soviet propaganda. *Sylvan Mystery Woman Slaughtered in Czechoslovakia.*

Paul turns the page. The remaining "Evidence" charts the post-War world in Europe. VE day and the tumultuous celebrations. A gathering in Wenceslas Square in Prague with lighted candles. Czechs greeting the Soviet army. The liberation of Auschwitz and Bergen-Belsen, where Josef perished. The infamous *Benes Decree* from Prague Castle which—as Karel had predicted—brought the wrath of the new Czechoslovak government onto Sudeten Germans. The subsequent horrors of the wild *odsun*, when tens of thousands of Gypsies and Czech-born Germans were forcibly driven from their homes, from their country, some drowned in rivers, some hanged, all of it recounted without pity or outrage in the American newspapers.

Tucked in the back is Karel Čapek's obituary in the *Prager Tagblatt*, dated December 19, 1939. Is it mere irony, Paul wonders? Mere irony, or something else, that Karel died within a week of the Christmas day the old Sudeten groundskeeper prophesied in that other Brunn, 1942? In the *first iteration*. In *this* iteration, though, the cause wasn't simple pneumonia. While walking with his wife near their Vinhorady villa, Karel was shot in the chest by an outraged reader of *Lidové noviny*, a Social Democrat—a Communist—angered by Karel's endless warnings against Totalitarianism. He died in his wife Olga Scheinpflugová's arms. A state funeral was planned, with a procession to the historic Vysehrad cemetery and the rock where Princess Libuse prophesied the birth of Prague. At the last minute, the procession and all public ceremonies were canceled by the Benes government.

He was laid to rest at night, without a service.

After the war a tombstone was added next to his, inscribed:

> *Here would have been buried*
> *Josef Čapek, painter and poet.*
> *Grave far away*
> *18 02/1887 to—04/1945*

From a good thought everything else flows forth, as a matter of course.

Schoenberg said this only hours ago, while leading Paul down a bare hallway to a narrow door. "This place," removing a key from his pocket, "is an empty, silent space I have created for God." The door was solid oak. The lock clicked. He gripped the knob and had difficulty turning it at first. It squeaked open on rusty hinges.

A scent of dust, and something acrid.

Schoenberg stepped into darkness, and beckoned. Paul felt the close, dry air on his face, smelled the wine dregs, and the dust. A small lamp was switched on, revealing an oblong room. "This, Herr, the *caesura room*."

An oaken table almost filled the narrow space. Eight chairs—curiously unmatched, of steel, wood, plastic—surrounded it. Wooden racks, pressed against the four walls, crowded the chairs. "In here, we created an empty space, while we sailed the decahexachords into the past."

On the table sat an ashtray littered with cigar butts, several unwashed whiskey glasses and a nearly-empty bottle of *Bols* gin. A fine haze of dust covered everything. At the opposite end of the room, over what might have once been a window gazing upon begonias and rhododendrons, a black wall shone with Hebrew letters.

Noting Paul's attention, Schoenberg said, "My method of composing in twelve tones, Herr Haas, has always served the *Sacred*." He walked along the racks, searching. "God's greatest creation is the work of Art created by man. Others do not comprehend this. Nor do they understand why my sacred works, be it *Moses und Aron*, or *Die Jakobsleiter*, or *Modern Psalm*, are *incomplete*." He halted, drawing himself upright. The racks did not hold wine bottles. Rather, they were built for rolls of paper, and had a whiff of alchemy. "A lack of certainty, Herr Haas, a lack of closure, these things are at the heart of our Judaism. An awe for the mysterious. But there is one work, Herr Haas, that I did complete."

From one of the smaller slots Schoenberg drew out a roll of paper, and, with hand trembling, removed the black ribbon and unrolled it. "This was the first *decahexachord*." Paul took hold. He carried it into the pool of lamplight—a string of knotty chords in purple ink sprawled across the length of the paper, forming not Hebrew letters but star-like patterns, crisscrossing one another and linking up in chains. "The final rendering was greatly reduced, of course, with fine tempering."

Paul whispered, "But how?"

Schoenberg's eyes flashed. "The idea was started, Herr Haas, by a *gift*." Briefly, he smiled. He returned to the racks. "A musical manuscript retrieved from Czechoslovakia, from the Ghetto Terezin, after the War in the *first iteration*." He withdrew several sheets of brown paper in a protective plastic sleeve. "The title page of the composition, as you can see, is rather extraordinary in its design." Gently, he set it down beside the roll. "Herr Haas, you named your work *Al S'Fod*."

The musical notation formed *Hebrew letters*. It read left to right:

Do Not Lament for chorus, 1942
souvenir of the first and last year in the Terezin exile.

Paul's legs lost all tension. Pulling out a chair, he sat down heavily.

The old man said, "I was doomed to die this day, had I not revealed this truth to you."

"Goodnight, Dad . . . Mom says goodnight, too."

Too late, he registers Olga's soft voice in the hall. He rouses himself from lethargic thoughts, stands up, goes to the door, opens it. The light flicks out beneath her door. The house is dark and quiet. "*Dobry vecer, Olinka,*" he says softly, yet striving to be heard.

The silence is aching. He feels the absence deep in his chest—Sona, Olga, gone—then she responds, just as softly, "*Night, Papa.*"

He goes back into the room and gently shuts the door before checking the clock on the desk. *11:16.* His headache is gone, but the cigarettes have left his body and his long, heavy limbs feel tweaked and unpleasantly hollow. Standing at the desk he opens the satchel and gently pulls out the old, almost decaying pages.

He reveals staves drawn in his own hand on the coarse brown paper, notes and penned words providing bass and treble voices in chromatic unison, in fierce unison.

Do not lament, do not cry
at a time like this,
don't lower your head,
work! work!

61

In 1938, a letter had arrived at Delmonica Drive postmarked Brno, Czechoslovak Republic—his last communication from Karel. "*Things are worse daily, Pavel. Have we failed?*" Inside was another letter—Air Mail from England, the thin blue onionskin containing a letter to *The Brothers Čapek and Haas*, in Wells' English cursive. '*Maybe a certain cringing immunity may be possible for a few years more if Eastern Europe and France are thrown to the wolves. Then, in a state of extreme disadvantage, the British Empire (and the USA) will come to its last accounting.*'

Slowly, almost unnoticed, the door to the *caesura room* swung shut. The dust irritated his eyes. The low-lying smell of gin and wine, of spent cigarettes, of stillness and isolation . . .

Schoenberg waited. "Herr Haas?"

Paul stood up, folded back the cover page on the brittle brown paper, as though to silence the angry chromatic chorus. "I must . . . " He yanked open the door. Once free of the hallway, into the large living room, he breathed deeply. "I must go, Herr Professor."

Yet he paused before a framed black-and-white photograph. Words carved on a gravestone.

Schoenberg was pressing the satchel into Paul's hands. "I have placed your things inside, Herr Haas. Please."

Taking it, Paul could not look away from the inscription.

```
S A T O R
A R E P O
T E N E T
O P E R A
R O T A S
```

He could not understand the words, only the dizzying palindrome that bound them.

"My disciple Anton Webern's memorial stone." Schoenberg's voice, at his shoulder, grew stronger. "Before us, Herr Haas, music could move in many layers, but always in three directions. The harmonic line, up and down, and melodic line, forward."

```
S A T O R
A R E P O
T E N E T
O P E R A
R O T A S
```

"But with our system, we created *inversion*, *retrograde*, and *retrograde inversion*. And music was forever changed." He walked past Paul and opened the front door, revealing the path of stepping stones, the incline, the street. A fresh breeze. "And with the discovery of the decahexachord, I found I could command the very substance of existence in four directions. *Sator arepo tenet opera rotas.*"

```
S A T O R
A R E P O
T E N E T
O P E R A
R O T A S
```

"What does it mean?"

The old man's brief smile was not found in his sad, haunted eyes; the eyes, Paul later realized, of a man who no longer belonged; of a man who, even more than Paul himself, had lost everything familiar, including his beloved wife. A far traveler.

"It translates, Herr Haas, '*The Sower Arepo Keeps the Work Circling.*'"

Paul stands in the middle of the study. The Benny Goodman, long over, continues to turn, the needle hissing on its inner band like distant surf.

I must know. I cannot dwell on what Schoenberg says. There is another. At least one other I can ask. I must talk to him—Schoenberg's Devil Incarnate. Now.

In Hugo's Wheeldex he finds the card easily: the Brentwood address of Igor Stravinsky.

Chrysalis/Mayfly: Oh—oh—oh! (Stops). I proclaim the era of life. I command all creation: Live, for the kingdom of life has come. (Whirling). Oh—oh—oh!
A few last mayflies: Eternal, eternal is life. (They fall dead).

—*The Insect Play* by Karel and Josef Čapek

5. THE INVENTOR OF MUSIC

The house at 1260 North Wetherly Drive—flat-roofed, of simple gray and green slate—slumbers on a steep bank of evergreen and begonia.

As the cab continues up the winding road, Paul remains at the curb, dressed in his best suit coat, tie, trousers and shoes, with the Oxford snap-brim snug on his head. The tumult on Sunset Boulevard is muted. Behind him, crickets chirp in the eucalyptus. A crescent moon silvers the asphalt. During the ride he wondered if a composer famous for his globetrotting would even *be* in California, let alone at his Brentwood address on a Friday evening. The driveway is empty, but he is encouraged by faint light wavering behind lace curtains. Reaching into his pocket, past the gently-folded *Al S'fod* manuscript, he plucks out the Chesterfields pack and taps out a cigarette. Lighting it, he stares at the house, the empty driveway, the candlelight behind the curtains. He wonders: how crazed will he seem, knocking on the door, disturbing the peace at 9:30 at night?

Sator, arepo, tenet . . .

Blinking the words away, he cannot rid himself of circling conundrums. Schoenberg and the decahexachord. *Yours was the last that we attempted. And the most momentous*, he said. Yet the stave flower, sent back through time only three months ago, surely failed. It flung them—he, Magdalena, Karel, Josef and the others—only eleven years into the future. Across Time, but not across Space.

A lack of certainty, Herr Haas, a lack of closure, these things are at the heart of our Judaism. An awe for the mysterious. But there is one work, Herr Haas, that I did complete.

Tenet, opera, rotas...

"*Pavel*," Magdalena gazing up at him, in the Augustinian Monastery's little garden. "*I haven't been born yet.*"

He had come to believe that the stave flower was the *tool* through which the *Sylvan Jeanne D'Arc* was born. That, by meeting It—the *Geist der alten Natur*—Magdalena was transformed. Gideon and Max and the others debated that point in Gideon's house on Krenova Street, and in the years after, the Obstinates Redux came to believe it; however mystifying that belief might be.

A breeze stirs the palm trees.

Later, Paul will wonder at what point he became certain that a figure was standing on the porch; indeed, that the figure had been observing him from the moment he stepped out of the cab and donned his hat. The porch is in shadow, yet something darker than the shadow is standing there, staring down. He can either depart, having been merely smoking a cigarette, or he can approach the house, and the watchful figure. The moment teeters in the balance on the steep hillside, against a chorus of drowsy crickets.

The nicotine calms him, firms his resolve. He drops the cigarette to the pavement, squashes it with his shoe.

The angle of the driveway seems steeper than it should be; he is ascending the heights of Brentwood. Abetted by the nicotine, his heart pounds; he becomes acutely aware of his pulse against his shirt collar, the tightness of the hat on his head. But he is certain, now. A man is standing on the porch. Paul wants to wave and say hello—to change from silent intruder to harmless visitor—but he's entranced by the inevitability of the moment, and by the famous details of the figure coming into forceful clarity: the bantam-weight stature, the rumpled suit and tie, the broad shoulders, and knobby cranium, the strong nose upon which perch heavy and black-framed glasses magnifying enormous eyes; eyes which observe the intruder's approach with calm detachment. As Paul places his shoe on the top step, Igor Fyodorovich Stravinsky—chameleon composer of the *Le Sacre, Petroushka, Les Noces, Dumbarton Oaks*, friend of Picasso and Diaghilev, exile of St. Petersburg and Paris and Vienna—wrenches his ample lips into a Cheshire cat smile. One of his hands tightens on a cane, the other seeks to take both that Paul offers. He says, upward, in deep, glottal, Russian-tinged English, "You are *un app-ear-ari-tion*, my *deeer*."

"Maestro."

Stravinsky's hand, disproportionately large for his body, is dry and hot. "Maestro *Haas*." A slight, somehow charming, bow.

"I . . . " The rest dies in Paul's throat—dies as he begins to grasp the presence before him, Igor Stravinsky, the second most revered composer of his youth, and somehow a *co-conspirator* in the most troubling moment of his life. "I . . . was uncertain whether to disturb you tonight." He adds, while noting how the lace curtains glow in the butter-yellow candlelight, "You were expecting me?"

Stravinsky shakes his famous knobby head. "I am an adept *hear-er*." A formal gesture, with thumb and forefinger lifted to what is a very large ear. "The arrival of the cab. The door *slammink*. These things *rouse-ed* me." A scent of pine issues from the partly open door. Incense. And, as Stravinsky leans closer, a scent of gin. "Inside, *please*."

His host steps uncertainly backward, swinging open the door. The cane is used in another gesture, presenting an expanse of beige carpet, plush couches, teak end tables and Tiffany lamps—a living room like many in Hollywood but for the many ikons and religious tableaux crowding the tables and fireplace mantle; from a dozen different vantage points, the portraits watch Paul's entry: the serenely Russian Orthodox eyes of Justinian and Theodora. "We will share a *drink*." Stravinsky ambulates toward the wet bar, adding over his knobby shoulder, "Gin?"

"Thank you, yes." Paul removes his hat. He feels the regard of those dozens of ikons in the swaying candlelight. "I am... quite overwhelmed, at meeting you. And that you know my name."

"I have *Bols Gin*, you see." Stravinsky offers a toothy, yet nervous smile. "Very hard to *hold*, in this country."

Paul thanks him again, recalling the dusty bottle in the caesura room. He watches the broad shoulders of the little man, head bowed at the bar.

Another far traveler.

The room is quiet but for the whisper of the candle flames, and the clack of the gin cap being set firmly on tile.

Justinian and Theodora, in blue and gold raiments, watch from every corner of the room as the old man steps back. A single glass with melting ice sits beside the bottle. Stravinsky searches for a second glass—his Cheshire cat smile growing once more, twitching nervously—as he spies one on the coffee table. Approaching it between the couches, he lifts it saying, "Please. I have no *clean glasses*."

"That is fine, Maestro." Paul tightens his grip on his hat; a moment later he spies a hook and hangs his Fedora on it.

"Do you speak French, *Monsieur* Haas?"

"*Oui*."

"*Bon*." He sets down the bottle. "I am more comfortable in this language than in English." A pleased exhalation, as he turns, bearing in his large hands two tumblers half-full of gin and ice.

"Thank you, *Monsieur*." Paul takes the glass. "I hope I'm not intruding on your evening."

"My wife is at our daughter's for the week. My assistant is about his own affairs." Stravinsky gestures to the nearer couch, and seats himself on the farther. "I am alone tonight."

Yet Paul knows the great man is lying.

Seating himself on the couch Paul becomes profoundly aware not only of the dozens of languid, watchful ikons, but some other presence in the house. A box of weathered yellow cardboard roughly the size of a manuscript box, bound with thick rubber bands, sits on the table like unfinished business.

"*Monsieur* Stravinsky, do you know why I am here?"

"A friendly visit?" The Maestro slurps deeply of the gin.

"I was speaking today," Paul ventures, "with Professor Schoenberg."

Stravinsky's reaction is sudden: he grips the tumbler tight, begins coughing while rapidly blinking watery eyes. Recovering, he offers a thick-lipped sneer. "*No.*" This said as much to the table, and a portrait on the table between them, one facing the great man. "*Do not speak* the name here, *Monsieur.*" And sets his glass down heavily; glass on glass. "Do not speak it."

Paul strives for calm, but the nicotine has ebbed, and the candlelight shivering in his peripheral vision has taken over his entire body. He sets down his glass. From his coat pocket he withdraws the brittle, folded paper. The paper he has yet to fully reconcile.

This is yours, Herr Haas.

Paul lays it down past his tumbler, in the middle of the table. *Al S'fod.* Stravinsky lifts his chin and looks elsewhere. In candlelight, the Hebrew letters lurk in the blue tint of the page. "*Monsieur*, he showed me the decahexachord."

Stravinsky reaches blindly for the tumbler. The faint clink of ice on ice, as he drinks.

"The decahexachord, which you helped create, and which you and the others sent back to me."

"This man, this *Viennese chemist* . . ." Large hands grasp and regrasp the tumbler. "He has broken a *sacred promise.*"

"He was frightened, *Monsieur.*"

Stravinsky refuses to look at the paper. "The *other*'s methods. The *twelve tones.* There is *much to explore there.* I have always said as much. And this . . . was to be our starting point."

"*Monsieur* Stravinsky, I mean you no disrespect. But I am confused. I hope to find answers."

In response, Stravinsky's head inclines. He crosses his legs and folds both hands on his knees. Candlelight reflects in his large glasses, and the man—other than his outsized head and hands and clothes—seems shrunken. He reaches for the photograph and twists it for Paul to see. A head and shoulders portrait of a man Paul's age, whose long face and strong nose bear a strong resemblance to the man before him. "*This, Monsieur*, this was the *cost* to me. My son, Soulimina." He blinks rapidly then rises to his feet, walking to the fireplace and the ikons gathered there. "My son."

Paul gathers up the manuscript paper, folds it, and replaces it in his pocket. "*Monsieur* Stravinsky, I—"

"It was a *game, Monsieur* Haas." His trembling hand touches a bronze coin on the mantle, moving it back and forth. "Only a game. I greeted the money that was paid me. I greeted the *challenge* of the game, for I am *an inventor of music*. And this creation of ours—this was a grand invention by the foolish expatriates." He straightens his shoulders.

Paul presses: "I must know, *Monsieur*. Why your attempt to bring me from Brno to here failed. Why I was carried only eleven years forward, and did not leave Brno. As though . . . a force had drawn us there, so that the Magdalena might . . . "

"The flaws—they were the punishment!" Again, he touches the bronze coin with trembling fingers. "We played the game for a day, only, and realized too late that his formulas and equations had made the endeavor a tragic achievement, *Monsieur!*"

He turns. His face is despondent. At the same moment candles flicker. A breeze stirs through the room. Paul feels it against his face. A window open? Down the dark hall? He gazes down to where candlelight barely touches a lone door.

"*Monsieur*, how many others were saved?"

With Justinians and Theodoras at his shoulders, Igor Stravinsky girds himself. And seems about to reply when an out-of-tune piano strikes a D, in the room down the hall.

The note lingers, and Stravinsky turns to the many Justinians and Theodoras. They seem to hold back a response in their eyes. And the moment lingers, as the candlelight trembles down the hallway.

Returning to English, his host says, "These questions, my *deeer*. You must *inquire-ed* them of others."

"Your friends, are they here tonight?" He turns to the hall. "Is it *Monsieur* Werfel? Or Huxley?" And when no response comes from the door, he says, loudly, "*The Sower Arepo Keeps the Work Circling.*"

Stravinsky, at his shoulder: "You must *leave me at once, please*! My assistant *Bobbee* will soon be returning."

But Paul starts down the hall, into shadow. The wood creaking under his shoes. "Is the machinery here? I must see it. I must know how it was created."

"You—" A hand grasps his jacket.

"Who are your guests, *Monsieur*?"

"You cannot—"

The day's many conundrums have led inevitably to this moment, it seems: the old and famous man tugging violently on his elbow, swearing now in glottal Russian. Yet when Paul reaches for the knob and finds it locked, the urge to strike it with his shoulder—to break the wood and shove inside and perhaps injure whoever lurks beyond—evaporates. The door remains shut; the room beyond, silent. And his *hero*, Igor Stravinsky, is now a sad, frightened man gasping for breath. "*You . . . you must leave! At once!*"

He heads back down the hall, but stops at the mantle. What he had thought a gold coin is actually the end of a key. Stravinsky is at his side, is grasping for it even as Paul snatches it up.

"No!"

And Paul stares down uncomprehendingly, at a key entirely familiar, of baroque and unlikely shape; its haft decorated with a cameo profile of the Maestro's beloved Olga.

The key to the *Baseform Scasovani Generator*.

Stravinsky's trembling hand relents. He steps back. A long moment later, in a calm voice, he says, "Each of us, *Monsieur*," as Paul walks toward the front door, away from the many candles which gleam in Stravinsky's imploring eyes. "Each of us faces *Divine retribution*. All for meddling in this game. To me, a beloved son. To others, a wife. A brother. A sister. And even . . ." He follows, and says with great emphasis, "A *child. Yes, even a child. A boy not yet six.*"

An image flickers into Paul's mind. A photograph of a boy with brown hair combed carefully across his pale serious forehead, and eyes the same color as his father's.

The corner of its dustless bronze frame bedecked with a black ribbon.

"We found ourselves upon an exceedingly high tower, so that I seemed to touch the clouds. Looking down from this tower, I saw a city beautiful in appearance, shining, and prodigiously wide-spread, but not so great that I could not discern its limits and boundaries all around. The city formed a circle and was surrounded with walls and ramparts, but instead of moats there yawned a gloomy abyss, to all appearances boundless and bottomless. Light shone only above the city, while beyond the walls it was pitch dark."

—*The Labyrinth of the World and the Paradise of the Heart*
by Jan Amos Komensky

6. MENDEL'S GARDEN

At two a.m., the doors to Studio 3-C stand open, drenching the pavement with scarlet light.

A new cyclorama depicts razed black hills, shattered black trees and a sunset sky bright as arterial blood. The trees, ranked in forced perspective, rise prominently in the mounded background like tiny black signums of distress, while in the foreground a burnt-out Skoda sedan rests on its hubs under a red-and-gold swastika flag. It's a nightmare that might have leapt entire from Soviet propaganda posters of the Sylvan Massacre, or from earlier German *Volkisch* imagery, the pan-German romanticism that cleaved, at the Massacre, into pan-Slavic fanaticism.

Amid the assembled horror, incurious, and out of place, a dozen men in short-sleeves labor with hammers, screwdrivers and lathes, on ladders, in the rafters, on their hands and knees beneath the set. A few men smoke cigarettes. Everyone works quietly. Their tiredness is akin to the ever-present buzz in the air from the red-gelled lights. *"Yes. Good."* Hugo's voice rises from the lowering smoke. *"Very good."* Calm, controlled. *"Match it up with the illustration."*

Paul stands amid the scene, his right hand in his pocket, gripping and regripping the key.

"Hey, Paul." A greensman lugs a charred tree limb encysted with sickly vines across the stage. Over his shoulder, he adds, "Tell your brother to let us go home."

Hugo emerges from behind the charred hillside. "Who? Ah!"

Paul's hat dangles from his left hand, nearly forgotten. He waves it and treads carefully up the sloping floor, following his own red-tinged shadow. His shoulders brush against a giant tree, while those ahead of him seem to shrink at his approach, until the last is no taller than his elbow.

"Paul." Hugo wipes his hands on his shirt. "Been at the studio all this time?"

"I was out."

Snapping his suspenders on his rounded shoulders, Hugo squints. His salt-and-pepper hair is mussed as ever. Sweat glistens on his forehead and his eyes are bloodshot, due as much to the Benzedrine as the unending toil. A note of concern enters his voice. "What's happened?"

This last hour, while walking Brentwood's dark streets, while riding in the taxi to the studio, Paul had wondered just what to say to Hugo. The urge to confront him, to demand answers, had finally yielded to a great sadness, as well as a great love. Gesturing with his hat he says, in Czech, "We must speak, brother."

Hugo narrows his eyes. The moment lingers. Then he shouts, "Everyone! Coffee break, okay?" He claps his hands. "Fifteen minutes, huh? Then we'll finish up and be ready for tomorrow's shoot!"

From the crew comes scattered applause and weary hurrahs as they climb down, stand up, shuffle out, leaving eddies in the red-tinged smoke.

Hugo lifts his chin and scratches a slight beard that no longer seems boyish, but mangy. "You look tired, Pajo."

Hugo *is* Hugo, Paul tells himself. Hugo has *always been* Hugo, yet this man before me is another solitary traveler.

Along with Schoenberg, and Stravinsky, he has stepped out of Time. Paul manages, "I'm *sorry*."

"Pajo, I don't understand." Hugo steps closer.

"Sorry for what?"

Paul takes his hand from his pocket, and holds up the key.

Hugo's body freezes, but for the slow rise and fall of his sloping shoulders. A moment later, after a quiescent nod, he turns and climbs slowly into the treescape.

"Herr Schoenberg cabled me this afternoon," says Paul. "I just came from *Monsieur* Stravinsky's house."

Hugo hooks his thumbs into his suspenders and lets them go with a snap. "Stravinsky?" Turning back, he pulls a cigarette from a Chesterfield pack, sets it between his lips, and lights it. Hugo exhales, peering through the smoke. He offers the pack. When Paul doesn't move he says again, "Most strange, eh?" He nods, and smokes. He approaches the shattered black bough of a tree, and with a self-consciousness that would have been humorous at any other time, he rests his hand on it. A long moment later he says, "Three months ago, Pajo. Three months, five days, I'd lost you for good."

The simplicity of the statement is chilling. *Three months, five days.* And its ancillary: *Three months five days since Zikmund Richard Haas had died. Three months, five days* of what Sona had called *Hugo's recovery.*

"Six years you'd been gone, in that other life." Hugo draws deeply on the cigarette and exhales toward the rafters, where beams of red light strike and grow stronger. "And I was here. In '43, I was reading about that part of the world in the L.A. Times." He waves the cigarette in a circle. "Alone. Surviving. Starring in bit parts. Narrating propaganda documentaries for our American Foreign Service."

Paul begins to speak, but Hugo cuts him off with a wave of the cigarette. "Can't say how many hours I spent on the phone to New York, begging the Czech consulate for word of you and Father. Lenka and Zikmund." A rise and fall of his shoulders. "And all the while . . . all the while hearing the rumors of *transports,* of ghetto camps where the Jews were herded up like animals." Hugo's dark, plangent voice drops to a near whisper. "I was here." Now, a full shrug. "And I don't think I ever felt the moment. In 1945. When was it, December? When you died, murdered at their hands."

Hugo turns the cigarette toward his mouth and blows on the ember. "I wasn't there for my big brother. Even after the war ended the news was vague. *Gassed at Auschwitz. Whereabouts of the deceased body unknown.*" He seems to study his many-sprawling scarlet shadow on the cyclorama. "I lit a candle for you, brother. I said goodbye. And I survived with my 'career' of bit parts, even directing a few shameless little Z-grade movies. Until the package arrived last year, postmarked Paris, France."

He walks closer to the background, standing among waist-high trees. "I had refused to speak to them, afterwards, you see? Those who knew you, then. After lighting the candle, after saying goodbye. The survivors, they wished to see me, wished to tell me about you and your last years, but I refused, Pajo. I could not face them. I said no. I told them to go away." He turns his back to Paul, but raises his voice. "Then, one evening last year, I found the package in my bungalow. A film reel. The note said only that it had been smuggled out of Soviet Czechoslovakia. It was unsigned. So, I drank most of a fifth of scotch and threaded the film onto the movieola." A circular gesture with the cigarette, before he draws on it again, turning to face Paul. "It was this time of night. I was alone in my bungalow. The film was Nazi propaganda about Theresienstadt, one I'd heard about, but never managed to *see*. *The Fuhrer Gives the Jews a Gift of a City*. A *farce*, Pajo, staged by the Germans. Here were their happy Jews in a Ghetto paradise, free to pursue their sports, education, and the Arts, music especially. And *you*, Pajo, *you* had a starring role." Hugo pauses, and his eyes might be watching it again, floating in the air. His voice becomes rich with irony. "A *concert evening*, all the smiling Jewish prisoners in attendance, while Ančerl and his orchestra played a piece you'd written at the camp, the *Study for Strings*. Fierce, angry music. Stravinskian. And for a few seconds—seconds I ran back and forth there, on the movieola—the film cut to you, Pajo, the *guest of honor*, in the front row." He strolls back among the rising trees, shaking his head. "A scarecrow in a borrowed suit. And yet, alone among those unfortunates playing along to the camera, your anger shone in your immobility, in your crossed arms, in your grim expression, in your eyes. Such anger for this farce. How *galvanizing* to see that." He reaches the burnt-out Skoda and kicks it with his boot. "Soon after, other packages arrived. Possessions of yours. And a musical manuscript."

Paul rouses himself from a vision of his Arcimboldo self. "*Al S'fod.*"

Hugo nods. "And what could I do with that? Bury it in the bottom drawer? Frame it, as I framed Zikmundka's photograph? No, I wanted someone to see it. Someone who would understand it. And who better than your childhood heroes, who live here in Brentwood, eh? The immortals Igor and Arnold? I took it to Schoenberg first." Hugo drops the cigarette and grinds it. "And so I began this miracle." He shrugs. Any more of an explanation is left unsaid, as the smoke lowers over the razed trees.

"I'm sorry, Hugo. For Zikmund."

Hugo attempts another shrug, but it's hollow. So he insists with his voice: "I was *lucky*. Luckier than Schoenberg. Or Stravinsky. Or the others. How could I feel sorrow any more than I had?" He smiles wryly. "I stepped out of that room in Schoenberg's house to find not only *you* here, but Lenka, as well. I had abandoned Lenka and little Zikmund to their fates, fled the Nazis after making that anti-fascist film. So to know that here we were thriving? Even that, Pajo, was an extraordinary gift." He studies the burnt-out hulk of the Skoda.

"How many were saved, Hugo?"

Hugo's attention falls on the red-tinged limbs, and the crooked scarlet shadow falling behind him. "Before I started this project, I was *fading*, brother. Becoming more like a shadow every day, as though I might vanish in the California sunlight, never to be seen again. As though I no longer had any place in the world." With a sudden, theatrical flourish of his right arm, his wrist and hand set the smoke swirling—a gesture familiar from boyhood, conjuring this set, this studio, this city from a makeshift stage in the darkness of Father's shoe shop in Brno. "Your return, Pajo, that was my first inspiration. And this story, this *fairy tale* from the War, that was the second. You spoke of it, and Sona and Lenka, too. The strange stories out of our homeland. Of Magda, and the Sylvan massacre. Our group—Schoenberg, Stravinsky, Werfl, Huxley and the others—they made sure I could tell this story, in my little film. Yes, Pajo. It was worth it."

"Hugo. *How many were saved?*"

He gently lays a hand on the thorny branch, his eyes shining. And grows quiescent in that way of his, allowing a long pause before he replies. "*Only you*, brother." A whisper: "*Only you.*" Then delivers another flourish, which sets smoke swirling. "And yet, this, too. This . . . incredible victory, however small. This . . . *conjuring.*"

A street lamp casts a rhomboid shape on the bedroom ceiling. Sliding into the sheets across from Sona, Paul feels its strange glowing angles banish the palindrome from his thoughts, all the evening's worries subsiding under the gentle ticking of the clock, in the quietness of the house around him. Sona stirs. She murmurs something indistinct and draws a deep breath, her pale arm lifting from the sheets. She asks sleepily, "Finish what you needed to finish?" The skin behind her cotton gown scorches his body as she moves against him. Dizzied with her fragrance, he kisses her warm neck. She laughs, then pulls back. He senses her studying him in the dark. "What is it, Pavliku?"

Desire and dread mingle in the yellow rhomboid. He yearns to hold Sona, to push himself inside her, lose everything in her dizzying heat. Her hand rubs his chest. Soft strands of hair tickle his cheek. "You haven't brooded in a while."

"*Sonicku.*" Softly, in Czech, he says, "Tell me something. What do you remember most . . . about home?"

She replies in English. "Odd question." Smiling. The faintest exhalation, as her hand rubs his chest. "You haven't asked odd questions in a while, either." She stretches again, and relaxes into the mattress. And sighs. "It's Hugo, isn't it? He's pulling you into this obsession of his."

"No, *manželka.*" He whispers, an invocation to the yellow shape above. "*Just tell me, what do you think about, when you think about home?*"

"Hmmm." She moves closer to him. "I should say something like, *I remember the first time I saw you, Pavliku.*" Her hand moves lower, on his stomach, now. "I should say, I remember Mama, and Papa. And Olinka's birth." She draws another deep, somnolent breath, and, exhaling, says, "But when I think of home, I find myself thinking, always, of *crowds*."

"Crowds?"

He feels her nodding. "Never a single person. Never a face, or the house, or your papa's shoe shop, Czech Shoes at the Rabbit. It's a crowd in the Cabbage Market. Or a crowd on Masaryk Street, outside the hospital." She stirs. "Strange, isn't it? I don't think a day's gone by since we came here that I haven't had such memories rise up. Whether I'm working with a patient, or at lunch. Or even now."

"What do you see, Sonicku?"

The street lamp not only casts a rhomboid shape on the ceiling, it also filters an infinitesimal amount of light onto her skin, striking her eyes. Solemn-eyed Sona, the thinker. The bright young medical student, who had charmed him from the first moment they met in the Brno Beseda. "*I see Prague*," she says. "On that last day, before we left on the plane. Hradcany on the hill. The Little Quarter swarming with people. Karel's villa in Vinhorady. I smell the wet iron in the air, and hear the church bells in the streets." She stretches. "You never see such spires, hear such bells, in America." A stretch. "Maybe that's why I think of it."

He shuts his eyes.

She murmurs, "He can't have you tomorrow."

"Huh?"

"Hugo can't have you tomorrow. Or Sunday, Pajo. It's running you ragged." She kisses his shoulder, his ear. "I won't let him take you."

In the long shadow cast by the Monastery wall, against rain-dappled begonias, petunias and peas in the wild garden, she sits on the marble bench with her gloved hands folded on her lap, in Brno, in 1931.

"Magda?"

She looks up. "Pajo." In shadow, her hair retains its reddish glow. She smiles wanly. "What are you doing here?" He pulls open the small gate and steps through, into the Monastery's narrow, chastely-untended garden. The wilderness of autumnal asters, of Michaelmas daisies, pushes against the low, black-iron fence. "Sona told you where I was?"

He nods. And, feeling as though he were disturbing some holy silence, he sits beside her among drooping red and yellow blossoms. Bees dart and dip, busy on this late autumn day. Behind them, choristers sing in the Monastery's hall. The organ's tones mingle with the buzzing of the bees, and the noise of the city center to the northeast is lost, and found, and lost again.

She wears a light blue coat and skirt, like a schoolgirl.

"We're going to England next month, Magda. Karel and Josef and I."

Her lips part, but she says nothing. Once again she gazes at her green gloves.

He says, carefully, "Would you like to come with us?"

She glances up. In her eyes, the wondering questions and the answers, too—they're all apparent. Then she rises and walks three paces amongst the flowers. This quietness is something new to her personality; but it's not timidity, or fear at her transformation. Pavel can see the changes most clearly when she's playing. She has not given up the flute. Indeed, she has given over more of her time to Beseda concerts and work at the Real Gymnasium II; her playing has a calm strength to it, a seriousness, without the playfulness of earlier years. As Pavel understands it, this is what she brought back from Brunn, 1944. This, and a desire for solitude—something that troubles Sona, who often finds her in remote corners of Brno, like the Augustinian's garden, or some grove atop Špilberk Hill, or in the underground casements that, *once upon a time*, had consumed the undesirables of the Empire.

My village is dead, she had said.

He watches the bees darting and dipping among the blossoms.

"This is a marvelous garden," she says, startling him. "Don't you think?"

He nods.

"The Monastery lets it grow wild. In honor of Mendel." She tucks a strand of hair behind her ear. "This was *his* garden, you know."

He feigns to look for the remains of the famous Glasshouse in the courtyard; the 30 meter by 6 meter foundation in the rain-soaked concrete.

"I don't want anyone else to know, Pavel." She lifts her right hand to scratch the back of her left. "Not yet."

"As we agreed. Of course. We've begun writing our narratives, Josef and I. Max will translate them into English, and then we'll show them only to Mr. Wells. You won't be mentioned, of course. Karel thought, if you wished to come along with us and speak with Mr. Wells . . . " Pavel shrugs. "We haven't much proof. The booklet from the theater. And our testimony."

She tugs at her left glove, slowly revealing the pale skin that retains, however faint, the greenish cast. A condition that Sona—ever the logical doctor—has striven to cure. "I can't testify to much, Pavel." She adds, solemnly, "Only that . . . that I haven't been born yet." A smile. "And I have to wait until then. I can't risk it, by letting others know."

I haven't been born yet.

"I've told you, haven't I?" She touches a white rose. "How, when I was a girl, Mother liked to say I was *destined*."

"Yes."

"My sister, too."

"Because of the color of your hair, wasn't it?"

"She said it marked me." A bee hovers near her hand. When she raises it, the bee flies in tandem, darting with her as she moves it left, right. She smiles as the bee darts away. "And when I was six, the Maestro heard me play at a Gymnasium concert. He strode up to Mother and said, 'This girl must be enrolled at the Conservatory.' And when my mother showed she didn't understand, he shouted it. *'This girl is destined for great things, Madame! She will one day be the greatest flautist in our lands!'* Magdalena tugs off her other glove. "He frightened me so, Pavel. I was always terrified of him."

"All of us." He tries to draw another smile out of her.

She turns slowly amid the drooping flowers and drowsy bees. "After Mendel died, nobody knew what he'd discovered. Did you realize that?"

"Yes."

"It took them years to raise a statue. And now they keep this garden wild. I like it this way."

"I do, too." Pavel studies the shadow of the monastery on the damp foliage and the brilliant sunlight on the grass beyond. *She is decided*, he tells himself. *We must honor her decision not to come to England.*

My village is dead.

"Pavel, I *feel* them." Her soft voice is nearly lost in a sudden breeze whispering through the twigs and branches. "*The green and growing things.*" She kneels amidst the weeds, leaning forward, her hair spilling across her shoulders. "*They're down there, now.*" She runs her hand across the clover. "*Not even seedlings, but present, inside themselves.*" She gazes up, and her eyes shine with something like fear. *"I'm worried, Pajo, that I won't know until too late, when they're born."*

"A treat, instead of a treatment, for what ails you!"

—slogan for Old Gold cigarettes, 1949

7. SUNDAY

On Saturday, Sona had rented a station wagon and driven the family up the coast to Capitola.

Most of Sunday is spent on the beach, where Paul, in striped short trousers and a loose cotton shirt, manages to lose his thoughts in the brilliant sunshine and the calming thunder of the surf, in the mini-dramas of Olga and several of the local boys—ten-minute Straussian operettas of interest and estrangement—in William's discovery of the surf as a creature of benign malevolence, churning up endless strange objects for his scrutiny.

Paul manages also to twist his ankle in a hill of loose sand, a mildly painful injury that is treated with playful seriousness by Sona, who sets up triage on the *chaise-longue* under the polka-dot umbrella; applying a cold compress of ice from the cooler, administering aspirin and a beer and a gentle kiss on his ankle.

Sona gains a lovely dark luster over the course of the day. She does not press him for conversation: this is her therapy, the infrequent holding of hands, the murmured request for more lotion on her shoulders, the funny anecdotes about doctors and nurses at work. And while he feels detached from the worries of 13 Friday, he cannot prevent thoughts of a poem from recurring in the endless parade of combers, in the endless forward rush and hissing retreat of the ocean.

Power, plow, sower, sow

Once upon a time, he had deemed himself a Protektor: his destiny, as apparent and unshakable as Magdalena's, revealed in the Holy and Awesome 72-letters of the stave flower. Yet with his marriage to Sona, and with Olga's birth, and then, to his surprise, William's, his role had changed. *These* were the people he was meant to protect. From *a place of greater power*. He sees Josef's smile, as they stood under the Cedar of Lebanon in the garden of the Vinhorady villa.

> *awake and labor,*
> *redeem and be redeemed.*

"Papa!"

Little William, dripping wet in swim trunks, strides toward the blankets on which his parents lay. "Look what I found!"

Sona raises her sunglasses. "Oh, William, not another crab . . ."

He holds it up, grinning proudly. "It's for Papa!"

"Ah!" Paul musters great enthusiasm, extending his palm and catching the proffered gift. A smooth round stone, ebony with glints of azure, still wet and shiny from its ocean bed. "Why, that's *marvelous*, William. Thank you."

"I dug it up! The water almost got my legs!"

"Nothing for me, Willie?" Sona wipes his face with a towel, then throws it around his shoulders. William gives a smirk that mimics Olga's, then hastily kisses her cheek, tosses off the towel, and stamps back to the surf line. "Stay near the shore!" She settles back on the sand, smiling. "That is *quite a stone*."

Nodding, Paul lifts it close to his eyes, peering at its now gargantuan surface sprawled against the glittering, blurry ocean, and—thinking yet again of Wells, of the rainy strand—he ponders a vision as large as H.G.'s, of this little rock being rolled and rocked and carried about for millions of years, in the act of being shaped and polished and hidden, dormant, in high and low tide, one of countless others on this beach perhaps intended to remain here for millennia, only to be unearthed by a child's curiosity. Pure chance, to be plucked up across the breadth of eternity.

awake and labor,
redeem and be redeemed.

Yet had not he and Magdalena, Josef, and Karel, and the others, been plucked up with great intent? All of them to play a part in the unfolding drama of Time. And only he, Pavel, awake at this moment to question it, in the tangerine sunlight.

> "While Haas's source of inspiration in the last two decades lay in the Moravian folk song, his compositions from the fearful years 1939–1941 are marked by his adherence to the old Czech chorale to St. Wenceslaus. What makes it noteworthy is that here was a Jewish composer finding solace in the invocations: "Let us not perish, us and our descendants, Saint Wenceslaus."
>
> —*Music in Terezin* by Joža Karas

8. STAR OF THE UNBORN

Late Monday morning, he compiles the full pencil score with cue sheets and instructions for the copyist. Gathering them together, he tells himself for the fourth or fifth time that this project—this commitment—is now *complete*.

He tugs open the curtains.

Sunlight hammers through the window. A flotilla of Louis XIVth mirrors is being wheeled past, the shuddering reflections too bright to bear. Dazed, Paul collects his pencils, puts them in the tin along with the eraser, and stands up. He dusts off his trousers and checks his wristwatch. He'd told the music department he'd deliver the pages before lunch. He's early. So he returns to the closet and searches the contents for a heavy cord sweater and scarf, taking them down from their hangers then folding them carefully on the sofa with the other items. He adds heavy shoes, the compass, the currency, and packs them all into a satchel that he closes up and sets inside the closet. Then he snatches up the long cardboard tube he'd noticed earlier that morning—one of William Menzies, marked with the Universal crest; it's now empty of the blueprints it contained. He replaces the cap and tucks the tube under his arm.

At 11:55 he delivers the papers to the music editor, who invites him to lunch. But Paul refuses—he's on his way to see Hugo.

St. Vitus Cathedral rises beside Hradcany castle on a painted hill, its sooty, crenellated spires cutting into a luminous gray sky. The crown of Prague sits over a tableau of the Little Quarter and a finely-wrought miniature of the Charles Bridge in black and gold, complete with every famous statue. In the foreground is a foreshortened stretch of cobblestone, the side of a Prague brownstone bedecked with red and black swastika flags at eerily nervy angles, with shafts of sunlight cast by scrims of luminous fabric.

Beyond grips and extras and greensmen, Hugo stands below the stoop, speaking quietly but with broad gestures with Dick Widmark—their dapper, wiry Gestapo agent in black leather. He does not notice Paul, and the others merely nod, accepting his presence.

Paul is able, easily, to approach one of the lowest scrims, to run his hand along the fabric which, as he suspected, is parchment.

In another minute, it is done.

"*Dobry den, Pahn-ay Haas,*" says a light, amused voice behind him.

Paul turns. "Miss Simmons, I . . . "

Dressed in a yellow peasant skirt, the actress now possesses the brilliant scarlet hair of *Kameradschaftsbund* mythology. She fixes Paul with violet eyes. "*Yahk se mah-tay?*"

"I am very well, thank you. You look . . . stupendous."

"Why, thank you, Mr. Haas." She clasps a golden alto flute.

"Ah. You are armed with Magdalena's weapon."

She lifts the embouchure to her lips. "I'm the Pied Piper of Prague, I suppose." For an instant she becomes Magdalena in the orchestra pit, smiling up at him. "And I feel as uncomfortable about it as my Czech, I'm afraid. I wish I could play."

"Then you would be entirely too talented."

Her expression becomes serious. "You'll be writing her melody, won't you?" She lowers the flute.

"I—" Paul strives for a response, then finds himself striving to hide the pause. He places the cardboard tube under his arm and says, nonchalantly, "Hugo and I have not yet discussed it."

"I feel foolish, really, pretending to play when I'm not sure what it sounds like."

He recalls a strange, melismatic melody of twists and turns. "A Moravian folk song, surely," he says, following it somewhere in the air overhead. "Tinged with the East."

Hugo's voice intrudes, not distinctly enough to be discerned—laughing at something Widmark said, clapping the actor on the shoulder. A prop man hands the actor a submachine gun while gaffers raise lanterns around the scene to shine like reflected street lamps in the wet cobblestone.

"What about my dress?" She steps back two paces and twirls her peasant skirt.

"It's very lovely."

"But is it the sort that *she* would wear, Paul?"

"In real life, Magda was a very modern girl. But in the . . . the myth that grew up, yes. The ikons that have been smuggled out of the U.S.S.R portray her this way."

Her eyes grow suddenly solemn and serious, emphasized by her low bangs. "Just now I called you Paul but your name is Pavel. Do you hate people calling you Paul?"

"No, Miss Simmons."

"But we should call things what they are, I think, Pavel. Like this," she gestures with a slender white arm, to the castle on the hill. "It's *Praha*, isn't it. *Praha*. But we call it Prague. A much uglier name. Like *frog*."

"It's *make believe*," he says, almost a whisper, while cupping William's cool round stone in his pocket. "Actually, Miss Simmons, Magda never went to Prague, much. She and the others fought the *Wehrmacht* nearer my hometown, but the studio chiefs said to make it Prague, since nobody's heard of Brno." He adds, "It's the only concession that Hugo had to make."

Jean Simmons has not stopped scrutinizing Paul. "I want to know her *instinctively*, and make my portrayal *truthful*, Pavel. So I don't betray her memory. I . . ." Widmark raises the submachine gun, firing blanks toward the ceiling. She claps her hands briefly to her ears. "Oh, that *awful* noise." She takes him by the sleeve. "This way." Stepping gingerly over trailing cord, she leads him out the studio door. The walkway is comparatively quiet under a cloudless sky. Sunlight dazzles on concrete. "You have a very rich tan today, Mr. Haas."

He smiles. "My wife drove us to the coast this weekend." The thought draws his attention to the lingering pain in his right ankle.

"Sonya, isn't it? She knew Magdalena, didn't she?"

"They were good friends, yes."

She lifts the flute up to his shoulder, the gold keys winking in the sunlight. Confidently: "I'd like to speak with her." She places her lips near the embouchure. "I want to get the idea of Magdalena the Pied Piper out of my mind, Pavel."

Paul, thinking of his wife, cannot respond at first. Then says, "I am sure she would be thrilled to tell you all about her."

"I remember listening to reports on the BBC." She studies the cloudless sky. Paul marvels at the vividness of her hair, and how the scarlet strands contrast with her eyes.

My village is dead, Pajo.

"I was . . . well I must have been around fourteen, I suppose. And for weeks all they could talk about were the strange reports out of Czechoslovakia. Each one more *fantastic* than the last. And when I saw the newsreels . . . Grainy images. You couldn't quite tell how the trees had changed. They were so charred, and the bodies on the branches seemed, well, unreal." A moment later, "She didn't have a violent bone in her body, did she, Pavel?"

"No."

"And yet look at what she *accomplished*. Violence was committed, but . . ." She fixes him again with her eyes. "I wonder what *I* would do, if I were in her shoes."

"There were many brave people in London, Miss Simmons."

"Oh, *surviving* the Blitz. But just surviving, Pavel. Not fighting them, *directly*. That's what I admire about her. How she did it—well, that doesn't matter as much, does it." She falls quiet, and along with Paul, studies the sky for a time.

He says, finally, "There were many great people there. I was fortunate to know some of them."

"And the ones you knew . . . they didn't survive?"

He shakes his head.

Her voice is now as solemn as her eyes. "That's terribly sad, Pavel."

He grips the stone. "Yes, Miss Simmons."

Behind them, the door swings open. "Hey, Miss Simmons!" An assistant director waves his clipboard. "Hugo's ready for you."

"It's *White Mountain* time?" She smiles.

The young man's eyebrows jut up. "Huh?"

"Oh, never mind."

"Thank you for speaking with me, Miss Simmons."

"But aren't you coming in, Pavel? Hugo would love to see you."

He strives to fix her image in his mind; sunstruck, with hair nearly as bright as fire. "I have an errand to run." He offers, "Tell him, please, that the music for his *sleazy film* is delivered. And that I will see him later."

"All right." She waves. "*Nas-keh-leh-dahn-no*, Pavel."

"*Nashledanou, Slečna* Simmons."

✦

At the doorpost, he touches the mezuzah and then kisses his fingers. He knocks. Within the mansion, the whelm of chromatic chords ceases. Paul hears the grate of the piano bench. He has time enough to step to the side of the porch and check the tennis court. The gate is shut. The burden is laid on the red clay, draped with his winter coat.

Inside, footsteps. The *snick-snick* of the chain being withdrawn, the click of the doorknob being turned.

Schoenberg stares up, in the shade beyond. A genuine smile. "I had hoped, Herr Haas, you would come again."

"How now, you weathercock, I suspect you are minded to turn back!" Before I had time to answer, he threw a bridle over my neck, and the bit of Obstinacy which slipped quickly into my mouth. He remarked at the same time: "Now you will be more willing to persevere in what you have begun."

—*The Labyrinth of the World and the Paradise of the Heart* by Jan Amos Komensky

9. FIRST AND SECOND LIVES

"Am I interrupting your work, Herr Professor?"

Today, the *Monster of Modern Music* wears a beige short-sleeved shirt, freshly-pressed black trousers and brown loafers. His smile is genuine. He takes Paul's hand in his own and gently shakes it. "No, Herr Haas." His voice is no longer gray. Perhaps the fresh breeze has worked wonders. Or is it merely 13 Friday, receding with time?

Hanging his hat, setting the universal tube on a chair, Paul strives not to stare at the photograph of Anton Webern's gravestone.

SATOR
AREPO
TENET
OPERA
ROTAS

"My housekeeper has been by today. And so I offer you more pleasant surroundings than the last time." Indeed, the carpet is spotless, the furniture dust-free. *Menorah* and *Tehillim* gleam above the newly-washed brick fireplace. Daisies adorn the end tables beside the couches, and even the many expressionist self-portraits—newly dusted—stare out from the walls with more resolute power.

"Herr Haas, did you injure yourself?"

Paul gently shifts his weight to his left foot; his right has been aggravated this past hour, while carrying what must be carried. "A sprain. I twisted it in the sand this weekend." Blinking away a memory of Sona gently kissing his ankle, he forces his attention across the room to the piano. Score pages clutter the platen—new pages? Perhaps a new work?

Schoenberg gestures him to the couches and overstuffed chairs. "Please, Herr, sit."

He walks to the couch and sits down, happy to have the weight off his foot.

"Would you like a soft drink?"

"Yes, Herr Professor." He adds, "I would love one." He is pleased to find Schoenberg in good spirits, rejuvenated, and apparently at work. Now he must gather close to him what must be said, and decide precisely how to say it.

```
S A T O R
A R E P O
T E N E T
O P E R A
R O T A S
```

Sunlight brightens and dims. With dark clouds on the northern horizon, promising rain, he had nearly reconsidered leaving his winter overcoat, scarf and satchel on the tennis court.

"I find it amazing how the wonderful Los Angeles weather can turn so subtly awry." Schoenberg strolls to the wet bar. He lifts a bottle of Coca-Cola, gazing through the window, in the direction of the court. If he sees anything unusual he says nothing, merely cantilevers the cap off the bottle with a large opener, drops ice cubes into fluted glasses and pours the soda as though it is Champagne. Returning, glasses held in perfect balance, he says, "And so I *survived* 13 Friday, Herr Haas."

Paul stands up, takes the proffered drink, gives a half-bow, then reseats himself.

"Yet to do so, I had to burden you with my guilt and my responsibilities."

"*No*, Herr Professor," Paul says emphatically. "You opened my eyes."

Another smile flickers across the old man's face. Though still sparrow-thin, his bald pate speckled with liver spots, there is a gleam of life in those round, no longer haunted eyes. "I am glad you have come back, so that I may apologize correctly." He seats himself on the plush chair opposite the table dominated by two large books titled *Principia Mathematica*, volumes 1 and 2. Another, more slender book, *On Formally Undecidable Propositions of Principia Mathematica and Related Systems* sits amid sheets of yellow paper covered in equations and tone rows. Some are folded, some crumpled as though discarded, though still revealing tantalizing hints of work.

Tiny chords, sketched with precision.

"As you can imagine, my friends were quite concerned when the news of our visit reached them. They—and Herr Stravinsky—realized that it was for the best. We are old men. Tired. Frightened. Yet now, we are able to enjoy the sunshine, if only a little."

Paul sips the soda while Schoenberg contemplates his guest across the table.

```
S A T O R
A R E P O
T E N E T
O P E R A
R O T A S
```

"How have *you* been, Herr Haas?"

"My thoughts, Herr." After a pause, he continues, "My thoughts, Herr, have been running in circles since I left you on Friday."

Schoenberg sips chastely, then sets the fluted glass beside the books. "Then how about something to focus them. Do you play chess?"

On the way to the chess board beneath a Monet landscape, Paul pauses near another game board. It sits atop a bulky table of protruding metal struts, its surface delineated not by squares but by parallelograms, and stocked with small gold airplanes, green artillery pieces, red submarines, blue machine guns and silver bicycles.

Smiling, Paul reaches out and touches one of the silver bicycles. "One of your inventions, Herr Professor?" His leg touches one of the struts, and he becomes more interested in the table below; strange dimensions suggested by billows in the white tablecloth.

"You and I shall play the more orthodox version." Schoenberg gestures to the table beneath the Monet. But Paul lingers, lured by a vivid smell of printers ink, as though the twenty-by-twenty parallelograms were pooled with it.

"Herr Haas?"

He continues on.

"The guest chooses his color, Herr Haas."

Paul sits down in one of the narrow wooden chairs, facing white.

"Open, Herr."

Trying to brush aside the contrary thoughts that hector for his attention, he focuses on the finely wrought board of polished teak, with hand-laid ivory and onyx amid a filigree of painted gold, and remembers the long ago nights when Father would play both Hugo and him, beating them soundly. In later years, Hugo proved a more adept player than Paul—more dedicated, at least.

He wonders, suddenly, if Hugo has sat here? If Hugo played Herr Professor, in the days after delivering *Al S'fod*?

Paul advances a knight.

Schoenberg at least pretends to contemplate his first move. "Did you know my mother was Czech, Herr Haas?"

"No, Herr Professor." He adds, "Where was she born?"

"In Prague." Schoenberg holds a hand over the board, while he studies it. "In an important way I owe my life, my *first life*, to that part of my heritage. Were it not for the Czechoslovakian consul in Prague, my family and I would not have escaped Europe."

Paul sees Mrs. Premyekova, then, as Schoenberg advances a rook. The move, unexpected, focuses Paul's thoughts—much as the Professor had promised—until Paul notices the ink stain on Schoenberg's knuckles, and the ink under his first and second finger nails. "In that *first iteration*, in the summer of 1921, I foresaw our future quite accurately. That summer, I and my family were refused access to the spa at Mattsee. I wrote to my friend Kandinsky, warning of selective anti-Semitism, *a full decade* before the Reich was established." While Paul studies Herr Professor's ink-stained hands, Schoenberg continues, "*What does anti-Semitism lead to*,' I wrote, '*if not acts of violence?*" He touches the king's crown. "*Is it so difficult to imagine the Jews exterminated by the State?*"

He pauses, as though waiting for Paul to speak. Paul wants to say, *You foresaw the future, Herr Professor*. And Paul guesses that this is the point: *Schoenberg knows why I'm here*.

"And you worked to change it, Herr Professor. With the decahexachord."

"Yes, Herr Haas . . . though I failed. I attempted very large things, when I should have worked on the very small."

Numberless threats now occur to Paul, as he surveys the board. He marvels.

Schoenberg continues, "In Swedenborg's heaven, all directions are interchangeable. Remember Gabriel's exhortation to the masses: '*Whether to the right, or to the left, forward or backward, uphill or downhill, one must go on without asking what lies ahead or behind.*' It must remain hidden: it should, *must* be forgotten, if you are to fulfill your task."

Paul sits back. Then he stands up. He looks away from the board to the only other feature in the living room which has held his attention. "Herr Professor, I was thinking of something Magdalena—*the* Magdalena—said to me." He walks toward the other game board. "She likened her gifting to the work of the great Gregory Mendel."

"Indeed." Hands on his knees, Schoenberg is watching Paul.

"This was in 1935, Herr Professor. She had followers, by then. They met on Špilberk Hill. She would play music with others—with Rudolf,

Gideon and the other musicians who became her close guard in those years—play music by Martinu and Stravinsky in the tree shade. And though she was speaking of Mendel and his pea-hybrid studies, I think she was paraphrasing a piece of Karel's... Karel Čapek's. In *The Gardener's Year* he writes: *The future is not in front of us, for it's here in the shape of a germ.* It's already with us, unseen, in the earth, waiting to grow, and... and what's not with us won't be in the future." Small gold airplanes, green artillery pieces, red submarines, blue machine guns, silver bicycles. He looks past the board. "When I saw her, the last time," he kneels down, and lifts the hem of the tablecloth, "she was wearing the uniform of a Czech legion, with the—the white rose at her collar, like in the posters. And she said, 'It's like a germ, Paul. It was so small to begin with, and now, it's so large...'" Under the cloth are the metal struts and pinions of strange machinery. The ink smell is intense.

"Yet was it enough, Herr Haas?"

Paul lets the cloth drop. He stands up. "Herr Professor, I want their sacrifices to count for something. More than just by my presence here. More than just my... second life."

Schoenberg is staring past him, out at the sunstruck deck and the palm trees.

Returning to the chair, Paul takes up the cardboard tube and removes the lid. He quotes, "*It is the deed committed in good faith which ultimately counts.* Not the thought. But the divinely ordained deed."

Schoenberg's expressive eyes widen as the luminous parchment is removed. Almost a whisper: "And your *mitzvah*, Herr Haas, is to return."

There is not a question here. Paul nods. "To Prague, to 1935."

"And..."

"And work a good deed. A small one." Sitting down at the chess board, he thinks of a young man with demonic profile; a gifted composer who had not lived past his twenty-second year. "A visit to Prague, for only a few hours. One chance, Herr Professor. To give a composer a second chance."

Schoenberg straightens in his chair, and fixes Paul with his haunting, penetrating eyes. "*'From a good thought everything else flows forth as a matter of course.'* And you would trust me, Herr Haas?"

Paul seats himself, and looks at the board and its baffling implications. "I would, Herr Professor." Sensing the trap that has been sprung, he takes hold of his king and lays it on its side.

TWO: THE LIMPING PILGRIM

"In truth, I go from nothing to nothing, I merely wander within something. My path does not pass through places; it is a period of time, a tension in time or rather simply a state."

—*The Limping Pilgrim*
by Josef Čapek (1936)

10. TSAR OF THE FOREST

... and *out*.

Having slipped through a fold in the stave flower, Paul finds himself among beech and pine trees; branches brushing against his head and shoulders; the cold air ripe with rotted leaves. He swallows against a wave of dizziness. Grasping the bole of the beech tree beside him with his free hand, he struggles for balance. Shadow and sunlight shiver, and settle. As he straightens the trunks remain *not quite perpendicular*—he's standing on a hillside.

Above the trees, the sky is bright and cloudy.

He takes the satchel from under his arm, sets it down. The stave flower riffles in the wind, trying to leave his hand.

He had expected Prague, or its outskirts. But the wind carries only the sound of trees, and birdsong. No tramcars keening along their tracks, no car horns. No aeroplanes. The silence is profound compared to the sunny tennis court—the distant clamor of Hollywood on an early Monday evening. Noise that had surrounded him mere seconds ago. Standing in the warm, sunstruck tennis court—a warmth that remains on his skin. The ghostly feel of a sunburn on his neck. And on the balcony above him, huddled near the umbrella-shaded table, Arnold Schoenberg lifting a hand in farewell.

"*Do you trust me, Herr Haas?*"

Rolling up the stave flower is difficult.

The wings resist, flickering with their purple-inked mysteries. But he manages to gather them together, and rolls it up. Clasping it gently, he withdraws the cardboard tube from the pocket sewn into the side of his overcoat. The *Universal* crest dazzles blue on gold. A crow cries out, startling him. He uncaps the tube, carefully inserts the parchment, then pops the metal top on securely. For a moment, he hesitates. This is not Prague, certainly.

Do you trust me, Herr Haas?

This is *who knows where*, Herr Professor, he thinks, and *who knows when*.

He replaces the tube in the long pocket under his right arm, then takes up the satchel. His breath mists as he turns, and turns again. Beech and pine up the hillside, low lying brush. Nothing quite like Southern California: so he's been transported across Space. But what about Time? Tugging up his sleeve, he reads the silver-and-pearl Timex. Half past seven. Five minutes since he parted with Herr Professor.

He watches the second hand, ticking industriously.

The breeze, more forceful, more chill, rustles the high branches. A prickly fall of leaves sift down through the canopy.

Do you trust me, Herr Haas?

This might be Bohemia. Or Oregon, for that matter. And a decade ago? A century?

He spies another bird in the sky—perhaps a sparrow.

The California heat has departed his body. He tugs the heavy gray scarf around his neck, buttons his jacket, begins trudging downhill through the underbrush. In places he must grab the peeling white bark of beech trees to slow himself before he pitches forward.

Follow the slope of the hill. Find a source of water and follow it.

The air certainly smells fresher here. And the sky, when glimpsed beyond the trees, is empty of all but clouds. No aeroplanes, and in 1935 Prague airport had been busy. And the roads which crisscrossed the outskirts of the town had been noisy with traffic in these daylight hours.

Paul nearly trips over a buried log. His right ankle begins to ache, and he slows, and forces a smile. Admitting to a vague, if not entirely untroubled pleasure. To have come here, wherever this is. This miracle of movement. *Sung* by a chord across Time and Space. And if Herr Professor had erred in his computations—in that hour spent at the caesura room's table, poring over star charts and maps of the Earth, over volumes of handwritten almanacs filled with Schoenberg's neat and careful numbers—Paul might be anywhere on the globe. Any*when*. Yet there is no need to panic. *I'm unharmed. There are no threats nearby. I have simply stepped out of that world, and into this one. Now, let's find out what world it is precisely.*

Trudging downhill, he pictures the black wings of the printing press—the struts and platens, the reservoir flasks of purple and black ink, the baroque brushes.

In Swedenborg's heaven, all directions are interchangeable.

The large piece of parchment being set reverently into the holder, and with Paul's help, the great wheels being turned. The deafening clank; the smell of ink, the struts folding inward and around; the entire contraption swiveling on hidden bevels as though on gyroscopes, finally unfolding to present to their eyes the riven sheet of parchment whose lines contained the folds of a stave flower.

Remember Gabriel's exhortation to the masses: 'Whether to the right, or to the left, forward or backward, uphill or downhill, one must go on without asking what lies ahead or behind.'

Paul heads downhill. If he's anywhere near Prague, or any habitable city, then an hour's walk should be enough to determine it. Down through these ranked trees he should find a road, a river, a primeval gully.

Sator, arepo, tenet, opera, rotas.

Not a minute later, he breaks out onto a path.

Hopefully, he smiles. The path is wide, well-traveled, betraying signs of recent footprints. The brush on either side is beaten back.

He follows it.

With the satchel slung over his forearm, he slips his hands in his overcoat's pockets. In the left, his fingers find the stone from Capitola, still warm from the California heat. In his right he cups a dozen coins, Czech crowns of a certain vintage, similarly warm. In the satchel are his billfold with acceptable denominations culled from a shoebox of old money, as well as his old ID card from Brno, to which he had cemented the photograph from his Universal Studios badge. Additionally the satchel contains a canteen of water, two roast beef sandwiches, a compass. Enough supplies for a day or two. All the time he'll need, depending upon whether he is near Prague and whether this is 1935 or 1035.

Remember Gabriel's exhortation of the masses: 'Whether to the right, or to the left, forward or backward, uphill or downhill, one must go on without asking what lies ahead or behind.' It must remain hidden: it should, must *be forgotten, if you are to fulfill your task.*

How easily I've stepped through, Paul thinks. *How easy—and yet should it have been easy?*

To step away from Sona and Olga and William? To step away from Hugo?

He sees Schoenberg across the chess board. *And your mitzvah, Herr Haas, is to return.*

At first he thinks the *shout*, rising thin and naked in the cold air, is another bird, so high is the tessitura. But it's a human voice—a *young* voice, somewhere downhill, among the trees. He can only think of William in the backyard, cutting his hand on a nail. He is hurrying ahead, hoping it's still a bird and not a human voice, not a child in pain, but the cry comes again. He begins to jog, ignoring the pain in his foot, following the path on its low downhill curve, the pine and beech seeming to lift and turn as he passes, the breeze sighing strangely in the branches as the voice cries out a third time.

The path widens into a clearing. Low clouds impart a glow to the scene, while deep shadow remains beneath the boy. With black hair and torn black suitcoat, he lies on his back under leaning branches, and he is in motion, crabwalking on his elbows and heels. His breath smokes the air, his wide eyes growing wider still as he spots Paul, who halts a few meters away.

Paul, limping forward now, with his scarf fluttering across half his face. "Are you hurt?"

The boy's mouth is open, but no words come. His face is smeared with mud. Blood seeps through a scrape on his chin. "Are you hurt? Don't be afraid." At the same moment, Paul realizes he has been speaking in English; and that the boy is dressed in a Sunday suit of decades past. A moment later, he follows the furrows in the wet earth, leading from the boy's shoes toward the trees.

He tries Czech, with a calmer tone. "What's happened, young man? Are you hurt?" Paul, still gaining his breath, straightens up. Beyond the trees rise castle ruins, a low round guard tower, long-crumbled, and entirely familiar. "This . . . "

"I did not mean to," whimpers the boy in Czech; his eyes are wet and dark. "I did not mean to. I was only playing." He might be looking at the trees overhead. "They *moved*."

Paul pulls the scarf away from his face, tries for a gentle tone—the same tone he uses when William has scraped his knee and comes bleeding and crying. "What happened to your chin, and your hand?"

The boy begins to reply, then pushes back again, eyeing the beech trees, and a trampled white flower. "They *caught me*. My arm, my leg." He speaks with an Ostrava accent.

And Paul suddenly recognizes his face.

"He'll be angry!" The boy struggles to his feet.

"You . . . you are Kamila's boy!"

"I was only playing!" The boy staggers to the far side of the clearing, then runs down the path. Paul is too weary—too stunned—to give chase.

Kamila Stösslová's boy!

The foliage no longer stirs, the white flower no longer seems so signatory. Yet the castle ruins are entirely recognizable: the old castle above the village of Hukvaldy, in the eastern edge of the country. He remembers them well from a trip here with the Maestro's widow . . .

Below, he'll find the game preserve with its fallow deer, and the brewery at the edge of town. In Hukvaldy, Moravia. In 1928.

And Otto—Kamila's little boy.

Do you trust me, Herr Haas?

Another voice rouses him. A terse shout from the side trail. Incoherent, entirely familiar. "*Off! I drop them!*" Then a great thrashing sound, like a rampaging animal.

Paul follows, slowly.

White flowers cling sickly to the tree trunks. They tremble in the breeze, as though in reaction to that voice.

He tugs the scarf across the half his face.

"*Off!*"

As though in a dream, Paul staggers along the path to meet the Maestro.

In a clearing, against a backdrop of pale green pine and white flowers, the old man slouches on ancient stone. Clothed in rumpled tweed, his shoulders rise and fall. His head bobs as he gasps for breath, his crown of hair—the largest white flower of them all—rising and falling.

As Paul limps into the clearing the great head lifts. The eyes—those famous *restless dark flames*—fix on Paul.

The Maestro sits on the edge of an ancient fountain, amidst a battlefield. A sprawl of sundered foliage reaching out from the surrounding trees; tendrils like fissures splaying out from the fountain, the ground marked with furrows cut into the earth by the Maestro's heels, littered with small octavo sheets of paper. His walking stick, mud-caked, lies at his feet.

In the greater forest echoes a dying tumult, of earth raining down, of branches settling, and the fountain—ancient even when Hukvaldy castle was built—resounds with a long, low, almost inaudible roar.

"And so," the Maestro's shoulders brace his hands on the stone, and he stares up. His face is flushed. "It is done."

Paul strives to speak, but cannot. How many times has he faced this man in dreams? How many times has he found himself explaining, apologizing, answering questions whether in Pasadena or the bungalow at Paramount, or during the train trip from New York, or earlier, in the tumultuous months leading up to his exile?

He thinks of one particular moment, now. Perhaps the most poignant: at the premiere of his *The Insect Play* at the Metropolitan, when Olin Downes the music critic had come up to him all effusive about the Maestro and lamenting the Maestro's sudden passing; and Paul had wanted so very much to have him there, that evening.

Paul crouches and lifts the muddy stick, and passes it into the Maestro's hand. "Allow me, please."

His suitcoat is torn. His face shines with sweat, and there is a flush to his forehead yet an alarming paleness to his cheeks. His hand betrays a slight tremble, as he takes the stick. "A boy! Seen him?" He strives to regain his breath. His voice is there—sudden, vivid in its Lachian accent. "This tall! Dark hair! Please!"

"Yes, I found him." Astounded yet again at the sight before him, Paul presses the scarf against his mouth. He tries to ignore the battlefield, and the questions that rise from it. *What, Maestro? What have you done?* "He said his name was Otto."

Still gaining his breath, "Was he harmed?" He stuffs a sheet of octavo paper into the his pocket; a sheet covered with his fiery notation.

And so, Paul hears the Maestro's voice, *It is done.*

"He was . . . he was scraped, sir, but otherwise looked well. I sent him home, into Hukvaldy."

What *was done?*

The Maestro sinks against the edge of the fountain, whose roar has subsided to a deep, low tone. His short mustache is wilted, but a smile, however tentative, changes his countenance. Hands grasping and regrasping his muddy walking stick. "I thank you, sir. I am in your debt." He offers a hand.

Paul limps to the ancient stone, and sits heavily. "You are very welcome." Shaking it, he finds the Maestro's hand alarmingly hot.

"And you—you limp! Are you injured?" His voice gains a somber echo from the well.

Paul feels the unreality settling around his shoulders; he very nearly does not respond. "I twisted my ankle, weeks ago—" *Maestro*. He had nearly said *Maestro*.

He feigns curiosity in the well, thereby turning his face partly away. Staring down, he finds the faintest scrap of luminous sky down in the dark, and a lingering echo of his own voice. And finds, too, a realization. *This moment in Time:* young Otto going missing in the Maestro's forest, and the Maestro mounting an energetic search. *This* afternoon in Hukvaldy, with the chill air like brass on his tongue, marks the beginning of the Maestro's last days. The onset of pneumonia. Mere days remain.

Yet what else has happened?

"Its source is deep." The Maestro pats the stone with a trembling hand; trembling not from sickness, but from the aftermath of a great struggle. "It dreams of ancient times, until we wake it with our voices."

Four, maybe five days. Yes. Though Kamila pleads with him, the Maestro will refuse to see a doctor. And when he finally concedes to travel by car to Ostrava, the pneumonia will have advanced too far.

The Maestro brushes straggles of ivy and white petals from his tweed coat. Pulling a handkerchief from his pocket, he wipes his gleaming forehead. "It leads directly down to the luminous depths."

They moved. *They* caught *me. Caught my arm, my leg.*

One of the octavo sheets turns end over end, landing on Paul's shoe. He leans down and—careful not to lose the scarf—picks it up. He tries not to read it: the Maestro is watching his eyes, and would surely recognize the eyes of a composer who could hear what is sounding out on the paper.

A *scasovani* melody, surely.

"This is yours?"

The Maestro replaces the handkerchief, then takes the paper. "It is. Music. Do you read it, sir?"

Paul hesitates. "A little."

The eyes continue to study Paul's. Then the Maestro pats his chest, then gestures to the tumult surrounding them. "I am *Tsar* of this forest. This hill I call *Babi Hura*." A smile. His eyes twinkle. "And sometimes it is more lively than others. I am Dr. Leoš J⎯⎯, from Brno and Hukvaldy. And you—your accent is a strange *mélange*, sir. Yet you are Moravian at heart, yes?"

He nods. "My name is Paul—" Struggling for a surname, he merely says, "I've been in America this past decade, Doctor."

"America?!" Surreptitiously, the Maestro lifts another of the octavo sheets. It whips against the fountain's stone. "Where precisely, sir?"

"California."

"Indeed. California? On the western coast." He slips the paper into his bulging pocket. "You are a pilgrim, yes? And you arrive just in time."

From the rustling breeze, from the mouth of the ancient well at his back, a deeper cold seeps into his clothes. "Mr. Doctor J⎯⎯, Otto has returned home. And now you must too." He strives to stand with ease. "It is far too cold for excursions." His ankle aches, and his knees are weak.

"Yet I am quite warm, Sir." The Maestro pats his knees, and, leaning on his walking stick, surges to his feet. "And quite curious, now." He squints up at Paul.

"We will return to see Otto. And then you will join me and my dear Kamila for lunch, and speak of your mysterious life in California! Have you seen any Indians? Or ridden a stagecoach?"

"I . . . I cannot go with you, Mr. Doctor."

J⎯⎯ plants his stick. He has begun sweating again. The lobes of his ears are bright pink, as are his knuckles.

"Maestro, you must return indoors and take a warm bath, and find a physician. You are very ill."

"Ill? But—how do you know this?"

"Maestro, *you* must simply credit *me* this. If you don't seek a physician immediately, sir, you'll develop double pneumonia."

Wiping his forehead with his sleeve, the Maestro says in a soft, cautious voice, "I cannot see your face, sir."

117

"Maestro! You will certainly die."

A long moment passes, during which the ancient well sings like the lowest voice in the world.

"Who are you? Your voice . . . " He pats at the pocket of his overcoat.

"I am a Pilgrim, Maestro. A simple Pilgrim. If you do not seek a physician today, if you do not check into a hospital, then you will be dead within a week."

The Maestro's face utterly freezes. Mouth half-open. He leans more heavily on his stick. "You . . . appear from out of nowhere, pretend not to know me, when you do." His voice is uncharacteristically soft. "Yet you tell me . . . that I will die?"

Paul struggles to find his voice. "Yes, Maestro."

The moment pivots here, as the breeze rustles the fallen boughs, the ivy and white flowers.

Paul reaches up, under his collar, for the cord. And draws out the key. Sunlight gleams on the bronze haft, and the cameo of the Maestro's beloved daughter Olga.

"How . . . " The Maestro's eyes narrow. His mouth opens, but he does not speak. With trembling hands, he reaches into an inner pocket, fumbling, and comes out with . . . the same key. The key to the *Baseform Scasovani Generator* back in Brno. The key that he was fated to leave on the piano here in Hukvaldy, for that other Pavel to snatch up.

"Maestro, you *must* believe me."

"How . . . You must explain, sir. You must come back with me . . . "

Paul slips the key under his shirt collar. "Maestro, return to your cottage and tell Kamila to contact the doctor. You must go to a hospital. If you do this, I will visit you next week. To explain."

"Let me see your face, sir. Let me hear your voice unmuffled."

"Maestro, you must go now."

The Maestro stares hard at Paul's scarf, and his eyes. Then he pulls his coat around him, buttoning it. With a last glance at Paul and at the fountain, the Tsar of the forest turns away, trudges down the path into Hukvaldy.

Before following, Paul spies another of the octavo sheets caught in the ivy, and another. He picks up several, studies the Maestro's familiar hand, more agitated than usual, the ink blurring in its haste, the notes nearly running off the page. *Nápěvky mluvy* of some sort.

He stuffs them in his coat pocket.

For many minutes, Paul stands on the trail, the cold seeping into his shoes. He pulls down the scarf. His face is hot. He unbuttons his overcoat and draws out the cardboard tube.

Clutching the stone from Capitola in his pocket, he descends the path. The ruins of Hukvaldy castle loom, then are hidden by the trees. He recalls Schoenberg's voice. *"On this most cursed of days, my thoughts turn not to composers who are amongst us, and productive, but those we have lost. Those whose music was silenced."*

He draws chill air through his smile, and the path opens up, revealing the village of Hukvaldy with its church steeple and low cottages, its blocky brewery at the edge of the beet fields. In the distance, the Tartra mountains, out and out to Slovakia, and Paul cannot help but recall what he had seen last Friday—William Cameron Menzies's fever-dream cyclorama of the Moravian countryside. Here is a cyclorama he can walk into and into, and never meet its end. Excitement makes his heart pound.

The breeze rustles his hair and the collar of his overcoat. If he catches the evening train, he can be in Prague before morning. He can find Karel and Josef.

And warn them?

Or is my mitzvah already complete?

He continues down the hill, through wintry air scented with cheroot and chimney smoke.

At the small train station he buys a ticket to Prague, then asks the clerk if he can use the telephone. The clerk provides him with the number of village's only doctor. Paul rings it, and the doctor listens to Paul's story of finding the Maestro on Bila Hora then cuts him off in mid-sentence. "But you see his... his *friend* Kamila Stösslová has already called me, Sir," says the doctor. "She's very concerned about him, and I'm to visit him this evening after dinner." He agrees that the dampness and dire cough could be bad for a man of the Maestro's age, and pledges to do the utmost for Hukvaldy's most famous citizen.

And so the funeral bell will not sound.
 And so the black flags won't fly in Brno.
 Nor will the Maestro lie in his coffin for the young Pavel to file past.

At a pub beside the train station he devours a bowl of *gula* with lumps of sweet pork, onion and pepper in thick gravy, and bread dumplings; the food revives him deeply, as does a pint of hot cider, all paid for with ten Kc notes designed by Alfons Mucha from 1926; notes that look as though they've been around for decades. He studies the map of the Republic, the breadth of it no wider than that of California. Tonight he will journey from its eastern province to its western in little more than six hours.
 To Prague.
 Once aboard the train, installed in a seat in a warm cabin, now leaving Hukvaldy for the low hills of Freydek, he leans his forehead against the glass and whispers, *I am here.*
 I am here.

Great clouds of steam scud past the window, and the train blows its whistle long and low.
I am here.
I am home.

*"And in the stillness of rosy evenings
the glass foliage tinkles
the fingers of alchemists grazing it
like the wind."*

—*Praha* by Jaroslav Seifert

11. Z PRAHA

For the first hour of the trip, Paul strives to discern the landscape; slumbering fields of sugar beet, the silhouettes of onion-domed churches on hilltops, blackberry and honeysuckle massed with shadow beside the tracks. Tiny wayside crosses, lit by votive candles, flutter with prayers to the dead.

When they slow into Frydek-Mistek, into Moravska Trebova, into large, bustling Olomouc—the conductor announces each one in his characteristic Moravian accent, as prideful as a magician claiming these wonders beyond the windows, and Paul studies the crowds that wait patiently on the wooden docks under harsh sodium lamps. Each face is striking, the seams and scars, or the untouched smoothness, and the eyes that have always and only seen this place, this countryside, this country. They see him, now, climbing aboard, and some nod to him as a fellow traveler, but most do not notice.

It leads down to the luminous depths.

On his lap are spread the rumpled octavo papers, the Maestro's offering to the fountain. The notation is difficult to parse, but he hears vibrant runs of notes, strange chords. On the third sheet is written a single, indecipherable word.

With a rush of steam and a rolling jolt, the train begins again—

You ... appear from out of nowhere, pretend not to know me, when you do.

—Due in Ceska Trebova by 21.20, Pardubice by 22.19, in Golden Prague by 00.33. As the dockside lamps flick past him and vanish behind the land the window itself is now a trick mirror through which he must strive to stare, catching a glimpse of the Time Traveler in his black houndstooth overcoat—an artifact from the future, coated with the latest rain-repellent technology, according to the advertisement in the Pasadena Woolworth's.

He returns to the notation.

And so, it is done.

The mystery of Babi Hura becomes more alarming, the more he ponders it. The tumult of the forest, the vines that had snatched at young Otto—surely it is the *Geist der Alten Natur?* Young Otto had gone missing, out to play on the hillside, and the Maestro had presumed the Geist had taken him; so the Maestro had gathered up an enchantment—an enchantment in the form of *nápěvky mluvy*—to lure *Geist der Alten Natur.*

Which implies a more profound colloquy than he had imagined, between the Maestro and the force in luminous depths.

Reflected in the glass is the compartment's other occupant, one Frau Erun in frock coat and bonnet, a Viennese seamstress visiting relatives in Kutna Hora.

She had taken him at his word: that he was returning to Prague after some years aboard.

Frau Erun, upon seeing the tube, had taken him for an architect. She remarked that he had missed by mere days the lengthy ten-year celebration for the Republic, then had untied her bonnet, revealing graying hair, and pulled a newspaper—*National letters*—from her coat, settling in to read.

Staring past his reflection into the dark and flowing landscape, he contrives several storylines just as Hugo, languishing on the couch in Paul's study, would concoct the plots for one of his sleazy movies.

With a surreptitious glance at Frau Erun, whose face is hidden behind the *National letters*, he withdraws the wallet from his inside pocket, counts the bills, admiring the colorful design by Alfons Mucha replete with nubile Czech women and Slav Gods, each bill of proper antiquity. But shouldn't he have brought at least one of blatant *futurity*, if he needed to prove his claim as a Time Traveler?

He's pleased to find a Roosevelt dime in his watch pocket, dated 1935.

Frau Erun is now watching him from behind the sag in her newspaper, her eyebrows pinching above her narrow nose. While Paul girds himself for an onslaught of questions she says, with amusement, "Masaryk doesn't have an ounce of common sense."

Paul strives now for a response.

"Surely, Mr. Haas, you've been away long enough to realize that?"

He offers a smile. "Too long, perhaps."

"So," she lowers the paper and yawns. "What's your opinion of his relativism?"

"Perhaps, Frau Erun, I might read your newspaper, and then offer an opinion. I find myself in need of education on the matter."

She snickers, and yawns again, and hands the newspaper to him. "Thank you, Frau."

Then she switches off her lamp and settles back on the bench.

THREATENED GENERAL STRIKE BY METALWORKERS
FOOD SHORTAGES IN HANA PREDICTED TO WORSEN
SOCIALIST RALLY CLASHES WITH POLICE IN TEPLICE

The headlines remind Paul that the Republic, even at the height of its powers was never without turmoil. Yet Masaryk and his *pragmatist* government would—will—steer the ship of State through all these shoals. At least, he reflects, until Masaryk's death in 1936.

MASARYK REVILED FOR EXCESSIVE MILITARY BUDGET

National letters is a leftist paper, unlike the *Lidové noviny*—centrist

125

People's newspaper—and delights in every attack on the Masaryk administration.

Paul turns the page, delighting in an advertisement for the Bata shoe store—state of the art 1928 footwear it proclaims, over an etching of the company's nine-story Functionalist department store in the suburbs, its motto, "*Our Customer—Our Master.*"

On the Arts page he finds an article about Vinhorady Theater's new production of *The Seagull*, and an interview with Karel Tiege, the titular head of *9forces*. He skims these, along with the World News and editorials, looking for something about Josef or Karel, some indication that they are in Prague, and at work. He stops at a boxed, unsigned feuilleton on the last page entitled *The Castle Writer and Castle Painter Leave the Scene*.

"At the Klementium we had our last chance to witness Alfons Mucha's gargantuan and overwrought canvases, 21 in all, titled with all modesty the Slav Epic. *Meanwhile, at the Aventium Loft we have our first chance to buy K. Čapek's latest book titled* Conversations with T.G.M. *One does not doubt that Masaryk will ride his stately horse down from the castle to buy a copy, and perhaps take a last tour amongst those mammoth paintings of Princess Libuse and Jan Hus and the rest. In his* Conversations with Čapek, *he speaks of replacing* Austrian absolutism *with* Czech relativism, *and yet also reveals a dangerous stripe, telling us that his views on everything are multi-faceted, engineered to look at the problem from many angles, becoming so blind by so many solutions that no firm decision can ever be made. He complains that the Czech people are more used to criticizing their government than supporting it. If only T.G.M. could be as honest as Mr. K. Tiege of* 9forces, *who once wrote,* "Poeticism is the crown of life, constructivism is its basis." *Indeed,* 9forces *does not seek to merely write poetry, but to transform life into* "a magnificent entertainment, an eccentric carnival, a harlequinade of feeling and imagination, an intoxicating film track, a marvelous kaleidoscope that will relieve depression, worries, irritations while offering cleansing and moral health." *It seeks to make available to all the* "poetry of Sunday afternoons, picnics, luminous cafes, intoxicating cocktails, lively boulevards, spa promenades, but also the poetry

of silence, night, quiet, and peace." *All this cannot be found in Pragmatism, or Relativism, or whatever Masaryk calls it while gazing lovingly on Mucha's sprawling canvases. No, truth is the calling card of the Social Democrat. As Vancura has said, "Outside Communism there can be nothing modern."*

As for K. Čapek's book, perhaps the pages might be cut and rearranged by some of our 9forces *artists, thereby delivering a more fruitful literary endeavor. We refuse to believe anything this* Castle Writer *says, and offer a title for his next volume of nonfiction: Betrayals by Tomáš Masaryk."*

Paul rereads the paragraph, suppressing a smile, and with it feels some of Karel's life force in this country; his ability to summon the vitriol of the left and the right. It's no small irony, of course, that it's Čapek who gave the *9forces* their name, from a weed in his garden; nor that his own group *the Obstinates* served as a role model. But now Čapek and President Masaryk have grown beyond the perhaps boyish, perhaps violent, tendencies of Karel Tiege and the editors of the *National letters*.

He looks up to give Frau Erun his opinions on Masaryk's relativism, but by now she is lightly snoring, head tipped against her mink collar.

Soon he tires, lulled by the movement of the train. He settles back on the bench, head falling forward, bangs obscuring his eyes. He imagines that he might even sleep, yet cannot. Of course. In the lulling motion is an implicit truth: he's arriving. He hears it in the rattle of the window, the jostling of the bench, in the chug of the distant engine; feels it in his weary legs and his shoulders, in his teeth; knows the moment is here long before the conductor, striding the corridor, announces the first of the Prague suburbs with his proprietary cheer. Paul opens his eyes, brushes back his hair. He leans toward the chill window to find low hills east of the city under a starry sky. On high, a full moon welcomes him. He feels giddy. He clenches his teeth, he smiles. The train slows and the steam rushes back to obscure the moon as they pull into the first suburban station, yet even when the train sits motionless, chuffing on the platform while passengers embark, he feels the relentless motion. Soon enough they are underway, and the first of the suburbs is soon the last of them, and in the light of that full moon he glimpses a tiny spire, then a dozen tiny spires, remote, isolated under that sky and somehow too small, and precious in their smallness, the russet dome of St. Nicholas, the steeples of Tyn and St. Vitus growing larger like an invocation, while beside the train the Vlatva River unreels with him. He follows it for a moment as the tracks turn, then, as they turn again he finds Prague—*Praha, says Jean Simmons' remote and lovely voice, close to his right ear*—*Praha* rising up to greet the train, black and gold and silver in the moonlight. Trestles and tunnels overtake him, buildings both drab and modern block the view and soon he is within the city limits without being able to see the city, is slowing, and he lives within the beating of a great black and silver heart.

Inside the vast Wilson station, he bids a dizzied goodbye to Frau Erun and walks slowly through the station, among a crowd of metropolitans and panhandlers who take little notice of him. Climbing the stairs, he takes pleasure in snippets of conversation—*nápěvky mluvy* in robust Bohemian Czech, about a favorite dog, a broken lamp, a road in Ostrov, a headache. And then he is in the midst of Prague; the cobblestone streets and black-iron lamps, the granite storefronts, the statues. He smells the river, rich and loamy with a hint of excrescence and damp iron. He hears the aural breadth of the city, in distant car horns, in snatches of beer hall music. Frequently an automobile of lovely vintage drives past; less frequently, a horse-drawn fiacre. He yearns to walk the length of the city, from the Jewish Quarter to Vinohrady, but his ankle pains him. He has done much today; there is much still to ponder; he is not safe. These Praguers hurrying along to some early-morning rendezvous, this 16th century facade, these cobblestones—all of it is fragile. All of it has less than ten years of freedom left to it, fewer years than his son has lived. And somehow, the

Maestro was caught meddling at that fissure: what new dangers are opening up, unseen?

And I am here to help. As Protektor.

And, thinking of H.G. Wells at the Brighton Strand, Paul thinks, *I am the Time Traveler.*

Tomorrow, he whispers. *And tomorrow.*

He crosses the river into Smichov, opposite the embankment from the National Theater. At the Hotel Karel IV he procures a room with his vintage bills and signs the guest book *Paul Arepo.*

"Even gods have their seasons. In summer one may be a pantheist, may consider oneself part of Nature, but in autumn one can only take oneself for a human being. Even if we don't cross ourselves we all slowly return to the nativity of man. Every home fire burns to the honour of the household gods. Love of one's home is a rite, similar to the veneration of some celestial godhead."

—*The Gardener's Year* by Karel Čapek

12. THE VILLA IN VINHORADY

The bright keen and clatter of tram cars lifts him to wakefulness.

He stirs in the plush bed, squints at the furniture and the hazy gold outline of his Timex and the stone from Capitola on the bedside table. Remembering exactly where and when he is—Paul pushes himself up on his elbow. He smiles. Sunlight casts a long shadow across burgundy carpet to the coils of the hot water heater, whose heat he now notices on his bare arms and legs as he shrugs back the twisted blankets. Wiping at his eyes, he finds the cold wood floor with his feet, stands up and approaches the angled wall. Snug in the eaves of the old hotel, the room looks onto the gargoyles and parapets and rooftops of Smichov—a Dickens landscape. He opens the tall, pewter-framed window, ushering in a breeze redolent of rain-washed metal and chimney soot; ushering, too, a wave of nostalgia at a memory, some thirty years old, of his first trip to Prague.

I am Tsar of this forest. This hill I call Babi Hura.

How like a dream the day before now seems; and how dreamlike the continuity of that day to this. He remains here, in Prague, in 1928.

Below on the narrow cobblestone street a morning crowd hurries past. To the north, a church bell tolls; the half hour is soon marked by other bells throughout the city, and when the last of them lingers in the air, Paul closes the window and steps back, studying the room.

Last night his dreams had been of home—of 4111 Delmonica Drive, of William scurrying across the kitchen tiles like the elf in the Ajax Foaming Cleanser commercial while Olinka sang the jingle—and he feels a pang at the back of his throat, a momentary exclusion of where his right hand and left hand, right leg and left leg are; of being lost—an outsider forever lost outside.

Yet Sona is here, southeast in Brno. Five hours by train. Young Sona, who had chased him to the tram and brushed her hand between his shoulder blades to bid him goodbye; she, and Pavel. And Mother. Dear Mother.

He bathes, cleaning the Maestro's forest from his skin. Dressing, he surveys his accouterments. Satchel and cardboard tube, overcoat, beach stone. He need take only the wallet on his walk into Vinhorady. The key he places around his neck, out of habit. The rest is nondescript. Nobody would expect a stave flower, surely. But he cannot leave it behind. After some careful experimentation, he lays it out on the bed and folds it simply in half, then again. This shape is small enough to drop into his overcoat's inner pocket, where it expands against the lining of his coat, secure and safe against any rainfall.

Before leaving on his walk he telephones Ostrava and their municipal hospital. Posing as a teacher at the Brno Conservatory, he inquires after the Maestro's health.

Karel and Josef—I will find them today.

"*We'll be keeping him for a week at least,*" the nurse assures him. "Pneumonia was feared but the fever appears to be breaking. The patient is resting comfortably, if irritably."

Paul thanks her, briefly rings off then asks the operator to connect him to the Prague Conservatory. Striving to bring to the forefront the task that had originally guided him here, he asks after a student by the name of Gideon Klein.

While the inquiry is carried out, Paul strives to recall when Klein had come to Prague to study with Alois Haba. It's years too early, he's certain. Herr Professor has sent him back too far—sent him directly to save the Maestro, but creating difficulties when it came to Klein, who is surely still living in the Czech countryside, no older than little Otto.

Finally, the reply comes down the phone. There is no Gideon Klein enrolled.

The outlook is hopeful for the Maestro, he tells himself.

Walking south along the embankment, towards the Vinhorady neighborhood, with sunlight striking the river and the green trees, Paul cannot help but feel hopeful for the Republic as well. Dire thoughts are distant. The country is at its Zenith. The roads are busy with traffic. Tram cars spark and careen and ring their bells. The sidewalk is full of passersby, some out to enjoy the sunshine, others rushing to and fro. Statues from the Reformation, stained to a lush iron-green, watch with remote amusement.

Past the Old Town Square he finds a window full of *Conversations with T.G.M.* He stops and retraces his steps to the door, and enters.

"*Dobry den*," says the elderly bookseller.

"*Dobry den*," replies Paul cheerfully. He lifts a copy from the stack, after which the bookseller launches into a rhapsodic analysis of its contents; an analysis which continues even as Paul decides that bringing the book to Karel—if Karel were at home—would be too ingratiating, too uncomfortable for the Karel that Paul knew.

Instead, he ponders the shelves, slowing down at several Aventium covers with Josef's distinct linocut patterns. One begs to be bought. The bookseller wraps the book in brown paper and ties it with string, concluding, "He is our *little father*, even I, a man as old as myself. And it is like sitting at Tomáš's side, reading that book."

In Vinhorady, Paul marvels at the pastel-hued houses and Rondocubist apartments. Against a dwindling echo of cathedral bells, birds chirp in old oak trees. On the high banks to either side of the road, lavish gates hide the more affluent mansions. He recognizes landmarks such as a purple Belevedere mansion whose paint had been faded and chipping the last time he had walked here, under much older, sprawling oaks in 1936. Sona had held his hand at this very corner, had marveled at the wooden statue of the Madonna that now, today, is not yet standing here. He remembers it vividly because her voice had dropped low in mid-sentence as they turned the corner and the great double-Villa next door had been revealed.

And again, here it is, vaguely Romanesque and Gothic, entirely Arts-and-Crafts, with its wide, low peaked roof and its sturdy front columns marking the long front porch; a porch onto which opened, as though in a mirrored image, two identical front doors on the street called Uzka, which would later be named *Street of the Brothers Čapek*.

A garden slopes down to the sidewalk. Concrete stairs climb between massed rhododendron, helianthus and roses. Paul stops, clutching the parcel to his side. He stares up at the villa, listening to the birdsong.

Beyond the helianthus: a small movement. Over a cluster of red roses, a straw hat bobs up, then down. Paul feels his heart in his throat. A long moment later comes a soft clank, of metal on rock. A throat clears itself, then murmurs something. In response, a cat meows. The peace of the morning, the solitude that seems to lay over this garden and its occupant, leave Paul suddenly doubtful that he should intrude; Karel and Josef, and the Republic itself, must remain *inviolate*.

Then the straw hat bobs up. A face appears, staring over and through the helianthus, at him. A broad forehead and limpid, curious eyes in the brim's speckled shade. It is Karel, startlingly young. "Yes?" Head and shoulders rise up. After a visible grimace—one that makes the youthfulness of the face even more poignant—he stands up with the aid of a shovel's handle. He's dressed in dungarees. At thirty-eight years old, he could pass for a decade younger. "Looking for the master of the house?"

Paul's hands tighten on the parcel. "Mr. Čapek?"

Karel's shoulders sag a bit. "Yes?" He steps forward, squinting against the sunlight. "You don't look like a delivery man."

"I—" Paul decides against a half dozen different replies before saying, "That's a Victorian rose, is it not, sir?"

Karel smiles, his soft chin sinking into his neck as he nods. "You have a good eye. A gardener, are you?"

"Only on weekends."

"Ah, but we are all weekend gardeners. Or should be." He pauses, then. Curious about the visitor.

Before he can ask the obvious questions, Paul says, "My name is Arepo. Paul Arepo. I'm an admirer of your work, Mr. Čapek, especially your feuilletons on gardening."

This does the trick. Karel's smile grows easy. "Those are my favorites to write." His shoulders relax further. "And my work—my work is not going well at the moment. So your arrival is quite welcomed." He gestures. "Come up, please, sir."

Paul climbs the stairs, against the garden and the looming Villa, while in the rhododendron a gray tabby pokes out its head and meows at his passing.

"I've been spiriting my annuals inside, before the weather turns," says Karel. His chestnut hair, forever carefully combed and parted, is here messy and tossed by the breeze. "And I seem to be having only bad luck. All but three of my clay pots were mysteriously broken during the night. My spade is somehow misplaced. Perhaps my brother is using it in his studio for some painting or other."

Sunlight in the teeming garden dizzies Paul. Another cat—this one black, with silver-tinged ears—slinks out from the underbrush. As he climbs up, he's afraid he might trip over a cat, tumble into the leafy rhododendron and pine.

Beyond the tangle of helianthus and aster, Karel waits in sunlight, watches. Surrounding his fisherman's boots are clay pots, a spade, a pitchfork, and a satchel full of more tools.

The plaintive meows of a third cat serenade the sight.

After wiping his palm on his bib, Karel offers his hand. "Good day to you, Mr. Arepo."

"It's an honor to meet you, Mr. Čapek."

They shake. Karel's face goes rubbery, his mouth drooping like a movie comedian's. "Didn't take me for the servant?" He sounds a bit disappointed.

"I'm afraid not."

Karel attempts a shrug. "Nonetheless." He glances up at the sky. "Such sun today. The weather usually goes out of its way to disappoint the gardener. Prepare for sunshine and it's rainy. Prepare for black frost and you get sunshine. Today I was planning a mass evacuation of my more sensitive varieties, when in fact they would adore this last display of Indian summer." His hair riffles above his high, broad forehead. "Too bad. I've already begun. And I'm having difficulties with this *R. Lapponicum*." His right hand, gesturing, lacks the cherrywood holder and his ever-present Gaulois, though the yellow stains on his fingertips attest that the absence is only temporary. "It's a hardy plant, and sends its roots down deep into the soil." Stroking his cupid's-bow lips he mutters, "Perhaps it desires to return to the land of the Alpenhorn."

"Mr. Čapek, I would love to help."

Karel smiles. He squints against the sunlight and gestures now to the shovel. "There's the instrument. Though I don't always require my elders to do my work for me. And you're certainly not dressed for it."

Paul sets his parcel on the dry patch of earth, then lifts the shovel and approaches the frail-looking yellow and white flowers.

"I was going to ask my brother when he came home, but you've appeared like a visitation on the sidewalk, Mr. Arepo. You'll want to carefully dig—" And he describes the actions necessary.

While Paul carries them out, Karel explains, "I have a disability of the spine. *Via* subtle alchemy the bone is slowly turning to mineral, as in some fairy tale curse. Our Faculty of Medicine here in Prague calls it *Čapek's Disease*. And . . . Very good. Yes. Just a little further down, and we'll be able to cradle its roots."

"Yes, sir." Paul sets down the shovel.

"Call me Karel, please. And there's the pot, the target, once you lift it out."

As he cradles the flower, lifting it so that its delicate gray and white root system clears the edge of the hole, Karel waxes, "Vinhorady was once the vineyards of the Emperor. Our soil is disciplined and rich, and . . . Very good! Excellent!" says Karel. "Now, we'll take it inside. I'll pay you back with refreshments. Too early for wine, so we'll have to settle for tea."

<hr />

"I'm creating this garden from the ground up. From the depths of the soil. And to my despair, perhaps, I feel the need to *specialize*. First in asters and roses. Then in rock gardens, then thistles and thorny bushes, then in evergreens. Now, in rare alpine plants. Put it there, please. On the desk."

The interior of Karel's half of the villa is roughly as Paul remembers it, with Persian carpets heaped one upon the next, crowded against slouching sofa and easy chairs; carpets, too, are tacked to the wall, displaying their intricate geometries beside Josef's Cubist paintings and Karel's photographs of flowers and bicycles and lamp posts. Bookcases are packed with matter, some of it overflowing to the carpet, while the end tables are cluttered with gardening catalogs and a few stray copies of *Conversations with T.G.M.*

"God help me! There are still so many things in the world I haven't dabbled in yet. Crystallography, or the history of guilds, or the state of the national economy."

"I envy you your passions, Mr. Čapek." Paul steps around a wicker basket beside the door—makeshift storage for a dozen canes and walking sticks—and a hat-rack upon which Karel now hangs his straw hat beside bowlers and snap-brims. The *R. Lapponicum* tickling his nose imparts a slight fragrance but cannot dispel the aroma of pungent tobacco and of the ever-present cats; Paul must skip around a spotted Calico before setting his precious pot gently on the desk blotter.

"Very good, thank you, Mr. Arepo."

Straightening, Paul finds himself facing a poster for the Vinhorady production of *From the Life of Insects*. And for an instant, he feels disconcertingly dizzy. Afraid that at any moment, any movement might snap the string of this miracle.

Karel promenades further on, toward the kitchen. "As to tea, have you a preference? Chinese *Lapsang Souchong*, perhaps? Earl Grey?"

"The Chinese," replies Paul, following, but at a slower pace. At the bookshelf he studies the spines—Aventium titles, mostly, along with all nine volumes of Otto's encyclopedia, several of Palacky's *History of the Czech Nation in Bohemia and Moravia*, as well as the Encyclopedia Britannica. Karel's own works are relegated to the highest shelf, both galley proofs and hardbacks almost out of sight, but one volume is allowed a place of honor: a dog-eared 1918 copy of the journal *June*, with a woodcut cover by Josef. It contains Karel Čapek's translation of Apollinaire's *Zone*, perhaps the seminal event in the Czech modernist movement.

The calico pads lithely around Paul's legs toward a puzzling structure upholstered in remnant carpet—a Cubist scratching post.

In the kitchen, Karel stands beside the gas range, nudging the tea pot more securely over the burner. Beside him are two mugs, a tin and a tea infuser spoon.

"So, you are a gardener, Mr. Arepo. Tell me of your garden. I am always curious about how others organize the wild earth."

Paul sets the parcel on the counter. "It is most small." He smiles, picturing the backyard at Delmonica drive. "We have some Victorian roses, and rhododendron. Some grass to play on. In the summer we try to grow tomatoes." He doesn't mention the palm tree. "I would love to have such land as this."

Windows look upon the vast backyard—the rock garden, the fountain and more flower beds, a Cedar of Lebanon, as well as a spacious lawn framed by nine young birch trees. As every Czech patriot knows, they were planted by Karel in recognition of those who attend his famous *Patecnici*, or *Friday Circle*.

"Did you buy a book, Mr. Arepo?"

"Yes." He takes up the parcel and carefully unwraps the brown paper. "On impulse, at a shop near Old Town Square."

Green and silver sunlight streams across Karel's arms as he takes the book. "Ah, yes." His limpid eyes appraise the linocut cover while he speaks, reverently, the title. *"The Labyrinth of the World and the Paradise of the Heart."* Then, with a glance at the tea kettle, he adds, "Good old Jan Amos. The pedagogue's pedagogue. This will please Josef no end."

Paul takes back the book. "I would very much like to meet Josef."

"And he, you, no doubt. But before the water boils, you must tell me more about yourself, Mr. Arepo. Out of the way, Apollinaire." He nudges the gray tabby, which has appeared from nowhere, with the tip of his cane. The cat meows plaintively. "Three o'clock. You know the rules."

"I'm from Brno," says Paul. He's surprised how easy it is to speak the truth, yet does not plan to speak more. Not to Karel alone. At any rate, not now.

"I spent my formative years in Brno, living with my sister." From somewhere, Karel has retrieved his cherrywood cigarette holder and half a Gauloise. He opens a drawer and takes out a wooden match, striking it on the edge of the counter. "What do you do in Brno?" Lighting it, teeth clenched on the stem. Briskly puffing.

"I . . . I work in a shoe shop."

Karel shakes out the match. "You must *own* the shop, yes, Mr. Arepo?"

"Of course."

Karel nods and returns to his cigarette. Then says, around it, "Some men carry burdens with the air of a laborer. Some with that of an owner. You are the latter, Mr. Arepo."

The smell of the pungent Gauloise is another nostalgic surprise to Paul; somehow, the picture of Karel had been incomplete until this moment. They watch the tea pot and the cats. Karel smokes. He finally says, "You look like a man who has accomplished much, and who has much more to accomplish. A restless quality, perhaps. I've no doubt you have a more extraordinary resume than me."

Taken aback by the observations, Paul says, "You honor me, Mr. Čapek. But—"

Karel waves the Gauloise. "No need to explain. You've spared me having to ask Josef to help with the plant and have therefore spared be being indebted to my brother. You've also postponed the real work I wasn't looking forward to."

A low whistle rises to a shriek.

"Allow me, sir." Paul lifts the pot, and under Karel's direction, pours the boiling water into the cups over the spoons of *Lapsang Souchong*.

Paul sets the tea pot on a cold burner. "I must admit, Karel, I came here on a pilgrimage of sorts."

"To see me? This way, Mr. Arepo."

Paul takes up the book, holding it under his arm, then grabs both the mugs and follows Karel back into the main room. "You and your brother."

Karel detours to his Alpine rose. "Really? Just the two of us? Surely a pilgrim must seek something larger?" At that moment, footsteps sound on the porch. The door adjacent to Karel's can be heard opening, then closing. "Ah." Karel swivels in place and gestures with the cane. "And as though ordered to enter, stage left, my brother is home. Something larger, indeed. Let's disturb him." Karel raps the wall with his cane, on wainscot dented from similar summonings.

Faintly, a dulcet voice is heard, entirely familiar, even if the words are not. "*Atop quol, K!*"

"Quol, J!" replies Karel with a grin. Then, to Paul, "Sit down, Mr. Arepo. Please don't think us rude for speaking in a foreign tongue. It's a language which only three can speak in the entire world, our sister Helena being the third."

Heart pounding, Paul chooses one of the overstuffed chairs and lowers himself into it. He sets the book on the table beside him.

"You're favoring your ankle, Mr. Arepo. Is it paining you?"

"I . . . I twisted it earlier . . . "

Beyond the wall, the door bangs. Footsteps sound on the porch, and then Paul is heaving himself to his feet once again.

"You really don't have to . . ." Karel begins, then the door opens, and his brother steps into the room in gray suit and black tie, paint brushes jutting up from his breast pocket, the sleeves stained with brilliant ochre and saffron. Josef Čapek, rotund yet boyish, no older than thirty-nine, his eyes twinkling behind polished wire-rimmed glasses. "What's this? Oh. Hullo. A visitor?"

"Meet a man on a pilgrimage, Josef."

"Really?" Josef steps forward and offers a spry hand. "Pleasure."

"It's an honor, sir." He cannot help but grin. "I'm Paul Arepo."

"Arepo. Hmmm." They shake. The ochre and saffron on his cuff is matched by specks on the back of his hand. He smells faintly of turpentine. "Like the old palindrome, eh?" Josef smiles.

Paul is surprised by the buoyant youthfulness in Josef's face; the easy smile is not sardonic.

"Mr. Arepo says he's a cobbler from Brno." Karel approaches the wicker basket full of sticks.

"Brno? Did you check his papers, K?"

"Yes, I noticed the accent too, Josef. And he is in need of assistance." Karel rummages through the barrel and selects a carved stick of dark green wood.

"Where's your pilgrimage to, Mr. Arepo? Prague isn't much of a pilgrimage."

"Here, Paul. You may have this on loan."

Paul takes it: the haft of the walking stick is carved with an ancient, bearded faced.

"A water sprite," says Karel. Then, to Josef, "He brought a book you designed, brother."

"*I* designed?"

Paul lifts it from the end table.

"Komensky! Yes, yes. Then it makes a bit more sense."

"Sign it for him, Josef."

"Of course, of course." Josef pats his pockets, finding only paintbrushes. He scowls.

"Here." Without consideration, Paul produces his own pen, a 1948 Fisher Bullet Pen in solid aluminum from Carson's Department Store in downtown Burbank. Josef takes it, his eyebrows lifting. He stares intently at the sleek shape.

"It's called the Space Pen," says Paul.

"Fancy that." He studies the point. "Imported?"

"Yes."

Josef opens the book to the title page, which has, below the name of Jan Amos Komensky, *Illustrations and Engravings by J. Čapek*. As he signs, Josef mutters, "A rather authentic pilgrim, this Komensky." He writes in flowing blue ink. "Survived White Mountain. Came home to find his family dead. And so set out on the road." With a last lingering glance at the ball point—"Marvelous,"—he hands it back, then closes the book.

"Thank you, Mr. Čapek."

"Call me Josef."

Karel smiles. "How will you tell us apart otherwise?" And to Josef, "In a hurry to return to the theater?"

"Goodness, no. The scrims all came crashing down last night. Loose bolts or some such. We in the flies have retired for the day."

"Paul interrupted my work in the garden at an opportune time, and I've no wish to proceed yet to other, more bothersome chores. So let's go to lunch, yes?"

"Certainly, K."

"Paul?"

"Yes, Karel." He takes up the water sprite stick. "I'd like that."

"Good. We can talk about your facade over roast pork and dumplings, Josef's favorite." He glances at the clock. "I'll need a few minutes to change into better clothes. And if we take our time getting there, we'll be just in time for an afternoon glass of wine."

"The future is not in front of us, for it is here already in the shape of a germ; already it is with us; and what is not with us will not be even in the future. We don't see germs because they are under the earth; we don't know the future because it is within us. Sometimes we seem to smell the decay, encumbered by the faded remains of the past; but if only we could see how many fat and white shoots are pushing forward in the old tilled soil, which is called the present day."

—*The Gardener's Year* by Karel Čapek

13. FUTURE PRESENT

In the Restaurant of the Nine Cock's Crow at the edge of Vinhorady, a plate of pork skewers heaped with dumplings is laid before Josef by the languid-eyed waitress, while a platter of *svickova*—beef sirloin in cream sauce and cranberries—is set between Paul and Karel. "Enjoy, Mister Capek."

"Thank you, young miss," says Karel, who had diplomatically nudged the cuisine away from the pork for himself and his guest.

Three long-stemmed glasses gleam in the sunlight, with Josef's newly-drained. He refills his from a bottle, vintage 1922. "Wonderful," he says, then fills his brother's glass, and Paul's.

They have taken advantage of the clear skies to sit on the patio, with an audience of pigeons. Karel, having changed into a natty striped suit, and with his hair combed precisely and a flower from his garden stuck into his lapel, seems more familiar to Paul. Josef, his breast pocket now stuffed with pens, pencils and paint brushes, lifts his glass in toast. "To Paul Arepo and his timely arrival."

"To Paul Arepo," says Karel.

Paul lifts his glass. "And to the famous Brothers Čapek." The *young* Brothers, thinks Paul. Josef, in particular, retains the boyish roundness to his cheeks and chin, and his eyes sparkle with good humor. And though Karel's dandy exterior and drifting cigarette ashes are familiar, he seems smaller in the costume, someone still practicing to be the famous Karel Čapek that will one day be a nominee for the Nobel Prize.

"Wonderful town, Brno," continues Josef, after slurping down a mouthful of wine. "Become a modernist playground for architects, all your memorable Cubist apartment buildings and such. Puts the rest of the country to shame." He cuts into his sizzling pork. "Not so stodgy as Prague. Less pretentious on the boards." Josef sips again, then sets the glass down. "Though if you listen to the press, we're always at war with one another, aren't we? Nedjely and his ilk adore reducing us to lovers of Smetana and you to Dvorak. They warn of a dangerous Dvorak cult in Brno, while we venerate the grand old man of *Ma Vlast*." He pauses, gazing at Paul. "At least, when it comes to hops, we can lay down our swords and lift our cups." He does so. "I'm a huge fan of the Pilsner from your neck of the woods, Paul. Gets its flavor from those Taborites who settled down in your region."

Paul tucks into the rich beef sirloin and cranberries, so as not to smile.

"King of the old era, fellow by the name of Koranda the Heretic . . . "

Karel's fork grinds on the his plate. "Josef," he says, across the padded shoulder of his jacket, "Not at the moment, please?"

Josef grins like a cat. "Maybe Paul would like to hear the story."

"Actually, I know that story, Josef. It ends with good Pilsner being poured over the king's corpse, doesn't it?" He strives to remember the telling from Hotel Slavia, in 1931. "The punch line goes something like, *If you'd been alive, pal, you'd be drinking with us anyway*."

Josef gapes. Then laughs, loudly. Pigeons scatter. "Very good, Sir!" He leans closer. "Well, here's *another one*."

Karel rolls his eyes.

"*It's the Slavs*, Paul. Always the Slavs. They have that *tinge of cruelty* that makes my heart sing." He slurps his wine. Then: "Sixteenth century, or thereabouts. Hungary. You know, the *old old* days of the Hungarian empire. Didn't go in for the ambassadors and coddling that they do now. There was a peasant revolt under a peasant king. Hungarian margraves put it down immediately, of course." He forks some sausage, lifts the bubbling meat to his nose. "They built an iron throne for this peasant king. Heated it in a forge for hours and hours, 'til it was *white hot*." Josef grins. "Then they dressed this king up in ragged robes and led him in shackles along the processional aisle, all pomp and circumstance, *ha ha*. And they seated him rather forcefully. *Shoved a red-hot crown on his head, pressed a red-hot scepter into his hands.*" He eats the sausage and points the empty fork at Paul. Chewing, he says, "His screams could be heard in the next town. And *then*, you see . . ."

Karel lays his knife on his plate. "Is that not enough, Josef?"

Josef glances at his brother. A lingering glance, through which the smile grows broader. Again, the fork levels at Paul. "And *then*, Mr. Arepo, they *compelled his followers to . . . eat of his sizzling flesh.*" Biting into his sausage, he adds through a full mouth, "Feast went on for hours."

Karel sighs. "If I never have to hear that recounted in public again, Josef, I will be very pleased."

Church bells toll the second hour. Pigeons venture underfoot. And Josef, chuckling to himself, pours himself and Karel more wine. "That name," says Josef, slyly, around his glass. "Mr. *Arepo* . . ."

Karel holds up his hand. "Yes, no doubt there's a story behind it that would render it all banal." He bites on the cherrywood stem of his cigarette holder, regarding Paul across the table. "I enjoy the small strangenesses. For instance, you are from Brno. I do not doubt it. You speak of places there as a native would speak it, but your accent . . ."

"A tinge of the Continent?" Josef pulls a pen from his pocket and is doodling on a napkin. Fleet straight lines, curves.

"No. No, Josef. Nor what might be explained away as a learned Hebrew diction. The glorious monodies of the *Torah* and the *Cabala*. No." A pause, while he sets the cigarette on the table's edge and lifts a spoonful of cream sauce, slurping with pleasure. "I am currently writing a series of feuilleton stories for my paper. Mysteries. I am a great fan of mysteries." Karel has meanwhile managed to re-light his Gauloise, and now sends a plume of smoke up toward the linden branches. "They are

147

a hobby, I suppose. Mysteries, rather than solutions. I take great pleasure in giving my reader conundrums instead of solutions. I write whatever takes my fancy."

"I look forward to reading them," says Paul, carefully. They are among his most favorite of Karel's works—*The Tales from One Pocket* and *Tales from Another Pocket*.

"And your appearance in my garden this afternoon, Paul, strikes me as a similar sort of mystery."

Josef, peering sideways, continues to sketch a portrait of Paul hulking over the table, in Cubist lines and curves. Suddenly self-conscious on several fronts, Paul offers a laugh. Luckily, Karel is truthful in what he says; he does not wish the answers—not yet, anyway.

And Josef is busy doodling.

"Paul, will you be in town tomorrow evening?"

After a pause: "Yes."

"We hold little Friday night meetings at our villa, Josef and I."

"Yes, I've heard of them, of course."

"We invite friends over for chats about lively topics, and I would imagine that you would be able to contribute something."

Paul is surprised to find himself saying, "I'm . . . I'm doubtful I'd have very much to say to such enlightened men."

Of course, he could have much to say. In fact—could be saying much to Karel and Josef right now. Yet cannot. Cannot disturb this small and wonderful peace.

"Our group is varied, and relativistic. We desire men from every corner of our little country. I would not want it otherwise. We are all small men, and particles of the whole. You, Paul, would be most welcome."

"I will attend, Karel."

"Good. And now, Josef. Now, I must return to the villa and some necessary drudgery." He stands up.

"And I'll entertain Paul. You can stay, can't you, for the afternoon?"

"Come in, come in, *Mr . . . Arepo.*" Josef gazes sidelong and lingeringly at his guest. He nudges open the door to his side of the villa. "Watch out for *Demon.*" Demon is a cat, but facing the doorway is another demon—a long wooden mask of African origin surrounded by other examples of primitive art.

In the entryway, with another Persian carpet underfoot, Paul leans on the stick. He hears the tapping of Karel's cane beyond the wall.

Josef's half of the villa is, if anything, more cluttered than Karel's. The air smells predictably of turpentine and carbolic printer's ink. Instead of gardening catalogs the low teak tables are piled with trade journals and color wheels. Easels are set haphazardly here and there, with tantalizing works-in-progress. The walls are hung with Karel's photographs of apples, dandelions, gargoyles, guitars. Little of Josef's work is on view; instead, there are a few Picasso prints, a Mondrian, and a lush Alfons Mucha of Princess Libuse hanging—"*fondly,*" says Josef—upside-down.

"Yes, Lucretia, we'll find you some sardines," says Josef. "And yes, Raphael—" this to a white tabby who leaps onto the black ottoman that sits in the very center of the room. Gently, though betraying a bit of a sway in his stance, Josef pets the animal. "But later, *hmmm*? Give us humans some time to settle down. And perhaps share a smoke?" Josef's wire-rim glasses wink in broken sunlight as he glances at Paul.

"Yes, absolutely." Paul hadn't realized how much he'd been craving a cigarette since the moment Karel lit his Gauloise.

A black cat with emerald green eyes slinks past an empty easel. "Ah, and there's Demon. Wouldn't miss your tuna fish, would you, Demon?" The far side of the room has more easels and a tarpaulin across the floor. "I'm being waylaid, I see. Excuse us for a moment, will you, Paul?"

"Of course."

"Yes, yes. Yes, yes." With gentle gestures, Josef lures the cats into the kitchen.

Gripping the water sprite haft, Paul strolls to the far side of the room. In the comparative dimness—the drapes there are pulled, and the hurricane lamp that Josef now lights near the kitchen does little to dispel it—Paul discerns Josef's own work on the walls. In particular the colorful, vivid posters for *The Adventures of the Fox Bystrouska* and *Makropulous Thing*; the former of vertical red and green blocks, over which hover the Cheshire cat eyes and smile of the Vixen. Both posters contrast against the stark, black-and-white linocut sheets in the corner. Paul remembers it in Brno, a performance he'd not been able to attend but had dearly wanted to.

They had found the Maestro walking about in the upper circle, hands clasped behind his back, nearly invisible but for his shining halo of hair—

"Paul?"

He turns, startled. Josef, too, seems startled by this reaction; after all, he's only offering a cigar.

"I—thank you, Josef."

"A rather profound blend." Josef attends to his own, biting off the end and stowing it in his breast pocket.

"You have a marvelous apartment."

"Thank you, thank you. Not only an apartment but a gallery, of course." He reaches now into his side pocket, withdrawing what Paul had been curious to see since Josef's arrival—the silver phoenix lighter. "And the gallery," he continues, kindling the flame for Paul, "is also *a trap*."

Paul puffs the cigar to life, feigning complete interest in the ember. Then, without artifice, he savors the smoke, finds it calming him even as his eyes seek out the posters on the wall.

Josef, through a blue cloud, says, "My girl Jarmila always gravitates to the sculptures. She's a very tactile girl, is Jarmila. Karel, meanwhile, always putters over to his own photographs to search for imperfections." Josef draws again on the cigar, and exhales. "Which of course he always finds." A smile, which fades into something more serious, as Josef studies Paul's profile. "I was not at all surprised that my gallery had trapped you here, *Mr. Arepo*."

Trying for a puzzled expression, Paul says, "Oh?"

"Fan of opera?"

Paul nods, and smokes.

"From Brno, you must know him, eh? The Maestro?"

"How could I not?" replies Paul.

Josef nods, and walks past Paul, surveying the linocuts. Unlike the poster, they're not framed; they're raggedly cut and might be here only temporarily, while Josef works on them. He seems taken with appraising them but Paul knows this is a guise. "You can spot an artist by how he looks at things." He rights a can of spilled brushes on the desktop. "At times his gaze blazes brilliantly on the surroundings in order to fix them in the mind's lens. At other times, the glance is furtive, the artist spying from behind his trap, unwilling to let the subject dart away unseen."

Uncomfortable, Paul draws another lungful of smoke and exhales toward the rafters. Soon the sunlight through the window is tinged blue and Josef, bisecting that light with the shoulders of his jacket, is perched on a stool, observing.

"And right now, Josef, you are spying from your trap."

Josef squints, and smokes, and nods. Then says, "I know, somehow, that you are related to an artist that I know from Brno. An actor."

Even as he tries to remain nonchalant, Paul's entire body freezes up. His heart pounds, aided by the cigar's effect. "Really?"

Josef nods. "Your accent is from Brno and elsewhere. Your accouterments—the cut of your jacket, of your shoes, the collar of your shirt, and especially the device in your pocket—that marvelous pen, well, they're—"

Paul feels movement at his foot. A white cat rubs his trouser cuff.

"Nephilim is trying to understand you. Perhaps she too senses something beyond the ordinary muck of the Prague street on you." While the cat wanders toward the desk, and out of sight, and Paul merely smokes, Josef continues, "Your profile, your eyes and nose and mouth, is enormously suggestive, you see . . . "

Paul squares his shoulders. "Who do you think I am, Josef?"

Josef backs up against his rough-shod linocuts, as though to capture all of Paul in a glance. "You anglicized your first name. You couldn't change it, of course." The round lenses wink; then are steady. "Hugo speaks of you often." He adds, "And so does the Maestro J⎯⎯."

"But how could I . . . how could I be him?"

Smiling, Josef smokes his cigar evenly. Then: "Of course, you couldn't. So my reasoning went, you see. Hugo had mentioned an uncle. At first, I thought you must be this uncle. The resemblance was too strong."

"Michael Epstein."

Josef nods. "But you're not he, are you?" He looks away, looks to the nearest linocut, of a jagged street receding into a black sky. "Yet how can you be Pavel Haas?"

Paul has no intention of lying. Not to Josef. Dear Josefka, who in that other future had pulled him from the ruins of the Maestro's domeček.

And he recollects, from the faithful reading he has done over the years, a line of Josef's from a volume that does not yet sit upon the bookshelf. "*In truth, Josef, I go from nothing to nothing, I merely wander within* something. *My path does not pass through places; it is a period of time, a tension in time or rather simply a state.*"

"*Pavel Haas,*" whispers Josef, and scratches his chin with a now trembling hand. He turns to his linocut and studies it, lifting the cigar at certain aspects as though rethinking its composition. Paul can hear him muttering under his breath. When he turns back his cheeks are flushed.

"Josef?"

"Um. So, you are he. Yes. And, *why* are you here, Pavel?"

"I came . . . to speak to you. And Karel."

Josef's eyebrows lift. But, smoking, he says nothing. Finally, he meets Paul's whisper with his own. "*What year are you from?*"

Pavel reaches into his inner pocket. He feels for the coin, pulls it out and offers it to Josef. The Roosevelt dime dated 1935.

Josef mouths the date. "I can't imagine a . . . a more interesting signum than this."

"It was the oldest in my pocket, before I left."

"And what, Pavel, would the newest have been?" Josef does not look up from the coin.

"1949."

"*1949,*" Josef mutters. A frightened smile, which vanishes. He lowers the coin. "And tell me, Paul, *why* have you come back?"

"To warn you, Josef."

"Warn me?" He turns the dime over, and over again, then sets it on his trembling palm. "Of the future?"

Paul smokes, and holds the smoke deep. Then, exhaling, says, "Yes."

Josef nods. "Yet perhaps . . . perhaps I don't want to know. Not yet, at any rate." He glances up. "I have a few days yet?"

Paul smiles. "Of course."

"Good, then. Good. Maybe I will enjoy these days without having to worry about . . . your warning. Or perhaps, well, perhaps I cannot imagine hearing it and surviving?" He slips the coin in his pocket. "Perhaps not. At any rate. Uh. What . . . method of travel did you employ? You can tell me that much?"

Paul sets the cigar stub in an ashtray. "You might not believe me. The technique was inspired by the Maestro J⎯⎯'s theoretical studies. What he calls the *scasovani*." Paul sees the Maestro sitting on the ancient well amidst sundered foliage.

And so, it is done.

Josef puffs on his cigar. "I'm familiar with it, of course." He is silent for a time, walking round, staring up up at his linotypes. He walks to the window, and holds the coin in the sunlight, then sets it on the blotter. "Another of your Maestro's crackpot theories. But my sis . . . Lenca received a strange feuilleton for publication. Told me about it, or tried to. About how he found proof of it, supposedly, while on a trip back from Bratislava. In a village, high in the mountains . . . Crackpot story, apparently. And when the *Noviny* balked at publishing it, he sent in a whole boxload of supposed proof." Josef shrugs. "Didn't pass muster, apparently and was spiked." Josef stops, and studies Paul's face. "You haven't heard the story?"

"No, Josef."

"Of, hmmm, of a dead woman. A dead woman *brought back to life*? Of how the Maestro was stranded in the mountaintop village? Doesn't sound familiar? How he was sitting in a café, and heard the woman singing. And the next morning, after spending a night in the some mysterious mansion, the Maestro rises and walks like a forester into the woods. And there he finds her body, pierced through the chest by something like a giant thorn."

Paul can only think of Magda.

"Paul, you look quite surprised."

"I haven't heard this."

The Heartbeat of the World.

We never found it, Karel and I.

"How he encountered an elementary force high in the mountaintop. Awoke that *scasovani* of his. Brought it to life in his music. And then found himself back by the train as though the world had turned in a circle, and there she was, the dead woman, alive once again." Josef smiles wryly. "Funny. The Maestro couldn't see it, of course. He was too close."

"See what, Josef?"

"The young woman in the woods, killed, then brought back to life. The circle of events, with everything ending back at the beginning..." With his left arm, Josef picks up Nephilim, nuzzling the cat's fur with his chin, and walks over to the poster for *Fox Bystrouska*; the Cheshire cat smile smiles upon him. "Can't you see? It's the story of the opera he'd just finished. *Adventures of the Fox Bystrouska*. Right down to the old man's epiphany at the end, catching sight of a newly reborn Bystrouska." Josef's smile grows troubled. "And now you walk through Time, eh? Inspired by the Maestro's lunatic dream."

"The candle has its thief in the sun."

— *Zapisnik* by Karel Hynek Macha (1833)

14. THE FRIDAY NIGHT CIRCLE

On his approach down Narrow Street in Vinhorady, wielding the water-sprite walking stick, Paul feels all of Prague at his back.

The chill, sunny day has descended into starry night. The thoroughfares of New Town bustle with the outbound weekend traffic. In suburban Vinhorady, the houses are lighted, settled in, quiet. The rap of his stick on the pavement, the tread of his shoes, are crisp and clear as the constellations over the Vltava. The moon, three-quarters full, floats in the branches of an oak tree, ghosting his steps. Beneath his overcoat he wears a new suit bought with Josef's loan of a thousand crowns ("*We must acclimate you visually, Paul, to our quaint era*")—gray tweed with an arch bow-tie and celluloid collar, and on his feet, sturdy Belvederes from the Bata outlet in New Town. He has also bought toiletries to last him a few days—necessary days, he tells himself, to monitor the Maestro's condition. A phone call this afternoon to Ostrava had confirmed his condition was improving, leaving Paul concerned with what the Maestro might do once released from the hospital; surely he is obsessed with his meeting of the Pilgrim Arepo. Paul plans to travel to Brno before the Maestro returns, strictly to visit the archives of *Lidové noviny* and look for the feuilleton and notes. *If* Josef can arrange it with his sister.

As for tonight, he's now uncertain about his choice to

attend the Circle. If Josef had noticed the resemblance to Hugo Haas, then might the others? As far as Paul can remember, Hugo had never rubbed shoulders with the most famous members—like Karel's colleague at the newspaper, Ferdinand Peroutka, or the author František Langer. Nonetheless it's a risk.

Yet how can he resist the opportunity to witness one of these legendary evenings?

The thought draws a smile, shared with his companion the moon.

Soon the villa appears, lighted and active behind the rhododendrons and roses. Paul stops at the base of the stairs, listening to the many voices coming out the open door on Karel's side. He grips the water sprite for courage, and it's the stick that leads him in a slow climb. The air smells pleasantly of roses and pipe smoke and something roasting in the oven. "Paul?" Karel stands on the porch in a green-striped suit and white tie, a carnation in his lapel.

"Karel, good evening." Behind him, in the street, a car putters up to the curb; a cat darts past. As Paul reaches the porch, he and Karel shake hands.

"Good of you to come. How's the stick serving you?"

Karel's hair is meticulously combed but for an unruly lick in the back.

"Quite well, actually. My ankle feels almost back to normal." Paul reaches into his pocket. "I brought a present." He draws out the stone from Capitola. "For your rock garden."

Karel takes it. "Why, thank you." He turns it in the light, watching azure glints flaring from the ebony. "This has seen much water in its day. The ocean, in fact."

"I would be honored if it found a place in your rock garden."

"Absolutely. We don't have many ocean rocks here. The coasts of Bohemia are notoriously dry."

At the sound of a cane tapping the concrete steps, Karel looks past Paul's shoulder. "Yet another arrival. And—a surprise. Good evening!" He hands the stone back to Paul.

"Good evening, Čapek." From out of the rhododendron's shadows materializes a short, slender man, dapper in a black suit with a rose in the lapel. He wields a cane with his left hand, clutches a potted plant in the crook of his right arm. His shoulder juts up at painful angle, but his face, brightening as he nears, shows a grin. "Good evening," he says to Paul.

Karel points the Gauloise to Paul. "Acquainted?"

The other man shakes his head. "I've not had the pleasure."

I once saw you in the Maestro's garden, Herr Brod, thinks Paul. *And I recently read your essays, sir, on the Diaspora and the founding of Palestine, from my home in Hollywood.*

"This is my new friend, Paul Arepo," says Karel. "An owner of a shoe shop, and an astute gardener. Meet the writer, composer, editor Mr. Max Brod."

Max hooks his walking stick on his right forearm, then smartly shakes Paul's hand. "Herr Arepo. It's always pleasing to have a fellow Jew in company." He bows, then plucks up the cane and turns to Karel. "I bring a gift, grudgingly, on behalf of another—"

"Another gift."

"—and it is best I dispatch it now."

Karel surveys the potted plant, whose brittle branches are shorn of all but three leaves. "What is it?" With both hands, he takes it.

"I ran into Franz's old sweet girl. Milena." Brod smiles uneasily, his neat little mustache twitching. "She pressed me to *pass this on* to you."

"What's that in the soil?" Karel turns the plant in the light.

Tiny bones bristle up from around the base of the tiny plant, as well as three little wooden slats on which are written in black ink: *Left*, *Center*, and *Right*. "Curious."

"It's from her current beau, that fellow Tiege from 9forces."

"Very intriguing." Karel's smile is tighter than Brod's. "My brother will enjoy this. He'll be curious about the bones. Perhaps a rat? Or a parakeet? As to the plant, this is *petasites vulgaris* also know as *Devětsil*. A boon to beekeepers."

"Herr Tiege's way of saying hello. *Optical poetry*, he calls it." Brod adds, hopefully, "I don't think it's *entirely* hostile."

"No, no. Certainly not." Carefully, he touches one of the forlorn leaves. "I quite enjoy it. Perhaps I can plant it in the garden and rejuvenate it?"

Paul slips the stone back into his pocket. "May I?"

Karel passes it to him. Then, gathering up his cane and his good cheer, he ushers Max and Paul up the stairs and through the door of his apartment, which is smoky and warm, with the Persian carpets tidied-up and the furniture re-arranged, and five men standing near the framed paintings smoking and drinking wine.

Paul deposits his water sprite stick in the barrel.

Karel gestures with the Gauloise. "We've a few of us here already, as you can see." And, to the others, "Here's Max, whom you know! And this, this is my friend Paul Arepo. Meet František Langer, the writer. Josef Susta, the historian. Ferdi Peroutka, the journalist . . ."

Paul shakes hands with the gentlemen. They stare at the plant, until the last one, Vaclav Skrusny, lifts it from Paul's hands. "Fractured art. Looks like Tiege's work."

"It is," remarks Karel dryly.

Max says, "Josef here?"

"In the kitchen, preparing his famous Parisian apple tarts."

Drinks are offered by Peroutka; port wine is ushered into Paul's hand. Brod declines, and says generally to the group. "Hear about the earthquake today?"

Some of them nod.

"Earthquake?" says Karel.

Brod's reply—"Yes, in Brno."—stops Paul with the wine halfway to his lips. He and Karel share a glance.

"But nothing too strong," Brod continues. "Merely enough to ring the bell in the Capuchin monastery, topple some stalls in the Cabbage Market and leave some interesting marks in the ground."

Karel turns to Paul. "Did you hear about it?"

Startled, Paul shakes his head. "No."

"You're from Brno?" Max smiles. "Well, I don't think anyone was injured."

"Would you like to sit down, Max? That way, you'll get first choice. I recommend the plush velvet."

Max thanks Karel and ambulates toward the seven chairs circled between the fireplace and the desk. He says to Paul, "It seemed more of a splash of excitement than anything else." Instead of the plush velvet, he chooses a tattered Bauhaus, and sits. He removes a gold cigarette box from his side pocket, opens it and offers one to Paul.

"Thank you." As Paul takes it, he's trying to remember ever experiencing an earthquake in Brno. Temblors in Burbank, yes, in Brno, no.

Langer lights Brod's cigarette. Then Brod is talking to him and Peroutka about some literary agent all three seem to despise; Karel is examining a book that Susil has taken down from the shelf. And so Paul—stowing the cigarette in his pocket—moves toward the kitchen and the wafting scents of browning crusts and tart apples. He finds Josef in a dress shirt and tie, suspenders, tan trousers. His suitcoat is hung over the back of a kitchen chair. His sleeves are rolled up. He's loading delicate pastries onto a pair of silver trays, cats crying at his ankles. "There he is. Evening, Paul." Josef straightens up. "Well, you certainly look more ... contemporary. Marvelous."

"Thanks to you, Josef."

"Yes, and I've been painting all morning and baking all afternoon so that my thoughts don't spiral off into conundrums." Josef rearranges the pastries, then picks up a napkin. "I've formed my tarts into question marks, as you can see. Not that I mean to have my questions answered by you, Paul. No, no. *Ummm.* At least not right away."

"Of course."

"I can't stop thinking of Komensky. From the book you brought, I suppose." He wipes excess apple from the edge of the tray, then sets down the napkin and adds more pastries. "Those Spectacles of Doubt the Pilgrim wore. All day long I've felt as though I'm wearing them. Even at this moment. I can't see what I want to see directly. Only from the corners of my eyes, if you understand." He wipes his hands on the towel and meets Paul's eyes for the first time. "So, do you plan to ... reveal anything to the group tonight?"

"I'm not sure, Josef."

Cassandra's noose, he wants to say.

"Yes, well. If nothing else the food will be memorable. What's that?"

"A stone." Paul walks to the kitchen door and looks onto the spacious garden. "I'm going to add it to your garden."

"By all means. Then you can help me carry the trays in for our carnivale."

As they enter the living room, Brod calls from his chair. "Josef. Good evening."

"Doctor Brod. I thought I heard your voice. What a delight you could come."

"I mailed the typescript rather than carry it here."

Josef sets his tray down on the dining table, directing Paul to set his on the other side, past the *Devětsil* plant. "I look forward to it. A *new* Kafka. Imagine that."

"Something new?" asks Peroutka, breaking off his conversation with Langer.

Kafka? Hadn't he died in 1924? The idea threatens to meld with unrecorded earthquakes until Paul remembers that the new Kafka is really the old Kafka—*The Fortress.* The strange book which had become a *mandala* to the Robots. "It's taken me three years to sort out the drafts. He left it in a mess but I've managed to shape it nicely. Josef, do you think twelve linocuts are possible before deadline?"

Josef, setting an apple tart on a napkin, says, "Strangely, yes. I feel in the mood to work." He hands the tart to Susil. "Hullo, Susil. If you like them, thank *Madamoiselle* Yvette from Paris, who one well-remembered evening in 1916 . . . "

Peroutka says to Brod, "Have you thought of asking Karel Tiege for illustrations? He's dating Franz's old sweet girl."

"And what Milena says . . . "

Josef, studying the *Devětsil* plant, mutters, "Parakeet bones?" He passes Paul a pastry.

"Thank you, Josef. It smells wonderful."

"Gentlemen." At the fireplace, beneath a Cubist portrait of a mother and a baby, Karel squares his shoulders. He rests his hand firmly on his cane. He smiles, and his face goes rubbery for an instant. "Dare we sit down? And with Josef's wonderful pastries in hand—"

"Soon in stomach," says Susil, his mouth full.

"—yes, be sure to thank *Madamoiselle* Yvette. With his pastries in hand we will begin our circle. František, Ferdinand, Josef, Josef, Paul."

They seat themselves. Paul sits in a comfortable leather armchair, with Josef to his left and Brod to his right.

Peroutka, lighting a pipe, says, "So how fares our Republic this week, Karel?"

"Other than Brno," quips Ferdinand, to contrite laughter.

Josef, about to take a bite of tart, says, "What about Brno?" The gray tabby begs at his boots.

Karel says, "A minor earthquake."

Peroutka says, "Remember the whirlwind of 1871?"

"Really?" Josef glances at Paul.

"In Brno?" asks Susil.

"Wasn't it 1865 or such?" asks Langer.

Brod shakes his head. "1870, I'm quite certain. I have a client who loves to tell tales about it . . . "

Karel, who has been smoking during the exchange, now exhales above their heads. "No whirlwind this time. A minor event, to all reports. Let's pray that any damage is the sort that spade and spackle can easily repair." Karel squares his padded shoulders. "Now, as most of you know, I began these Friday circles in the firm belief that a *dialogue* is infinitely preferable to a *monologue*. And I, by myself, am a *monologue machine*." Karel smiles. "True, I have Josef. But our minds have grown so similar that we are in fact, a *duologue machine*."

Josef, with the tabby now on his lap, says, "Terrifying thought."

"And so I truly look forward to hearing the opinions of others. And—

Ferdinand, you offered a galvanizing topic at the end of last Friday's circle, and I would love to continue it now, for a time."

Peroutka nods. "Worldwide depression, yes. Hadn't we exhausted the topic?"

Max, lighting another cigarette, says, "I was not here to listen, sir. Nor was our friend Paul."

Peroutka straightens, lifting his chins. "Very well. The argument. The argument, as I recall it, sirs, was on the likelihood of another Depression such as we've seen in the Germanic lands since the War, and to a lesser extent here, in the first years of our great Republic." He voice deepens. "What is the likelihood of such a Depression, like a pathogen, *attacking the corpus of the entire Earth*."

Murmurs in the lowering smoke. Josef, stroking the cat, says, "Worthy of one of Karel's imaginative scientific tales."

Langer, whose politics are vitriolic, snipes at Karel. "Your centrist views would vanish like a will-o'-the-wisp, Karel."

"So quickly?" Karel lifts his eyebrows in mock surprise.

Langer nods. "Your ideology can only exist in peacetime. If such an event were to take place you would find yourself in a now *radical* center, while the dire emotions of the proletariat would drive the people to either side. I think—" Langer pauses. He and the others turn to the front door, which has just opened. A lean man in a black overcoat hovers on the threshold. His head is clean-shaven. A figure of menace, it would seem. But none of the others seems uneasy nor even surprised when—with a nod from Karel—the figure retreats onto the porch, dematerializing into shadow.

"*He* hasn't come in a while," says Peroutka.

Josef stands up. "I'll fetch another chair."

"He can have mine," offers Susil, in the burgundy.

Karel waves his Gaulois. "Keep it. The *old gentleman* is not choosy."

Josef returns with a nice chair from the kitchen and reseats himself. Then, they wait. Paul wants to ask a question but is mesmerized by the others' solemn silence, by the brittle ticking of the clock and by the crackling of the fire in the fireplace. Finally, above the yawls and meows of a dozen cats come unhurried footsteps on the stairs. From out of the shadows strides a tall, leonine, gray-suited, white-bearded, glittering-eyed old man, entirely familiar to Paul. The firelight gleams on his pince-nez glasses, thick white mustache and pointed beard, and on his bald pate the hue of polished rosewood. He tucks his oaken walking stick into the barrel and crosses the Persian carpet toward them.

He is the Philosopher-King come down from his castle.

Tomáš Garrigue Masaryk has arrived.

"Long live:

the liberated word, the new word, fauvism, expressionism, cubism, pathetism, dramatism, orphism, paroxysm, dynamism, plastic art, onomatopoeism, the poetry of noise.

Long live:

machinism, sports fields, the Central Slaughterhouse . . . the crematorium, artistic advertisements, steel and concrete!"

—*Lidové noviny* (Czech Futurist manifesto) by Stanislav Kostka Neumann

15. THE LABORATORY OF THE APOCALYPSE

"Glass of wine, *Senor*?" asks Karel.

Masaryk shakes his head. "Pipe will do, Karel." Josef, at his shoulder, helps the President remove his overcoat. "*Gracias*, Josef." Masaryk squares his boots on the Persian carpet, hands Josef his walking stick, then tugs the corner of his coat. Once again, he nods to everyone in the room; he seems to know each of them, but when he reaches Paul his head quizzically inclines.

"Meet Paul Arepo, Tomáš. A shoeshop owner from Brno."

"And a pilgrim," adds Josef.

Paul bows. "Mr. President. It is a great honor to meet you."

"Shoeshop owner and a pilgrim?" Masaryk nods and tugs on the ends of his mustache. "A logical combination, Mr. Arepo." Then, motioning once again to those who remain standing, he approaches the chair beside Josef's. "Please, gentlemen." With them, he sits down.

Brod inquires, "Have you heard anything new about the earthquake in Brno, Mister President?"

With a tone of mildness in his sonorous voice, Masaryk says, "I am told it was minor. Radiating from the depths of Špilberk Hill." Looking to Paul, he asks, "Near your shop?"

"No. On Zanechivka." Paul finds himself nearly telling the entire truth. *Zanechivka C 2, Mr. President. We're known as Czech Shoes at the Rabbit.*

167

Masaryk has removed a pipe and a velvet bag from his pocket, and now packs the bowl. He nods, and in the silence, the others sip their wine or smoke their cigars, while the fire crackles and the painted portraits jostle in the uneven light. "Zanechivka Street will remain bustling, as always, Mr. Arepo. I heard no reports of damages to commercial buildings, though a more complete report shall be transmitted to the castle this morning, with details of any financial losses or damage to city utilities," he waves his pipe in a slow circle. "And the like."

Josef proffers his silver Phoenix lighter. Acquiescing with a generous nod, Masaryk places the pipe between his teeth and accepts the flame that jumps into being. After drawing and puffing the tobacco to life, he says laconically into the rising smoke, "I interrupted a topic. Please continue."

"Yes, President." Ferdinand Peroutka, the journalist, settles in his Biedermeyer chair. "The likelihood of a worldwide depression." While Masaryk leans forward in the chair, staring into the fire, his elbows on his knees, Peroutka outlines the thesis of his argument, to which František Langer counters, with Josef adding a few laconic comments. Masaryk is quiet, intently listening. Paul feels untethered by the fire's shimmer, by the shadows, by the cats' eyes gleaming in the dark; yet he is held to his chair by Masaryk's presence. Earlier, during his walk into Vinhorady, he had felt all of Prague at his back. He knows now that it is seated not more than a meter away from him. Masaryk, is in the very truest sense, the Republic. He perches on a simple chair which is actually a throne. For the next few hours, the Republic is centered in this living room, is bantered and argued about, is discussed in conversation of a high and low order, and Masaryk, his potent presence and his calm, sits too in the eye of a future storm that swirls unseen around them, in the flux of Time.

As the conversation flows from the threat of worldwide Depression to the construction of new roads in Prague VII; from the worthiness of

Cuban tobacco to the pragmatic views of the new American president Coolidge, Paul is a witness. And for the most part, so is Masaryk. He seems more content to listen to the opinions of others. Peroutka, a member of the left, is eager to advance arguments about Social Democracy. Langer, a journalist through-and-through, steers the conversation to various attacks by both the right and left, on Masaryk as much as Karel. Brod speaks of Palestine, and the Zionist movement and its leader Theodor Herzl, whom Susil decries. From time to time Masaryk raises a monitory finger when one of the guests strays into talk deemed too metaphoric or outlandish. He interjects a short, concise comment, pats the orange tabby that sleeps on his lap and smokes his pipe.

The Friday Night Circle soon sits on the edge of Saturday morning. When the clock chimes twelve Karel stands up, girding his padded shoulders. "Well!"

Paul tastes the stale smoke in the air. He yearns for another cigarette, but resists.

Peroutka, Langer, Susil, Brod, all remain seated until the President nods and says, "A good talk, gentlemen."

With him, they all stand up.

"Yes, a very good talk."

Hats and coats are donned. Peroutka and Langer leave, off to share a cab. Susil bows to Masaryk and shakes Paul's hand, then dons his overcoat. When Paul approaches the barrel for his walking stick, Josef halts him with a touch on his elbow. Josef gestures to the others—Masaryk, who remains near the fire, and Brod and Karel leaning on their canes.

The old gentleman says, "I'm not ready to be locked up for the night yet, Karel."

Karel smiles and gives that slight nod that is, for him, a bow. "Let's enjoy the back garden, *Senor*. The crisp air will revive all of us."

Josef grins. "I'll light the lamps."

"I built a fountain since you were last here. And I forgot to show you the alpine flowers that I've resettled in the upstairs."

A buttery light throbs among begonias and roses, juniper bushes and trellised ivy. The hurricane lamps exhale warmth as well as light, altering the garden stirred by the night breeze into brief hints of a tropical night. Nestled on the edges of the small piazza, they light the wicker chairs but barely touch the tops of the beech trees—the trees planted to commemorate each member of the Friday Night Circle.

"Those were quite excellent tarts, Josef," says Masaryk, sitting beside Brod, with the oaken walking stick against his knee.

Karel, standing near the trellis, murmurs, "*Thank Mademoiselle Yvette.*"

"Marvelous young woman." Josef sits down between Brod and Paul, while a dozen cats pad silently across the piazza and amongst the bushes, where taller, darker figures can also be discerned.

"Karel, I must thank you, as well, for your new book."

"*Our* new book, Tomáš." Karel says to the others, "Mr. President agreed to split the royalties fifty-fifty if he could give his half to a dear widow struggling to support her young son." Leaning on his stick, he adds, "We have missed you these past months, Mr. President."

Masaryk acquiesces with a slight tilt of the head. "Your garden has changed since I was last here."

In the shuddering light and the shuddering warmth they survey Karel's garden. "Yes. Most of it is inside."

Masaryk, with his oak stick, points out a few plants, nodding appreciatively. Nothing is said for a time. Paul accepts a cigarette from Brod. Josef lights it. Then Masaryk gazes sidelong, thoughtfully, at Paul. "You are an *interesting* man, Mr. Arepo."

Surprised—abashed—Paul says, "But . . . but I hardly spoke in there, Mr. President."

Josef says, "Silence often makes the greatest impression at these Circles."

"If you *had* spoken up tonight," Masaryk pauses to light the pipe under Josef's phoenix flame, "what would you have spoken up about?"

The throb of the hurricane lamps darkens in his periphery. At his foot, the black cat sidles past and jumps onto Josef's lap. Josef absently pets it, while watching Paul carefully.

Paul straightens in the chair. "I would have asked, Mr. President, your thoughts about the future."

"Call me Tomáš, please." Masaryk smokes and nods, smokes and nods. "What, in particular?"

Paul suddenly remembers standing before another precipice, this one at the Slavia, seconds before asking Karel and Josef if he might adapt *The Insect Play*: the world threatening to tilt in either direction. "I would ask you, Tomáš, if you fear the end of the Republic."

Masaryk leans forward, setting his elbows on his knees and staring into the hurricane lamp. Paul notes the steadiness of his eyes flickering with the light. "Fear?" he says finally. "Do I *fear* the end of the Republic?" He lifts the hand that holds the pipe, and with the stem near his lips, he smiles. "Have you news of imminent danger, Paul? Or are you thinking of the future more in terms, say, of Karel's scientific prophesies."

Glancing at Josef, Paul replies, "In a way yes to both questions, Tomáš."

Masaryk smokes and is quiet for a time. Then says upward, "I accept a material world and a spiritual one. All history is an argument for *today*. All history is, as it were, *taking place today*. The present is a piece of history. The past and future are alive in us." A slight smile. He lowers his pipe and says, "We live every instant in Eternity, Paul. We shape it, from one moment to the next. Our Republic is an effort in *State-Building*. To create and perfect and to ... *deepen* something enduring." And a long moment later, "Therefore, what can be seen, ten years hence, Paul, is constantly in flux. By our hands."

And they contemplate this, the five of them. Josef strokes Demon's chin. Karel, fingering the handle of his cane, watches Paul intently. Brod stares away from the lights, into the garden.

Masaryk straightens in his chair. "Do you fear it, Paul?"

He nods. "I do, Tomáš."

"And how would it come to pass?"

171

In the shifting shadows, the shuddering warmth, Paul glimpses Magdalena in Mendel's garden. The dim red of her hair.

Tomáš, Karel, Max, Josef—they are each waiting for him to speak.

"A reconstituted Germany, in nationalistic fervor. A leader, who will use the shame of the post-war Depression to lift them up. And a claim against the borderlands of our Republic. One that no other country will dispute." He feels his pulse throbbing against his collar. "Soon Germany will conquer the Czechoslovak lands to Bratislava, and Poland—all of eastern Europe, and begin a systematic destruction of all Jews."

Brod stares intently at Paul. Josef, intently elsewhere.

"That's an interesting—and an ominous—thesis," Tomáš Garrigue Masaryk taps the bowl of his pipe against the edge of his cane chair. And Karel, fingering the haft of his cane, is searching Paul's face with his eyes, as silence grows, broken finally by Masaryk's voice. "Yet," says the President. He stares upward, at shivering stars.

Paul begins to speak, but Masaryk continues, gently, "We must not be fearful that only dire things lie ahead. Karel knows this. We must not be *impatient*. If we cannot reach out and touch it, we must not lose heart." He adds with an enigmatic smile, and a glance toward Karel, "*God's mills grind slowly, yet they grind exceedingly fine and for all eternity.*"

The aphorism is allowed to live in the garden shadows for a long moment, before Brod clears his throat and speaks. "I am reminded, quite vividly now, of the book I discussed with Josef earlier. My friend Franz's last work."

Masaryk stows the pipe in his pocket, sets elbows on knees and acquiesces to Brod.

"It's called *The Fortress*. Something he'd worked on for more than a decade. Never finished." Brod's neat moustache twitches with a sad smile. "I've managed to create a complete version. Full of nightmares precisely of the sort you speak, Mr. Arepo. One that came to him in a strange, and troubling, manner." Max Brod gazes up at the stars. Perhaps he intends to say something more.

Masaryk intervenes. "What was it they called Vienna, before the

War?" He glances at Karel, at Josef, at Brod. A professor waiting for his students to respond. "A laboratory of the Apocalypse?"

Josef gives a wry chuckle.

"A state, a republic, a democracy..." Masaryk gestures laconically. "The new Europe is like a laboratory built from the great graveyard of the World War." A glance in Paul's direction. "And a laboratory calls for the cooperation of all. Democracy—modern democracy—is in its infancy. Shutting our eyes to any threat—any *White Mountain* looming on the horizon—would be a grave error. Yet..."

Josef, hands in his pockets, says, "Tomáš, what if what he said were to come true?"

"But it *is* true, Josef. Of course. That, and a million other futures." He straightens, and as though in colloquy with the ringed lamps, if not to the cats that wander in his periphery. "We can worry about each one, and we can continue building on our army." He straightens in the wicker chair. "I am a *convinced pacifist*, Paul. Karel knows this. Yet I love the army. I desire peace—a practical peace, not a utopian one. I won't meet aggression unarmed."

The cold breeze feels colder; the fleeting warmth, cooler. Masaryk's pince-nez lenses flash in the lamplight. "Paul, you are... a most decent person."

"Thank you, Tomáš."

Only later—much later—will Paul learn that Tomáš's comment, about being a *most decent person,* was a very great compliment.

The garden stirs, lifting the brazen echo of church bells. At that same moment five men with shaven heads and black overcoats materialize from the birch trees. Masaryk pats his knees and stands up. "Being under constant surveillance is the part of the job I do not enjoy, gentlemen," he says.

"*Senor.*" Karel taps his cane on the gravel. "I thank you for gracing our circle tonight."

"Not at all. It was most enlightening." He shakes their hands, Paul last of all. "Good morning, Paul."

"Good morning, Tomáš."

While Josef and Karel escort the President of the First Republic to his waiting car, Paul stands with Brod, who is silent, clutching his cane, gazing up at the stars. Paul thinks of *The Fortress* and its eerie walled city. The enigmatic shades.

Brod clears his throat. "Theodor Herzl wrote a vivid parable, Paul, about a man—a world traveler, a hedonist, a dandy—who suffers a very deep cut on his arm." Brod lifts his arm, regarding the cuff and bared wrist. "As the doctors work on his grievous wound the man glimpses for an instant, amidst the blood, the *white hardness* of his own bone. The man, Herzl writes, feels a great terror as well as a certain *harrowing beauty* in that glimpse. For it shows him what he was eventually to be, standing before Eternity. And he becomes obsessed with his own skeleton, which he comes to call '*the Beautiful Rosalinda.*'" Brod's voice fades into the hiss and shudder of the hurricane lamps.

"*The Beautiful Rosalinda,*" echoes Paul. Before he can ask Brod any questions, Josef and Karel return. Josef has retrieved the *Devětsil* plant, muttering about how nice it will look buried behind the rhododendron.

"I will also bid goodnight," says Brod. "Mr. Arepo, perhaps you could call on me next week? I think our concerns are in tandem."

Paul shakes his hand. And doubtfully says, "I would like that."

"And Josef. I look forward to your reaction to the manuscript."

"Of course. Oh." Josef glances at Paul, then asks Brod, "Heard from our friend the Maestro?"

"Only that he's in the hospital, in Ostrava. Came down with a serious cold. The doctors worried it might conflate into pneumonia, but it seems to have passed."

"So he missed all the brouhaha in Brno?" mutters Josef, with a glance at Paul. He shakes Brod's hand once more. Then Karel escorts his guest to the street.

And when it's just the two of them, Josef pulls the Roosevelt dime from his pocket. "I phoned my good sis in Brno. She says the archives are in a bit of a mess, but she'll arrange for you to get access to that feuilleton of the Maestro's."

"Thank you, Josef."

Josef peers at the front of the dime in the lamplight, then carefully stows it in his pocket. They walk along the side of the villa accompanied by several cats. They find Karel on the steps.

"Paul, a most fine evening."

They shake.

"Thank you, Karel."

"How about dinner tomorrow? My Olga's coming to town. I think she'd like to meet you."

"Paul's going back to Brno, K."

"Oh, of course. Of course. I hope you find your shop in order."

"He could not say with any certainty in which direction New York lay; he had paid little attention on the way here. Finally he told himself he didn't have to go to New York where no one was expecting him. So he chose a direction at random, and set off."

—*The Man Who Disappeared*,
by Franz Kafka

16. Z BRNE

With the snap-brim hat tipped low on his head, Paul struggles to read the book. "*We descended a dark, winding staircase and entered the gate in which a large hall was filled with young people. On the right sat a fierce-looking old man holding a large copper pot in his hand.*"

The train jostles over ties; rain and soot spatters the window and he finds himself hovering over Komensky's great city, if not within it.

"*I noticed that all who arrived from the Gate of Life presented themselves before him and each, putting his hand into the pot, drew out a piece of paper inscribed with a word. Thereupon, he went toward one of the streets, either running and joyfully shouting, or walking with a sorrowful mien, complaints, grimaces, and backward glances. One read, RULE; another, SERVE; or COMMAND; or OBEY; or WRITE; or STUDY; or HOE; or JUDGE; or FIGHT.*"

He glances out the window at rushing blackberries massed beside the track. No second earthquake has been reported in Brno. Paul tries to explain away the first as something forgotten, barely noticed. Didn't he recall some sort of temblor from those years? Father complaining about the stock in the store all tumbled on the floor? But no. No earthquake. *Nothing radiating from the depths of Špilberk Hill*, as T.G.M had reported. Here was a unique event, and he, Paul, and his stave flower, was most certainly the cause.

Or was it the Maestro?

Paul shifts on the chair. He shuts the book, studying Josef's striking linocut design—a six-pointed star set within a circle, red on black, representing the six avenues of the City. The Maestro—being alive when he should be dead? Or if not the Maestro, then the *Baseform Scasovani Generator*, that improbable device of bulbous bronze installed in the corner of the Maestro's office; its chimes that had drawn the great tree from the garden?

Such thoughts are useless, and have been turning round and round upon themselves.

What has the Maestro been up to in his hospital bed? How has the incident on Babi Hura affected him? Will he now seek to build other machines like the *Generator*? Will he attempt to summon, more profoundly, the presence from the luminous depths?

Paul's hand is at his rumpled tie, touching the shirt beneath it, and the outline of the ornate key on its chain.

Why not telephone the Maestro? Why not visit Madame, and ask her directly?

Yet he knows he is risking much in merely visiting Brno incognito. Helena Čapková knows of his arrival—is expecting him. Nobody else can know.

The Labyrinth of the World and the Paradise of the Heart.

He opens the cover. For seemingly the hundredth time he rereads Josef's dedication; a dedication, he reminds himself, that Josef had written only minutes after meeting him; hours before Josef had determined the truth.

To Mr. Paul Arepo, Pilgrim and Sower. May you find the truth you seek in the City. Sator arepo tenet opera rota. Josef Čapek

Sator arepo tenet opera rota. The magic square of words repeating endlessly, as the train relentlessly chugs toward Brno. Once again, he touches the key. It's like a key from a fairy tale, perhaps from the George MacDonald tale that dear Olinka had read to him—she, his daughter, reading to him in perfect English that enchanting story, and asking him about the Russian fairy tales he had told her as a child. He misses

Olinka deeply. He wishes she were here to tell him in her sensible way—the beautiful echo of her mother's patient voice—what must be done. He imagines her thinking quietly for a time, and running her index finger down her long back bangs, drawing them away from her eyes. And she would tell him, surely, *don't get off the train. Don't go to Brno. Come home. Come back to me and William and Mother.*

The night before, in dream after dream, she had done just this.

He sits back, nudging the hat farther up his head.

He meets the eyes of the old woman from Hradec Kralove—Mrs. Tandova is her name; at her side, asleep, is Mr. Tand, a retired milliner. For the first hour of the trip, as they chugged through the Bohemian countryside, she had told him about her grandchild who was also a milliner, while her husband, sometimes speaking over her, had waxed fondly about his days in the patriotic Sokol movement. He had soon fallen asleep, and she had become rapt with her needlework. Now, above a scaffold layer of brilliant red and yellow, she smiles. "Mr. Arepo, you didn't mention if you were born in Brno."

He looks away from her; looks away so that he can lie to her but then he does not lie. "And I'm getting some lovely weather for my return." He gestures to lowering clouds over dark green hills; clouds with dark underbellies birthing a haze of rain.

"How long, Mr. Arepo?"

Rain strikes against the window, past sooty embers that have stuck and frozen to the glass. Focusing past it as the track begins a long curve and the smoke now whips like a conjurer's sleeve past the window, he suddenly recognizes the land. North of Brno. North of home. The Adamov forests, where he and Bakala and the Krenek brothers like to go hunting and smoking. "Fourteen years."

The Adamov forest, now silver-gray shining in the rainfall.

She begins to hum under her breath, then to sing, and Paul stares out; he is now the conjurer, willing the familiar contours of the land to appear, and only as she nears the end of the melody does he recognize it, and realize that she is singing it for him:

Where is my homeland?

"*Bohunice! NÁDRAŽÍ!*"
"*ŠTÝŘICE!*"
"*Trinita! Naschela!*"

As they stop in Brno's outlying suburbs Paul sits away from the window, studying the crowds on the platform, worrying that a familiar face will appear. But none does, of course. The crowds go about their business as on any other day, and look at him as significantly as they would have looked on the Pavel who lives in this year of 1928, in the town whose name the conductor now shouts down the length of the train car. "*Hlavni nadrazi! Next stop, Old Brno! City station!*"

Even having encountered the Maestro, Karel and Josef, nothing is as emotional as sighting the smoky sprawl of Old Brno, or Špilberk's red-roofed casements, or the neo-Gothic spires rising on Petrin Hill; spires that he has known since a boy in the Krenova suburbs; spires that were a familiar sight viewed from the apartment window on Biskupska Street, and that beckoned to him as the train pulled out of the station on that day in 1936 when he, Sona and Olinka departed for Prague.

And now, he asks himself, *at this very moment, is Pavel seeing the spires? Perhaps he's in the shoe shop? Or out with Hugo? Or mother?*

The train slows, blowing its whistle. Smoke no longer whips past the window but billows alongside, with the rain-swept streets beyond. The green stanchions of the station overtake the train; stanchions that in 1936 would be painted white.

Does Sonicko hear the train whistle? Now, at this very moment?

The train comes to a halt under awnings that silence the rainfall. He hears Olinka's voice in his ear, warning him not to leave the train. He stands up. He pulls on his overcoat, careful with its burden. He winds the scarf around his neck, lifts the umbrella and the satchel. He will stay only long enough to search the archives. He promises Olinka: *I will take the 6:30 train back to Prague.*

"I hope your office wasn't damaged, Mr. Arepo."

"Thank you, Mrs. Tandova. I'm sure it's fine." Somehow, she had taken him for an architect. "Good day."

She smiles. "Good day, Mr. Arepo." Her voice rouses her husband, who says goodbye too.

Rain pounds the cobblestone, beating the gutter water into silver waves. Umbrellas crowd the sidewalk. The trams shine along the streets, their windows fogged up, their passengers a vague yellow-tinged crowd.

Paul trudges north on Masarykova Street. His ankle is only slightly painful. He holds the umbrella low, wears his hat low over his head, his collar turned up. For the moment, his Bata shoes prove watertight. The brisk walk is a balm after the hours of sitting on the train; and he now heads straight toward his target, the *Lidové noviny* office at Ceska 6. Water drips from the cantilevers, a deliberate counterpoint to the thundering rain. Trudging passersby are mere legs and shoes and trenchcoats. Their voices, their Moravian accents, their poignantly banal conversations, draw his attention; three men sloshing through the puddles, obviously drunk, snipe about *stale schnitzel*. Two women laugh brightly, and run to the tram before it can pull away. An old man confides to his daughter about laundry left outside. Paul wants to lift the umbrella as each of these groups pass by, but remains fixed on the cobblestones. He allows only the few meters in front of him and to either side. The air, though, alternately chilly and laundry-warm, offers an evocative *mélange* of wet iron, of spilt beer and hot cabbage, of creosote, of French perfume. To his left the Church of Mary Magdalene chimes the matins, answered to the north by the Church of St. James, entirely familiar. Dangerously familiar. *I belong here. This is home*. He feels exposed, even in the downpour, even under the scarf and hat and overcoat; exposed like a bare iron rod to the clouds.

He expects to look up and find friends from the Conservatory, like Bakala or Chlubna, or customers from the shoeshop.

Briefly, to the left—the direction of the Cabbage Market—a tuba blurts a comical *oompah-oompah*, answered by a crash of cymbals soon lost in the hiss and rush of the rain. Paul lowers his head. Trudging on, he feels the spires of St. Peter and Paul at his left shoulder; he wonders if Hugo's at home rather than in Prague, or if he—Pavel—is in the shop with Papa and Mother . . .

A sickly yellow glow shimmers past him, winking on his shoes. A reflected shop sign. Gone, now. And in its wake he pictures the Cabbage Market full of scaffolds, and the Parnus fountain draped in tarpaulin and swastikas. His breath is hot against his face, muffled by the scarf; he tastes the acrid flavor of the wool, the threads tickling his tongue as he draws a deep breath—tasting of iron, of beer, of cabbage. Ahead, the street opens up into Svoboda Square. He feels it rather than sees it; feels it before he hears the walls coming to an end on either side, hears the broad expanse of rain-dappled stone. The swastikas live deep in the cobblestones, in the silver splashes of his Bata shoes. And he marvels that he might show a swastika to any of these passersby. He might *hang* a swastika here on the ancient stone spire of Morovy in Svoboda Square—the oldest part of oldest Brno, predating the city, marking where three ancient trading routes had crossed—and some might recognize it as a Slav symbol; or, if a person possessed Josef's knowledge of art and history, as a Sanskrit *svastika*. He might even walk south to the Jewish suburb of Krenova and hold the swastika up to passersby and receive only blank stares.

He dwells on this while he walks. Better than dwelling on Papa and Mother and Hugo alive in the city at this moment, and a warm dry house that awaits him only a quarter hour to the southeast.

Once through the revolving doors, out of breath, craving a cigarette, Paul is loathe to completely fold up his umbrella. More than cover from the rain, it is cover from the crowd, and there is quite a crowd in the *Lidové*'s lobby. He shakes his sleeves and stamps his shoes on the damp rug, leaving on the hat, tugging at the scarf as though he were about to take it off, yet keeping it on.

The lobby is overly hot. The smell of mint, paraffin and printer's ink hangs over the polished marble. On the walls hang framed front pages, as well as portraits of contributors. As Paul meanders toward the desk, trying to keep his hat brim low, he spies Karel's portrait beside Ferdinand Peroutka's.

The receptionist, a woman in her twenties, tucked away behind a small, sliding window, is thankfully unknown to Paul. "Good afternoon, sir."

"Good afternoon, I'm here to see Miss Helena Čapková, please."

She attends to her headset and wires. "Last name, please?"

"Arepo."

"Thank you." She plugs into the board, tilting the horn closer to her lips while managing also to gesture to a row of empty chairs. He walks toward them but does not want to sit on display to those coming in the revolving doors and to those heading up spiral stairs clutching sheaves of newsprint. Nor does he plan to hang his overcoat on the coat rack. Nor meet the eyes of those who are passing by. He hears Olinka's voice again, warning him not to step off the train. He studies more photographs—these of Brno in the 1800s, its veneer of later Hapsburgian largesse stripped away, betraying the Gothic and Baroque. Carts and horses. Cattle in the Cattle Market.

He pats his pocket for the cigarette pack, begins to take it out.

"*You must be the mysterious Mr. Arepo?*" asks a sly voice, behind him.

Paul turns, and—briefly—doffs his hat. "Good afternoon, Miss Čapková."

Her hair in a fashionable bun, she's wearing a dress-suit in stylish brown and gray stripes. She's younger, of course, than the last time he saw her—a brief hello in Prague that last day before the trip to America. And slightly younger than the *most memorable* time he saw her, in the early morning hours after the first performance of *R. U. R*, in 1931.

Youth gives her a greater resemblance to Karel, especially about the eyes and nose.

"So, Mr. Arepo, you want to penetrate the impenetrable?" Her smile is sharp.

Feeling a slight measure of alarm, he says, "I'm sorry? I don't understand."

"Read the impenetrable writings of our Maestro J⎯⎯, of course." She laughs brightly. "That's what Josef told me was your mission here."

"Yes. If I could, Miss Čapková."

"I would never deny dear *Peca* anything. This way. Down into the depths of Hades."

Her heels click smartly on the parquet floor. She leads him along a narrow corridor, where the bang and clatter of printing presses reminds him instantly of Herr Professor Schoenberg and the swan-wing platen of the printing press. Then she opens a narrow door on a stairway down, and cautions, over her padded shoulder, "We haven't quite cleaned up yet, Mr. Arepo. The quake, you know. The archives were thrown together like trees in a gale, and poor Vitek has been up to his neck sorting them out."

She swiftly descends, past bare light bulbs and walls painted a bright green.

"Peca was very generous in his details about you, Mr. Arepo. Which made me quite suspicious, of course."

"Of course."

She opens another door, this time into a low-ceilinged lair with wire-meshed lamps hanging overhead. The room extends into the far distance, broken at the front by a long counter. Overhead, pneumatic tubes hiss with cargo.

"Mr. Arepo to see the files, Vitek, as I promised. Here's the number."

A bald fat man wearing a green eye-shade sits at the counter, slowly sorting pile upon pile of blue paper. He grunts as Helena approaches. She produces a receipt.

The man gives a slow, sarcastic bow. "Great and Terrible Madame Editor Čapková, if you would perform the duties yourself, I would be forever grateful." And nodding to Paul, "And Great Sir Guest. No smoking, please."

"Look at him, Vitek. He couldn't possibly light a match drenched like that. We'll find him a warm corner of your little hell, eh?"

Vitek shrugs. Helena lifts a door in the middle of the counter and ushers Paul through, slamming it shut behind her.

The aisles of shelving are in various states of anarchy. Some still have their burdens mounded on the floor, while others have been returned to neat stacks and files. Helena, reading the paper as they pass under the wire-meshed lamps, motions them right, then left, then right, and finally stops before a particular shelf and a particular yellow box.

"Here it is," she says brightly.

"Why hasn't the Maestro taken these back?"

"Why?" She laughs, and lugs the box off the shelf. "Mr. Arepo, you can't ask *why* when asking about the Maestro. His quaint, harmless little madness isn't quite as easily charted as that. Perhaps he forgot. Perhaps he thinks we'll get around to publishing it eventually. Here." She passes it into his hands, and only then does he recognize the weathered yellow cardboard bound with thick rubber bands; he had last seen it sitting on Igor Stravinsky's living room table.

"Mr. Arepo? You can hang up your umbrella, at least?"

He does, awkwardly, on the edge of the shelving, then follows her to the promised "warm corner" of the basement archives, where sits a bare desk and chair, and a table lamp. A heating vent blows down from above.

"Now, just sit, and read to your heart's content. And if you find you must take something with you... Josef, in our private language, told me very certainly that you must be allowed to take whatever you like. I'll be leaving word at the desk with our cheerful Charon."

He offers a smile, and only now dares take off his overcoat. "I thank you, Madame."

"You've piqued my brother's sense of the reverent, Mr. Arepo. He's always had a soft spot for religious mystery. I don't think I'd ever heard him more serious."

"Perhaps," Paul offers, with a smile, "it was a bad phone line."
"Perhaps. Enjoy, Mr. Arepo."
She strides away.

"I feel as if my pen wanted to drop out of my hand. Breathless, run off my feet—I wait to see whether some little distant star will fall ringingly into my mind.

"Tame as a dog, fierce as a vulture, dry as a faded leaf, crackling like a breaking wave, sputtering like brushwood consumed by fire. Receptive to every stirring of the mind—and silenced by holy stillness."

—Leoš J—— to Max Brod

17. THE WHIRLWIND

With some semblance of drying out, and with his overcoat draped across the back of the chair, Paul seats himself, and stares at the box. It is certainly the same box he had seen in Brentwood, California, no doubt smuggled out of post-war Czechoslovakia. Plain, roughly the size of a manuscript box at Universal studios. He removes the thick rubber bands.

An unknown hand has written on the label in thick black ink: *Leoš J———, Giskrova 30/10 August 1924/ Notes and draft for feuilleton/not for publication.*

Paul opens the the box.

Atop a stack of papers secured with a withered rubber band is a small card—what in America is called a *calling card* and here is a *vizitka*. On the front is printed the Maestro's name, nothing more. Paul sets it aside, then takes out the bundle, carefully tugging off the rubber band which nonetheless breaks and falls to his lap.

The papers are varied. He feels the manuscript paper at the bottom, fixed with a rusty metal clip. On the very top of the pile is, strangely, a train schedule. Paul wants to set everything aside for the feuilleton but forces himself to contemplate everything in turn. The *vizitka*, with its cursive font, is charming enough. Turning it over he finds, in the Maestro's hand, a simple directive—"Read, please! Look at the evidence!"

The hairs tingle on the back of his hand as he sets the *vizitka* aside.

The schedule is from 1922. Czecho-Slovak Train Timetable. Unfolding it, he finds more of the Maestro's handwriting on the large map that takes up one entire side. In blue ink, a note beside Brno—"trip begun"—and a line going southeast to Bratislava, where a note reads, "Opera 11 November. Zuna conducts. Left 13 November for Prague." From Bratislava, a blue line heads north toward Prague, only to halt, and branch off in several directions, ending in question marks. Paul surveys the branchings, and how they leave behind the train tracks altogether. He examines the rest of the schedule for any annotations, but finds none.

He sets it aside. Next is a program book for the performance of *Káťa Kabanová* in Bratislava. The annotations here are more mysterious, little zigzag lines and symbols, as though mere mental thumb-twirling. Below the program book is a small stack of sheets. Familiar—wonderfully familiar—sheets from the composer's notebook, covered with speech melodies.

Paul hears them in the cavernous archives, against the faint buzzing of the lamp. A washerwoman's voice. Children at the train station. And another, labeled "Prevarication by a forester." They continue on the next page, and might be any random entries from the Maestro's vast collection of *nápěvky mluvy*.

Impatient, Paul sets them aside.

Next, on a large sheet of paper that Paul must unfold, is a hand-drawn map of the Maestro's domeček and garden. The positions of the box trees, the fern, the rhododendron are marked, as is the fence separating the domeček from the Conservatory, and the Maestro's table and chairs. Amid these things are a series of small x's that mean nothing to Paul, except to suggest these were places where Čert, the Maestro's devilish poodle, had been digging. He refolds it and sets it aside.

The next sheet stops him cold. Three staves, hastily drawn. Three separate fragments of melody, labeled for alto flute, trombone and piano. He has never forgotten them; never forgotten the leaping, melismatic melody from the flute, or the strange bending tone from the trombone.

And especially the icy clatter in the piano keys, which he had used, in another Brno, to draw *der Geist der alten Natur* upon him.

Hearing the echo of these in the air, he sets the sheet aside, and comes upon the manuscript pages with their rusty clip.

The Heartbeat of the World

1869—the 1000th year after St. Cyril's death. The celebrations at Russian Velehrad crowning the anniversary, the glorious passing, the lingering chalice. 1869 marked my 15th year, and my pilgrimage, when I and the other choral scholars from the Monastery journeyed to the distant city.

Cyril and Methodius, the sacred ground where these two great brothers had their post—I was not worthy to tread in their footsteps. But I went, a retired bluebird, and sang under Father Křížkovský's baton for the last time. Velehrad swarming with a pilgrimage of 40,000!

That day I bathed in the holy light of a Slavic empire, before skulking back into the shadow of the Austro-Hungarian.

In the garden of my little cottage, Cert runs circles round the rose bush. Usually he runs circles around my hens, shepherding the ladies away from the gate when students pass by to enter the Conservatory. Yet now he is out of sorts—by the sprouting of a little tendril in my rhododendron. A shy green tendril, peeking up near my shoe! What is this? What roused it?

Not long ago, in a land more distant than Velehrad, I brought pages bound with my blood into the depths of the forest. And there they were planted.

Here in my little garden, much to my wife's dismay, I planted pieces of truthful parchment, and look what grows! The tuber. See it peeking up in the shadows. A sentry of wild nature, asking me a question. But I know the answer. I heard it years ago, in the courtyard of the Augustinian Monastery. A great whirlwind tore through Brno. I, a retired bluebird, swirled with clipped wings through Abbot's garden, not realizing the danger to come. But when it came, I captured it too. An impact connection that penetrated to my very soul.

"Impudent youth!"

That long-ago day, Abbot Gregor Mendel shouted at me while Špilberk Hill seethed above us, as though the trees were troughs of ocean waves. The little garden of pea plants and begonias huddled under the black gate. "Impudent youth!" The sky gathering its shadows and holding its breath.

I had wandered the Monastery looking for our Abbot, and found him.

Abbot Mendel was Abbot of the Sky, that day. His scientific researches grew from things planted in the earth, yet now came crashing down from above. "Respect the sky!" he shouted, over the gathering din. "It is about to speak its pronouncement!

A pronouncement rising out of the earth as much as sky. A whirlwind, descending on Brno. Atomization and stratification, searing the air.

Atomization—have I not made myself clear? The scasovani is made up of atomization and stratification, leading to interpenetration. Atomization—those particles both visible and invisible that make up the world. On the simplest level think of the connection of two chords. The impact connection. It can be both minuscule—as if two smooth stones were struck together—or immense. The Whirlwind!

I felt them in my bones. Two notes of the firmament.

A whirlwind slicing the belly of our town. What a sound! I was as little to it as a leaf to a passing thresher. It took no notice!

But sometimes the Earth takes notice. Sometimes it bites!

As Cyril and Methodius wander far from Byzantium, I now wander far from Brno. To Teplice, to Vienna, to Bratislava. I chase my operas into foreign lands, and so I took the opportunity by train to Bratislava to hear Káťa Kabanová. How many years do I have left to hear it? A fiery performance, such as one can only hear in the Eastern lands. Zuna and his scorching baton! Yet the trip home was stymied by snow. Avalanche on the tracks, and so we were rerouted. Where?

Into the aether. To the very limits of the atmosphere, to a village whose name cannot be written. A place where the scasovani, the Heartbeat of the World, is stretched so thin it can be caught and held, and manipulated by the Slavic soul.

And there she died, the first time.

Why?

I caught her voice with my pen. Notes that dripped blood. And then I found her, poor thing, lying in the forest behind the old cantor's house, her breast ruptured with a giant thorn.

There in the village of the green baize hermitage they took her to another, older church deep within the alpine forest. I heard its strange little bell at midnight.

Bending, as the tuber bent under the weight of gravity as it lifted from the soil. I heard the bell again in daylight. I spied them from a safe distance, a procession of townsfolk carrying the bier with her sad remains.

Cert does not like invaders! He runs in circles! He barks loud enough to rouse the ghosts in the Old Seminary.
Away, Cert! I crouch, I peer. A tiny tendril which had not been there before, in the warm evening.

You curl your head above the grass, unfurl taller than the grasses, so I could see you. Roused by a strange piece of paper perhaps. Crazed notation that sailed down from the sky! Or had you been seeking me all this time?

High notes, low notes from the firmament.

The scasovani had revealed itself to me that day. In the whirlwind's voice. In the two notes thrumming in my head. I had pain ever after in my sinuses from its passing. The Abbot Mendel—crazed that I sketched its voice in his clerical book.

But I did not know what I had!

The whirlwind, the damage. 1000 windows broken in the Monastery. These were the impacts on my youthful mind.

Only later, only now, do I say: the scasovani is the Heartbeat of the World. Its purest power lay cupped in those mountain peaks at the edge of the Eastern lands. In this town that was of our world and another. They heard it, the folk of that town. In the cellar of the cantor's house I found hints of an older age. Far older, of both worlds.

Cyril and Methodius spent a winter there. I hear now, the Alderman's voice as he fabricated the story. I hear the truths between the words. Cyril and Methodius built the little church in the forest.

Cyril and Methodius had risen the giant thorn from the ground.

The Slav power—it's everywhere and nowhere. The town is lost in the mists. I cannot find it. North of Teplice? East of Semmering? Did that green baize church, those little colorful shops along the railroad tracks exist at all? Or were they masks that the scasovani held before its face?

Their whirlwind spun me around and out.

Cyril and Methodius, gone these last thousand and sixty five years.

Yet still with us. They shepherd us, as Cert shepherds the hens in my garden. They gave the gift of written language to the Slavs. They wrote it down and planted it in the hearts of the people. And the gift continues to grow up form the earth, and sail down from the sky.

Cert is made uneasy by this, as are the hens. Ever since the tendril peeked into my garden Cert pays more attention to the ladies, and less to the underbrush. He needs no written language to express his disgust.

Go! Away! Play!

Late at night I wake to the lonely tolling of a strange bell, far beyond Brno.

Paul turns back to the beginning and reads it again, then for many minutes sits lingering over a single marginalia in the Maestro's hand.

Climbing the last of the steps into the lobby, he tugs his hat low on his head and readies the umbrella. The satchel is under his arm. The overcoat, now only partly damp, is tight around his elbows and shoulders. He lights a cigarette, draws deeply on it, sets off for revolving doors—a thief making a run for it—when Helena Čapková appears close by.

"Mr. Arepo! Find what you want?" At her elbow stands a young man—drenched—lugging a huge plastic-wrapped camera on a tripod.

Paul stops. He squints against the smoke. "Yes, Madame." He eyes the spinning doors, and the silvery light that stutters through. "I found exactly what I wanted. And I'm borrowing it for a while."

She dismisses the photographer with the same motion she might a slow child. "To the dark room. Fifteen minutes!" she says after him. Then, to Paul, "Of course, of course. Keep it as long as you like."

"Thank you."

Walking Paul to the door she says, "Quite a spectacle. He's just back from shooting the circus."

"Circus?" He remembers the distant tuba on his walk over.

"Aftershocks, Mr. Arepo." She smiles. "In the form of the *avant-garde Poeticists*." Delighted at Paul's bafflement, she laughs—it's a recognizable variation on Josef's laugh, both gentle and ironic. "They're staging a circus in the ruins. Surely you've heard of 9forces? Comrade Tiege and our jolly Social Democrats? They're serenading the fissures! Marvelous story for tomorrow's front page, if we can get the pictures developed in time."

"Art runs across the stage on its hands dressed like a circus clown."

—Viteslav Nezval

18. ZONE

Umbrella tipped low, his hat brim tugged low on his head, Paul hikes resolutely southward on Masarykova Street, headed for the train station. The rain has eased off. Sun shines through breaks in the clouds, casting black shadows on silvery cobblestone.

He's listening for the circus but hearing the strange bending of the Maestro's bell. *Bending, as the tuber bent under the weight of gravity as it lifted from the soil.* The same strange bending Paul had heard on trombone, alto flute and piano: the music that had drawn the *geist der alten natur* to the maestro's sundered garden. bending He's hearing Cert barking at the intruder.

Smoking, staring down, he strives to recall what the Maestro had said that afternoon.

Indulge me, Pavel, in a bizarre request. Take these young musicians up to the atelier and serenade me with some melodies. Particles from my new opera—for inspiration.

Yet we were luring it. For the hour—or hours—that we played in the atelier.

And it worked.

Ceska Street widens onto Svoboda Square, which is crowding up with folk venturing into the sunshine. Paul keeps to the shaded edge, his thoughts roaming ahead of him, eager for faster motion than his stride—for the train. To be gone from Brno. But to where?

The town is lost in the mists. I cannot find it. North of Teplice? East of Semmering?

Paul's shoes slap the cobblestones. He hunches his shoulders and grips the satchel tighter. He is eager to look through the papers again, the marginalia especially. In the edges of the train schedule, and also in the margins of the feuilleton manuscript.

Indulge me, Pavel, in a bizarre request.

What had the Maestro told Karel? In the Slavia, after the premiere of *Makropulos Thing*? How time had been *twisted back* for him. He had shown Karel the tuber in a plastic sleeve. *"It is a far traveler, from somewhere east of Bratislava, grown from the luminous depths. A village I struggle to find again."*

And afterward, the Maestro had begun work on the *Baseform Scasovani Generator*.

The pavement is growing more crowded. People brush past, close enough so that he must lift the umbrella higher, exposing himself dangerously. He tugs his hat brim lower. He strives to give the look of someone in a hurry, someone lost in thought, which he is. He hears cymbals clashing. A tuba, blurting. And focuses on the cobblestones. The single marginalia had taken a moment to decipher. A most unexpected word, crossed-out, and one very familiar.

~~Hilsner~~: *T.G.M.!*

Paul has reached Orli Street. To avoid an oncoming lady with a pram he steps leftward. Then seeing the edge of the Cabbage Market ahead,—a sparse crowd, a series of wooden fences—recalling the earthquake, and the talk of damage, and the sight of dire scaffolds that had once, and would perhaps again, fill the square—he slows, and heads toward it.

Tuba, trumpet, drums, cymbals—four musicians play demented spa town melodies against a disorderly din of picks and hammers. The musicians, huddled at the northern edge of the square, are dressed in velvet jackets and oversized shoes, their faces painted. The tuba man twirls in place.

Paul, in a simultaneous instant, registers both the youth of the Cabbage Market and its damage. Though empty of the stalls that had been ever present even into the winter months, the expanse of white stone and the baroque splendor of the Parnas fountain stand equal to his youthful memories of them; all except the buckled stone in the center, currently fenced off by wooden barricades. A dour policeman stands nearby holding a club, eyeing the crowd who seem to have been drawn out only recently by the lapse in the weather.

Amidst the throng the 9forces are made vivid by their uniforms—comical black trenchcoats and bowler hats. A dozen of them roam the crowd, acrobats and mimes tossing red balls into the air. Atop the fountain, one is victoriously seated. Long-legged, with a shock of yellow hair under his bowler, this man proclaims:

"A charlatan from out of the dusk

"Praises tricks to be performed!"

He lifts a camera from his lap, pausing to snap a picture down at the crowd—a puff of magnesium—while the band plays its drunken melody, culminating in brash clashes of the cymbals. Then continues.

"From platform height the harlequin

"Wanly salutes the audience!"

It's Karel Tiege, architect and photographer, leader of 9forces, and the man who sent the strange little gift to the Friday Circle. But he's more intrigued with what is behind the barricade. The zigzagging fissure on the west side of the square. The results of the earthquake which had begun on Špilberk on the day of Paul's arrival. Yet he's careful in his inspection. Surreptitiously, he glimpses it from under his hat brim, raising and dipping the umbrella, catching sight of the torn earth beyond pick axes and hammers, beyond the mounds of gleaming stone.

"Magicians from Moravia
"Some fairies and some sorcerers!"

One of the workers stands in the fissure. All that can be seen of him is his head, and from time to time a chunk of muddy rock being thrown out. Others are wheeling off wheelbarrows, while outside, two of the Poeticists skulk in their oversized black garments, and near the barricade they lob a dozen red balls that bounce and ricochet. The policeman laconically chases the pair off. Some in the crowd applaud.

Indulge me, Pavel, in a bizarre request.

A woman, passing by with a friend laughs gaily. "A ray of sunshine!" The laughter flaring strangely, due to the acoustics of the square and the tilt of his umbrella and a sudden rush of breeze. To Paul's right, and moving southward, a man striving to be heard over the music: "Tomorrow, they say. František promises tomorrow!" From the opposite direction: "Tiege! The fellow Tiege." Two men trudging past in time to the clashing of the cymbals.

"The one there, on the fountain!"

And his cohort, speaking in mock tones, "Photographs of his. Strange stuff! Ghosts in the negative."

"Ghosts?"

"Yes. Took pictures up at Špilberk yesterday, and they say a hundred poor souls appear in what were empty casements."

A soft, warm voice, close to Paul's left elbow says, *"Hello."*

"He brandishes with outstretched arms
"The star he unhooked from the night!"

Paul does not turn. He stares resolutely ahead.

"Good afternoon," says the voice, just past his umbrella. Her tone is good-humored and curious. Strands of her red hair stir in the breeze.

He should walk away, yet cannot move. His heart begins pounding.

"Hello?"

"And all the while a hanged man rings
"A cymbal with his hanging feet!"

Then her hand, her slender fingers, are gently grasping the edge of his umbrella, and lifting it slightly. He has to look. She is peering up from under, with a cautious smile. "Forgive me, sir," she says. She wears a yellow slicker, as well as a blue bonnet on her head, from which her long red hair escapes. Beneath the slicker is the pale blue of her coat, and the darker blue of her long skirt. Even now, she clutches her flute case. "But is your last name Haas?"

He does not want to speak. "Quite a sight," he murmurs, finding his mouth dry. He draws a deep breath and nods toward the barricades and the workmen—who are tossing red balls out into the square—hoping to redirect her attention. His hand tightens on the umbrella's handle, a lick of static electricity in his gloves, accompanied by hissing cymbals from the band.

"Do you know Pavel Haas?"

A dozen more red balls are lofted high over the Cabbage Market. Children run toward them.

He glances south, towards the alley through the Capuchin monastery, and east toward Kvetinarska Street, the avenues of escape. Then he begins to walk away. Her shoes click on the pavement. She moves up alongside, young, with a shy, but forceful, smile. She squints. "The resemblance is most strong."

He stops. He looks at her directly then. Narrow shouldered and, even with the bonnet, shorter than he remembers her. And her face. At first, he sees it through accumulated memories of her, through the portraits in *Kameradschaftsbund* leaflets and Sylvan Uprising newsreel footage, through later Soviet ikons as well as Jean Simmons' portrayal; then all of this falls away.

She, too, is studying him. Her brave blue eyes narrow, then widen. He shakes his head but cannot muster an argument to the simple wonderment in her face.

"Say something." Her hand, which has not yet drawn blood, reaches for his sleeve. "Your voice, it's . . . Pavel's."

A red ball goes bouncing past him, chased by a child and the child's mother. The crowd, drawn by the band and by Tiege, who is now silently taking pictures from his perch atop the fountain, is growing larger. Once again, Paul starts to hike toward Kvetinarska Street, aware that she's staying at his side. "Where do you know this Pavel from?" His feigned innocence falls flat.

"Pavel graduated the year I started." She smiles. She squints up at him, then lifts the flute case. "I stopped in to see him at the shoe shop on Tuesday . . ."

She tugs his arm then. The umbrella, which he'd been holding at an angle, drops to the cobblestones and he stands revealed. "When I left my apartment this morning, I told myself that something extraordinary would happen before the sun set."

Beneath the bonnet, her hair whips in the breeze, the same breeze that rocks the wooden barricades and sends the red balls in every direction across the square.

"Why do you suppose that was?"

She is quiet for a long moment. Then when she speaks, her voice is soft. "I often think that way. And I'm usually wrong." He hears her smile. "Yes. Not today."

He looks directly at her.

"Pavel?"

She stands before him, not an actress, not a *Kameradschaftsbund* idealization nor an ikon nor the *lovely murderous maiden* who had died fighting the Nazis in Strektot. It's Magda. His friend from the Conservatory who was always running through the halls late for class. Soon to be Sona's good friend, a girl who knew her future would be with her instrument, and who had unrealistically set her sights on the first chair in the Vienna Philharmonic. The Magda who, one day, would be thrilled to be in the pit band at the theater on the Ramparts for a production of *R.U.R.*

She says, "Your voice, it's *his*." His hand is tapping nervously on the satchel. "Say something else."

"Okay." He eyes the crowd. "Let's get a cup of tea."

"At the Slavia?"

No. Nowhere she would normally go. Where they might meet familiar faces. He gestures upward with the umbrella.

"On Špilberk. Is the outdoor café . . . still there?"

She nods, smiling. "It's going to be sunny, I think."

The *Pohadka* café sits halfway up the hillside, a small house in the style of the 19th century National Revival with a high and intricate gable, painted furniture and floral patterns on the doorposts. Today, it is vacant of patrons. Dripping birch and elm trees sparkle in the sunshine.

He chooses a table under a green awning, in the darkest corner; the oaken floor underfoot is damp. The table affords a view of sunlit Brno spread out beyond the trees. Out of breath, Paul sets his satchel on the table, his umbrella beside the chair. She sets her flute case beside his satchel.

He lights a cigarette.

The proprietor, a heavy-set woman unknown to Paul, brings Magdalena a *limonade* and Paul a tea, then retreats indoors.

As Magdalena sips from her straw, sunlight dapples her hair, free from the bonnet. It strikes too the smattering of freckles across the bridge of her nose, freckles which would begin to fade in a year or two. Again, he's struck with the urge to leave her here, to walk to the train station and return . . . where?

To Prague?

To Burbank?

Sipping the tea, he recalls the Maestro's fueilleton, and especially the strange marginalia. The questions lure him further into the country, in this year of 1928. The lure of finding the secret to the Geist der Alten Natur. Yet Magda . . . *did the stave flower draw her to me, as it drew the tree in the Maestro's garden?*

"Don't worry, Pavel." She sets down her *limonade*. "I won't tell anyone."

He takes off his hat, runs his fingers through his hair. "I'm called Paul."

This draws from her a tentative smile, radiant nonetheless. And her eyes once more roam his face. "Why are you visiting, Paul? And from . . . where?"

Magdalena, green-shouldered, clutching her flute with vermilion fingers. "My fingers are stronger than before, Pavel. I can play. Let me play."

He ignores her second question. "I came to Brno for some papers." He lifts the satchel, hoping to draw her scrutiny away from his face. He sips some tea. "I hoped not to meet anyone I knew."

"It's amazing, isn't it." With her elbows on the table, she leans toward him, and is silent for a moment that seems endless. Then says softly: "Where are you going?"

"I'm not entirely sure." He adds, "I may be taking a railway trip. Northeast, perhaps."

"And you're looking for . . . for something extraordinary. Aren't you, Paul?"

He lifts his coffee cup but sets it down when his hand trembles. "Most extraordinary."

Or have I found it?

Below, the bells begin to ring in St. Thomas and St Michael and St. James. In Brno Cathedral. Two o'clock. Paul nearly tugs back his cuff to check his Timex. The bells fade into the fainter sound of a circus in the Cabbage Market. She's staring down at her folded hands. The pale pink tips of her fingers become white, as she clasps. "Don't you think it's extraordinary that I found you?"

He murmurs, "I shouldn't have lingered in the market. I was heading directly to the station."

"I want to help you, Paul."

He shakes his head. Drums his fingers on the table, then withdraws them into a fist.

She continues, brightly, "But I know a lot about trains. I'm always riding to Ostrov and Vienna." She sits back, folding her arms. "And I bet, where you're from, you've forgotten some of the things about this country. How long has it been since . . . since you were here, Paul?"

"Magdalena, you have a job here *and* school."

She smiles triumphantly. "But it's the weekend! Let me come with you for the weekend. I won't miss any work or school."

When he says nothing, she sips her *limonade* and takes to looking out at Brno again, or maybe not Brno. She's staring at the sunstruck raindrops falling from the birch trees.

Pavel, I am made of green and growing things. They're being born inside me.

If she was drawn to me by chance, then should I turn her away? If by the decahexachord and the *Geist*, then shouldn't I honor its wishes?

"After the weekend, Magdalena, you return here."

She nods. "But we'll find it, Pavel. Whatever you're looking for. I know because I've dreamed it."

*"The Czechoslovak railroads are the
arteries of our Republic's beating heart."*

—Pamphlet, Prague, 1924

19. CROSS ROADS

He dreams of Burbank.

He staggers along sun-drenched Pasadena Avenue in winter coat, snap-brim hat and scarf. Gleaming Packards amble down the hot asphalt; in every curve and angle they're emblems of futurity. Paul gasps past the scarf, struggling to breathe the hot, oily air. But the scarf, scratching his neck and chin, is also inside his mouth. He tastes the wool on his tongue. He tries to spit it out, fumbles with his fingers to draw it out, but the scarf is wedged in deep. He chokes. The end of the scarf flutters in the hot breeze. He manages to tear some free—not wool but parchment, fluttering from his fingers, carried off behind him. He spits and tears, and more comes out, the course and brown paper covered with black ink. In his shaking fingers: black ink forming characters that have run with his saliva.

He gazes at the front windows of a Woolworth's: his reflection battling the scarf, bent double in desperation, trying to breathe. Bits of paper float away.

"Fella!" A policeman stands at his side, tapping a Billy club to the top of his German boot. "What's your name, fella?"

Paul spits and struggles with the scarf. "Puh..." he manages, pulling it free.

"What's that, fella?"

He tugs the scarf from his neck—the winding parchment like a burial shroud, covered with Hebrew letters. "Paul..."

"Paul what?"

"Paul..." He struggles to say it aloud yet cannot. It is lost on the paper, the torn saliva-wet paper being carried along the sidewalk in the breeze. "Paul..." he struggles. "Paul..."

Paul H——.

The flute, in hesitant, feather-light tones, plays the outline of a leaping, swirling melody against the clattering of the train compartment. Paul awakens on the jostling bench.

Seeing him awake, she stops.

He blinks at the sight beyond the window. The long low hills tinged pink and russet by sunset, unreeling; is startled new by Magdalena with the flute at her shoulder, her lips at the embouchure. She sits across from him in her rumpled blue coat, the contents of the *Lidové* box spread across her lap.

But where did she learn the melody? He's about to ask her as the dream fades, torn away like the shards of smoke beyond the window.

He clears his throat, wipes his mouth. "How long?"

After a pause she lowers the flute. "An hour, at least." On either side, her bench is cluttered with vintage train schedules and maps drawn from her bag; a bag stuffed with umbrella, yellow slicker and more maps—so many that they have erupted volcanically from the bag onto the bench. Now, she sifts among them for the flute case, and sets the flute gently atop it.

Returning to the *Lidové* box, and running her narrow fingers across the papers, she says, "Do you remember that tune, Pavel?"

"Of course." He coughs again and unaware that he's doing so reaches for the postal tube in his overcoat pocket, but the overcoat is folded beneath his hat on the bench beside him. "I was surprised to hear it again."

Her eyes grow serious as she studies the paper. Not Jean Simmons's violet eyes, but nonetheless startling.

He's dizzied by fragments of the dream that remain, and more so by what's happened, which moves now with the swiftness of a dream. Tiege in the square, quoting lines from Apollinaire, Magdalena's appearance at his elbow and her sudden, unstinting confidence that she must go with Paul. He blinks away an image of her in the Monastery's garden. "Oh, yes."

The carriage is mostly empty; at the far end a Babushka who had climbed aboard in Pisen, with a hen in her lap. It is no longer so noisy, or at least not heard over the rattle of the tracks. He draws a deep breath, scratches his chin, then yawns again, enjoying the clatter and momentum of the train, dizzied by the smoke thrashing past in brilliant orange.

Magda rootles in her bag. Its embroidery is charmingly modern—of an airliner soaring over Prague. She retrieves one of the schnitzels they had bought from a vendor at the station. "Hungry?"

"Later." He adds, "Thank you, Magda."

She unwraps the paper and, scrutinizing him for a long moment, takes a bite then returns to reading. She turns page after page and becomes involved in it to the extent that she forgets—and then remembers—to close her mouth as she chews.

Watching her, Paul feels a tinge of regret. Regret at having taken her from her young life and into what must be a foolhardy venture. Yet he's also fascinated—bewildered by the turn of things—to watch her examining a mystery from a new angle.

Even as she sits in Mendel's garden, green hands clasped on her lap. "They're down there, now. The green and growing things."

Turning a page, she murmurs, "He always frightened me."

"The Maestro?"

She nods. And a moment later, "Do you believe what he wrote here?"

"Quite poetic, isn't it."

Her head tilts; she gazes out the window. "I like the bit about Cert," she says. "Always liked Cert. I'd bring him biscuits, and feed him when the Maestro wasn't looking." Once again, she meets Paul's gaze. "Do you suppose he really did find the little tendril in his garden?"

Paul attempts a shrug.

She smiles. "And he asks . . . " She searches the page. "He asks, *Have I not made myself clear?*" Laughter, now. Bright, easy. And she says directly down to the feuilleton, "No, Maestro, you have not!" She sets the remnants of the schnitzel back into the bag, wiping her hand on her skirt. "Why didn't you go see him and *ask* him what he meant?"

Paul ponders. Should he mention Hukvaldy, the hospital? "I didn't want to involve him, Magda."

"Or me."

He nods. "Or you."

"And . . . and you came back here, because of this?" She lifts the page.

He begins to answer, then decides to study the sunset.

"Oh. Okay. I won't ask anymore. Not at the moment." She spends more time with the fueilleton. Then, "But what does he mean here? He wrote 'Hilsner' and crossed it out, then 'T.G.M.'"

Surprised that she would alight onto that single marginalia, Paul says, "Have you heard the name before?"

Hilsner. She says it silently, then shakes her head. "He wrote it right beside the most ominous part, didn't he. *And then I found her, poor thing, lying in the forest behind the old cantor's house, her breast ruptured with a giant thorn.*"

"Leopold Hilsner."

Her eyes narrow. "I . . . may have heard it."

Paul hesitates to tell the story. Through the window, pine trees whisk past, hoarding shadows. "Hugo used to tell it when we were boys. To frighten me." He adds, "It's the ultimate horror story for a Czech-Jewish kid."

She sets the *Lidové* box atop her maps, and folds her hands on her lap. Waiting.

"It . . . it happened the year I was born, or roundabout. In Veznicka. A young woman was found in the forest." He pauses. "Hugo could tell it so vividly, Magda. I'm not Hugo."

"Go on!"

"She was found in the forest. Murdered. Her throat was cut." He shuts his eyes, remembers Hugo whispering the story to him, in the dark, bed to bed, in their childhood home. "Her throat had been cut ear to ear, and her garments torn. Nearby... nearby was a pool of blood and some blood-stained stones. The men who discovered her body were convinced it was ritual murder. Hilsner had been nowhere near the scene, but they blamed him. He was slow of thinking, and itinerant, and most important, he was a Jew."

"*Blood libel,*" she says.

He nods. "In Hugo's version, he would tell of other murders that had happened near Brno, and how the blame was placed on young Jewish men from our street. Just a tale, to keep me awake at night. But the truth was just as disturbing. And Veznicka wasn't so far away. Hilsner, and other Jews—many others back through the centuries—were singled out for similar crimes, and hanged. Or worse. The legend grew that Jews murdered Gentiles for their blood."

Magdalena's fingers worry on her lap. "But Pajo, the woman, the one the Maestro found dead in the forest—she was *reborn*, wasn't she." She says it flatly, matter-of-factly. Paul remembers the fox's sly smile in Josef's *Bystrouska* poster; Josef suggesting that he, Paul, had been drawn along by the Maestro's dream.

He glances out the window but the pine is dark and all he sees is his own worried reflection. "I think the Maestro realized there was no connection the minute he wrote it down. So he scratched it out."

"But why write *T.G.M.*?"

Paul smiles at another bit of the story falling into place. Hugo hadn't included this particular detail back then. Why destroy the ominous mood? "Hilsner was tried several times, and finally found innocent. Tomáš Garrigue Masaryk represented him." The scent of Masaryk's pipe smoke returns to him; the calming presence of that great old man in the garden. He smiles. "He was a young lawyer, then. When nobody would take up the case Tomáš Garrigue Masaryk did. And won the trial on appeal."

We live every instant in Eternity. We shape it, from one moment to the next.

When he looks up, Magdalena is looking perplexed. "But then... who did it? Who murdered the girl?"

"Hugo liked to say—and remember, this was Hugo, the dramatist, twelve years old with a lantern under his face—he liked to say that it was a spirit in the woods. A creature far older than Jews or Gentiles. One that *must feed*."

This brings a smile, however conflicted.

Maps are spread beneath the ceiling lamp. The dark outside the windows has shrunk the space around them and heightened the faded colors on these schedules and maps from a decade or more earlier. A 1924 Prague to Bratislava schedule is unfolded between them, and Magdalena traces the stippled line across the length of Moravia. "Was it east to Kromeriz and Zlin and onward?"

"North of Teplice," he reminds her. "East of Semmering."

She holds up an admonitory finger. "Or so he thought." Then points to the map. "But the line comes back this way, doesn't it."

Paul smiles at her enthusiasm.

"The mountains he speaks of must be the sub-Carpathians, of course." Her careful, cautious eyes; Paul glances over at her reflected profile. Somewhere beyond the glass, in the far distance, fires shimmer atop the rolling hills and are gone. "Past Zlin. Past Rinz." Her brow furrows. "No. That doesn't make much sense." She turns to her bag; the map begins to droop between them. "But... but there are tracks that were *discontinued*, I think." She rootles among the schedules. "This is from 1917. I got it on my tenth birthday." She smiles, and while he struggles to keep the map level between him, she adds, "Aren't you glad you brought me along?"

"Yes, Magda."

She unfolds the schedule atop the map. "This is from 1917 and I think we'll find . . . that tracks are discontinued, and that towns changed their names after the war. Not just from German to Czech, Pajo." She falls silent, reading the columns. "Here, at Rinz. It's called *Epishev*. See." She taps. "Epishev, and there's another line heading east into the sub-Carpathians." Triumphant, she lets map and schedule sag onto the floor between them and sits back amidst her bench's clutter. "But we'll have to change trains at Zlin. We should arrive in about two hours, I think. Our luck will hold out in the northeast. Only . . . "

"Only what, Magda."

"Only it might be wrong. Those tracks aren't shown in any other map."

As they near Zlin, the train stops more frequently, picking up passengers no doubt headed into Bratislava. The languages are predominantly Slovakian and Hungarian, and Paul finds himself listening to Magyar vocal inflections, and strange speech melodies, set against Slovakian words that are close enough to Czech to understand. Magdalena remains poring over the feuilleton. "Do you know of any 'green baize hermitages' in Moravia?"

"I might. If not baize, then certainly the color that it evokes. St. Nicholas in Prague."

She tucks strands of red hair behind her ear. "*To the very limits of the atmosphere, to a village whose name cannot be written,*" she reads. "*In this town that was of our world and another.*" Her hands fall to her lap.

"Oh, Maestro, you are so frustrating!"

Surreptitiously, Paul tugs up the cuff of his jacket; the Timex's luminous dial reads 9:35. They are due in Zlin by 10:30 according to most of the recent schedules. As he drops it, he notes Magdalena glancing up, looking at him and his wrist unabashedly. Perhaps she would have said something had not the inspector appeared in the car, a tall gray-haired man in a blue and gold suit; he smiles amiably at the passengers, pauses to check tickets a few benches down. As he nears Paul and Magdalena, she lifts her hand. "Mr. Inspector?"

He pauses. "Yes, young miss." He grips the back of her chair and leans courteously over. He wears a briskly trimmed moustache. A gold chain, from the pocket watch hidden in his vest, swings with the motion of the train.

She glances at Paul. "We're looking for a village. Maybe you can help us."

"If I can, young miss."

"Good! We have some facts about it, but not a name."

"Very well." He, too, glances at Paul, with some amusement. "What are the facts?"

"Well, we got the facts from a friend who's rather old and uncertain. But it's definitely a village high in the mountains, perhaps at a summit. The tracks stop right up next to a line of colorful shops, and in the distance there's a cathedral with a *green baize dome*." She pauses, expectantly.

"It could not be a cathedral, of course, like our Brno cathedral. Such a thing could never be lost. It must be a monastery or a hermitage or *poustinia*." Paul adds for the benefit of the inspector.

"Green, eh?" The inspector strokes his moustache with his free hand, gazing past her through the window. "It might be Orli, perhaps. They have the lovely cathedral—what's its name? But that's not in the mountains."

"No, it's not Orli." She adds, "We're thinking its in the sub-Carpathians. And a friend of ours was diverted there, while returning on the train from Bratislava to Prague. This was five years ago, and so we think it must have been the Green Bratislava to Prague express." She offers up the old train schedule.

"Hmmm." The inspector takes it with some amusement.

"North of Teplice. East of Semmering."

"East of Semmering? That's quite a large area, young miss."

"Exactly! Now," her eyes beam, and she straightens on her chair, "isn't it likely that our friend was taken on tracks that aren't being used any more? Tracks that might be used if there were an avalanche—which was the case for our friend?"

Once again, the inspector strokes his moustache. "If tracks weren't being used any more, they would be in disrepair, most certainly. I don't see how a train could be easily transferred to them in the case of an avalanche." Before she can speak again, he says, "I've been working this route to Bratislava for the past seven years, young miss. I haven't heard of such a thing."

She mutters, "But how could a railroad line, and a village, just disappear?

He thinks for a moment. "There have been tracks that were discontinued after the war. Due to irreparable damage, as I understand it, in the hinterlands, or lines that were not of great need anymore in our new Republic."

Magdalena grins. "Do you know of any? Any leading into the sub-Carpathians?"

"We're nearing Zlin. The next stop after that is Honak, near the border. If anywhere, it might be there." He hands her the schedule. "The stationmaster there is a pleasant fellow, very knowledgeable. We can ask him." He tucks his hand into his pocket and draws out the gold pocket watch on its chain. He unclasps the cover, squinting down. "We're due there in forty minutes, young miss. I'll come by and give you warning."

"Thank you, Mr. Inspector."

"Most obliged. Young miss, and sir." He nods, and continues on his duties, leaving Magdalena with a radiant smile. She nudges her bag and train schedules away from the window and moves close; her breath mists the glass. "We'll go there, Paul. That'll be the place." And wiping the glass she whispers, "Look, the mountains."

But in the lighted cabin he discerned only her profile, unnerved by something utterly familiar: her unerring and almost unearthly conviction.

"You can smell the dust, Miss Marty. It is the dust of history . . . "

—The Makropulos Thing
by Karel Čapek

20. THE FIERY ANGEL

Magda smiles. "How's your foot, Pajo?" Steam swirls around them, hazing the sickly yellow glow of gas lanterns along the platform. The train becomes indistinct on either side; a backdrop worthy of one of Hugo's sleazy films.

Pulling the pack of Chesterfields from his pocket, he puts his weight on his right foot. "Good." It had pained him only slightly descending the short flight of stairs.

"But you're still limping."

He lights a cigarette. "Only from sitting so long."

"Hullo!" The train inspector has stepped down beside Magdalena and is waving into the dark. Beyond the platform rises a tall narrow building with a faded Czechoslovak tricolor below the gables and a water tower alongside. A fellow in ash-gray clothes is swinging a water crane towards the locomotive. He pauses to wave. "That is František," confides the inspector, drawing Magdalena by her hand further away from the train. "He will be able to answer your question."

"Thank you, Mr. Inspector."

Paul regards the town, or what can be seen of it. Beyond the gas lights, rooftops huddle against foothills whose presence is more of an absence to the eyes. The air tastes metallic; from the train, perhaps, or the wet cobblestone underfoot. He senses the mountains nearby.

"Here he comes."

The fellow approaches, holding a shuttered lantern. "Hey, but it's Pietr," he says, in Slovak-tinged Czech.

"Good evening, František." They greet one another and speak of their duties to be dispatched. Then the inspector gestures to Magda and Paul. "They ask me a puzzling question, these two. They seek a village that might not exist anymore. They seek old tracks that might have been destroyed in the war, and I told them you of all people might know." And to Paul, "This is František the stationmaster."

He lifts the brim of his dirty hat to Magdalena. "There are tracks, and nearby too. But they are overgrown, young miss."

She asks, "Do you know of a village, Mr. Stationmaster? High in the mountains, with little shops along the track and a green baize hermitage dome?"

His smile broadens at the eagerness of her details. Cloaked in the swirling steam, he lifts a hand to his chin; his face is grimy and his bright, limpid eyes narrow, dropping first to Paul's satchel, then to his shoes. "Ah! *Bata!*" While the inspector chuckles, František spreads both his arms and recites, "Bata! *Our Customer—our Master!*" And laughs heartily.

"We take František into Prague once a month," explains the inspector. Then, lifting out his gold watch and growing more serious. "Tell them, František. Is there such a village?"

"There are tracks, yes. And a village I am not sure. Tales, certainly. I am not the one to ask for certainties. My beloved father . . . " He crosses himself. "The War destroyed much."

The inspector, glancing back at his train, says, "There is an inn here, my friends. You could stay the night and investigate in the morning. The inn is open this season, is it not?"

The stationmaster squints at Paul; and seems to hesitate. "Yes—the *Fiery Angel*, above the tavern, called also *Fiery Angel*."

Magdalena says firmly, "Yes. We'll stay the night."

"We return tomorrow—"

"At 1:45, right, Mr. Inspector? The rest are all non-stop."

"You know the schedule very well, young miss."

Paul nods. "We'll stay. Thank you, Mr. Inspector."

"Treat them kindly, František."

And František, still taken with Paul's shoes, nods. "At the *Angel*, down that street and around the corner—ask to try the Moravian Sparrow! Tell them František recommended it!" He rushes back to his water tower while the inspector, after tucking his watch back into its pocket, shakes Paul's hand and then kisses Magdalena's. "I hope you find what you are looking for."

"We will. And thank you."

Following the stationmaster's directions, they walk into the town, among quaint, close-shouldered houses that might have stepped out of the 19th century National Revival. Gas lamps provide the only illumination. At this hour, most of the houses are dark, or glimmering with the faintest of candlelight. The breeze, sighing through the streets, carries with it the scent of pumpernickel and hot cider and the sounds of music, growing stronger as they round the corner.

The *Fiery Angel* is awash in light. The sign protrudes over a motorcar a mere decade old, and a modern bicycle is tipped against the low planter box along the wide windows. From inside come voices and laughter, and the sound of a cimbalom, a violin, and, strangely, bagpipes.

Magdalena hurries her step, swinging her bag and her flute case in turn. At the entrance she fumbles her flute case into her other hand, and opens the door for Paul. They step into a long low room, a fire roaring in a fireplace reflecting off the low beams overhead. The scent of baking bread joins that of spilt beer and nutmeg. A warmth surges around Paul, lifting the collar of his coat.

A dozen tables—surprisingly crowded given the hour—occupy the long space before the fire. A bar with bar stools is mostly empty; the tender, a plump man with sparse black hair and red cheeks, white shirt with tight suspenders, waves a towel from behind it. "*Nazdar!*"

Some of the patrons show interest in the new arrivals. A group of old men playing a game of Taroky pauses as Magdalena walks to the bar. One gestures to Paul in greeting. Near the fire, a boy perched on a stool plays the bagpipes while two girls seated beside him play cimbalom and violin; the sprightly tune is redolent of Lachian folksong perfumed with eastern scales.

Paul sets the satchel on the bar and sits on the stool. Magdalena perches beside him; she tests the bar for dryness then sets her bag and flute case side-by-side. "František sent us," she says.

Paul adds, "Have you rooms for the night?"

The tender pauses; he studies Paul's face. Paul feels an uneasiness he's not felt since he was a boy. "Did you arrive on the train?"

"We did." Magdalena folds her hands on the edge of the bar. "The Moravian Sparrow comes highly recommended." She smiles at Paul.

The tender relaxes his shoulders. "Ah, yes, it is František's favorite."

"We'd both like a serving," says Paul. "And two rooms, if you have them."

"Please. Make yourselves comfortable." He wipes the bar with his towel. "Would you like a drink? Young miss?"

"One tiny little beer, *prosím*."

"And you, *Pane?*"

Paul takes off his overcoat, careful to keep the postal tube inside, and drapes it on the bar beside her bag. "What do you recommend?"

"With no regard for your head in the morning? The *fernet* is outstanding!"

Another patron further down the counter lifts a glass of dark liquid. "*Na zdraví!*"

"*Fernet?*" When he was younger Paul had often favored the bitter herbal liqueur with cigars. "We liked to call it, *varnish for your coffin*. Tonight I'll have a beer, please."

While Magdalena shifts on her stool to listen to the musicians—bagpipes, cimbalom and violin vying with the clatter of falling sticks in a game of Taroky, the conversations at the other tables and the crackling fire—Paul studies the portraits behind the bar. None of Masaryk; he wasn't expecting any. In fact, none of any angels, fiery or otherwise. He's surprised to find a faded photograph of Emperor Franz Josef, then notes the tiny holes throughout: a dart board. Beside it is a target of the Hungarian king, and next to that an etching of more ancient vintage, a king perhaps, in a low crown. But largest of all and resplendent in its size, an abstract painting of whirling greens and blacks, sparked with yellows and reds and whites.

"Here you are." The tender sets down a stein of golden Pilsner in front of Paul and a small glass in front of Magda.

Paul thanks him and lifts the stein. He finds he's actually both thirsty and hungry; the beer is ice-cold and bracing and somehow sweet. He takes a long draught, eyeing the painting—or rather, a tapestry, its loose threads contained behind tarnished glass—whose whirling, bristling design might almost be the work of one of Josef's Obstinates.

"*Na zdravi*, Paul." She's watching him closely, the beer held in salute.

"*Na zdravi*, Magdalena." Carefully, they clink their glasses. He drinks; she sips.

"I've been calling you Pajo. I'm sorry."

He shrugs. "I am Pajo as much as Paul."

"I think . . . " She studies her glass, moving it a few millimeters to the right, then to the left. "I think I've been taking this pretty well. I mean, I haven't been pressing you for every detail. Or asking you all the questions that I've wanted to."

"Thank you, Magda."

"The last time I saw Pavel . . . " She glances over, to make sure she can continue. "The last time, which was on Tuesday, he was riding his bicycle to see Sona. He's quite taken with her, even though she's with another man."

A *bicycle*. Paul smiles at the memory; first of his beloved Gartvaas three-speed, then at the many times he had ridden it to Sona's house.

"So . . . did you marry her, Paul?"

Instead of responding, he takes another draught of beer, hoping she'll be drawn away by the music, which has continued cantering swiftly through its strophes.

"She's always wondered if you'd ask her."

Paul sets down the beer. And nods. "Yes, Magda."

"And where you're from Paul, she lives with you? And are there children?"

"Yes. Two."

"And . . . you left them? To come here?"

"You have many questions, Magda." He glances at the surreal tapestry; drawn by its whorls of color.

She's curious, yet she does not seem to notice the uneasiness in the room. Or is it just his own imagination, his own latent sensitivity to his Jewishness?

He remembers H.G. Wells: *The part about the pogrom . . . I would sit on that card. Some people are uneasy with the Jewish question, some are, quite frankly, bored.*

~~Hilsner.~~ T.G.M.

"Magda—"

She's lifted the cardboard tube from his overcoat. "I'm not going to open it." She holds it gently in both hands, and turns it so that the bright yellow and red Universal globe catches the firelight. She mouths that word: *Universal.* "What does it mean?"

"It's English, Magda." He translates it and this word, too, she mouths.

"And *in the Hollywoodland.* Is this where you live?"

He pictures the house on Delmonica Drive, and the cluttered living room, Sona and Olga and little William. "Yes."

"And were you happy there?"

"I was happy, Magda."

"But sad, too?"

Her glance is penetrating, unnerving. He nods and turns away. He sips his beer instead of saying these things aloud. Carefully, she replaces the tube in the long pocket. And turns on her chair to watch the musicians.

Plates clack down on the counter. "Moravian sparrow, sir and young miss!" Succulent lumps of pork, moist potato dumplings and tangy sauerkraut. Paul grins as a large spoon is laid down for him, and a linen napkin. The mingled scents assail his memory; how he and Hugo would sneak into a Brno tavern for this dish, certainly as forbidden as as the cigars and beer that accompanied it.

"Wonderful. Thank you, sir." He lifts the spoon. The tender lingers, watching as Paul digs into the side of a dumpling, gathering up pork and sauerkraut and shovels it into his mouth. The potent tang assaults his taste buds and the hearty, thick textures are a joy to chew. He nods, and eats, and seems to please the tender, but he's thinking of Sona and William and Olga, and a moment far distant where they wait for him on a Monday evening.

To distract himself from such thoughts, he decides something closer to the here and now: that tomorrow he will take Magdalena back to Brno. Yes, they will search for tracks, and ask questions about the village, and when the train arrives he will climb aboard with her and ride back to Brno and send her off. Then he will return to Prague and perhaps to Home. Again, he's staring into the tapestry. The threads have a luminous hue and in the firelight seem to quiver, as though the tangle of blacks and greens are in motion, the boughs of a forest, perhaps.

Clapping startles him, as had a moment of silence just before: the music has ended. The card games and conversations temporarily halt, while near the fire the three young musicians take a bow. Magda too is clapping, and now turns to the bar and her flute case. She takes it up, and turning back to the fire, raises it. The musicians take notice and the young man with the bagpipes waves at her to come over.

"Do you mind, Paul."

"Please."

She opens the case and draws out the sections of her flute which she deftly assembles. "Can't you see it?" Climbing off the stool she gestures past him to the tapestry. "It's a stag!" As if magic words from a fairy tale have been whispered the animal materializes in front of him, woven of those dark threads: the many-antlered stag amidst its forest, majestic, serene, unforgettable, staring out.

DR KOLENATY: *Run up to the funeral parlor and tell them to loan us a crucifix, candles and some black cloth. And a Bible. Hurry.*

VITEK: *Yes, sir.*

DR. KOLENATY: *And find me a skull.*

VITEK: *A skull! A human skull?*

DR. KOLENATY: *Man or beast, it doesn't matter. As long as it represents death.*

—The Makropulos Thing,
by Karel Čapek

21. ALOIS KRÁL

The music begins, spurred on by the flute. Magdalena stands beside the black-haired youth with his bagpipes; he grins shyly. His instrument is not comparable to the Scottish variety. Against its soft, almost sweet drone the cymbalom player strikes a slow, circular rhythm against which the violinist offers counterpoint. Unbidden, Paul identifies it as what the Maestro would term *Popevny*, second in his three tiers of folksong categories. At the same moment, Paul recognizes the tune; the Slovak folk song *My River*.

"Lovely young woman." The tender wipes the already clean bar. "She cannot be your daughter, eh?"

"No." Paul straightens on the stool, picks up his spoon. "A student of mine." After another bite of Sparrow, he adds, "We're from Masaryk University in Brno, on an ethnographic expedition of sorts."

"Eh?" The tender sets down his towel. "An expedition?"

Deciding that the tender's watchfulness is for a reason other than anti-Semitism, Paul says, "We seek a village. One which a fellow teacher, a composer, once visited, somewhere in the mountains near here. He's very keen to find it again." Paul wishes for Magdalena's enthusiasm in narration. "Your stationmaster, František, said there are disused train tracks here in town, and that . . . that they led into the mountains but were destroyed in the War.

"Ah, yes. The War. Of course." A plaintive smile. Then the

tender looks out toward Magdalena, and they listen to the melody she spins, both gossamer and grave. Behind his shoulder, the tapestry catches the firelight; the stag stirs in its forest.

"The war didn't really touch you in Brno or Prague, eh? But here. Devastation."

"And elsewhere. In the mountains?"

He nods. "A graveyard. We were *occupied*, you see. The Emperor's army reached us late in the winter, and they were already sorely tested by the enemy. They stationed here, and sent their troops into the mountains to hunt. So many townsfolk were killed."

"And you've heard then, Sir, of a village? It would have sat high in the mountains, with little shops beside the tracks and a hermitage dome of green baize . . ."

But the tender is listening to the music. Or pretending to. Magdalena's flute chases the cymbalom up and down a Dorian scale. Paul glances over his shoulder. She is lost in the music, the flute, winking golden as she moves it up and down, her body following the line of the music. The girl at the cymbalom, with blonde tresses as long and lovely as Magdalena's own red hair, wields the small hammers over the metal plates with now-dizzying speed. At the surrounding tables, conversation has dwindled, though the card players continue their Taroky, the clack of their sticks in defiance of the song. Under the sputtering gas lamps on the walls, under the long low oaken beams that crisscross the room, men of middle to older age in woolen suits and loosened bow ties, the women in folk dress though a few wear modern clothes and Paul has a sense of the community holding forth here in the oblong room, close to the fire and the music.

Though in a far corner, at a smaller table, a gentleman sits by himself. Like Paul, he seems apart from this community. Sparse white hair, a trim white beard. A black suit that hangs on his shoulders. And something frozen in his attitude.

"A village, you say?"

Paul turns back. "Yes. Does it sound familiar?"

"The War." The tender shakes his head. "It destroyed much near here."

"This village could not have been destroyed. It definitely existed five years ago. And the train tracks there were in use, in case of an avalanche." Though he hears Magda's *Oh, Maestro, you are so frustrating!*

"Most of those who visit us, Sir Professor, are interested in the direction opposite the mountains. The spa called Celanda, with its moist peat bogs." After a pause, "But there were stories told of villages that were lost, too, you see? Lost in the war, in the aftermath. Forgotten, when the Hungarians and the Czechs and the Slovaks divided up the spoils." The tender stands near the dart pocked portrait of Franz Josef. "What a shame, the things he did to us." A gesture with the towel at his Hungarian accomplice. "And him. But we are used to it. We turn over in our sleep, and wake up with a new king."

Paul thinks to mention the *National Awakening*, but the tender has walked past the glimmering stag to that other portrait, the ancient one. "All the way back to Samo."

The Samo Empire. Paul knows little of this ancient tribal realm.

"We lost most of our town's men in the war. And had to rebuild the structures. This place, it was born in the aftermath."

Paul loses himself with the stag in the whorling black and green of the forest and then jumps at the sudden clapping; the song has ended. Tearing his eyes away from the tapestry, he turns on the stool and joins in the applause a little dizzily. Magdalena, red-cheeked, takes a bow, then shakes the hands of her fellow musicians.

"Very talented, she is," says the tender.

As the applause dies down, Paul returns to his Sparrow. "Yes, she is."

He does not observe Magdalena whispering to the others; only later will he hear her recount how she had outlined what song to play, from her head. He hears only the results. Magdalena's flute, by itself, spinning the eight notes of leaping, swirling melos.

He turns. Magdalena is staring at him and playing the melody from the Maestro's feuilleton. Then she plays it again, while the bagpiper chooses a drone on the tonic, and the cymbalom player carries forth the tritone at the end of the haunting phrase. Paul wants to tell her to stop; but of course does not. It is remote, somehow. The Maestro's domeček and the ivy-choked piano; the clattering hue of the *scasovani* in the air.

Der Geist und Alten Natur.

Here she draws those eight notes into new life and projects them further into variations, while the violinist, assuming the *kontras* role, sends the first phrase into the foreground, wistfully, against which the bagpiper's drones. Here, the tune is not pleasant, not the lyrical or *popevny* tune; rather, it is redolent of the *boyatyrsky*, the heroic, the oldest stratum of folksong.

The crowd, however, treats it as another serenade.

Gripping the edge of the bar with his right hand, Paul turns back to his plate.

The tender has returned to his other customer, setting a freshly poured Pilsner down before him.

Distracted by the music, which continues to grow, Paul raises his hand. When the tender is in earshot, he asks, "Have you followed the old tracks into the mountains?"

"I?" He laughs. "I would rather take the deer trails or the road into Bratislava. Better than to travel back into that hell."

"Do you know how far they go, before the damage?"

A shrug. Then the tender is distracted by something beyond the bar. Paul notes motion, turns to see the tiny silver coin flying through the air; it strikes the flagstone before the fire and is enough, apparently, to cause the cymbalom player to hesitate with her hammers, and the bagpiper to pull away from his instrument. The violin ceases and only Magdalena is left playing for but a few measures before she too ceases.

The conversations and the card playing continue. The only lull in the room, besides the musicians, comes from that far corner, and the gaunt white-haired figure seated there. His arm, which had been poised up near his head, now drops to the table.

Almost immediately the violinist begins a new melody, taken up by cymbalom and bagpipe and then by Magdalena; another sprightly *popevny*.

"More Sparrow?"

"No . . ." Paul reaches into his suitcoat, pulls out the wallet, from which he draws a ten crown note. "Thank you." He gropes for his satchel.

"Thank you, sir! And when you're ready for your rooms, you have only to ask."

Paul stands and lift his overcoat and their other belongings. Then goes to meet the stranger.

A long face, fringed at the bottom with the clipped white beard. Tall, gaunt, he sits rigidly in the chair though his eyes do not betray that rigidity. Eyes of a languid gray hue, they observe Paul's approach from a distance. Firelight struggles past beams and columns to tease the weathered wood behind him.

Paul's impression upon reaching the table is of a man whose sparse white hair and clipped beard betray an almost military bearing; he has none of the softness of the old men playing cards. Yet, too, he has not their haleness. He sits in the chair like a thing abandoned. So, not only a man apart but a far traveler, surely. As forlorn as Herr Professor or Stravinsky.

"Good evening." Paul bows. "May I join you?"

In response, the stranger gestures simply to the other empty chairs. Paul sets down the bag, lays his overcoat carefully on one chair and seats himself on another. "You have a wonderful town here."

The other man smiles. An old scar on his right cheek adds, somehow, a tenderness to that smile. He replies in German, "As you can hear by my accent, Herr, it is not my town."

Paul strives to cover his surprise with a smile in return. "Herr, I am Paul Haas of Brno. I apologize if I've offended you."

"You made no offense, Herr. I have long enjoyed the beauty of the country hereabouts. It is obviously not your town either." He lifts his glass; some green liqueur catches the faint firelight. "What brings you here?"

"I and my student—she's the flautist—"

"Ah, yes," says the stranger. "A lovely girl."

"We seek a village hereabouts." Paul does not wish to rush into questions; the man, who has not offered his own name, and seemingly will not, sips his drink and watches Paul. "We do not know much about where this village might be. And for some reason, Herr, I think that you might be able to help us." He pauses, wishing for a cigarette or a beer to hide behind. "Are you well traveled much in this part of the country?"

A shrug. "I am old enough, that wherever I sit for he night, there is my home."

Old, yes. But in the shifting firelight he is old one minute and no older than Paul the next.

"I've been told that the village I seek no longer exists."

"No longer?"

"Yes." While Paul speaks of the village high in the mountains, of the colorful shops along the railroad tracks, of the green baize hermitage, the stranger's rough finger draw a slow, cautious circle on the side of the glass. Old and yet not old, he raises his hand. "I know of the village."

Paul sits forward. He finds himself tripping on the German: "I . . . I am . . . that is wonderful, Herr. Have you seen it?"

"I have."

"The tender says it was destroyed in the War, along with the tracks that leave this town and head into the mountains."

The stranger nods, and then startles Paul again by saying, softly, "It is dead now."

Tote.

In the silence that follows between them, filled in by cymbalom, violin, bagpipe and Magda's flute, Paul cannot help but think what she had said—would say—to him, as she emerged into the Maestro's sundered garden.

My village is dead.

His heart begins pounding. "How do you mean? Dead?"

The old, not old man lifts his glass and stares into the green liqueur. Is it the trembling firelight? Or does his hand now tremble? He sets the glass down. "Dead, Herr Haas, in the truest possible sense. Dead, by which I mean its townsfolk are in their graves, or no longer there. The town is forgotten, the land itself has . . . has swallowed it up."

In the firelight, the man's eyes betray slightly different hues. One gray, and one silvery gray.

"And was it . . . during the war, that the village was lost, Herr?" Applause startles the air; the music has stopped, and the crowd cheers and raps the floor with their boots. Yet Paul cannot look away from the man, whose left eye, surely, is false. "When were you last there?"

The eyes, silver and gray, lift past Paul's shoulder. Paul senses Magdalena's smile before she steps up beside him, saluting him with the flute as though with a sword. "Were you listening?"

"Yes." Paul stands up. "It was most beautiful."

Her face is radiant. She clutches a garland of white flowers, and now struggles to place it on her head. "The cimbalom player is terribly talented, isn't she? Hello," she says to the stranger.

He struggles to rise, then seats himself. "Fraulein."

"May I present my student, Magdalena."

His eyes widen. He seems to look at her anew. "It is an honor, Fraulein. You play beautifully." He motions Magda to sit down in a vacant chair.

"This gentleman," says Paul, in Czech, "knows of the village."

"That's wonderful!" Unaware of the strangeness of the man's reaction, she dismantles the flute. And then says, in German, to the stranger, "And what is your name, Herr?"

He stiffens in his chair, raising his chin. "My name is Alois Král, Fraulein. I was once a forester."

"When were you last there, Herr Král?"

But Král watches Magdalena, who has finished packing away her flute and now sits with hands folded on the table. "How long have you played, Fraulein Magda?"

"Oh. Years. I'm so very old, as you can tell."

The old yet not old man echoes her smile.

"But please tell us, Herr, about the village."

"It was many years ago, Fraulein."

As she leans over the table, she reaches up to adjust the garland. "Were you born there?"

Paul is struck by this question; insight or innocence? The Forester's pause leaves Paul wondering, until he remembers the vivid impression he'd had. A far traveler. And Král's answer resounds with it. "My birthplace is lost to me, Fraulein. Or rather, though it exists, I cannot go back."

Exile, and far traveler. Paul sees Schoenberg in the Hollywood sunlight, grasping at Beethoven's skull.

"But where?" asks Magdalena.

"A pleasant village in the low hills of Austria, Fraulein."

"Herr, what can you tell us about this village in the mountains?"

"It is a dead place," he says to Magdalena. "Nobody lives there anymore."

"How far away is it?" she asks, then glances up, over Paul's shoulder. The tender stands there.

"Compliments of the house, young miss. Another tiny little beer for you."

"Thanks!" She takes it. "You have a wonderful band here."

He bows, and, after a lingering glance at Král, returns to his bar.

Magda, with the glass in hand, urges the Forester to speak.

"It is perhaps two days travel from here, Fraulein."

She sips. "And why did it die out?"

"It was an old, a very old, village, Fraulein. It had died out and been conquered, and been reborn, many, many times over the centuries. This last time, well..." He lifts his hand, spreading his long fingers as though grasping at something that is no longer there.

"We want to go there," she says.

He nods; his eyes, gray and silver, shining in firelight.

Paul, uneasy yet unwilling to let the chance evaporate, says, "Can we hire you, Herr Král, to take us there?"

"Please, Herr."

Král draws another slow, cautious circle on the side of his glass. "It would not be easy. Horse, and dray. The paths are old."

"We understand. We would pay for your time and transport and supplies, Herr." He adds, "Name your price."

Almost imperceptibly Alois Král leans back against his chair lost in thought. Gray and silver gone as he shuts his eyes. "Perhaps merely the price of returning." Mismatched eyes fixing on Paul. "Though we will need to purchase supplies for ourselves and the animals. And perhaps some brandy."

"You will take us?"

A slight nod; acquiescing. "If you mean to go."

"We do mean to go, Herr."

The old yet not old man grips the table firmly, then shoves back his chair. "You are spending the night here?"

"Yes," says Magda, brightly. "And you'll take us tomorrow?"

"Yes, Fraulein. We will meet an hour before sunrise." He rises—or attempts to. He falters, but not from drunkenness. He lunges for a crutch that leans against the wall. Grunting, he grabs it and with stately movement rises to his single leg. His left trouser is pinned at the knee. "I will have my dray and horses waiting by the train dock."

Then he departs, the firelight teasing a crooked shadow from his green and gaunt form.

"The rooster wakes me in the morning. He 'sings' such a strange melody that I haven't yet been able to take it down."

—*Leos J——— to Kamila Stosslova 1918*

22. THE ETERNAL ROAD

The wagon is simple, with a bench wide enough for the three of them, a spring-board footrest with new bronze casings. A weathered sailcloth is nailed to a wooden frame behind them, providing cover for bedrolls, a rucksack of dried food, Austrian army canteens, jars of jam-pudding and fruit supplied by the tender's wife, an ax and other tools, along with Magdalena's bag, Paul's satchel and Herr Král's crutch. Sitting between Paul and Král, Magdalena holds the flute case on her lap with the same care that Paul clutches at the architectural tube in his overcoat, and she tries to maintain the white garland in her hair despite the side-to-side rocking of the wagon. A pair of white-maned, brown-spotted nags, with bells around their necks, pull the wagon easily along this first stretch of pathway; below them lies the town in morning sunlight, its bustle of peaked roofs remote as dolls' houses.

Král sits hunched forward, his leg braced against the footrest. He wears a green longcoat, a white shirt ruffled in the manner of two decades earlier, gherkin green trousers and a black boot. His greeting on the railway platform had been terse—"*Guten morgen, Herr, Fraulein.*" Under the dying gas lamp, in the cold pre-dawn, he had hobbled around the wagon, securing stays, running his hand along the wheel rims, then tending to the nags. Paul and Magdalena had helped him load the supplies, delivered in a wheelbarrow by the sleepy-eyed tender.

Ahead loom mountains. White peaks, the color beginning to bleed as the sun climbs into the sky. Gorse and hayflower on the sloping hillside in the windless morning. Magdalena's enthusiasm, her joy at the nags—she had petted each nose in turn and asked their names, and fed them the sugar cubes she had taken from the bar during breakfast—her pleasure at being on a winding pathway with the mountains ahead of them, at the fresh cold air and the hawk circling in the rosy sky—had all been tempered by Král's reticence. But she was gradually wearing him down; or perhaps it was the fact that the village was behind them, almost lost from sight. Král, the exile, was returning.

And Magda presses, "Can I ask—did you visit this village after the War, or before?" While waiting for Král's reply she studies the wagon's jagged shadow on the hillside, swaying as they sway, streaming over the rock and ever climbing.

"I did not say I was a visitor, Fraulein."

"You *lived* there?"

His scar twitches; a slight smile. "For . . . many years."

She turns wide, startled, amused eyes to Paul. Then back to the subject of her interrogation. Her schoolgirl's coat, with beads of dew on her upturned collar, glows violet against the red of her hair. "Why did you go to live there, Herr Král?"

Another long pause. Paul has turned his attention to the blue-white peaks in the distance, what the fog once concealed, the rising sun now burnishes.

"I was a soldier, Fraulein. In the Emperor's army, against the Prussians."

"Near here? And you . . . you chased them into the mountains. And you . . . you found a village, like you told Paul?"

"You tell it better yourself, Fraulein, most certainly." He clucks his tongue, and with hands on the reigns guides the nags around the gentle sweep of the hillside, ever upward.

"And you lived amongst them?" She catches the garland, just before it falls.

He nods curtly. "I and a few others of my regiment. They were badly injured and did not last the season, but I was luckier, my injuries were slight and I settled in as forester to the community."

"And . . . what happened, Herr Král?" She leans imperceptibly toward him. "Why did the village . . . die?"

Magdalena is mistaken if she thinks she's going to get a clearer answer than the one given last night. His next words, some minutes later, caution them to the deteriorating path; the cart begins jouncing from side to side, and Král threads his right arm through a leather strap that might have been put there for just this reason.

Ever upward they climb. Foothills vanish to escarpments of gorse, and then to cliffs that, by mid-day, become white with snow, and deep with blue shadows. The path narrows, becomes a switchback. The nags do not slow, but lift and turn their heads as they trot, their ears twitching, their bells ringing more thinly at this altitude.

Magda opens a jar of sugared apples. They share them, eating quietly. Paul's thoughts linger on the town they've left behind, on the kind tender and his wife—who had provided the fruit and jam this morning, as well as a bin of charwood bedwarmer the night before; a comfortable if small room with a fireplace. On the wall had been more lithographs of that ancient ruler Samo, as well as others that Paul could not identify. When he slept he dreamt not of them—not of past glories—but again of Burbank, again choking on the *shem* of paper that crumbles in his hands.

Paul pulls low the scarf to eat the sugared apples; now he is reluctant to wind it tight around his neck and chin, even with the chill breeze. As he takes the jar from Magda and turns to set it back in the box, he recalls the tender's wife, and how she had asked him to bring the jars back to the *Fiery Angel* upon his return; and this thought—of return—makes him uneasy. Until now the journey has been one-way. The only return is that *via* the stave flower, back to Herr Professor's tennis court. But now he is bound to Magdalena—and both of them to Král.

Beside him, Magdalena draws her coat around her and allows herself to be jostled against the jostling seat. Paul feels regret at having brought her here; more, a deep, troubling responsibility; a growing sense that she is now his to protect, this 'daughter' who had once played alongside him at the Conservatory; a daughter as precious as dear Olga.

He retrieves a peasant blanket from the back of the cart and throws it across their laps, then he sinks back on the bench and watches the pathway emerge from turnings in the hillside, watches the unchanging mountain peaks that have moved without his having realized it—a jagged outcropping that had been poised far, far above the nags' ducking heads is now at his shoulder, and a new tableau has opened up.

Král guides and goads the nags. With left arm bracing his legless side, he grips the reins, leaning slightly forward as though creating their momentum from sheer concentration. A gray eye, almost phosphorescent, fixed on the path. Compared with last night, when the forester had seemed abandoned to his chair, Král has now grown larger with the task at hand. The exile, returning to the village that had become his home? Paul is not certain he believes that tale. There is more to it, certainly. He ponders and without realizing it he draws the scarf across his lower face and neck.

Clouds the size of airships float by.

Some time later, Magda murmurs, "How far have we come?" She holds the garland—now a bit careworn—in her hand.

"The foothills are well below us." Král's left eye glinting silver in the sunlight. "We will reach it by tomorrow."

At sunset, they stop the cart so Král can rest and feed the nags. Paul helps Magdalena down and she stares up and around at towering blue-white peaks and the dome of sky in which the first stars of evening are aglow.

"Tell me more, Paul," she says, yawning to clear her ears.

"More?"

"About home."

"I told you already."

"You're worse than Král." They stand a dozen paces from the cart. Their driver is speaking with the animals while a breeze roves the mountaintop, nearly covering the sound of her smile. "Maybe not worse. But certainly mysterious." Her cheeks are red from the cold, and her eyes watery from the altitude. "Why did you come here, Paul? Just because you received that . . . Universal . . . object?"

Paul smiles and shakes his head. He thinks for a moment, then unbuttons his coat part-way and reaches inside. He finds the plastic sleeve and withdraws it; the brown paper, and the fading ink which forms Hebrew letters that are also musical notes. "I came . . . because of this."

She takes it, frowning.

"I was given it, and told that, in another time, that *I* had written it."

She reads aloud the words below the title: "D*o Not Lament for chorus, 1942. Souvenir of the first and last year in the Terezin exile.*"Then, breathlessly, "*1942.*"

He nods.

"But . . . but what does it mean? *Terezin exile?*"

"Magda, remember the story of Hilsner?"

A whisper: "Yes."

"It's not just a quaint story. Not just a bedtime tale that Hugo liked to frighten me with." He watches her read the manuscript, her brow furrowing with seriousness. He very nearly doesn't tell her; does not want to stain her with such knowledge. "Within ten years from now, Magda, the same hysteria and bigotry will flare up again. Against every Jew and Roma in Europe."

She glances over. Her expression breaks his heart.

"There will be war, starting here and in Poland and spreading. Masaryk won't be alive to defend us. He dies in '36. A war will overtake us and the world. A war and a pogrom. Millions will be murdered in Auschwitz, Treblinka, Baden-Baden. In little more than a decade . . . " His voice has dropped to a whisper.

"*Ten years?*"

"And so I came back. To do . . . nothing much at all."

She studies his face. He's reminded uncomfortably of Miss Jean Simmons. "A decade?"

"Yes, Magda." He takes back the paper and slips it into his pocket.

She lifts a hand to her neck, silent, and her thoughts, brimming in her eyes, are her own.

When he wakes from a brief, dreamless sleep, night has drawn a curtain across the mountains. Král claims that the horses need no light to find the trail, yet at Paul's urging he stops the cart to light and hang a lantern from the brace above the bench. Its swinging glow, as they clatter upward—ever upward, along gorse and sea-worn rock—lulls Paul. The peaks rise invisible but for the sound the breeze makes as it roves through, a bewitching keen and whistle that never falls silent, that is always modulating and growing in beguiling ways that makes sleep difficult.

Magdalena stirs. She says she is going to try to sleep in the back, amongst the blankets. Carefully she turns in the rocking bench and climbs over. Paul now has an emptiness at both shoulders. He decides for wakefulness. Breathing deep of the cold and utterly clean air, he straightens and runs a hand through his hair and turns to their driver. "Herr Král," he says, loud enough but not too loud. "You have not told me the name of this village."

The bells on the nags ring thinly; he counts twelve such rings before Král responds.

"Villages such as it, Herr Haas, have many names."

"Many?" He wraps the scarf tighter around his face and clutches the tube containing the stave flower closer to his chest. "Tell me one, Herr Král."

"I cannot."

Paul studies the profile, the scar that does not twitch but is immobile, fixed just as the eyes remain fixed on the path ahead of them.

"Tell me then, how did you come upon it?"

"How?"

"Yes. Can you answer directly?"

Now, the scar twitches. A long moment later he says, "Would you like to hear a story, Herr Haas?"

"I would, Herr Král."

And to the drowsy rocking of the cart as it climbs, ever climbs, slowly, and with many pauses, Herr Král tells his story.

"I lived my first fifteen years in a village in Kerne, in the hinterlands of Austria, Herr. Comparable, perhaps, to the town we left behind. Forests of teak and pine and oak. Scattered lakes. My father was a forester and his before him, in service to a once-great family. I had a girl. Her name was Maria Suzette. And I had a dog, a black pinscher, named Terni.

"Have you ever had a dog, Herr Haas?

"And even at that age, I was a forester like my father. I knew the trails, and the breadth of the land. I believed I understood the . . . the way of things, if you understand me, Herr. I pictured my life and those of my forefathers like the rings of a new fallen oak. I could trace them, and with my imagination could trace where mine would lead. But of course I would lose it all, in the span of a single day.

"When had the news reached us?

"You will not credit this, Herr. That I knew little of the Emperor, and still less of his Archduke. Perhaps it was a logging train that brought news of the assassination. No matter. I gave it little thought, although some of the women in the village were weeping at the news.

"Yes, Herr, I was fifteen. I was a youth, and knew little of the outside world. I told your companion about a Prussian war but that was a lie.

"Do you wish me to tell my tale, Herr Haas?

243

"There were plans to make ceremonial wreaths to ship on behalf of our employers. That would be that, I thought. I did not understand why the Hapsburg grenadiers marched into our village, or why the women wept again.

"They swept me up like a leaf in the wind, Herr. I and a dozen others. We were given swords at first. They had no rifles for us. And so I found an ax that reminded me of the one I had left behind. And even when I was given a rifle I kept the ax at my side.

"I need not tell you about the horrors of that War. Those of us who survived the battles in northern Austria pressed on.

"By what compass we followed, I cannot tell you. I could not attune myself to these new boundaries and borders. It was the land that spoke to me, even more than it did to my unlucky comrades.

"Melee after melee, we stalked the land. By then our commander was dead, as were those who had been my friends in the village. To fight the enemy we used our hands, our knives, and my ax. We hoarded our ammunition, and always fled into the mountains.

"It was springtime. It was cold, yes, and more than half of us died on the trek. It was an escarpment twice as tall as the one beside our cart, Herr, that I climbed. And found the hidden valley. And what lay inside it. The forest, and the structures, and the people. Yes, Herr, a railroad track. A green baize dome, as you have said.

"I fell. I fell down the other side of the escarpment and cannot remember what happened to those who were with me, all I know is that I never saw them again.

"I woke in a great forest. Ancient trees, you see?

"I must have wandered there for many days, before the villagers found me. And even after they . . . cared for me, I was considered to be apart from them. Not an enemy. But a stranger. And I, more comfortable in the forest, found my home there.

"You must credit me this, Herr. I tell you the truth, now.

"This was an ancient place. Many empires had grown and died around it. It was the crux of the land, of the continent. You are right, the brothers, Cyril and Methodius, traveled there in the ninth century. They brought their religion, but like the empires it would grow and die, too. They brought, too, their gift of the written word. They gave us the alphabet, and the power of the written word. And such the village hoarded.

"Let me speak, Herr.

"Yes, the brothers were of great importance to the village. The village, Herr, holds such truths.

"Do not tell the Fraulein this story, Herr. It would only unnerve her. I have spent many years more in the village than I have in the outside world. My years are longer there than here.

"There is a place I found, that first day . . . But now, Herr, all is gone.

"All power is dead."

Todt.

"Some sort of revolt in the body, in the blood, is being prepared."

—*Leos J*—— *to Kamila*
10 February 1922 vol 2 425

23. SPIRES OF BLACKEST MIDNIGHT

The scar twitches, but Král does not smile.

"You think I tell you this story to amuse myself, Herr Haas?"

"No." Paul says in a low, level voice as he grips the back of the bench. He is aware of Magdalena's red hair glowing in the lantern light, spreading out from beneath the blanket pulled over her. "I have seen it. Years from now."

sator, arepo, tenet, opera, rotas.

For the first time the old yet not old man gazes upon Paul. Paul says nothing.

The moon appears, winking over a jagged summit high to the right. Paul had not sensed the mountains drawing so close. Moonlight pours down the sheer rock and lights the road—surprising in the variety of green and brown rocks that sparkle as the horses draw near them.

"Beautiful," says Magdalena, sleepily, at his shoulder. She offers the canteen. He takes it—glad that he has the task of drinking rather than commenting on the strangeness of the landscape: the path of sparkling stone unreeling from out of the mountain.

He offers it to Král, who declines; then hands it back to

Magdalena. She remains wrapped in the blanket, leaning against the side of the wagon. Then, a few moments later, gazing up and around, she says: "I've dreamed of this."

"Just now, Fraulein?"

She shakes her head.

Král's good eye gleams, then darkens.

The blanket slithers from her shoulder as she lifts the flute case onto her lap. "When I was a girl." Moonlight burnishes the instrument. She assembles the pieces with practiced hands then brings the embouchure to her lips, conjuring a low, hesitant D. As Paul turns to face the path she begins playing, with long and solemn lines, Debussy's *Claire de Lune*.

With daybreak the snow catches fire. Sunlight dazzles on towering crags. It chases the blue shadows from mountaintops, leaving the path all but invisible to Paul's eyes.

The path becomes more treacherous and Král more belligerent with the nags. Against the ice-blown wind Paul wraps the scarf around his face. Magdalena huddles under the blanket, shivering. Král, his face barred by his writhing collar, drives the nags onward, their breath smoking the air and torn away, their bells ringing thinly, vanishing in the booming gusts. The glare is oppressive. Paul shuts his eyes, braces himself against the sting of ice on his forehead, and soon grows queasy at the side-to-side bustle of the cart. He stares down at the dark wooden footrest or the red and white wool of the blanket, but the peasant weave is gathering crystals, each an echo of the snow glare surrounding them. Král makes noises under his breath. The leather creaks in his hands, as he tightens the reins. His guttural voice is lost, then found, in the breeze.

Paul feels Magdalena shift beside him. Her hand nudges his arm under the blanket and Paul looks up. From out of the shimmering glare, towering shapes cohere, marching with eerie grace on either side, gray and black shapes—spires, bristling from the mountainside.

"*You see it, Pavel? Am I imagining it?*" Across space and time, Josef speaks to him. They walk along Rooseveltova Street, toward the theater. "*Spires of blackest midnight, eh? They encircle Karel and the others.*"

The cart leans and rocks. Wind drives hard. Behind them, an empty jar shatters.

Magdalena shouts something, but it's lost in the din. Her hair whips like a fleck of fire. She stares up at the spires. Král gives them no attention: he is intent on the nags, and the buckled path; he shouts and whistles, and draws the reins left and right.

You see it, Pavel? Am I imagining it?

The cart tips dangerously to the right; Magdalena is thrown against him; Král loses grip of the reins. Paul grasps at the bench and feels himself falling inevitably out but Magdalena clutches at his coat. His shoulder strikes the seat and—in the mad buckling—he fights to upright himself, and then clutches the cardboard tube to his chest. The nags veer leftward; a spire veers into view. Král lunges for the reigns but cannot stand. Paul struggles up. He feels as though he stands at the top of the mountain, with all of it behind him were he to fall. Dizzied by bells to the left and right, by the grinding wheels and the snow-spangled brilliance all around, he pushes against the footrest until it sticks then braces himself, reaches forward to the leather straps whisking above the snow; grabs. Then pulls himself back into the cart, helped by the buckling momentum to crash back into the seat. Magdalena passes the reins to Král.

He shouts, he tugs. The cart is righted. They pass small between the procession of stone.

Ahead, the mist clears. Blue and white sky stretches into the distance. The summit is reached.

Descending, they find a dwindling breeze.

The snow-white brilliance is damped by the blue of the sky, while hundreds of meters below are the trees, and a fog-bound valley. At first Paul thinks the ghostly gray pallor is due to the mist; but nearer, as the cart and the nags are drawn down, ever down the switchback trail, the pine reveals itself to be desiccated. Bare, dead trunks and branches, a snarl of undergrowth clinging still to the mountainsides, descending in ever-thicker ranks to a mist-strewn plain below.

"Home," Král mutters, his hands gripping the reins.

In places, spires break through the dead trees. They shine, sharp gray and black. Paul counts fifty-five in the nearby sweep of forest before the trail enters the trees and everything is lost to sight. The breeze, sloughing in the peaks above, is muted, forlorn. The bells clang loudly, the wheels grind on the dirt and sing, sparking, over stretches of bare rock. The tree limbs hang lifeless, sketching sharp and narrow angles through which the sky shines. And the air grows warmer, but tinged with a sickly odor.

In the underbrush can be seen the bones of small animals.

The trail is treacherous, and the nags become obstinate, slowing or halting completely when the a fallen trunk blocks even half the path. His legs and arms stiff from the tumult near the summit, Paul nonetheless volunteers to clear the brush. The work is not hard; the boughs are eaten away; hardly any strength is required to topple them aside. He and Magdalena climb down by turns, and soon the path appears to level off, the trees to grow more sparse. Smoother ground awaits them, and through the boles he can see—a hundred meters below, or less, the low white structures of a village and a hemisphere of shining green.

"I've dreamed this before," says Magdalena.

Yet when they finally emerge from the forest, onto a field of brown grass, he cannot find the baize dome, nor even the profiles of a town. What lies before them is tumbled stone and low white walls, with spires lifting, tilted, from the earth. "No railroad tracks," murmurs Magdalena, drawing her coat around her though the air is much warmer now. Indeed, almost balmy.

The nags whinny. The leftward one staggers. Král clucks and tugs on the reigns, and the cart comes to a stop at the edge of the ruins.

Paul wants to ask Král if this is the town he remembers; if this is the town that the Maestro J——— had visited. But the scene, wide, desolate, dead, mesmerizes him. He climbs down from the cart—his back and thighs aching. As Král staggers on his crutch to the fetch the buckets and feed, Paul helps Magdalena down, and they stand there, staring at the ruins.

Paul strives to find the green hemisphere he'd spotted from the hillside.

"The nags will need a full day for recovery, Herr."

Král's voice is strangely at odds with itself. Distracted, yes. Unnerved, but also harboring a deep pleasure.

"Is this as you remember it, Herr Kral?"

Král hooks the feed bucket under the muzzle of the first nag, then he stops, and balancing on his single leg, surveys the ruins. "Not as I remember it."

"What . . . what happened?"

But Král does not answer. And Paul has no patience to wait. He tucks the Universal tube under his arm, fetches his stick from the cart and, leaning heavily on its water-goblin handle, he walks with Magdalena into the ruins.

"What are you thinking, Magda?"

She's been quiet, stepping with him over the low foundations of chalky rock, over the dead gorse and crabgrass.

"How old?" she says, finally.

Paul is glad to speak. He feels the need to reason things out, to set aside the eeriness of the low and fallen structures pierced by the towering spires. "Older than the town our Maestro visited."

"The towering rock." She gestures at a spire with her flute case. "You weren't surprised to see it. You've seen it before."

He nods. "In Brno."

"Br—" She stares at him. "A decade from now?"

Paul lets the rapping of his stick reply.

They round another of the long, low foundations. They find no sign of human occupancy; no kindling furniture, or moth-eaten clothes, or bones. Beneath the sighing mountaintops, the ruins express an age that beggars Paul's imagination. Yet Král had been here as a youth, ten years earlier? The conundrum does not point to the forester having been untruthful. Rather it draws Paul's thoughts back to Herr Professor and the great clanking swan-wing platens of the printing press; to the puzzling equations that had warped the *scasovani* and delivered him to Prague, 1928. Here was something surely tied into it, and perhaps what had drawn him to this time and place.

Here were primeval ruins built upon the memory of a pleasant, trackside village.

Paul changes direction: a flash of green. He and Magdalena climb over the low, jagged walls, step through gorse, the mountaintops dizzy on all sides—and emerge onto an emptiness. No gorse, only bare brown stone. Ahead of them a much larger foundation and in front of it a depression in the earth faceted with emerald hues.

It might hold the cart and nags entire, with room on all sides. As Paul walks the gold-etched boundary the facets flash and recede, and in the lowest part of it a dark red hue prevails.

Paul stops, and Magda alongside. He crouches. A broader band of gold marks the ground here, inset with shapes the size of human feet. And carved into the gold is another shape, that of a knife, or sword.

Magdalena straightens. She places a hand on his shoulder and then he hears it too.

Behind them and from out of the distant, dead forest a small, plaintive bell tolls a second time. With a strange, upward bend to its echo.

There they stood in the moonlight, like a vast army surrounding our camp, shaking their innumerable silver spears defiantly, formed all ready for an attack.

—*The Willows*
by Algernon Blackwood

24. BLOOD OF THE SYLPH

The bell tolls again for a fifth time as they near the cart. Eating from their buckets, the nags shift and nervously turn their heads at that strange, upward bend in the decaying tone.

Král is gone.

They stand there until the bell rings again. It emerges from the mountainside forest to the left of the path. Its initial tone, which sounds like small-throated bronze, is C minor, while its echo climbs most of an octave before fading into the breeze.

Simultaneously, Paul and Magda start walking toward it. A seventh time, and an eighth, it tolls, as they cross the dead grassland toward the trees. Paul wants to shout for Král; shout his name as clearly as he, by ringing the bell, is shouting theirs.

Yet the stately intervals between tolls does not suggest danger, and it's too long to suggest a summoning.

By the time he reaches the trees, with Magdalena a pace ahead of him, he's not even certain it's Král who's ringing it.

"Magda." *Slow down*, he intends to say. But as she glances back over her shoulder, smiling, he vividly recalls Magdalena in that other Brno, walking toward the linden tree.

Pavel, do you see . . .

Sinking into green and silver shadows; her white arm reaching for the *shem*; snatching it up even as the silver branches close around her.

She slows; she must, for there is no proper trail. But the tenth toll comes from ahead, and above, where the desiccated trees grow thickly. There is barely enough room for them single file, with Magdalena leading, now climbing, up through the trees, and Paul striving to hold onto the walking stick and tube. Branches arch overhead, cutting sunlight to a gray dimness, and shadows live in the leaf-mold and dried mud. His shoes compress them, compress shadows and lift a faint fine dust that smells of rot. The bell tolls.

"Magda..."

But she's hurrying ahead—where the boles are larger and the branches form interlacing archways; not a vaulted hallway of trees but a hundred hallways set one upon another in dizzying array. Between and through and among them they weave; ahead, in dim gray shadow, the mountainside grows larger. He's tiring. He struggles to catch his breath. His thighs ache at each climb yet Magda grows more nimble, her red hair like a lure that he follows amongst the trees. "Slow down, Magda."

For a final time the bell tolls and its lingering, upward-bending echo is as vivid as the initial toll, and seems to live beyond the trees just ahead.

The forest ceases. Magda steps into a clearing stippled with dead roots and Paul follows close behind her.

"Is that..."

Blue shadows dwell in the lee of a stone-roofed structure, its high narrow windows dark like brooding eyes, its leestone topped with the Byzantine cross.

The narrow, oaken postern is undisturbed, the edges sealed with moss. The air reeks of mildew. Algae stains the filigreed hasps. At the foot, beside one of the cart's lantern, is laid Král's crutch.

Magda moves up. "Is he inside?"

"Král!" The loudness of his voice startles him. He relaxes his grip on the walking stick and the Universal tube under his arm, and listens to the absolute silence of the trees.

Magdalena walks the perimeter; Paul follows. She gestures to the high dark window, also undisturbed, and at the back, which is featureless and closed, like a mausoleum, she runs her fingertips along the marble. Her shoulders shiver, she pulls her hand away. And they reach the front with only silence. No bell has tolled, yet Paul is braced for it. He glances up at the Byzantine cross.

He studies the trees; there are no pathways out there anymore. The vaulted branches have closed up, surely.

Král is not here.

She stops on the flagstone.

"Magdalena, did you dream of this, too?"

She clutches her flute case to her chest and with her free hand lifts a bronze clasp. She tugs, and pushes. Dust rises up, swirling onto her blue sleeve. "*But how did I dream of it?*" Her tone has changed. Speaking to herself. No longer giddy at the strangeness of it, she's left with fear. "*How could I?*"

"Step back."

Magda does so, holding the flute case with both hands.

"What is this place?"

He sets down the walking stick and the cardboard tube.

The smell of mildew hints of many seasons of rain, snow, sunshine. Paul heaves his shoulder against the postern. It shudders. Dust envelopes his head. Holding his breath he heaves again: it moves a few inches before grinding to a stop on broken tile. He straightens, gasps for breath.

Aware of the expansive hush of the clearing, of the moon, lonely high above the mountain peaks, he turns back to the door and once again heaves against it. This time, hinges groaning, it moves a solid meter, into darkness and stale air.

Magdalena is kneeling, her flute case beside her. Lifting the lantern, she lights it. With a last glance over his shoulder, Paul retrieves his possessions, and steps through. She follows him, the light casting his shadow across a silt-stained floor while higher up it flows over glittering hues of scarlet, cerulean, umber brown, with lichen more black than green. "Careful. The floor is slippery. Here . . . " He leans the stick and tube against the wall, and takes the lantern. The space has no remnants of benches or altar. He lifts it high. Friezes leap out from the oblong walls. Figures draped in gold robes stare across centuries. Mountains loom against vermilion skies. A yew tree lifts its branches. A glittering stream wanders a glittering forest. As Magdalena steps carefully past, he approaches the lower half of the wall and a pair of golden figures with long, serene eyes, enrapt in a forest. Paul feels the closeness of the walls. He unwinds his scarf, unbuttons his jacket.

"Cyril and Methodius," whispers Magdalena.

But she's looking at the opposite wall, and a newer frieze. There, in glittering raiments, the Byzantine brothers stand side by side. But on this wall . . . The golden, long-eyed faces possess the strangeness of those ancient portraits of Samo. These are less human than Dryads, or monsters from the Russian fairy tales his mother used to tell. He blinks. The forest of silver-gray branches behind them seems to promise an Arcimboldo revelation; something leaping out, unexpected. He looks away suddenly, not wanting to see, looks up; and there it hangs, from an ancient wood beam. A bell. As he lifts the lantern, the light swarms its dusty throat. The edges betray a hint of bronze, blackened with age. No clapper hangs within. If it had, it would be little use: one side of the bell is gone.

And Magdalena drifts along the wall, plucking at the lichen. She reveals Cyrillic characters, set along a black boundary halfway down. Or rather, not Cyrillic but *Old Church Slavonic*. He recognizes it from the Maestro's *Missa Glagolitica*.

"Look." Magdalena kneels down, beside the smaller figures of the other brothers; the lower portion of the walls is an older frieze, surely. Even the rock has a different hue, as though the top were built later, when the Byzantine cross was added. She's plucked away the lichen, baring mountain peaks of simplified green and gold. Peaks that clearly represent those above the village.

Beyond the letters, the frieze portrays a line of people. The brothers—not Cyril and Methodius, but taller with long blond hair again in glittering lineament.

The lichen patters softly on the floor as Magdalena clears it away from mountains and streams and a stag, lonely, amidst perfectly represented linden trees. She steps back, breathing through clenched teeth. The blood beats in his ears. He wonders at the connection between the two; one on the right, showing a journey; one on the left, an arrival. And if it were read from right to left . . .

The wall ends there, but perhaps continues where he had begun, on the wall opposite the door with its high narrow window. He turns about.

His lantern finds the brothers staring out from a blotches of lichen. Paul sets the lantern by his shoe and begins, like Magdalena, plucking away at the clumped, moist lichen. The tesserae feel smooth and cold to his touch. In the fainter light, shining up, details emerge with startling vividness. The mountains above them, and a bird—perhaps a hawk—flying in the fractured blue sky. A gold chalice, over Methodius's head. A sword at Cyril's side. And below, bright crimson.

Paul kneels. He brushes his hand across, obliterating the lichen which reveals a broad swath of crimson over which the Brothers are standing. A swath that leads from the mouth of a golden bowl, like that in the center of the ruins. Larger and larger as his hand sweeps over the wall, fingernails digging in.

A lake of blood.

What is this place?

Magdalena steps back from the wall.

She breaths through clenched teeth, feeling a sudden cold along her shoulders. *How could I have dreamed it? Even this. Even this picture and the way the picture moves in the light.*

All her young life, she's believed she was fated. Mummy, Papa, and most of all her sister Jina, who would comb her hair and say that it marked her as uncommon. That she was destined for something far beyond Brno.

And the voice. I remember the voice. Where is it?

My village is dead, *it said.*

When she opens her eyes, she finds Pavel crouching close to the frieze. Pavel, who is not Pavel. Whom she was drawn toward by the music in the market. And now—

It and I am made of blood. We are blood. You are blood.

Scarlet tesserae surround him. He is rapt in the task of clearing away the lichen. He doesn't even notice the folded, coarse-brown paper in its plastic wrap—*Do Not Lament*—falling from his pocket. *A decade, he'd said. All will end in a decade. War, and pogrom. The destruction of the Republic.* He does not notice when she walks toward the door, does not turn to look as she steps under the low lintel out into the cold.

What is this place? she asks, clutching her instrument case close to her. *Why did I dream of it?*

She walks across the clearing toward black trees.

My village is dead.

She'd anticipated the church but not exactly what lies in the woods. Had she? The dream was long-ago and she as a girl had dreamed many other dreams. But always the mountaintop and the linden tree and the strange pictures and the voice.

Jina, combing her hair by candlelight, always more mature and more favored in Mummy's eyes, but she would fall rapt, as she combed. *"You'll live far from here, Magda. You won't have to live on Giskrova Street, or spend your life working at the tannery like Papa. You'll be famous."* And the Maestro, that terrifying old man. *"She will be one of the great musicians of the new century, Madame!"*

But Pavel—Pavel says that only ten years hence and all will be lost. That's why he's here.

My village is dead.

And now she was leaving it behind. As she reaches the brittle dead trees she finds a path. Not quite as wide or forgiving as the path that brought them here; no. A branch jabs her shoulder, snapping off. She ducks under another, her hair is clawed back from her eyes, but yes, there is enough of a path to follow. Moonlight drizzles with luminous shadow as she moves through. She feels a measure of relief when the church is lost behind her; the church a place of death though Paul did not feel it as strongly as she. The dead woods have closed up behind her.

My village is dead.

Branches crack under her shoes. Smaller branches scratch her hands as she snaps them off and moves forward. The church is gone and the village is further gone, and ahead of her the mountainside rises toward the peaks. And she is headed along the path—toward where she should be. She feels it with a poignant rush, like her first kiss with little Pietr on Yellow Hill. The path may be no path at all, in fact, she is now certain that she has lost it if there ever was one—is making her own path through the brittle wood that gives way, even as her hands and face and neck are scratched. Because ahead of her, moonlight falls heavy. Another clearing. As she is expecting, it materializes before the tangle of branches. Another stippled field. Tangle wall

In the center sits a stone well. Dark, crumbling stone. A sickly scent. She remembers the one outside of Strektot—dating from the Hussite age, and built of granite. Said to be deeper than the distance walked from Brno to Prague. And this one is older, no higher than her knee. Approaching, she feels a moist breeze redolent of deepness and darkness; a smell like the inside of her flute; smells like metal and saliva. And now she hears the metal in the sounds, too. Like little slivers of brass tinkling one on the other. Yes, even in the moonlight she can see the green and—she breathes deeply—she smells the sap and tinge of growing things. She sinks to her knees, setting the flute case beside her. She touches the soft tendrils and the tiny leaves, then she places her hands on the cold, hard stone.

Thinking of the wide golden bowl in the center of the village, she leans forward.

Her hair falls down on both sides of her face. The strands tremble in the breeze. It lives down there, the sound. It doesn't get any louder because it's so far away. Listen. It speaks.

Magdalena smiles. She feels the green expanse basking in the moonlight, and the silvery beats, like the agitated dreams of minerals.

Then the young woman is standing beside her.

Her legs are bare. Her peasant dress riffles in the breeze. She smells of iron. She reaches down for Magdalena and speaks in a low, murmurous voice.

A lake of blood. It covers the wall from side to side.

Paul pulls his hand away from the last of the frieze, then clenches it in a fist to stop the shaking.

Rising from the banks of the lake are linden trees, wisped at the tip like green flames. And behind the linden, the same forest of silver-gray branches that extends above, near the gold, long-eyed figures. Yet the forest is not a forest; the limbs are the gnarled limbs of a figure. Paul sits back, follows the form up the wall, a towering figure that requires hundreds of tesserae to portray, a figure shaped like a talisman of convolute branches, its arms unnaturally long, its neck a bundle of cord, its face without eyes and only a huge, gaping maw that hints of decay and destruction. This behind the golden, long-eyed figures. The Arcimboldo image he had feared would leap out at him.

And below the lake—

He moves to where the wall meets the floor. The mold and slime is not so thick there; the lantern light shines on more tesserae, blood-red. The frieze continues on the floor. Paul straightens onto his knees, then stands up. He begins using the heels of his shoe to scrape off the sediment. With each passing a swath of image is uncovered. Heart beating in his throat, he kneels once more and sweeps away the clumps of lichen and mold and dirt. The lake of blood surrounds two long, narrow rectangles the length of the floor, bordered with elaborate design.

His chest grows cold. Not a church, but a crypt. He kneels upon it. And moreover, glancing around, he finds himself alone. "Magda?"

Moonlight shines through the doorway. Beyond, framed in the oblong door, the empty clearing.

Paul stands up. He drops his walking stick, its echoing clatter ricochets from wall to wall and does not quite die away. From out of the sound emerges the lonely timbre of a flute, rising and falling in a leaping, swirling melody.

The floor shifts beneath him—he falls to the ground, the lantern tipping over, the light swelling up and the friezes sparkling, much as the doorway—which Paul now sees on its side, his head lying helplessly against the crypt tiles—is flickering with light. He looks away. He forces his eyes to the frieze and the unearthly creature, its mouth writhing in the strange radiance. A bird flick-flying through the vermilion skies, the linden boughs twisting as moonlight stutters in the doorway—moonlight and sunlight—as Magdalena's flute reels through the melody, fierce and sharp and unrelenting, the church pitching like a storm-tossed ship.

He tries to shout her name but cannot. Cannot form words. Cannot close his mouth for what's inside it. A blackness writhing like the creature's.

Two of them, one inside the other. Prostrate, unable to move, even as he tries to remember his name.

Pavel.

He struggles to speak it. Then merely to think it, entirely.

Pavel H—.

He spits blood, feels it drying on his lips and chin, as the moonlight bathes the forest.

Pavel Haas.

When he can stand—dizzy, nauseous, with the tinnitus making every step a burden—he approaches the door.

Sunlight streams through. A warm breeze.

Magdalena's garland trembles beside the door.

"*Mmmmgda.*" He struggles to speak. Fighting the urge to vomit, he braces himself against the ancient wood of the door. Sunlight in the clearing, and brittle, leafless growth crowded beyond, under a blue and cloudy sky. Mountains, clear of snow, rise up sharply.

He staggers outside. Unbelieving of the warmth and the feel of sunlight on his face. He walks into the clearing. He finds his balance. He straightens his shoulders and breaths deeply. His foot does not pain him.

"Magdalena!" His voice echoes with the strength of two.

The breeze sloughs through the distant peaks. He tastes metal. Turning, he gazes up at the mausoleum's lonely front.

Overhead, a hawk soars in the blue sky.

"Pavel?" She appears around the corner. Her face and hands are bloody with scratches, but she appears unharmed.

"Magdalena." He blinks, unbelieving. She wears a garland of green leaves. "What . . . what happened."

She smiles, and takes his hand. "A *decade*."

The cart sits where they left it. All that remains of the nags are bones and hide.

She leads him to a fount of fresh water that revives him. They search the cart for anything they can use. A jar of jam-pudding and one of peaches are still good, the Austrian army canteens are intact but empty. They eat, then take the canteens and fill them from the stream.

He notes the blood beneath her skin; the green tinge to her fingernails.

And they walk. He doubts at first whether they can make it, but finds his energy returning. At worst, his Bata shoes have shrunk. They pain him after the first eight hours, but even then there's no urgent need to stop. He doesn't miss his satchel, yet is pained at the loss of his Terezin manuscript, and comforted to have the Universal tube and its contents, intact.

She refuses to tell him more about what's happened. She spends long moments staring at him. She tells him, with that eerie confidence, that they will make it out of the mountains alive.

By moonlight, they climb the escarpment toward the summit. In the swirling mist, more than once, he sees the form of a man with two legs hovering at a distance, with a dog at his side.

The next morning at the summit, they wonder at the mountainous landscape stretching out to the horizon. With little rest they descend. Paul, drinking long draughts of the cool, clear water from the canteens, believes that they soon will be dead. They walk through the day, pausing only for brief periods. On the morning of the second day, as sunlight spears across rolling green hills, they spy a pickup truck parked by the roadside below, its vintage surely closer to 1940 than 1928. Emblazoned on the door is *Slavonic Geological Survey*. Not far away they find the surveyors beside a lone anthracite spire, measuring it with a battery of equipment.

By evening they have arrived back at the railroad tracks and the geologist's base camp, in late May, in 1938.

ONE: WHITE MOUNTAIN

"Speech melody calls for a Czech in the bosom of his land; it calls for his life, rolling through the centuries with equal sorrow and harshness."

—Leos J——

25. A PRAYER FOR PEACE

The headline in the *Lidové noviny*, date 23 May, reads *"MASARYK'S REIGN WILL CONTINUE, PROMISES BENES."*

Will *continue?*

Astounded—so much so that he fails to thank the train inspector for fetching him the newspaper—Paul returns to a photograph of an aged, yet hale Masaryk, captioned, *The President in February, before falling ill."* Then, in the faltering sunlight, he reads, *"Though President Tomáš Garrigue Masaryk has remained in a comatose state for an entire month, Vice President Benes announced today from Parliament that he would continue to fend off efforts to remove his superior from office—"*

Magda, at his elbow, whispers, "He's still alive?"

"—quoting Dr. Ales from the Prague Hospital that 'Masaryk's condition is grave but not vegetative, and though induced by diabetes it cannot be said to be permanent."

"What does it say, Paul?" Her schoolgirl's coat is on the seat beside her, over her green-stained flute case. Her sleeves are rolled up, her forearm laid on the sill in sunlight. She has drunk her fifth glass of water which the inspector was kind enough to bring.

He reads her the article. It goes on to say that the strongest opponent to Masaryk is Conrad Henlein—a notorious name to Paul, the leader of the Borderland *Sudetendeutsche Partei* and the *de facto* head of the local Nazis after the Germans took Austria in the bloodless *Anschluss*.

Dr. Klenz—the geologist who drove them into the village of Strenhov—could tell Paul little about current events, other than the earthquakes and the odd geological formations that had been thrusting up along new fault lines. The one near Strenhov was the furthest east yet discovered, though many had appeared between Prague and Brno. The rock was not sedimentary and seemingly alien to the geological crust of the countryside.

"Brno's where most of us are," Klenz had said. "You headed back there?"

"Yes, Dr. Klenz."

And the man's eyes had softened. "I envy you that, Mr. Arepo."

At Polda, fifty kilometers out from Brno, Paul disembarks to buy a recent newspaper.

At this early morning hour, the village square facing the train tracks is swarming with demonstrators. Whistles keen, voices shout epithets, yet none is distinct enough for Paul to understand. Even the placards, lifting and swaying above the heads of young men, cannot be clearly seen.

As he makes his way along the edges of the crowd, under bright lamplight, Paul spies a kiosk and a row of newspapers. Some of those in the square are clearly waiting to board the train, but the railway employees are holding them back for the moment.

A scuffle breaks out behind him. In the kiosk, an elderly woman with gray-and-ginger-hair leans over her wares, anger causing her plump cheeks to spasm. "*Hooligans!*" she shouts, then seeing the koruna in Paul's hand says, "Bless you, sir, yes. A paper?"

She hands him the *Lidové noviny*, dated May 14, 1938.

SUDETEN CRISIS GROWS

In Karlsbad, Konrad Henlein demands Masaryk be removed from office

Paul strives to catch a glimpse of the scuffle, but the smoke from the engine rushes across the platform. The paper riffles in his hands. "How long has it been going on?"

"Only this morning. They swarmed in. Both sides. I'll be glad to see them go!" She spits.

"SdP?" asks Paul.

She sneers, revealing brown stained teeth. "Yes, and *KB. Völkisch scum.*"

He bids her good day, then turns and hurries back along the edges of the crowd, eager to be aboard. But the crowd has grown unruly.

Metal strikes the cobblestones. Somewhere within the suddenly surging crowd a placard floats up, a black-and-white photomontage in the style of 9forces. Konrad Henlein's face divided in half, with a donkey's hind-end in the middle. As it bobs above the crowd a beer bottle flies across and smashes in the square behind them. Another placard shows a welter of WW1 Tanks and statues from the Charles Bridge; it is striving to stay above the crowd while hands tear at it, then something strikes it.

Paul squints against the smoke. He's ducking left and hurrying along the track when a young, blond man with sharp cheekbones materializes out of the crowd. He stalks alongside, a dangerous gleam in his eyes, the ends of a black armband twirling in the breeze. "*Juden!*" Blood runs from his ear.

Paul sees the wink of the knife a moment before it strikes. His attacker—reeking of gin and sweat—is pressed against him, growling in his ear. Paul twists back, feeling the bite of the blade on his right hand, against the newspaper. Without conscious thought he swings with his left hand, catches the youth on the jaw and sends him sprawling. Shards of a broken blade fall on the cobblestones at his feet. Then a hand grabs Paul's shoulder. "Here!" It's the inspector, rushing him toward the stairs, up into the train.

"Sir, are you harmed?"

Paul, stunned, collapses against the rail. The inspector is lifting the paper. It had been folded in thirds, and the edge is tattered and torn and smeared with blood.

"Your hand." His knuckles, apparently. Paul feels no pain. Beyond the staircase the crowd is a distant din of shouts and bright movement. The inspector ushers him fully into the car and closes the door.

Paul flexes his right hand. The cut is minimal. The knife had apparently impacted the newspaper and glanced his left hand, which now throbs at the knuckles. Though stunned, he decides he is entirely unharmed. Indeed, very lucky.

"You got the better, sir. Knocked him out cold."

He draws a deep breath, feeling a surge of elation. Adrenaline causes his heart to pound fiercely. He manages, "In my youth, I was often mistaken for a boxer."

"I can see why, sir. Don't worry, you won't be bothered by them. They're being restricted to the last cars."

Unbelieving, Paul turns back to the village square beyond the window. "They're coming with us?"

"Yes. To Brno."

Paul presses his hand on the handkerchief the inspector has offered. "Why Brno?"

He barely catches the other man's smile. "They say Masaryk's there, sir."

Magdalena stands up as he approaches. She notices the bandage the inspector applied. "Are you hurt?"

He lifts the newspaper. "The newspaper cushioned the blow."

She looks a little wonderingly at him as he sits down; looks at him precisely as he had looked at her, during the long hours of their walk from the mountain peak.

"Who are they?"

Peering out the window, he tries to find the youth he struck, but all that remains are the fragments of the knife blade on the cobblestone. "Youths," he says. "9forces rabble and Borderlander rabble, letting out some aggression." He fails at a flippant tone. He sits and unfolds the newspaper, pulling away the cut portion with his blood on it. "No doubt there's more to learn in the paper."

She sits in the window corner of her bench, leaning her forehead against the glass, looking out at pine trees and distant mountains. "How long. Until Brno?"

"Due to arrive at noon." He unfolds the newspaper.

SUDETEN CRISIS GROWS

In Karlsbad, Konrad Henlein demands Masaryk be removed from office

A photograph of Henlein, dapper in his uniform, recalls the parody in the 9forces collage. He hopes they managed to bring it—untorn—onto the train. He no longer hears the policeman's whistle or the thrum of an angry crowd. They have grown sedate, each group sent to its own carriage. The train shudders. Steam swirls.

Riots suppressed throughout Brno

Masaryk's location in the city unknown

The woman at the kiosk has her wish: the rabble has departed Berenska.

Visitors from 18 countries descend on city

Security TIGHTENED for upcoming concert

In the bottom corner of the page he spies a boxed article. A shiver descends his spine.

A PRAYER FOR PEACE by K. Capek

I have always welcomed the warm weather and with it the dizzying invasion of flowering gentian, delphiniums, asters, phlox, roses, chrysanthemums, centaurea; and never more so than now, in these dark hours. On my lawn I have a cedar of Lebanon twice as tall as I am: I greet it as a friend.

Yet I write this from Brno. Here, in this little capital of Moravia, in our little Czechoslovak Republic, we have attracted many great entities these last tumultuous months, both human and perennial. Some we greet with great huzzahs and claps on the back, some with an eye toward their strange tubers and towering blossoms, while others—a troublesome minority of the human breed—we wish to show the door.

But my target is not entirely the expected one. Let me say what the Old Gentleman would say himself, were he able: Violence cannot be tolerated in an enlightened Republic. Neither can intolerance be tolerated. *Those who seek to put the marksman's target squarely between the eyes of the Borderlanders are mistaken. Yes, they have been partly to blame for riling the calmness of this little town. Yes, they have sinister grievances—* misguided *grievances I believe. But we must also keep in our crosshairs any group—any* Czechoslovak *group—which seeks violence on the other. Not in our little town. Not in enlightened Republic.*

These are miraculous and terrifying times. The earth itself jumps and quivers, yielding solemn stone pronouncements. Geologists are giddy with delight, as am I! What manner of rock is this, and what great movements in the sedimentary layer allowed its birth?

Some, like our friends the 9forces, *treat the panorama of newborn rock with sardonic irony: a message of warning from mother earth about the motherland, a reaction to the Anschluss. Others, the misguided SdP youth—as Czech as you and I—have been lured by the* Kameradschaftsbund *with its romantic Germanic mysticism, a* Volkisch *fever dream that turns its back on the realities that will greet a freed Sudetenland. 9forces, Kameradschaftsbund: youths all. And youths should be allowed to make mistakes. But in these crucial and dire times, mistakes can be fatal. Sudetenland, dug up entire from our Republic, would be transplanted in the diseased soil of a new Pan-German Empire. Freedom from the Republic? No, tyranny under a dictator. And the Republic is stronger with Sudetenland as our arm. We will not give up the idea of solving the differences between our peoples. T.G.M. would not—and will not—give up. And I, born and bred in those lands, know with utter certainty that they belong to us and we to them.*

We can allow thoughtful discourse in our little city, but not the sorts of riots that have plagued our town this past week, violence stamped on both sides of the coin. Spurred on by the rascal Henlein and the Dictator in Berlin, our Sudeten problem has become the Sudeten Crisis. Our only consolation is that the world is taking notice, drawn as much by the geological wonders as the political perils.

And how marvelous, and terrifying, that an upcoming concert event in which I am intractably involved, should be seen as a looming matchstick, waiting to be set afire.

Let us pray for President Dr. Masaryk's swift recovery. Let us pray for peace in our little town, in our little Republic, the peace of small things. Let us weave a spell of kindness and serenity around the venerable facade of our Theater on the Ramparts.

Paul lowers the paper. Countryside rolls past; Magdalena's head is tipped against her folded hands and the window; her eyes are closed. He gives himself over to the lull of inevitable motion. Brno an hour away and he and they, drawn to it.

WILD GROWTH BAFFLES HORTICULTURALISTS reads the headline, and the article catalogs the various outbursts over Brno, centering mostly in the city center and around Špilberk Hill.

At the bottom of the page, announcements proclaim a wealth of events at the Beseda house, including a piano recital by "young Gideon Klein, direct from Prague, in a program of Brno's great composers."

Gideon Klein.

Paul straightens. Another shiver.

Gideon Klein, direct from Prague.

He's looking past the newspaper at the plain black-and-white wrapper of an LP. *Music from Theresienstadt, 1941-1944. Paul Haas/ Hollywood Symphony Orchestra, Ken Darby, Hollywood Bowl Chorale and Soloists.* And on the back, a photograph of sardonic, handsome Gideon Klein, seated behind a concert grand.

My mitzvah.

He sees Herr Professor on the balcony in Brentwood, huddled near the umbrella-shaded table, lifting a hand in farewell.

"Do you trust me, Herr Haas?"

On the next page, an article proclaims that the British ambassador will be arriving in Brno today, along with his American counterpart, adding, *For the concert*. Recalling the headline about security tightening for the concert, and the remark in Karel's feuilleton about the concert and the lit match, Paul reads ahead for answers but finds none in the article; nor the next, regarding the Agrarian Party's dissolution.

Yet the answer has been in his periphery the entire time, at the bottom of the page.

It seizes his eyes. It shakes him harder than the train.

"Boura shook himself and rose. It went on snowing more thickly, more steadily, and the trampled field with the large footprint ... was disappearing under a new layer of snow. 'I won't let go of it,' said the snow-covered man. 'The footprint that is no more and will not be,' Boura finished the thought, and they set off on their separate routes, in opposite directions."

—*The Footprint* by Karel Čapek

26. THE BEAUTIFUL ROSALINDA

"*J*anáček*,*" Paul whispers. "The Maestro *Janáček* is alive."

He remembers a dream, a nightmare, of suffocation; struggling to speak his own name and spitting the wet paper of a torn *shem* on the pavement.

Janáček.

Why does it feel so strange to whisper it?

With the sunlit hills slipping past the window, Magda drinks a cup of soda water. "The Maestro must be eighty years old."

"Eighty-one."

"And are they going to go ahead with the premiere if there's violence?"

He recalls what the train inspector had said, before Magdalena awoke. "*I'm not a fan of opera, sir, and I bet most on this train aren't. But we're damned sure following this one.*"

Magdalena ponders; demure in the blue schoolgirl coat, the red hair tied tight behind her head. Solemn eyes, reminiscent of Miss Jean Simmons, a girl in London yet to be greeted by the Blitz.

"Look," she whispers.

In the strong sunlight, a spiny outcropping of rock is draped in 9forces posters.

As they reach Terna, and the suburbs of Brno, the landscape surges with green and silver foliage. At first, pressing his forehead to the warm glass, he thinks it part of the pine forest encroaching on the town. Yet these are not the vertical chevrons of pine but the sprawling horizontal of alien ivy. Church steeples rise from it. Roadways, bared like canyons. This is not the violent aggression familiar to him, but a bucolic settlement of greenery. How long had it taken to advance? How many weeks or months before the locals accepted it into their streets, striving only to keep it back from the doors and roadways?

Sitting back, he finds Magdalena pressing her hand to the window. The flute case nearly slides from her lap, unnoticed, but Paul leans across and takes it.

"What do you think of it, Magda?"

"*It's beautiful.*" Her whisper fogs the glass.

The train slows. On the platform a dozen or so young men—in the blue jackets of 9forces—mill about under the nervous watch of a dozen or so police officers. The conductor steps down from the cabin behind them and begins to direct them, even as cheers erupt from the windows and policemen scan the cars further down, jerking and gesturing with their sticks. Boarding is swift; the 9forces are accepted into their cabin, which resounds with cheers. The policemen relax their shoulders; the conductor bounds back on board the train.

Beyond, at the edge of the village square, under brilliant hurricane lamps, two men hack the undergrowth with machetes.

His first glimpse of Brno is the green-stained spires of the Peter and Paul.

Paul tugs the snap brim low on his head, then holds Magdalena's hand as they depart the train into the crowd. Steam rises and obscures the length of the platform. Voices shout welcomes in French, English, German. As they cross toward the long, low building figures rise and fade into the steam and the smoke; he hears rowdy taunts; but there will be no riot. At least not here, on the platform.

Placards and montages float down from the carriages, held aloft by invisible young men, met by similar placards and montages by those waiting on the platform, interrupted by solitary swastikas and Sudeten flags. Yet not clashing.

As the steam clears and the old, young, peasant and cosmopolitan head toward the Train station proper, and the cabs and trams beyond, the presence of Authority becomes apparent. Policemen with hard helmets and white sticks lurk in the doorways. Phalanxes of soldiers in the crisp blue and gold of the Parliamentary Guard stand at attention, and the troublemakers from the train nod and smile as they make their way peacefully to the cobblestoned streets.

Cabs, startling in their modern vintage of bulbous and shiny black, purr at the curb. From many points, radios—wirelesses—transmit the announcer of Radio Brno, who announces that Solnici Street shall be closed off from 4 p.m. to sunrise. Trams fill up under the glare of arc lights: a newsreel crew in suspiciously American garb—vests and wide trousers—a suspicion confirmed as Paul nears them and hears, in bracing vividness, the New York accents of a cameraman and the sound boom operator.

He pulls Magdalena past them. Scanning the crowd of new arrivals for familiar faces, wanting to keep to the shadows; wanting to reveal himself to the Americans.

Several streets over a German voice hectors over amplification. The SdP boys hurry off in that direction. A booming whistle from the north: another train arriving, no doubt from Prague.

As they follow Orli Street he sees no sign of wild growth except in the gutters. Green stalks longer than crabgrass in which cigarette and cigar wrappers are caught, fluttering. Farther on the ivy becomes apparent on the buildings. He smells the loam, faintly, under the stronger stench of gasoline and ozone.

Špilberk Hill lurks behind the downtown clutter. The red-roofed castle is lit by spotlights which catch a Czechoslovakian flag.

"Where do we go, Paul?"

He lets go of her hand and tugs his hat brim lower over his eyes. "Are you hungry?"

"I can't go home." Something in the tone of her voice immensely sad to hear; the voice of another far traveler.

He's about to say, *Let's go to the theater*, when he spies a short, slender man in black, wielding a cane—Max Brod on the other side of the street, chatting with a woman and a Parliamentary guard. But of course he'd be here, to attend the concert for the Maestro's benefit.

Startled, he slows, the crowd surging around him, cabs rumbling past. Paul cannot help but think of *The Beautiful Rosalinda*. And when he turns back to Magdalena she's not there.

"Magda?"

He looks left and right, then hurries forward. Men and women and guards and policemen on the move, but no splash of red hair. Her hair had been hidden, of course, by her hat and the collar of her coat, and the only blue he can see belongs to the Parliamentary guards. Resisting the urge to shout her name, he chooses the most likely direction—north, to the theater—reassuring himself that she is not a stranger here, not in danger. She will come to the theater, eventually.

He stares down at his shoes, seeking solace in that thought, his fingers flicking, gripping into fists.

I did not drag her along with me to the village. I did not seek her out. She attached herself to me. She felt the flux and flow of Time.

She had to go.

She is here. She is safe.

Here, with most of Prague's security to protect the ailing President, surely she will continue to be safe.

Until then, I must go. I must find Karel and Josef. And the Maestro.

I must see the Theater on the Ramparts.

Swathes of cyclone fencing surround Malinovského Square. Beyond, the theater lifts its familiar Grecian facade, the statues atop the lintel floating serene over the pillared columns. Only as he draws closer does he see the sooty stains on the white pilaster, the boarded up window in the upper floor.

A banner strung above the portico proclaims:

> WHITE MOUNTAIN
> JANÁČEK/ČAPEK
> STARTS MAY 15

The buildings opposite the theater are dark. Here, the damage is more apparent. Many windows are boarded up, walls painted over with whitewash through which, ghost-like, swastika's glower. Though the theater is alight, and the front doors open, the square is empty. Tonight, Brno is active elsewhere; in the Cabbage Market, surely, where the German voice, fainter, continues hectoring the air; and the 9forces perhaps at the base of Špilberk, shepherded by the police and the army.

Paul slows. Hands in his pockets, he studies the Parliamentary guards who stand, smoking, in their crisp blue uniforms; uniforms commissioned by Masaryk from Alfons Mucha himself, who delivered a dash of fairy tale along with fustian.

Across Malinovského, a man approaches struggling under a bobbing thatch of alien greenery; strange fringed leaves scattered with yellow dots. He wears overalls and boots, with an unlit cigar dangling from his lips. Paul doesn't recognize him but sees him for what he is: a stagehand, and so he walks towards the man and smiles and offers to help him carry the fronds inside. The man, eyeing Paul, nods, the cigar jutting up and down as he hands over half his burden. The stalks are heavy, the broad leaves catching the wind, and stinking slightly of resin.

"Thanks," says the man, and together they approach the guards, who barely look up from their cigarettes.

Paul climbs the stairs with another of those misplaced pangs of homesickness; this time for a much older Brno and a production of *R*.

U. R. The facade looks the same but for a darker patina to the columns, and the pair of Parliamentary guards just inside the door. These two are not smoking, are attentive, and studying both Paul and the stagehand.

"For Mr. Čapek," says the stagehand.

"Okay, Pietr." The guard nods. Then, "Know this guy?"

Pietr slows, and around his cigar says, "No."

The second guard holds up a stick. "Who are you?"

"He just came along and took them," says Pietr.

"Let me see your papers." The first guard steps close to Paul, eyeing his torn suitcoat and bandaged hand.

"Please, I need to see Mr. Čapek. Josef. Tell him Paul Arepo is here."

"You don't have papers?"

"Keep your hands out of your pockets." The second guard steps closer.

The greensman, bustling off across the green and gold tiles of the atrium, snipes, "Arrest him."

"Why did you try to break in here?" asks the first guard.

And before Paul can reply, a voice echoes down the distant stairway. "There they are. Almost too late."

"Josef!"

"Step outside," says the first guard.

"Josef!"

Stout, and forty-one years old, in gabardine and ivory brogues, adjusting tortoise shell glasses that are no longer new, Josef says, "Huh?" He takes one of the fronds and weighs it appreciatively.

"Do you know this man, Mr. Čapek?"

"Well, I'm not sure, if it's a delivery . . . " Josef freezes on the stairs, his mouth half-open. "Is that . . . are you . . . oh my."

"Hello, Josef."

Josef Čapek continues down. The stagehand and his green burden climb past him, while Josef descends, faster. "Is that you? Pavel?"

"He called himself Paul Arepo, Mr. Čapek."

"Yes. Yes. That is his name, too. Certainly a surprise, yes. Please, gentleman, let him inside. This is the man who inspired our little operatic evening."

"Ah, the beautiful land, the beloved land, his cradle and his grave, his mother, the only land, the land given him as his birthright, the broad land, the only land, the blood of her son flows over her."

—*May* by Karel Hynek Macha

27. WRITTEN IN FIRE

And as Josef comes close his face loses its composure, eyes widening, cheek twitching, mouth opening to speak. He stops. Behind the large glasses his eyes roam Paul's face and his clothes and his hands clutching the satchel, and a moment later the strange frond—forgotten—begins to tilt in his arms. Paul reaches for it.

"Yes, Josef. It's good to see you."

The artist's brow furrows. He takes hold of the branch once more and recovers his poise, nodding once, reaching with his free hand to the paint brushes sticking out of his breast pocket. "Well. Indeed. I was just telling K―― these are extraordinary times."

Discomforted by Josef gaze—as though he's seeing more there than he can recognize—Paul steps back and pretends to take stock of the theater's lobby; then, in a swoon of gold and green, under a great pennant now being hoisted into place by two workmen on ladders—the Czech tricolor—his interest becomes genuine. He falls back through time, if only in his mind. He is fourteen, here with Uncle Michael to see *The Dogheads*; the opera by Kovarovic less memorable than the Deutsche Stadt-Theater's statuary and the breadth of the lobby with its high windows and its carmine-scalloped staircase. And he is sixteen, invited by the Maestro Janáček to a performance of *Her Stepdaughter*, seeking out the great man in the darkest corner of the theater—"*Young Pavel, I am hiding. Do not reveal me, please.*" He is thirty-one, and in rehearsal for *Rossum's Universal Robots,* on the night that Karel and Josef give their blessings to a future *Insect Play.*

Beyond the tricolor flag, workmen are waxing the floor, wiping the mirrored pillars, polishing the statues of Calliope at the base of the staircase. And from above, at the top of the grand staircase, men in the uniforms of Czech radio are lugging boxy equipment and cables into the theater.

Doors opening, closing, and from somewhere within comes the chaotic sounds of an orchestra tuning up.

Paul whispers, "*Is the Maestro here?*"

Josef chuckles. "He fled the scene two days ago. Hasn't returned." Studying Paul's profile, until Paul faces him directly, Josef adds, "He sends his amanuensis from the Grecian villa with corrections, but otherwise he says he's done with it."

Josef begins to walk across the green-and-gold parquet tiles. He gestures with the fronds.

Paul follows. "And how is he, Josef?"

"Still a crank. An elderly crank, a bit like Prospero, or perhaps Lear—if Lear were a Lachian groundskeeper. Hmmm?" Josef begins to slowly climb, shifting the fronds over his shoulder like a workman shouldering a shovel. "It's charming really. He'd had the wind out of his sails since that immortal beloved of his—that Kamila—proved so very mortal. Said he'd never write another opera. Spent his time writing those baffling feuilletons. But the Naciste really riled him up. Our good sis Helena suggested he work again with Karel, and K. had just the strangest story that lit a fire under him. Crank recovered."

Nearing the landing and the double doors leading into the atrium Paul says, "Where is Karel?"

"He's off visiting Masaryk and worrying about his speech tonight—on live radio, you understand, right before the performance."

"Where—"

"And Masaryk's location is a state secret." As he reaches the top, Josef halts. He gathers his breath. "Paul. So you went here to Brno. Back then, in 1928. And what did you find?"

Distracted by a choir of cellos emerging from the din of instruments—cohering with a jittery phrase that is unmistakably the Maestro's—Paul thinks for a moment. "I found a map, Josef. And someone to help me."

"And you've . . . " Josef tears his glance away from Paul's face. "You've gone from nothing to nothing."

Paul nods. "My path does not pass through places. It is a period of time, a tension in time, or rather simply a state."

Josef smiles. "Extraordinary. Don't know how we'll explain you to anybody—K. most of all. Luckily, there's a . . . change in your features, isn't there?"

Paul says nothing.

"Well." Josef blinks, and seems to become more alert. "Well, let's be on. I must deliver these, and see to a few niggling details." He starts walking. They pause at the double doors as the radio men lug in more cable, but Paul is listening and not looking; is hearing the orchestral warm-up from which leap, with vivid profile, the Maestro's familiar tongue. Yet somehow sharper, almost frightening in its intensity.

"Doing a rather good job, she is," says Josef. "Young Miss Kaprálová. Not too long out of the Conservatory, and someone that the elderly crank has—shall we say—warmed to?"

At Josef's approach, the guard lifts a hand. "That cutting, sir. I don't think we can allow it in the theater."

"Preposterous." Josef shakes it. "It's quite dead and the ideal color for the underwater city."

The guard attempts to muster a response, then his epauletted shoulders straighten. "Very well, sir."

"Good. Come inside, Paul. Let's show you what we have in store."

Ahead, through the pilasters surrounding the main floor, the stage glows luminous and strange.

A hanging scrim of midnight blue caps a background of pale white forming the top of a triangle, or the negative image of a mountain; behind and in front hang smaller partitions of black and silver over a wide and low expanse of rich vermilion. Intruding on the solemn strangeness of Josef's design, stagehands mill about the stage, shifting free-standing curtains cut like giant blades of saffron grass. Closer, in the empty, expectant seats, two women push noisy vacuums; in the boxes to the right and left workers are polishing the caryatids and statuary and the Czech tricolor bunting is being hung from the Presidential box.

But Paul's attention settles on the long railing below the stage, and the pit. Voices lift up, and the occasional sawing of a cello.

"Here." Beside him, Josef holds up a plastic envelope containing a small coin. The Roosevelt dime from 1935. "It's no longer of shocking vintage, of course." He turns it this way and that. "Yet how strange to see that year approach and then fade, and now," he shrugs, offering a plaintive smile, "it's just an old American dime." Noise from the stage draws his attention. Josef squints, adjusts his glasses and seems to take in the scenery anew. "I have a sickening feeling in my gut. I thought it was the scenery but perhaps it's everything else." Carefully, he stows the coin in his wallet and replaces the wallet in his pocket.

"It's a beautiful design, Josef."

"Yes, it is rather." Josef begins to walk the aisle with Paul alongside. To the right and left, hovering at the edges of the auditorium, lurk the fanciful guards in their fairy tale outfits as well as men in dark suits with revolvers clearly bulging in their suit pockets—the state security detail, perhaps. "To say I found the project inspiring . . . well, that hits below the mark a little. The story dates back to our earliest days, you know. Karel invented it one memorable evening, 1918, just after the founding of the Republic. And now . . . " Josef slows once more. "Well, it's become more than it should be. A political event. Everything, all the luminal strangeness of these past years—as the nightmare became real in our local neighborhood and in all of Europe—everything seems to be leading to this evening. And, well, you're appearance. I suppose I was anticipating something. I have to admit I'm frightened."

"So am I, Josef."

"No. No, you have the look of someone who knows the secrets, Paul. You always did."

Paul doesn't know how to respond to that, so he focuses on the pit; on technicians hanging microphones on stands. Through the rails he glimpses the conductor atop the podium. She has a bobbed haircut and her arm, lifting into view, is slender.

In the world he had left behind, Vítězslava Kaprálová had been the first female graduate of the Conservatory. By this year she had moved to Prague. Her *Military Sinfonietta*—in homage to the late Maestro's own identically titled work—had been a huge hit in Prague and London, where she'd conducted the Philharmonic to rave reviews. After the war began, in Paris, she had died of tuberculosis.

But here she is, not working in homage to the Maestro, but *with* him.

"Can we check the levels, Maestro Kaprálová," says a radio technician onstage.

She nods. "Yes. Did everyone hear that?" Her voice is enthusiastic, bright with a nervous undertone. "Let's try the new pages. The opening."

Pages rustle in the pit. Voices murmur. Closer, Paul begins to grasp the size of the orchestra. Sixty musicians, at least.

Approaching the second row, Paul feels everything fade. He's remembering the theater as it had been in another time, the *Hansel and Gretel* stage scenery, the old man Hottinger standing amidst the fairy tale forest. The pit where he and Josef, Karel, Magda, Rudolf and Elizabet and the others had huddled, uncertain, in that terrifying future; where the stave flower had been folded, and the transformation occurred.

"Figure one. From the top. Can we have silence in the auditorium?" She says, louder, to someone in the warrens below the stage, "Can we have the vacuum cleaners turned off?" There is a smile in her voice. "Play the pianissimo as softly as you can. We're going to test this rig out."

The technician grins. "Can't play softly enough." Then, after a chat with a colleague standing incongruously amid the wide vermilion sea, he says, "One moment for the transformer to heat up."

"Of course."

A moment later a young man rushes from backstage and announces the order to the seats; the ladies turn off their cleaners. Microphones are lowered once more.

"Josef," Paul says softly. "What was the Maestro's inspiration?"

He smiles. "*You*, of course."

"Ready?" Maestro Kaprálová raises her baton. "From the top, figure one, please."

Josef mutters, "I just hope the theater is still standing tomorrow."

From the depths, and distant, the trombones intone a soft and broken motif, divided left and right, with the low strings providing blocks of chordal background, dark as the midnight blue in Josef's backdrop, modulating in ponderous, crazed, yet muted, counterpoint. Shaped by Maestro Kaprálová's close and careful gestures, her right palm patting the air as though to lower the sound physically by sheer will, then—with the baton in her right hand striking at the slumbering giant—the trombone motif grows larger, faster, its patchwork driven into brighter and higher realms with bright piccolos and nervous violins in the upper registers.

And Paul is startled by the breadth of this live music, by the Maestro's voice so suddenly and strangely conjured before him, both entirely familiar and foreign. He grasps a recognizable melody in the lower strata of the music, the Hussite hymn *Ye Who Are the Soldiers of God* lifting up the crazed patchwork then vanishing, as the orchestra launches into a cheerful chorale bathed in Moravian folk modes—an outburst which surely signals the raising of the curtain in the first act—and Maestro Kaprálová, with fierce gestures from her slender arms, draws the music larger and larger into the auditorium.

Then extinguishes it by lowering her arms.

"That opening was inspired by a whirlwind," says Josef, climbing the stairs at the edge of the stage. The frond sways over his head. "Or so he likes to say at every chance. Struck in olden times here in Brno."

The technicians are back at work with microphones, the musicians are chatting and tuning their instruments while young miss Kaprálová pores over the score. In the flies, the stage is cluttered with pieces of scenery. The group of men and women hail Josef; he hands the frond off to nervous glances, ordering that it be placed in the "third act underwater grotto affair," then Josef leads Paul into the backstage area. Nobody takes notice of Paul and Josef walking into the wings, past fantastical hanging backdrops that reek of wet turpentine, past more of the fairy tale guards and somber security men, under ropes and stays, around stacks of radio equipment that hum with irritation, past the odd bit of furniture—a wooden table, quite ordinary but for its absurdly long legs, laden with beer mugs and plates of cold sauerkraut and sausage; a ziggurat of mossy green rock encrusted with barnacles the size of biscuits; a shop window out of old Prague, with fanciful letters reading Vikarka Inn—to the more mundane clutter of the extreme backstage, where Josef's designs hang from corkboards and the long low tables are crowded with paint brushes and knives and hammers.

"Will everything be ready on time, Josef?"

He chuckles. "We're being broadcast around the world, so we have little choice in the matter. Luckily, the world will only hear, not see."

"Mr. Čapek?" An underling advances with a host of questions.

"Paul, I shall return. In the meantime, you might want to read the *Times* of New York there." Tugging at his lower lip, Josef wanders back onto the stage.

Paul approaches the magazines and newspapers at the edge of the table; *Paris Match*, with a cover painting of Karel and Josef, and a copy of the *New York Times* dated a week earlier, folded open to a photograph of the Maestro.

His great thatch of white hair is no longer so great, but he still possesses the sparkling eyes and the tubby figure, and wears the same familiar tweed coat and tie. He's posed in the corner of his garden, beneath fronds of alien origin.

JANÁČEK'S *WHITE MOUNTAIN* WRITTEN IN FIRE
The Czechoslovak composer's new opera set to premiere in Brno

by Olin Downes

Upon meeting the 80-year-old Leoš Janáček in the garden of his little cottage in this Moravian capital, one is struck by his smile, both youthful and hard-won. This is the composer, after all, who labored for the first five decades of his life in obscurity, before his peasant opera Jenufa broke into the international repertoire.

And today the composer, whose seventh opera *White Mountain* is set to premiere in Brno's Theater on the Wall next Wednesday, and later in Prague and Paris, is inspired by the dark events of our world.

One has barely shaken his hand before the composer, through the translator, inquires about the latest news of Hitler's aggressions. This from a man who had found himself at the center of a 1905 German Volk-stag riot in his hometown, doing battle with his walking stick against fixed bayonets before spectators wisely spirited him away. Though Janáček's step is slower than our last meeting ten years ago, his speech is just as swift—energized, no doubt, by the strange horticultural wonders that have introduced his beloved Republic, and in particular his homeland of Moravia and its capital Brno, to the wider world.

"This!" he says, gesturing to a towering tuber in his little yard, while a small dog barks at his heels. "It is an admirer of music, as you can see! It is drawn as they all are to our Moravia by our heartbeat. Our passion. We have been roused, and will not meet aggression unchecked!"

Janáček, who is quick to point out he holds honorary doctorates in both philosophy and earth sciences from the local university, is more than just fond of this horticultural oddity. He believes he is responsible.

The tuber he points to is just a sample of the foliage that has baffled and amazed horticulturalists and geologists from around the world. The vines and tubers, fronds and alien topiary might have stepped out of the planet Mars, but Janáček has never been more down-to-earth in his concerns.

"I'll light a fire under my countrymen!" he says, offering me a seat at his garden table. "Twenty years ago I wrote an opera," referring to *The Excursions of Mr. Beetle*, "in which I tried to rouse a nation of Oblomovs, sated, fat, lazy. Here, I seek to wake the nation and the world to the danger posed by this lunatic in Berlin. In my opera, every note is dipped in blood. These motifs came from the very soul of us. They marched out one by one onto the paper, inspired by the horrendous situation that is brewing. We Czechs had many friends in Germany. My professional career and success depended on many great men in Germany and Austria like Klemperer and Kreisler, and now these men are being forced out."

He becomes agitated, pacing back and forth while the translator finishes her work. Then he seeks to assure this reporter that his opera is not propaganda. "It is fantasy. From the mind of Čapek. You have seen his plays, yes? His robot play? I was charmed by the idea of starting an opera in a tavern. I myself am a teetotaler, but I am fond of the atmosphere. And before long our protagonist, who is a sort of pilgrim, arrives at the River Vltava in Prague, and meets a water sprite!"

When I suggest an homage to his countryman Dvorak's *Rusalka*, he waves me off. "I admire Dvorak greatly, but the inspiration here is different. Čapek's work satirizes the crazed Reich in Berlin. Here, it is an underwater realm that might seem far away, indeed fantastical, but in fact it reaches into the heart of our country via every tributary and streamlet! Blood flows in this water, right at our feet. And though its source is beyond our border, the danger is here."

"I wish to say more about this pilgrim," he says, again before the translator can finish. "It is a strange character. He is an unlikely man, who proves the savior. Where does he come from? Who can say. But he is Czech through and through, and like every common Czech man and woman out there, will waken to the danger and work to save our country!"

The composer's wife soon appears, and offers us tea. We go inside the cramped yet lovely cottage that has served as their home for the last twenty years, and the Maestro is soon engaged in demonstrating to this reporter the various machines that he has designed; machines of unusual operation meant to communicate with what he calls the "scashovanee."

"It is the rhythmic essence of existence. It is here in my voice. And I hear it in your voice, too. Look, I write it down." And here he dabs notation furiously upon a napkin. "With these machines, which I have built with the aid of Dr. Novak of Brno, and later with the help of the faculty of Masaryk University, we have broken through to the primal elements that exist in the life force. With these, we have touched the luminous depths and the effects you see in my garden. I have brought this new life to Brno and it will serve as backdrop for my new work, *White Mountain*."

But a line of communication definitely exists between Janáček and a fellow pioneer of sorts, the composer Henry Cowell.

Janáček is an honorary fellow of the California Iconoclasts based outside San Francisco, and before leaving on my trip to Brno I paid a visit to this "woolly man of music."

"Dr. Janáček possesses the greatest talent in opera today, of course," Cowell, a hale sixty-two year old, proclaims on his sunny patio amid the Northern California pine. "But he's also the most important theoretical mind in music. He is not an extremist like the brilliant Schoenberg, nor a chameleon like Stravinsky, but his approach is uniquely vectored. His studies into speech melodies have led him to important discoveries, the gist of which won't really be understood for decades."

Another Californian admirer is the composer Paul Haas, a student of Janáček's who settled in Hollywood some ten years ago. Haas's *The Insect Play*, also based on Čapek, premiered with great success at the Met in 1935 and has proved equally viable in Chicago, London and lately Los Angeles. It can be argued that its style—

full of bewildering pace and the use of short, broken motifs that resist conformity—owes much to his teacher. "Maestro Janáček was the crucial influence in my career," concedes Haas, thirty-seven with a wife and two children, in his Pasadena home. "It was he who suggested I emigrate to America. Opera companies who have tasted of his strange works have been interested in hearing my own. I have been lucky here to encounter many great musicians and composers, but the Maestro stands higher than the rest. His music is full of truth. His new work, I believe, will speak a great truth which must be heard."

And the New York area will be able to hear that truth next week. *White Mountain* will be broadcast on the Mutual Broadcast system, 8 p.m. on May 31."

When Paul looks up, Josef is standing beside him.

"Let's go see K."

"Our time confronts us with a fantastic problem, so fantastic our imagination could never have conjured it up. At a time like this one can only survive, save, if one has the courage to consider something even more fantastic not only possible but achievable."

—Arnold Schoenberg

28. THE ARCHITECT OF RUINS

For Josef, the Pilgrim's presence is the ultimate expression of the strangeness that has overtaken Brno. Worrisome, miraculous, profound, and yet supremely *natural*.

As Paul sits beside him in the Tatra 77's back seat, studying the riotous vines that cling to the theater's facade as though it's new and strange to him, Josef studies Paul. He wonders at the subtle changes to his profile. Is it merely Josef's memory—the passage of ten years, the river rushing past, to so speak, and he not remembering the curve and striving of the waves? He wishes now he had access to a sketch he once made, in the Nine Cock's Crow, to compare the august shape of that nose with this one, and the wider mouth here, and the strong yet younger chin. Perhaps some Cubist dimension has been breached, beneath the skin, seismically. Or is it merely the fact that Paul does not look ten years older; that Josef's mind, grasping for the change of Time, and finding its puzzling opposite, is stymied? Yet the voice is the one he remembers. Isn't it? The phrasing, both soft and strong. Adding to all of this, Josef is now certain that the clothes Paul wears are the same he had bought for him the day before the Friday Night Circle with poor Masaryk, back in the golden years of the late '20s, before the ominous flowering of the '30s.

He is a signum, Josef muses, as surely as the Roosevelt dime that Paul had given him, once upon a time.

The Tatra purrs along Divadelni, and Josef strives to sink into the cushion, to shut his eyes and rest, but remains straight as a whip. "Much to do," he murmurs, touching the brushes in his pocket. Policemen, seeing the approaching car, blow their whistles to clear a narrow passage. The crowd—a jostling amalgam of grins and sneers, raised fingers, clapping hands, whirled tricolors and snapping swastikas—surges close then retreats to the blue-uniformed back. Ivan, their driver from Valassko, is speaking on the radio.

Josef leans forward and taps the partition glass. Ivan slides it open. "Can you take the *indirect* way?"

"Streets are locked down," says Ivan, who is usually such an inspiring fount of Valachian swearwords. "Getting pretty thick, Mr. Čapek."

Josef nods; he recalls the announcement on the radio, something about corridors of traffic being kept for dignitaries going from their hotels to the theater.

A scuffle to the left, in front of an apartment building. A bottle shatters on the street, spraying green fragments. Five youths—three in the blue uniforms of 9forces, and two in the tan swagger of SdP—tussle on the cobblestones. Behind them, looming across the facade, is another of those bland Tiege montages—photographed and scissored faces framed in strong diagonals, of Czech men, women and children. Then they're left behind, and the scene is overtaken by foliage. Josef spots the Michaelmas hybrid with its yellow blossoms—the flower that had so excited K. that he'd scaled the south flank of Špilberk to obtain a specimen, much to Lenca's consternation.

The rumors had begun months ago. The first solid evidence had arrived from Helena and the offices of the *Lidové noviny*. At first the articles had been relegated to the back pages; the front was taken up with Masaryk's ill health and the ramifications for the country. Yet they were enough to capture K.'s interest. "*Weeds, Josef, of the strangest hue and shape, in the Krenova suburb of Brno.*"

"*Really, K?*"

"*Yes, look at this picture Helena sent me.*"

"I thought you hated weeds, K."

"This is something different brother. Care to take the train down for a few days?"

And so they had toured the outlying towns of Bohunice and Syrice, and then the Krenova suburb, Josef quickly admitting that yes, this was *rather odd*, wasn't it? *Rather like something from your scientific fiction, K.* And K., well, he had gotten dangerously over-stimulated, exhausting himself by relentless excursions and long interviews with local horticulturists and geologists. His feuilletons, which had been reprinted as far and wide as the New Zealand and Des Moines newspapers—both, by charming coincidence, named *The Register*—are to be collected into a companion volume to *The Gardener's Year* titled *The Year of Unusual Gardens.* Though to K.'s irritation, the overseas publishers want to credit it as by the "*Master of Czechoslovak Science Fiction.*"

The vector neither of them had foreseen had come in the form of a telegram to their hotel.

Misters Čapek! Come to my little cottage for tea. I wish to discuss the incursion that I have drawn to Brno and its ramifications for the health of our country.

Dr. Ph. & Geo. Leoš Janáček,

"That crazy crank," Josef had murmured. "When did he become a doctor of geology?"

Yet the meeting—during which the Maestro made the extraordinary claim that he, along with an array of machines built in conjunction with the Brno physicist Novak, had summoned the wild growth from the *luminous depths*—had failed to be as startling as it might have been. By then, K. was well aware that something entirely unique was underway. Dr. Ph. Geo Janáček's was no crazier than others; in fact, his mention of a Californian Pilgrim, who appeared amidst one of the very first incursions, had been a startling lure to Josef.

From this, the idea of an artistic collaboration had coalesced. The opera *White Mountain*, had grown as the only sensible communication between them.

Five months of slow invasion. Five months of miracles from the Maestro's quarter, climaxing in the, well, so-far-unending climax of Masaryk's *not* dying.

"Josef?"

Josef, staring down at his turquoise-spattered hands, blinks a little blearily. "Huh?"

Paul—the young and yet not young Paul—says, "Not dying?"

"Oh?" He's dizzied by the momentum of the car, which has picked up speed. Almost as fast as a jog, now. "Muttering." He shifts on the seat. "No, what I wanted to ask, well. Hmmm. Yes, well, I'm a little taken aback by your appearance this afternoon, on this particular day."

"As am I, Josef," says the Pilgrim, with startling effect.

"Did you . . . choose this day to return? For the opening night's performance?"

The Pilgrim's face—that grave Jewish profile that is somehow as young as it was and quite different—knits up perplexedly. "I did not choose."

Josef blinks, touching the brushes in his pocket. "It's a happy accident then, and well timed. The other VIPs have been arriving all day."

"I saw Max Brod, Josef. At the train station."

"Yes." Josef nods. "Yes, that sounds right. They're all dribbling in, aren't they. Here for the sights outside the theater, if not inside." He ticks off with his fingers. "In the last few hours, we've received telegrams confirming, oh the mayor of Prague, the deputy Prime Minister, Mr. G.B. Shaw of London, and the British ambassador. H.G. Wells should be arriving soon after." Noting Paul's reaction, he says, "You should meet him, Paul." And when the other man says nothing, "Karel and I are dining with him tomorrow. Can you . . . stay that long?"

A smile. His brooding eyes brighten a bit. "I'd like that, Josef."

"I as well, Paul," Josef says, arranging his brushes by feeling the bristles, the sables to one side and the mohairs to the other. "If the theater is still standing. If we . . . survive the opening night."

"Tram cars are burning," says Ivan over his shoulder, honking his horn to clear a startled youth.

"Again?"

Ivan sets down the radio handset. "On Jakubska Street."

To Paul, Josef says, "They stuff them full of car tires, douse them with petrol and, whoosh!"

Beyond Paul, another of the Tiege bombardments unreels against a building, vying with the *svastikas* and the weeds for wall space, and Josef supposes he prefers them over the former if not the latter; these simplistic, puerile images are serving a purpose. And Tiege himself is somewhere in town, stirring up more trouble with his wife Milena— poor Kafka's former sweet girl.

Paul suddenly stiffens, lifts a hand toward the glass as though to grasp at something floating by.

"It's—"

He seems ready to jump out of the moving car, until something else catches his eye—ahead of them. A repeated image in Tiege's collage. An image of a red-haired young woman captured through a long lens. She's standing in a square amidst rubber balls, looking a little lost. It's a famous image in Brno, reprinted in the local paper.

Alarmed by Paul's sudden anxiety, he says, "Karel Tiege. Stuff's all over the city."

"The girl."

Josef nods. "Yes. Local. They call her *the one who disappeared*. Walked out of town never to be seen again, or something. A musician, wasn't she?" And when Paul says nothing. "Did you know her, Paul?"

"She went with me."

Josef feels a shiver down his neck. "Went?"

"She's here." He turns back to the window. "Somewhere."

"Went together?" To *where*? The Maestro's little village in the mountains? How far have you traveled, Pilgrim? A vision lifts through Josef's volcanic imagination: of Cubist landscapes, of dimensions opening up and Paul rearranging himself to step through.

A figure—blue uniform—rushes up beyond the window. Ivan honks, swerves the mighty Tatra. The 9forces comrade runs alongside and slaps his hand against the window, twice. Red paint, and the double smear forming something like a glowering sun.

The apparition falls away, and back.

Josef's hands are shaking, yet he cannot stop from rearranging the paint brushes in his pockets. He says, under his breath, *"cannot let things spin out of control."* Then, pleadingly. "Paul, tell me. All of this. This world we find ourselves the actors in. Is it anything like what you know, from your other future. From 1949?"

Paul runs his hands through his thick dark bangs, brushing them away from those amazing eyes. "Masaryk shouldn't be here."

"You're right, of course."

Paul looks over.

Josef says, "He should have died months ago."

The Pilgrim waits. And Josef is pleased, for once, to be holding the answers. He gazes through his window at a throng of SdP outside the Church of St. James the Greater, then shuts his eyes, settles back. "Have you read Mr. Poe's *The Facts in the Case of M. Valdemar?*"

"No."

Touching his brushes, the sables and mohairs, he says softly, "Then . . . then let me tell you a little fairy tale."

JOSEF'S TALE:
THE UNDYING WOMAN

She was dying Paul. His beloved Kamilka, whom he had loved since the day she sat down beside him at the spa and said he looked lonely. She was married, of course, but in her chaste way—her impossibility at loving him back—she became his safe amour. She inspired his works, and yet never responded to his invitations to attend the operas and string quartets that bore her dedication. Until the final years, that is.

She was there Paul, when *The Dead House* premiered in Brno. And though the opera was a bleak utterance, she filled his heart with a warmth unsurpassed in his lifetime. He built a room in his country house for her and she, out of kindness for the old gent, stayed there in the summertime. And while there were predictions of many great musical works to follow, the Maestro instead devoted himself to her happiness, as well as, behind the scenes, devoting himself to his investigations of the *scasovani*.

After his attempts to write about his experiences were met with skepticism, he kept the matters close to his chest. He and that Brno physicist Novak continued work on a number of ever-odder machines—machines that would probe and wick the pulse of the natural world.

But the nature of his explorations—and their intensity, changed in the autumn of 1936.

She was dying. There was nothing that could be done. Yet to the Maestro J——yes, Paul, we cannot refer to a mage in a fairy tale by his full name, for the name is power, and must remain hidden—the Maestro J—— who had lived a full eighty years and counting, the idea that his immortal beloved was very mortal and would die at the age of thirty-seven—unthinkable. His passions, which had always driven him to extremes, now pushed him in laboratory experiments. And it was mere months later, as Kamila slipped into a coma, that he unveiled his machine at Masaryk University. The *scasovani suspension field generator*, he named it. He convinced Kamila's husband to allow it to be tested on her; it would suspend her, while doctors worked to find a way to cure her body. The horns, the table, the keening bright bell of the *scasovani*—they enwrapped her body. And Kamila, his muse, lay in its embrace. At first, the signs were hopeful. But it soon became apparent that the complexities had not been solved. J——, in his passions, had overreached himself, and she fell from his grasp and died.

Madame J—— took pity on her husband. For the umpteenth time they reconciled. At least, she suffered him and he suffered her, and they lived together once again in the little cottage. The Maestro tried to turn his back on the *scasovani*. But, to hear him tell it, the *scasovani* vied for his attention. Not as directly as it once had—with Kamila's little boy and the appearance of his California pilgrim to the rescue, no. But it communicated, from the luminous depths. And when the tenor of the body politic began to change in Europe, when the dark clouds rifted on the horizon, he fell back into his work, convinced that they were linked.

And when President Masaryk was diagnosed, the Maestro returned to his *scasovani* suspension machine. It was a matter of patriotism, of the very future of this country, to keep alive the man who embodied it in every way. The president's daughter agreed, and in Masaryk University they built a machine that far surpassed the first; and President Tomáš Garrigue Masaryk became *Monsieur Valdemar*, and hovers between life and death to this day.

In Spiritus Sanctus, Amen.

On Jostova Street black smoke billows from a queue of trams. Police contain the crowd behind barricades while firemen fight the flames. With much use of the Tatra's horn, with vivid gestures and expletives, Ivan drives them past the brouhaha. Smoke overtakes the car; Jostova Street vanishes but for policemen materializing out of nothing, waving them on to clearer skies.

At Komenského Square, the police give way to soldiers and the Presidential guard. To the west, at Špilberk's northern flank, the noble facade of Masaryk University—capped by a Sokol hawk ready to take to the air—is surrounded by a makeshift fence topped with barbed wire. Armored personnel carriers block the street, where the crowd is much larger than yesterday. One thing is certain: Masaryk's once-secret location is now known.

"Out of the fucking way," mutters Ivan, veering around two soldiers who stumble onto the curb. But his forward progress is halted by a vintage tank. "Sorry Mr. Čapek, we're not getting any closer."

"That's fine, Ivan. Really." Josef rolls down his window; a Captain leans in. "Josef Čapek as arranged, and guest."

A warmth redolent of pollen and flowers wafts down from Špilberk Hill, which takes up half the sky. In strong sunlight, skeins of smoke rise from bonfires south of the city. The same sunlight, nearer, highlights patches of vivid color on the hill, new patterns that had not been there yesterday. The nearer side of Špilberk has attracted the densest growth, and Josef knows why.

The Heartbeat lures it.

Beside him, Paul walks slowly, a little dazed. He acquiesces when the guard approaches and insists that he be searched. Josef watches with interest as the postal tube is taken from the overcoat and opened to reveal, well, the *shem*. Not unfurled. Nothing dangerous there, no. And the Pilgrim possesses no weapons.

They are ushered through.

The tumult, the sound of horns and cries, the massed buzzing of crowds, is at a distance. Here, the sun warms their necks, and the air is fresh with the helianthus and aster that climbs the University's granite facade.

They trudge up the stairs. At the top, two Guards in gold-fringed navy blue salute with ornamental sabers: twin bars of golden light, slicing the air. Josef blinks. He marvels at their Alfons Mucha fairy tale uniforms.

"*Once upon a time,*" he says to them, bowing.

On the second floor a marble corridor stretches into the distance, entirely empty. Yet as they walk along, Josef hears the Heartbeat. He feels it, as he had that very first time, tickling at his ear. And the Pilgrim hears it, too. That great Cubist head is tilting, striving to hear past the clicking of their shoes on the marble floor.

On either side, doors open onto lecture halls which reign in silence; silence but for the beating of a faint gold bell somewhere in the aether limits, growing more intense as they near the end, where a wide rosewood door is flanked by two solemn guards.

"Is my brother here?" Josef asks quietly.

"Yes, Mr. Čapek. In the viewing room."

"Fine. We'd like to see him, please."

And the first guard grasps the ivory handle and opens the door onto an outer room, where stand two ladies. President Masaryk's daughter Alice is by the ivy-tendrilled window, while Karel's wife is near the door to the inner chamber. Ever the diva, she says, "Josef, why aren't you at the theater?"

"Hullo, hullo, dear Olga. Well, it's quite a parade out there right now. Is Karel in? Good afternoon, Madame Masarykova."

She, young and beautiful, strikingly intelligent, bears the mystery and strangeness of her father's fate with aplomb, bestows a troubled smile. "Good afternoon, Josef."

"Madame Masarykova, may I present a friend of mine and Karel's, and the worse for wear. This is Paul Arepo."

The Pilgrim bows. "It's an honor, Madame."

"I hope you weren't injured, Mr. Arepo."

Paul glances at Josef. "No, I am quite well."

Olga Scheinflugová, the star of Barrandov studios, says meanwhile, "He doesn't need distractions right now, Josef."

"I'm afraid we must, my dear." Josef leads Paul to the wide padded door and its swan-wing handle. He turns it, and enters the anteroom to the domain of *Monsieur Valdemar*.

Dim, of rose-petal wallpaper and cream carpeting, outfitted with three Louis XIV chairs fit for the company of the President, the room is a mere viewing chamber, quiet, facing an oblong window looking into the sapphire gloom of the inner sanctum, where, as though afloat in midnight essence, the white-bearded form of President Tomáš Garrigue Masaryk reposes on swathes of black fabric. The bed that he lies on is hidden from view, as is most of the medical equipment that monitors his life force. Likewise, suspended in midnight, a dozen old gramophone horns from past decades—encircle the Presidential form at various points, and it's from these pearl-shell mouths—as well as further acoustic marvels hidden in the floor and ceiling—that the Heartbeat issues steadily and forever into the chamber.

Every time he steps into the viewing room Josef is overcome by the sight and sound and awed by the *morbidity* and *wonder*—by the sense of a struck chord held indefinitely, buoyed by that fleet and distant chime; or better yet, by the feel of a play frozen in mid-act, in mid-sentence, the actors motionless onstage with arms lifted and mouths open and the words forever hovering somewhere between footlights and audience. He feels the tickle in his ear and on his skin. He senses a mood both funereal and magnificent—the suppression of death, the suspension of a natural principle, the baring of that primeval pulse the Maestro deems the *Heartbeat of the World*.

Paul steps forward as in a dream. He cannot quite believe it of course. Who could? The austere profile of T.G.M., the moustache and beard grown long like Rip Van Winkle's . . .

K. sits in one of the chairs, in mute attendance. His right hand worries at the haft of his cane. His hair gleams with freshly applied pomade; it's neatly combed and parted, with a lick of hair standing up in the back. As Josef draws near, he sees that K. is only half-dressed for the festivities, in pressed black trousers and shined shoes, white shirt, cummerbund, suspenders. But his shirt is unbuttoned at the collar and he's rapt with the note cards he holds with his left hand, mumbling the words of his speech.

"Brother?"

After a pause, he says, quietly, "Oh, Josef. Did you hear anything from the Maestro's assistant?"

Josef waves his hand. "No doubt stuck in traffic." He waits, but K. doesn't look up from the cards. "K? I brought a visitor."

Brother's first reaction is a darkening of his brows, an *I don't have time for this* sort of scowl. Then his face grows long and freezes. How wonderfully expressive, as he studies the new visitor against the tingling, tickling pulse of the heartbeat, against the faint gold bells tart on Josef's tongue. "Who . . . " Karel blinks and blinks, and grasps his walking stick and lumbers to his feet. And looks once more at the Pilgrim. Yes, he too has difficulty recognizing—and then reordering—the identity before him.

"Hello, Karel." The familiar voice clinches it for K.

"Paul . . . " K. leans on his stick. "It cannot be." His mouth hangs open. Approaching, he squints up, then mutters a line—yes, from Apollinaire—"*The clocks in the Jewish quarter are running backwards.*"

"Indeed Brother."

"Paul . . . " Muttering through his fingers. "But how?"

"Well said," says Josef.

The Pilgrim offers his hand; K. shakes it.

"Mr. Arepo, what has . . . ? Why are you here?"

And Paul, with grace and quiet in his voice, says, "I've come back to help you, I think."

"We each carry in us, willy-nilly, the primordial pagan, the primitive caveman; we are fascinated by fire. The man who has never stared into a glowing stove on a winter evening, who has never burned old papers, squatting before the stove in the reverent attitude of a savage, who has never in his life made a bonfire in the fields and danced around it, is perhaps not descended from old Adam but from someone else. Perhaps his ancestors were hatched from frog-eggs or fell down with the rain, like the ancestors of vegetarians, total abstainers, and other superhuman beings. And the man who has never made the mystical, fiery sign of eight with a burning match has never felt the awful and felonious ecstasy when man's petty fire breaks its chain and flies up in a mighty blaze."

—*Fires* by Karel Čapek

29. APOCRYPHAL TALES

"But... where," Karel mutters into his fingertips, "where were you?"

Paul is made uneasy by Karel's gaze, by the naked wonder and fear made more eerie by the glass partition behind him and the body of President Masaryk suspended in that ever thinner, ever finer, *scasovani* chime.

"Paul?" Josef, too, is waiting for an answer, and Paul realizes that he must tell it; that his love for the Brothers demands that he be honest, as far as he can be.

"Most far."

Karel gestures to a chair. He and Paul sit, while Josef goes to the wet bar and pours a glass of seltzer, handing it to his brother as though it's a desperately needed medicine. "Drink it down, K. And don't lose your speech."

Karel manages to sip the seltzer and rearrange the cards on his lap. Josef fixes two more glasses, then seats himself on the other side of Paul.

Masaryk, entombed in that *scasovani* chime, is in mute attendance.

"Paul... what happened? Where have you been? You must tell me."

"The Maestro's village. The one he wrote about in his feuilleton—I found it."

Instead of replying, Karel sips again of the seltzer.

Paul says, "It changed me."

Karel shakes his head. He blinks with great exertion, as though to clear the fog from his eyes.

"*All of this—everything—*is a wonder. I write about fantastical things, but I have no great wish to live them."

Josef sighs sympathetically.

"I cannot quite believe the fecundity of nature around this town, or the flux of recent events. I cannot quite believe I'll be addressing the world in little more than four hours." Karel struggles to his feet. "Time is the essence here yes, stretched out for the old Senor. But it seems also to be collapsing for me, all the hours coming too quickly, and now . . . you. You say it changed you. What changed you, and how?"

Paul grips his knees. He struggles to put into words, to say it so simply. The church, the tomb. Magdalena's song beyond the threshold.

And those glittering, long-eyed figures in the friezes?

"I cannot say it so clearly, Karel. Not yet. I'm sorry."

"I, too, have trouble with mysteries. Josef knows this. He kept the truth from me, knowing what my reaction would be. Yet once the Borderlander crisis began, and the world began to follow the prophecy you told at my garden party, Josef showed me the coin you gave him. And told me a strange tale."

Karel is rearranging the cards; and for the time being, his concerns draw closer to the present moment. "Josef, the Maestro promised he would send his assistant with those additions to my speech. I would like have my words somewhat memorized before the event."

"Delayed by the brouhaha, most likely. Unless, that is, the Maestro has procrastinated. Remember how he snuck changes into *Makropulos* right under the conductor's nose? If he had a telephone—"

"—but he doesn't. And so I have another worry on top of the others." He pats his breast pocket, where the flimsy paper is about to fall out, and plucks out the topmost one. "These blasted telegrams. Alerting me to the many arrivals, invitations to this dinner and that, as though I could even begin to think about tomorrow. And I received this a little over an hour ago." Without looking over, he hands the telegram to his brother, who plucks it up.

"From Tiege?"

"Yes."

Josef is silent for the space of five distant chimes, and Paul lives it with President Masaryk in his suspension. "It's rather dry for him, isn't it?" Josef passes the telegram to Paul. "Where's the optical poetry?"

"Yet just as sinister, Josef."

TO: KAREL ČAPEK
FROM: KAREL TIEGE

BE CAREFUL TONIGHT ČAPEK STOP I CANNOT BE TO BLAME FOR ANY DISTURBANCE OF YOUR OPERA STOP BUT 9FORCES WILL NOT ALLOW THE SDP AGGRESSION TO GO UNCHECKED STOP WE WILL FIGHT ON BEHALF OF WE AS ARTISTS STOP THE DESCENDANTS OF YOUR OBSTINATES STOP VIOLENCE WILL BE POETRY.

Paul is handing the telegram back to Karel when the door opens: Olga enters.

Karel says plaintively, "Any word from Klein?"

"Forget about him, Karel." She frowns at Josef and says to her husband, "If you're satisfied with the speech as it is, then so be it."

"It's not the speech, Olgicku, but the matter of my presentation." His face grows longer and he attempts one of those rubbery, movie comedian scowls. "I'm afraid my voice won't carry to the back of the theater, let alone the world. Any news from H.G.?"

"Let's call him, shall we? Everyone should be here. Madame Masaryk has departed for the theater and I think we should take her cue. Including you, Josef."

Josef sighs and stands up. He takes the glass back to the wetbar. "I'll telephone the gate. Make sure they haven't held back our assistant with the addendum. Paul?"

Olga nods, pleased.

"Goodbye, Mrs. Čapková. Karel."
"Goodbye, Paul."
"Mr. Arepo."

He hovers at the doorway, with a last look at T.G.M. He genuflects; a gesture that Olga seems to find too private; she turns away.

The heartbeat, Josef had called it. Yet to Paul, the *scasovani* chime brings intense memories of the Maestro's sundered garden in that other Brno; and nearer memories of the new opera and the trombones intoning their soft and broken motif, in midnight blue, from the depths and distant.

"A moment, Paul, while I make the call." Josef walks to the telephone while Paul stands listening to the heartbeat that trembles in the air. The *scasovani*, calling as it had once called to him in the theater. But here, it is tamed, ordered.

Paul's attention is drawn to the window and its ivy. In the dying sunlight the tendrils glow golden. He approaches, studies the lacework, then stares through at the cordon of tanks, at the crowd beyond, their shadows are thrown sharply forward as are the grander shadows of Red Church and the Besední dům. Then he notices a lone figure below the house—the red of her hair, the blue of her coat.

He hurries from the room without bidding Josef goodbye.

"Such, then, is the time in which we live: a time of iron and fire, or perhaps not even that; a time of a secret poison, which is surreptitiously poured into the drink of the condemned, so that it could strip them of their selves even before their execution and send them out, transformed into liars and cripples, to the ridicule and mockery of all."

—*The Age of Iron and Fire* by F.X. Salda

30. THE WOMAN AT THE WELL

Once through the gate, he hurries into the crowd, squinting against the setting sun for her red hair, her blue coat. He emerges on the far side of Husova Street. The shadow of the Beseda house darkens the lion-colored cobblestones. She's not at the fringes of the crowd; logic would suggest she's walked back through Old Brno, in the direction of the theater, but he remembers Sonicku in 1931, concerned about Magda and her moodiness, her lonely walks through town; how she would seek out the most remote and unoccupied places, whether Mendel's garden, or Špilberk's casements.

He turns to the hill. In the slanting sunlight, the trunks of the oak and linden stand sharp, cloaked in wild color.

He approaches the path and begins to climb.

With every switchback and every tier of trees surrounding him, the sounds of the protest grow faint and the shadows lengthen. Dappled sunlight. A thrush singing in the branches overhead, somehow reassuring. He peers up the hillside at the higher switchbacks, but is not dissuaded when he sees only the overgrown path, the wild trees and ivy and a hint of the stone castle above him.

At the same time, he revels in the climb; in his newfound energy, his sharpened senses. He's able to feel the presence inside him, abiding.

Pavel, I feel them. Magdalena, kneeling in the Abbot's garden. *The green and growing things. They're down there, now.*

Not even seedlings, but present, inside themselves. Gazing up, her eyes shining with fear. *I'm worried, Pajo, that I won't know until too late, when they're born.*

<hr />

The castle's red roofs gleam with sunset; the pale stone swarms with shadows from the oak and linden trees that line the paths outside. A hush descends.

This evening, Špilberk seems to hoard centuries around its walls.

It exists in the thirteenth century, when the first stones were raised; and centuries later, during the Thirty Years War, when it was rebuilt as a Baroque fortress. It exists as the castle that was partially destroyed by Napoleon, and as the civilian prison it became in 1820—the Hapsburgs' notorious Dungeon of the Nations.

And from out of the hush rises a flute's melancholy tone. A melody, thin in the air. Echoing from somewhere above the windows.

Paul follows it, heart pounding. The sound teases his ear. He turns a corner, finds it empty. The granite floor extending into shadow. To his left, the flute's melody lifts again, no longer in leaps and swirls but in a slow and cautious line, as solemn as Magdalena's eyes.

He follows leftward, around disused barracks and a short alley, hearing it ahead of him then behind, with overtones his ear cannot explain, weighted with something low, like the chord played on an organ's lowest stop. Rounding yet another corner, he suddenly finds it. The golden flute, and Magdalena.

She sits on the edge of a low stone structure, a well. Known as the deepest and most ancient well in Moravia, its mouth is capped with a lattice of steel. In her blue coat and long skirt, she inclines the flute over the wellhead, her hair wisping in an upward breeze from below.

Reverently, Paul approaches.

Her lips, pursed over the embouchure, are chapped but also of a deep red. Her coat is undone, and the blouse beneath it untucked. She appears tired, though this is refuted by the low, strong, steady pulse of music that she plays. Her cheeks hold a faint blush.

Her eyes meet his.

Softly: "Hello, Magda."

The echo of that airy tone rises from the well.

He does not want to sit beside her, is uneasy both at interrupting her and at the idea of leaving.

Her strong fingers, moving over the flute's keys, possess the faintest green tinge to them; and green, too, the veins of her delicate inner wrist.

Many minutes later, when the melody has yet to be resolved, she stops. It lingers for a few seconds longer in the depths of the well, and she, with her head tipped, seems to listen to it as a voice responding to her own. Then her pale blue eyes lift to his. She says, "Paul."

"I was worried about you, Magda."

She lowers the flute into her lap, staring once more down into the well. "You shouldn't be, you know."

"Where did you go?"

She's quiet for a long moment. Her hair wisps across her pale neck. "I just walked," she says. "Walked around the city. And I saw..." She looks up.

Paul sits down beside her, both with their backs to the well, facing the courtyard.

"On the train, Pajo, you told me the terrible things that would happen in a decade."

"And so... you brought us here?"

She has no reply. She merely stares down at her flute, her fingers working at the keys.

"Magda, we haven't spoken much about what happened. In the church, when you wandered off."

"It was a crypt," she says.

He struggles to put into words what could not be said to Karel and Josef. "A crypt is where the dead lie, Magda. But I felt them, their presence. Those who were under the stones."

"*Yes.*"

"And I've felt . . . one of them inside me ever since. He's wraith-like. He haunts my every thought."

She looks over, bravely studying his eyes.

"I wish I could speak with him, Magda, but I can't, so far. I feel him most when I fall asleep. I'm back there at that little ruined church, standing over their graves. And I realize I'm here on their behalf."

"Yes."

"Have you felt them, too, Magda?"

She shakes her head. "I wish I could see them." In a wistful tone, "I'm all alone." And when Paul says nothing, she adds, "*She* sent me here."

"Who?"

"The woman at the well."

He senses, then, the shaft of empty air behind them; senses it deep down into the earth. He blinks away a welter of images: grainy newsreel footage of the *Sylvan Uprising*, *Volkisch* and *Kameradschaftsbund* leaflets. "And did she tell you what you're supposed to do?"

She smiles. "Only *play* my flute."

"And . . . nothing else?"

She turns away from him, towards the main castle building. Her hair whips in a sudden updraft; the cold moist breeze which reeks of the deep earth. "The casements are waiting, Pajo. Can't you hear them breathing?"

Yes, he thinks.

"They're waiting to eat many thousands of lives."

"And . . . are you here to stop it?"

They sit together side by side, listening to the voices from below. As shadows lean across the courtyard the sky darkens and stars begin to gleam in the broad clear sky overhead.

He's not sure how long he's been watching them: the searchlights stabbing up into the air from Old Brno. He's been thinking of zeppelins and the stench of cordite, the Maestro's cottage in ruins, Josef and Bohu trudging back along the midnight streets to the theater and Magdalena emerging from the ruins of the tree whispering, "*My village is dead.*"

"Paul?" She hasn't spoken, hasn't moved, for some time. As the lights draw his eyes, the well had drawn hers. She's been staring through the black lattice into the utter darkness, while the currents stir her hair.

"Yes, Magda?"

"You must go."

He nods. Standing up, he thinks he understands: she wants him to be at the theater to witness the performance, and what the performance will wreak. He says, "Tomorrow," and she nods, clasping the flute—its burnished gold the brightest thing in the dim of the courtyard.

Only after he leaves her, descending the switchback trail, does he understand what she really meant.

He must go. He cannot be there, for whatever would be happening.

With this, he stops. He nearly returns to her. Once again he feels the pang of separation. But he is no longer caretaker of her. She has grown into herself. She has heard the green and growing things; and she is about to be born. But into what? The Sylvan Jeanne D'Arc? The heroine of Soviet mythology? Or something else, as different from her previous selves as this Brno is different from the others he has known?

Her flute lifts the long, searching melody, familiar to him. She must have heard how the people speak of her.

It's a song from the Maestro's cycle, *The Diary of One Who Disappeared.*

The sun sets
The shadows grow.

The lines, from a song cycle, return to him.

Oh, what shall I have lost?
Who will give it back to me?

Though heat remains on the hillside, along with the thick loamy scent of soil, the wind is chill. As he reaches the second switchback, the sounds of rioting return to him. Farther away than Masaryk University, west, in the direction of the theater.

How late is it? Have the celebrities and distinguished guests already been ushered inside? Has Miss Kaprálová lifted her baton? Paul cannot imagine he will gain entry into the theater. Josef will not be there to rescue him from the guards. And so he considers another destination.

The Maestro is surely at home this evening. Is surely hiding in his cottage in the same way as he would once have hidden in the highest, darkest corner of the theater.

I will go to him. The Maestro. I will tell him what has happened. I will tell him who I am.

Voices reach him, close-by. Young voices. Laughter, then hushing up. One says softly, in German, "Hear it?"

"Up there, yes?"

Paul freezes. In the dimness he makes out their figures—four youths with blond hair, in the tan uniforms of the SdP. They skulk up the trail. "I don't hear it."

"Fuck you! All you can hear is explosions."

Laughter. Their footfalls grow louder as they reach the switchback. Paul steps into the trees. In shadow, he is certain, he will not be seen. Young, with arms swinging as they walk, they are cut from the same cloth as those other youths on the train platform.

"Sshh." One holds up a hand, tilts his head. "Listen."

But it's not Magdalena they hear. He's gesturing down the hillside, then toward the trees. They, too, hide, a dozen paces from Paul. And together they listen to footfalls on the path. From out of the dark comes a small figure, hands in the pockets of his coat, hurrying up the trail. Dark hair and face, staring down. He halts suddenly, as the three youths appear in front of him.

"Little kike out for a walk?"

The other two laugh. One reaches into his pocket, producing a length of pipe.

The small figure, a young man not much older than a boy, his hectic pace halted, now stands still and watchful.

"What you doing out, Jew?"

"You know what could happen to you?" asks another, in an unbroken voice.

And the figure opposite them says in a calm, yet sarcastic tone, "Fuck you, *Naciste*. Out of my way."

Paul is as stunned as the three youths; but they react quicker than he does. They separate and come at him from three sides, low. In the tussle, their opponent pulls his hands from his pockets and starts swinging wildly, but the youth with the pipe strikes a glancing blow to the shoulder, and the dark-haired boy staggers.

Paul steps out. He hulks down the trail toward him, immediately drawing attention. Three startled faces at his approach, and the other bent over double. One says, "What is that?!" The other two dash down the trail then upward, into the brush. Their leader follows.

Paul reaches the youth, and helps him straighten. His dark hair is mussed. Blood runs from his nose and lip, which he wipes with his hand. His eyes are afire. His face, demonic. "Shit!" He pulls free of Paul, rounds on the others who are now scampering up the hillside. "Fuck you!" He tugs the side of his coat, straightens his tie.

"Are you hurt?"

"Had worse." He regards the blood on his knuckles, then wipes it on his jacket. He bears a bruise on his forehead that is not recent.

"You should be more careful," says Paul.

There's something demonic about the boy's smile; bared eyetooth, like a fang. "Bad night for a Jew to be out by himself."

Paul gestures to the town beyond the trees. "And so you are headed indoors."

"I was talking about *you*. Josef sent me to fetch you in."

"You . . . you're from the Maestro's?" Paul looks the kid up and down, startled. Then, still unbelieving, he struggles to reconcile him with the remembered photograph on the back of the plain black-and-white 78; of the young man seated behind the concert grand. "You're his assistant?"

Do you trust me, Herr Haas?

Gideon Klein lifts his knuckles, trying to see the blood welling up. "You know a lot."

Paul smiles. "I know that you should take care of your hands. They're your livelihood, after all."

They start walking down the trail. "Yeah?" He chuckles. "Josef didn't say you looked like a Golem." And glanced over his shoulder. "Acted like one, too. Thanks."

"Yes, yes, the White Mountain is soaked in human blood. If the Moldau did not flow so fast it would still be red with blood, even today. Wherever you lift up a stone on the bank, you will always find little leeches underneath. That's because at one time it was a river of blood. And they are waiting because they know that the day will come when it will feed them again."

—*Walpurgisnacht* by Gustav Meyrink

31. THE THEATER ON THE RAMPARTS

"So you know my name, Mr. Arepo?"

"You're Gideon Klein."

Klein hunches his shoulders, trudging with Paul along the edge of the crowd. "Have you heard me play?" The question lacks bravado, is charmingly tentative.

Paul glances sidelong as his guide. How old is he now? Eighteen? By the time he's twenty-two, he'll be famous throughout Prague.

"Yes. You're excellent, Gideon."

"Where? Where did you hear me play?"

Paul pretends to be fascinated with a surge of rioters near the Red Church; it gives him time to conjure up a reply. "At the Beseda."

"Yeah? Why don't I believe you?"

"You're a composer."

Gideon laughs. "You don't know my sister, do you? You can't. She's back in Prague." But before he can follow up with a question, Gideon halts. He gestures with his chin. "Car's gone."

"The Tatra?"

He nods. "Josef's returned to the theater already. We'll have to walk."

They set off down Solnici Street, empty but for the ivy and the torn Tiege collages.

"I didn't expect you to be a Jew."

"Oh?"

"What were you doing up there?"

"I was visiting a friend," says Paul. He finds her, in the collage. The one who disappeared.

"And this friend. He's still up there?"

He recalls the telegram: *Violence will be poetry.* "She."

A few paces later. "And you're not worried?"

"I'm more worried about you, young Klein."

Klein laughs. He walks briskly; though smaller than Paul he's now a few paces in front of him, and grins over his shoulder, tousled black locks trembling in the breeze. "Fuckers. Want to kill us all, you know. Liquidate us."

"You've been in fights with them before."

"After my last concert." He adds, "At the Beseda. But I've barely gotten my hands dirty, compared to others." *Violence will be poetry.* "Last month I saw Theodor Herzl in Prague. A speech about the Zionist movement."

Paul nods. He remembers Brod's story of the *Beautiful Rosalinda*.

"Forget these SdP radicals. They're pawns. A distraction. The Germans want to extinguish us. Cleanly. Methodically. Herr Schoenberg told me—"

Paul stops. "*Arnold* Schoenberg?"

"Yes." Surprised at Paul's reaction, Gideon stops as well. "You a fan of his music? Or do you hate it?"

"I like it. Very much."

"Not many do. For my crown, he's equal to the Maestro."

Attempting nonchalance, Paul starts walking again, and asks, "When did you last speak with him?"

Alongside, Gideon shrugs. "We haven't spoken. We correspond. My sis Eliska sent him a few of my compositions. He wrote to me saying how much he likes them. And last letter he told me how he knew fifteen years ago that the Germans would be pulling this."

"At the spa at Mattsee."

Gideon narrows his eyes. "Yeah. How'd you hear that?"

Paul gestures vaguely. "I must have read it somewhere."

"Well, Herr Schoenberg is very interested in what the Maestro's up to. Says that the Maestro's lucky to have two assistants like me and Vitzky."

"He is," says Paul. "Very lucky."

Under a starry sky, demonstrators throng Malinovského Square, raising signs and fists and tricolor flags. Gideon and Paul get no closer than Orli Street. In the sway and tilt of the searchlight beams is revealed the steady line of well-dressed gentlemen and women, walking slowly along a line of Parliamentary guards, up the staircase and into the lobby. Tatras, likewise cordoned by police, idle slowly down Dvoraka Street, which is entirely restricted from everything but traffic to and from the city's hotels.

The Theater on the Ramparts is surrounded.

"Ten thousand easy," says Gideon, lighting a cigarette.

Paul spots three armed guards atop the theater's roof, and another five on the mid-level balcony. No doubt the entire building is so guarded. Tonight, Paul muses, the theater is truly on the ramparts.

"Should we try the back?" asks Paul.

Gideon shakes his head, hunches his narrow shoulders and sidles along the edge of the crowd.

"Can you see who it is?"

"Mayor and his wife?"

They duck past a Movietone crew filming the exterior. "Get a long-shot," says an American voice.

Paul hears snatches of French and German.

"*Le concert commencera bientôt.*"

"*Das Konzert beginig bald.*"

He hears catcalls and curses as another limousine arrives at the entrance. Cheers greet the newcomers stepping from the car. Paul tries to see but the way is blocked by placards.

A man lifts his little girl. *"The concert will soon begin, Elena."*

Elbow to elbow, the crowd jostles to the very limits of the square and beyond. Danger is anticipated by the policemen and paramilitary men with batons and rifles; but the riots that have exploded around Brno are muted here. It's almost as if the theater's stately facade and the well-shod guests are tamping down the flames. People are remembering their manners, at least for the moment.

"Hey, we have passes," shouts Klein, pushing aside a much larger man, who gazes darkly down then relents when he meets Paul's eyes. Gideon lurks and jumps up to see the new arrivals. Paul is worried about the boy injuring his hands—those dazzling, wondrous hands that would play to great acclaim in the coming years.

"Our luck, Paul!" he shouts over his shoulder, and bustles through the crowd as another limousine pulls up.

"Who?" shouts Paul, but settles for merely following. They're well into the square, near the drive in front of the theater. Somewhere behind them a gun or a fireworks resounds in distant streets, but there's little anxiety, only applause.

"Maestro!" Gideon shouts, and surges ahead, his smoky dark suit and tie flapping.

Paul follows, looking for the Maestro's vibrant white hair. Atop the theater, the guards have taken notice. One with a rifle aims at Gideon.

"We know him!" shouts Gideon. "I'm with the theater and we know him!"

The man Gideon addressed—tall, angular, with a lovely brunette on his arm—is not the Maestro Janáček.

"Maestro!"

The man scowls, then tentatively, smiles. "Gideon? What are you doing in this dangerous place?"

"Trying to reach the promised land. Care to escort us?"

The man notices Paul behind Gideon, then is taken up by the crush of guards and escorts who begin to push Gideon away.

"No, no—stop! This is Gideon Klein, assistant to Maestro Janáček." His commanding voice and his urgent gesturing halt the guards. "He and his guest will come inside with us."

"Thank you, Karel." Gideon grins up at Paul and shakes himself off. "See, told you I could do it. Come on, this way. Let's not get too far behind." This as they begin climbing the stairs after their savior. "You know him, don't you?"

"We haven't met," says Paul. "But I'm aware of his brilliance."

They follow Karel Ančerl, conductor of the Czechoslovak Radio Orchestra—and in another time, another place, conductor of the band at Theresienstadt—into a lightning-struck lobby of photographers and camera crews, of joyful laughter, Champagne toasts and nervous guards amid the carmine and gold splendor.

※

"We would rather have it in Prague, of course," Ančerl says to a reporter, who accosts him five paces into the theater. "I do not wish to emphasize a divide. The Dvorak/Smetana cults of past days are vanished in this new cause. Brno is where Janáček's heart is, and it's a joy to see it come to life here. We—"

A hand takes hold of Paul's arm. Gideon, likewise, is detained. The guards pull them aside as Gideon explains that he works for the theater. He is allowed to retrieve his papers from his pocket, then relaxes his shoulders as a steward in dress-coat approaches and explains to the guards that both of them are welcome.

The steward is the same one who spotted Paul that morning. "You must take the back way," he says after the guards move on. "The opera is soon to begin."

"Is that Bartok?" Gideon rises to his toes, then jumps to see over the crowd.

Paul struggles to spot the composer in the crowd, but he's distracted by other familiar faces. Ferdinand Peroutka from the Friday Night Circle, smoking a pipe and nodding at something being said by a blue-haired woman in a silver gown. Max Brod, leaning on his cane, talking to a couple in magisterial tuxedo and fur coat dress—who might be the Vice President and his wife. And, surrounded by a dozen tungsten lamps, Herbert George Wells, his walrus moustache newly trimmed, his glasses sparkling as he nods and speaks and nods and speaks again.

Then they've entered the hall leading underground, into the warrens. Gideon knows the guard at the door, and is ushered through without trouble. The din of the celebration gives way to the more anxious sounds of footsteps on the floor overhead, of the hum of mercury vapor lamps and a rumble that might be—that probably was—the stage machinery being tested.

"Eh? Paul? Gideon?"

"I found him, Mr. Čapek."

Josef, in tuxedo with a wilted tie, stands beside a scrim of striated turquoise—an undersea vista to which he is adding a few late dabs of green. He turns, and studies them up and down. "What happened?" He is surrounded by paint-daubed young people who seem to have gathered for some last minute pep talk. "Gideon—you're injured. Again."

"I'm okay, Josef." He removes a handkerchief from his forehead; the scarlet mingles with the vermilion, as he waves it. "Dry."

"And Paul—"

"Hello, Josef."

"Paul. Yes. Yes." Josef passes the brush to one of his assistants, then takes hold of a rope as though he might fall to the ground; but for the tuxedo he has the aspect of a sailor in rough seas. "Thank you for finding him Gideon."

"What happened?" This from the young woman in a black tie and tails—the conductor Kaprálová, her bobbed haircut high above her slender white neck, her bright and nervous eyes filled with a sudden concern. "Gideon? Not again."

"Vitzky. Don't worry." Gideon takes her hand, and kisses it. "Your hand is cold. How are you feeling?"

"Ready." Then, a further note of concern, as Gideon adjusts the carnation at her lapel. "Does the Maestro have anymore changes?"

"None. And if there are, I won't pass them along. Are you nervous?"

"Incredibly," she says. Glancing briefly at Paul.

Gideon smiles. "I won't introduce you two now. After the concert, yes."

Josef steps forward. "We have—I've been given the signal for five minutes." He touches his breast pocket, fingering his brushes. "Maestro Kaprálová, you should probably go to your pit before they drag you there."

To the clapping of the stagehands, she sets off for the staircase into the warrens; Paul's eyes continue to follow her even after she's gone, he remembers the spiral staircase into the seamstress's room, the narrow passage into the pit and the three steps up to the conductor's podium, with the vast and expectant audience behind.

Gideon grins. "Aren't you going to give them a speech, Josef?"

"Yes," says one of the young painters. "A speech Mr. Čapek."

"A speech!"

"Speech!"

Josef touches his breast pocket. He adjusts his eyeglasses. *"And yet . . ."*

"And yet," repeats the crew.

"I suppose I should offer something more substantial." He nudges his glasses up the bridge of his nose. "Perhaps I should mention the great Thomas Edison. Yes, Edison. He haunts the ramparts as the ghost of Poseidon was said to haunt the temple at Delphi. In fact, when the theater was being built, one of his first electric bulbs was enclosed in a decorative copper vault—quite lovely as I recall—and set in the closing stone." Josef scratches his chin with vermilion fingers. "It is sealed with his promise of the future. The future, yes. Not something vague, but something to be shaped. By art. By light, by shared understanding. Right, Pavel? Er, Paul?"

"Right, Josef."

Josef's speech falters and in the interim Paul hears the musicians tuning up, tossing up Janáčekian phrases that collapse into the general run of scales and trills. And he notes Gideon Klein watching Paul keenly, even when Josef continues.

"Perhaps a prayer is in order. So that we may all survive the evening, ha ha. Though I'm not one for prayer. But, well, we had one back in the old days that may apply." Josef tugs at his bow-tie, clears his throat. In a low voice he intones, "Long live the liberated word, my friends. Yes. Long live fauvism, and expressionism and poeticism. Long live dramatism and Orphism. Long live paroxysm and sports fields and the central slaughterhouse. Long live dynamism and the plastic arts. And yes, long live Thomas Edison, and steel and concrete, and the poetry of noise. *Amen.*"

Applause breaks out; Gideon and Paul join in, and Josef clasps the rigging in the gale, shouting, "Death to tank treads! Death to Empire!"

A throat clears. All heads turn to Karel Čapek, dapper in his tuxedo and tails, a carnation at his lapel, his walking stick polished to a high gloss, like his shoes. Standing stiffly, his chin impacts against his bow tie, a look of playful consternation on his face. "Goodness, Josef."

Olga Scheinpflugová, in a silver gown with many strands of pearl at her throat, hovers protectively at Karel's side; she's distracted by someone near the curtain; a prompter.

"Hello, K. Just giving them a pep talk, like in the old days."

"We were a little drunker in the old days," replies Karel, leaning on his cane. "Paul. Good to see you here."

Paul says, "You look very polished, Karel."

In the auditorium, applause breaks out. Maestro Kaprálová must have ascended to her podium.

"Yes, well, this suit is rather holding me up." Karel glances over at Olga and the prompter. "Let's hope it continues to do so. Are we ready?"

"Soon," says Olga. With a disapproving scowl she reaches into his tuxedo pocket and withdraws, by the haft, the starter's pistol, handing it to Gideon.

"Mr. Čapek, Mr. Čapek, places please," says the prompter.

Josef galvanizes himself into action. With silent wavings of his arms he disperses his underlings. Olga leads Karel to the edge of the curtain, leaving Paul and Gideon by themselves, amidst the hanging sea-blue scrims.

"Care for a sidearm?" he offers it to Paul.

"I'd rather not."

Gideon shrugs and sets the pistol on Josef's desk. Behind them, silence has overtaken the hall, broken not by an introduction for Karel—who yet hovers in the wings—but by the crowd itself singing *Where is My Homeland*.

"Are you from Brno, Paul?" Gideon is staring askance at him.

The many-hued voices, unpracticed, unfocused, rush the backstage and infuse these strange scrims and sets—the sea-green grotto, the immense tavern table, a sea-scallop bicycle—with a hymn of another time and place.

Paul pretends to be rapt in the moment; and so does not reply to Gideon's question. And Gideon seems quite rooted. Paul feigns distraction, and so does not reply to Gideon's question. He lowers his head as the anthem plays out. Moments after, the applause rises, thunderous. Paul pictures Karel against the curtain, beneath the painted lunettes of Czech history, in front of the cameras and the crowd, nodding in that abrupt manner of his, lifting his free arm.

The applause continues, growing louder, the scrims begin to sway. Gideon grins, and the floor vibrates with great poundings as though all the well heeled in the audience are stamping their feet; or perhaps it is Wells ascending the corner stairs to the stage, for when Karel begins to speak, it's to welcome the Great Man.

"With you here, H.G.," Karel's voice echoes tremulously; indeed, it can be heard in the back of the room, "I know that we have embarked upon a remarkable evening together." Then, in broken English, Karel adds, "I wish to welcome those from our great ally of England to this, our little theater. And to those listening abroad in America, welcome."

"*We are here tonight, my friends, to attend a fantasy opera. I stand before you the co-author of the libretto, with my modest brother Josef. A fantasy opera, written in a land that seems to have sprung from fantasy. Perhaps that is why I have been asked to address you.*

"*I am often asked to proclaim the horticultural strangeness in our land a work of science fiction, as though my fictional Newts had raised it from the earth. But no. In fact, it is the work of Nature, not of Newt. The XXth century has done horrors to the earth, and is preparing us for many more horrors to come. And so the earth is responding.*

"*Or is this fantasy, on my part?*

"*Tonight, before this premiere of the Maestro's magnificent opera, I would like to offer a little prayer for peace, a prayer for little things, for lasting things.*

"*Tonight, here in this Theater on the Ramparts, we Czechs and English, we French and Italian, we Americans, we Canadians, we Australians, we Norwegians, we Icelanders—goodness, who am I forgetting—we have been brought together by large, turbulent issues. They carry us along like a land wave. We marvel at it. We are frightened by it. This century seems to pride itself on big things. On a recent trip to London—my second—I was enthralled by the underground railway and by the Parliament chambers and by the bustling streets. They seemed a necessary encounter, in a way, to help me wrap my mind around other big things that swirl around us at this point in history. We live in an age of vehement political entities to the right and left, and yes, they exist to the right and left of us here, in our little country.*

"*But tonight, I ask you all—and I ask also you who are listening to my voice in lands faraway, and those of you watching me on your theater screens* many days after this premiere—I ask you to reflect on little things. For we are a country that prides itself on its littleness.

"Big things bring us together, but at the same time they separate us. And they separate us cruelly. There are terrible wars between people of differing ideologies in the world. But never over little things. Never would associations of, say, people who breed long-haired rabbits wage violent war against associations of people who train carrier pigeons. Never would a class revolution arise between collectors of postage stamps from the Caribbean versus collectors of postage stamps from, oh, Saskatchewan. Around small things is an atmosphere of sacred calm. Roses, pigeons, dahlias, chess, cameras, canaries... Over small things a sacred peace hovers. Over small things we can find clarity. Over small things, we can see the truth of the larger world.

"And so, I ask that today, in this very small capital of Moravia, itself within the small but precious Czechoslovak Republic, I ask that you meditate on small and peaceful things."

"Paul. *Ts-ts*." Gideon prods his arm. "Come with me."

"Where?" He watches a blue submarine flower, twice as tall as he is, being wheeled past by nervous stagehands.

Gideon's eyes shine in the indirect light. "Before they close up the doors for good. Let's go to the Maestro's."

"Walk there?" He thinks of Tiege's telegram.

Gideon nods. "I think he'd like to see you, Paul."

They share a long moment in silence, before it's broken: Paul walks toward the back door.

The guard sighs as he unlocks it. "Crazy out there, Klein."

"Sorry. Have to." Gideon looks over. "Right?"

"Right," says Paul.

*"The jackal howls outside
the wind is blowing there,
lie down, my son,
sleep, sleep."*

—*Lullaby* by Gideon Klein

32. AN OVERGROWN PATH

Paul expects a noisy crowd beyond the door. Instead, but for the stentorian tones of H.G. Wells and his translator through speakers relaying the proceedings from inside the theater, the street is hushed. The door shutting behind them startles him with its loudness. He feels momentarily dislocated, remembering another time when he had stepped through that door into eerie silence; of another Brno overcome with grayish ivy and the signs of occupation.

"*It is our duty,*" says Wells, "*the duty of the Pax Humana, of the European nations, of the United States, to hold out with solidarity to our Czech brothers and sisters.*"

Gideon jostles him, then hurries to Dvorakova Street. Following, Paul senses the crowd in their strange hush; soon revealed as he and Gideon reach the edge of the theater. They stand there, hundreds upon hundreds, in Malinovského Square, staring up as though Wells were reading to them from the rooftops.

"*We must shape the shape of things to come,*" says Wells.

The evening is warm. The air carries a tang of bonfires and the plush sweetness of flowers. Wells' voice echoes along the narrow streets. "*We, the righteous. We stand with you tonight, Pane Čapek. All civilized people are here to stand with you tonight."*

Applause filtering through the loudspeakers seems to rouse the crowd behind them. Clapping like the rustling of startled birds, mixed with coarser cries and cheers and catcalls. Gideon, grinning sardonically, says, "The *Pax* has been broken."

Behind him—plastered against an entire storefront—is one of the Tiege montages. Up-close, the immense, grainy images are hard to comprehend—part of a face, a shouting mouth, a bayonet blade. Paul recalls the telegram and its final line, VIOLENCE WILL BE POETRY. He rushes past it, then stumbles to a halt. Not at the rustle of ivy choking the sidewalk, as Gideon seems to think at first, with a worried glance at Paul's shoes.

Paul stares up at her.

Magdalena, that day in the Cabbage Market, in her schoolgirl coat. Staring at something past his shoulder. On the poster somebody has scrawled in tall red letters: SHE HAS RETURNED.

Gideon says, "You've seen her today."

"Yes."

"On Špilberk."

Paul nods. Surprised, he looks at the young man.

"Do you worry about her safety?"

He begins to walk; Gideon follows.

"No," Paul says at last. But when Gideon signals that they turn right, to follow Ceska Street to the Maestro's cottage on the northern edge of town, Paul continues across Svobody Square, toward Špilberk. The tail end of a crowd can be seen, walking slowly through the street in the same direction. When they reach the edge of it, Paul hears snatches of conversation.

"It's she . . . "

" . . . came back . . . "

" . . . she's back . . . "

They speak softly, chaste, as though at worship. *"The one who vanished."*

"*Magda.*"

The voices almost inaudible against the distant broadcast of the American ambassador's speech.

As Paul and Gideon pass the Hotel Slavia and Špilberk rises into view, there comes to the air, blending one into the other, the lonely thread of a flute's melody over the thin and ever forward tumbling chime; the *Heartbeat of the World*.

This time it's Paul who takes Gideon's sleeve, leading him away from the crowd and to the north, back towards the Maestro's cottage.

The trombones, down distant streets, intone a soft and broken motif. The Maestro's *whirlwind*. Low strings lift in blocks of choral background, and the midnight blue they conjure is found in the sky over Kounicova Street.

"At last," says Gideon, stepping high over the ivy-choked cobbles. "He cannot rewrite it anymore."

The buildings here are dense with overgrown foliage. Moonlight silvers the trumpet vines that frame a doorway like natural filigree. From every vantage, flowers open their mouths to the moonlight, and Paul remembers the horns that float above President Masaryk's body; from those horns the Maestro's opera carries across Brno, the broken motif of *Ye Who Are the Soldiers of God* lifting in that strange patchwork as the Moravian folk song catches fire; yet distant, yet muted.

Lights gleam behind ivy and curtains. Some windows, open on the warm evening, are laced with tendrils of recent growth.

"Paul, have you ever read *The Fortress*?"

Surprised, Paul replies, "By Kafka?"

Gideon nods as he stares down; with his right hand in his pocket he seems to be weighing the pistol he no longer has.

"I haven't." But the others have, of course; Max Auspitzer and Gideon Weiss and the other Robots.

"I'm reminded of it tonight."

The breeze rustles the ivy, grass, tuber, petals. The growth has been chopped back here, at the edge of the cobblestone, yet rises in silvery surges near the walls.

"Tell me, Gideon."

Gideon smiles. "I'm told I often lecture. I'll try not to do so now."

"Please."

"Its narrator is a young man. From clues in the text, we can suppose he is about my age. Kafka never names him completely, giving him only a single letter. K., of course."

"Of course."

Gideon is quiet for several paces, seeming to decide his words in the rustling ivy. "I'm thinking of one passage in particular. The narrator is walking to a rendezvous. Where? You've no doubt heard the basics of *The Fortress*. Perhaps you saw Josef's illustrations? A city much like Brno, but set down in a landscape that is constantly changing beyond its walls. He likes to climb the battlements—battlements much like the remains of the oldest gates on Krenova Street—and peer out at mountains that had not been there the day before.

"He is haunted by nightmares. Though it's never stated so baldly, he becomes certain that what others consider a fortress is in fact a prison. All are deluded by this, yet all, with their genteel calm, refuse his wish to leave. Even his sisters."

Gideon pauses; perhaps to listen to the tenor voice—from an open window overhead, and from a dozen points behind them—singing bawdily of the river and the river sprite.

"He becomes certain," he continues, "that all of them are not only prisoners, but bound to be delivered one by one to the center of town. There, rather like Comenius's city, there's another structure. The little fortress, it's called. And though he has no proof, he's certain that he and his sisters and all those he loves are due to be exterminated there." Gideon lifts his hand, waving off the thought. "I'm lecturing, Paul. I apologize. There's one certain scene where he goes to visit a certain Prospero to tell him what he believes. It's nighttime. The streets are deserted. The Prospero's house is surrounded by a fantastical garden, and in the garden there's a dog named Shade."

Paul, surmounting the ivy with more difficulty, smiles, thinking of Cert.

"The dog is gentle, of course, but by the end of the novel there are other entities called Shade. Of no importance to my tale. I'm striving to—this Prospero, this mage, he's a little man with frightening diction, wild white hair. Frightening, really, to the young man. And he likes to say that he, once upon a time, was the architect who designed the little fortress, the entire city. The Fortress. He's an artist. And well, he's so much like—"

Gideon stops. Paul, who had been staring down at his shoes, looks up to find it rising from the cracked surface in the middle of the road. Gray in moonlight, green in shadow. An oblong head, a body with long arms that brush slowly against the cobblestones.

"That's recent," says Gideon, continuing on, watching the strangely-shaped tree sidelong. "It wasn't here two hours ago."

Paul wants to gesture to the music in the air—even as he's distracted by it, wanting to stop, to listen to the tenor and lyric soprano who, in vividly short melodic lines, are arguing about water sprites and Pilsner.

"It looks like a sentinel."

"A sylph," says Paul.

Gideon mutters *"A sylph,"* and glances over his shoulder at it.

"You've told me a story, Gideon, now let me tell you one. A little one my mother liked to tell." And Paul tells of the green sylph that appeared on the path of her old home village in Russia, hearing her voice as he tells it, seeing her, younger than she must be at this moment, at the house. He tells how the sylph's appearance portends that the old Czar is dead, that a new one has come, that nothing will ever be the same again.

345

But his story falters before the end, as the Conservatory rises into view, greener than he remembers it, laced with ivy, of course, and hemmed in by riotous growth. The same growth spills through the black-iron fence beyond it; the Maestro's garden lifting gold, green and yellow boughs close to the height of the Conservatory roof.

At their backs, the music has faded. A peaceful stillness settles over the garden.

A Presidential guard stands just inside the gate. Under broad green fronds and white flowers, he might be just another fantastical growth himself.

He steps forward, nods to Gideon and unlocks the latch, allowing the gate to swing wide. Gideon steps through, but Paul hesitates. Through the tubers and trunks, the cottage's bay window gleams with warm light. He's standing, too, in that other Brno, where the cottage had basked in moonlight, its windows broken, its flat roof damaged, its dark patina darkened further still.

Paul hears the sound of a radio and, inside, the barking of a dog. Not Cert, of course. Perhaps Cipera, the Pinscher? And Madame Janáčkova. And the Maestro, inside.

His heart is beating in his throat.

"Paul?"

Paul nods and follows Gideon in.

Fern fronds brush against his ankles. Though a path has been maintained, crossing the wild garden diagonally to the porch on the left, the fronds and leaves and flowers lean close overhead. Paul must duck to clear a fragrant blossom. He feels the path close up behind him even as it opens ahead; the Maestro's white table, where he would sit on many summer afternoons, remains beside the porch, chastely attended by the garden on all sides. The door stands open, while a mesh-screen door—a new, and no doubt necessary accouterment, is closed.

Paul studies the bay window, and the lamplight gleaming behind a curtain of lattice ivy. He sees movement; again, his heart beats in his throat.

At the door Gideon pauses and knocks gently.

A dog barks. Tail wagging, it appears, leaping at the mesh to Gideon's offered hand. "Cipera, Cipera, do not worry. I bring no more additions. It is done. Finished." He straightens. "Good evening, Madame."

"Mr. Klein."

In a soft voice, Gideon says, "It is true, Madame, I hope?"

Zdenka appears in the lamplight. Her careworn face is gentler than the one Paul had known—in that first iteration. But worry knits her brows, and deepens the lines under her eyes. Then a scowl, as she sees Paul. "He doesn't want to speak with anyone," she says, *sotto voce*. "Except Dr Vymola, about his shingles."

Gideon pulls open the screen door. "This isn't a reporter, Madame. I bring an old friend of the Maestro's."

She backs up, while Cipera leaps and barks. Paul wants to pet it and say, "Cipera, remember me."

"He does not want to see old friends, either, Mr. Klein. I insist."

"Madame, he will want to see this one."

She yields to the men now standing in her hallway, muttering a curse, shaking her head and walking the three paces back into the kitchen.

Gideon gives him a knowing glance, then gestures to the little hallway. But Paul cannot quite believe in that hallway, nor the parlor full of lamplight, nor the strange tintinnabulations that now become apparent in the close confines; the *Heartbeat of the World*. He is suddenly fourteen, summoned here from the Conservatory to see the Maestro; he is twenty, here with Osvald and Bretislava after class; he is thirty-one, alone in a ruined building . . .

"*Paul.*"

Gideon is down the hall. He steps out of view, into the study. And says gently, "Maestro?"

Terse, hushed, entirely familiar, a voice replies, "*Sssh! My music!*"

347

"An unknown old man stood in my room. It was Sunday, still quite early. A moment before, I had been sleeping deeply. Was I still dreaming? This head with its high, beautifully domed forehead, twinklingly serious big open eyes and curved mouth ... A name sounded in my dream: 'Leoš Janáček.'"

—Max Brod on his first encounter with Janáček

33. THE HEARTBEAT OF THE WORLD

He sits at his desk under green-shaded lamps. He wears a worn, white jacket that shines like his hair—snowy hair that yet thrives in various vertical directions, though sparser on the pate. The lamps are perched here and there on makeshift shelving, and his eyes catch fire from them as he gazes at the ceiling. His face, more seamed and wrinkled than before, basks in thoughtful chiaroscuro, his moustache dragging down at the corners of his mouth. His ears, ever large, are larger still with massive lobes.

One hand is raised for silence. He sits rigid, listening to the sounds that issue from the Philips radio atop a cluttered desk; its luminous green dial is but one of many in the cramped room; instruments of curiouser construction that seem part of the ancient Baseform *Scasovani* Generator in the corner; bronze, leather, iron, with copper tubing and Victrola horns hanging down from the ceiling, softly projecting the *Heartbeat of the World* in different cycles and tones.

The far and near—the luminous depths and the depths of the Theater on the Ramparts—fill the small office not only with sound but with small movements. On the Ehrbar piano, on the bookcases, stacked near the Maestro's chair, in the corners: little needles flick, diodes flash, gauges swing right to left, while the tenor voice sings of blood in the Vltava, and how the blood flavors the Pilsner of those who crowd the taverns.

"Maestro," intrudes Gideon, hovering at the door.

The hand raises, fingers stiffen. "Look! You see. A nine point jump," he murmurs, then turns to the desk and a booklet sitting there. In furious scrawl he records the numbers. "Ever since the baton was lifted! The *scasovani* has been responding in increasing proportions."

Gideon looks helplessly at Paul. Then, "But the night is very quiet, Maestro. The crowds—both enemies and friends—are engrossed in your opera."

"Yet there is great work being done, Mr. Klein, *underground*." The eyes twinkle. He turns stiffly in his chair back to the desk and the radio.

"Maestro? I brought a visitor to see you."

An irritable wave. "I said no visitors. Please. Until tomorrow I am turning away everyone. Even Mr. Wells, whom Čapek wants to bring by after the concert. Nobody!"

Paul senses movement behind him; Zdenka, hovering in the hall, awaiting an order to throw the guests out.

"Please, Maestro. Make an exception for him. He's . . . familiar to you, yes?"

As the Maestro turns from the radio, as his eyes fix on Paul's face and his brow furrows, Paul tries to speak. Yet he is sixteen, once again, nervous, afraid that any answer will be wrong. But then the years wash away and he is fifty-one and strong. Most strong. "Maestro. It is I."

The Maestro's arm drops to his lap. He squints up. "You?"

Paul steps into the study; a single step before his knees encounter another module of equipment, but he feels the lamplight striking his face. And more importantly, striking the key that he now lifts out from under his collar; the green key with its cameo of Olga, glinting in the light as it turns and turns.

The Maestro's head inclines; towards the piano, and to his daughter's portrait above it and the identical key that hangs there.

"*You.*" A whisper.

The Maestro blindly grasps for something; a walking stick. He heaves himself to his feet, his hair glowing green then yellow then white as he straightens. Against the music, against the distant icy clatter from Victrola horns that seems to set the domeček to canter like a ship at sea, he strives for balance. "*My California pilgrim?*"

"Leoš?" Zdenka, in the doorway. "Is there a problem?"

A smile—swift, forceful—appears beneath the wilted moustache. He whispers, "*No, Zdenici.*" And to Gideon: "Take her, please, into the kitchen."

"Come, Madame. You can show me the recipe for *pig's chin.*"

After a pause, she retreats with Gideon at her heels.

"*You.*" Leoš Janáček reaches out to touch Paul's sleeve. "You are *real.* Yes. As I always knew."

"I am most pleased to see you, Maestro."

"That day, you saved me and lit a fire beneath me." He gestures expansively. "All this because of what you showed me that day. I wrote of our encounter but they would not publish it. And now Čapek's sister says it is lost from the files—"

"I have it, Maestro."

"You?"

"*The Heartbeat of the World.*"

The eyes soften. Then something like fear darkens his face. "And who . . . what are you? Sent from the *scasovani?*"

"I—"

"You seem different to when we last met." He steps even closer, peers up. "You have not aged, yet . . . "

"I have found your village, Maestro."

And at this, the Maestro can only stagger back into his chair, slump down beside the radio while mumbling to himself, "My village?"

"The green baize hermitage, the little row of shops. The church in the forest."

"You found it?"

"Yes, Maestro. It was . . . in ruins. All but the little church in the forest."

The Maestro rubs his chin, staring down at the peasant carpet. "And a bell, ringing. From there, its source?"

"A holy crypt."

"Cyril and Methodius . . . ?"

"No. Even older, I believe."

"You *found it*," he whispers.

Paul hears combers of ocean waves on the shore; he thinks of Capitola before recognizing the sound for what it is. He gestures to the radio. "They are applauding, Maestro. The act has come to a close."

The Maestro's eyes snap wider open. He fumbles for the notebook on his desk, turns to some of the nearest dials, then his shoulders relax. "I cannot worry myself with science at the moment." He adds, cryptically, "If you had told Abbot Mendel that I would one day follow in his footsteps . . . " He turns down the radio volume, leaving only the icy clatter and stirrings. He straightens. "Tell me! Tell me your story, sir!"

And in a hesitant voice he begins the story of the Pilgrim, carefully, starting with the trip from Hukvaldy to Prague to Brno, and his subsequent movements through Space and Time. And for perhaps the first and only time in his life, the Maestro listens and does not interrupt.

"I took it on faith, sir!" Now standing, the Maestro leans on his cane. "My dear Kamilka. I strived to find the secrets of the *scasovani*, to preserve her life." He gestures to the portrait hanging beside Olga's above the desk; Kamila Stösslová at his side in their Hukvaldy garden. "I tried, yet failed. But always I thought of what you told me that afternoon. I knew that I was on the trail of it. Just as it knew, sir!" He stops, panting.

"Please Maestro, sit down."

But the Maestro has wheeled about and now forces his way to the corner of the study—past the bulky and unusual machinery whose lights blink like Christmas displays. He sets his cane aside; it clatters to the carpet. Paul hears Gideon in the kitchen—in fact he sees him peering through the door that opens on the bedroom in between, and Zdenka also, anxiously peering before Gideon shuts the door.

"Maestro, can I help you?"

He holds it firmly in both hands—a thick notebook, privately bound, overflowing with octavo sheets. "I trailed it! In here!"

Paul sees where the Maestro intends to place it and pushes aside the desktop clutter.

"That afternoon, while I was waiting for the doctor—" he turns back the cover and presents the first page. "My Californian! My Cyril and Methodius from out of nowhere." A speech melody, and Paul's own words scrawled in the Maestro's vivid hands.

If you do not seek a physician today, if you do not check into a hospital, then you will be dead within a week.

"And the doctor—he told me, a week longer, and *poof*! Goodbye, Maestro!"

Paul gestures to the chair; the Maestro sits, grunting. His hands anxiously tap the pages. "And here, it began. A newfound involvement. For you came to me moments after it appeared. And howso sir, if you were not connected to it?"

"I have some theories, Maestro. But other than that I can assure you I have no connection to it."

But to you, Maestro, yes.

Paul thinks of Magdalena reaching for the stave flower; Magdalena disappearing into the branches of the tree.

"Your writings, Maestro. They are things of power."

The Maestro peers at Paul, trying to discover a lie perhaps, but finding none, "Your voice." He turns the page. "I tried to work it out. Its familiarity. But failed, sir, because you had the scarf muffling your lips."

"But not now, Maestro."

"No." His snowy brow furrows. "Not now."

"Maestro, I can show you. My own . . . instrument of power."

I must show you.

He is aware of Klein opening the door; Klein, who in another time and place had inspired Pavel Haas to write something, *anything*, in the Fortress Terezin.

"What is this?"

Paul opens the lid. "It's merely the carrying case." Then, gently, he reaches in and feels the parchment. In the many days of its confinement, the paper has changed. It has assumed the same curves as the Universal tube, so that when Paul tugs it out it comes easily, its many folds and points now swept back like the petals of a newborn flower.

"No..."

He had expected a reaction from the Maestro—but only after he unfolded it. Here, only the faintest of purple flecks are visible on the silvery paper, but the Maestro's visage has been galvanized. His shoulders go back, yet he leans toward the stave flower. Reaching with a shaking hand. "How..."

"This is the instrument, Maestro. Of my travel."

"Kafka..." He touches it with trembling fingers.

"A *shem*," says Paul. "A gift. Inspired by your theories, Maestro. Written by a... an admirer of yours." He recalls Herr Schoenberg on the patio, in the luminous sunlight.

As he gently separates the seams, revealing more of the tiny, innumerable staves, the piano groans low in its strings, and then the many instruments in the room begin to vibrate and ping and light up. And the Maestro too lights up.

"How..."

The stave flower unfolds between them, the Maestro and he opening it gently, larger and larger. Gideon has stepped into the bedroom, closing the door behind him. His eyes are large. He hovers uncertainly in the distance, and Paul wants to say, Gideon, you helped to inspire this.

Plower, plow. Sower, sow.
awake and labor,
redeem and be redeemed.

You put the pen in my hand, at Terezin. You exhorted me to write, Gideon.

From the Victrola horns the heartbeat triples. The windows rattle. In the corner the tuning forks on the Baseform *Scasovani* Generator chime in sympathetic vibration.

"We should not unroll—" Paul begins.

But the Maestro must see more. "The young man brought a scrap—" he says, and unfolds another corner, while the room shivers with movement—glass tinkling, Gideon grabbing for support on the door jamb, and somewhere far off Zdenka is crying out. Something shudders beneath the domeček, while past the salon, outside the bay window, something stirs in the garden ruins, lifting up, bristling and black and huge, sprouting leaves of silver.

"Leoš Janáček was waiting for me in the small garden of the Conservatoire. He sat among the bushes, with thousands of tiny white blossoms shining round his head; that head of his was equally white, and seemed to be the biggest of those flowers. He smiled, and I immediately knew that this is the smile which life presents to us like a gold medal for bravery in the face of the enemy; for bravery in sorrow, adversity and hatred."

—Rudolf Těsnohlídek

34. CEKAM TE!

By the time they reach the front door—having calmed Madame Janáčkova to a degree where leaving her is possible—the garden has ceased moving.

Paul steps out. Immediately he feels a steady rain of dirt particles. Leaves tussle and fall in the moonlight. Farther away—and yet nearer—the radio has begun its broadcast of Act 2, strange and nervous strettos in the low strings and high woodwinds that gild the branches of the huge new growth as surely as does the moonlight.

He knows it, of course. The tree had greeted him in that other Brno; had taken Magdalena away from him. Yet there is a difference this evening. The silver and black leaves—pointed, sharp—are not yet tinged with blood.

Atop the Conservatory roof, beyond the decorative balustrade, a good dozen Parliamentary police gaze down; and from the windows too; the Maestro's hidden security now in plain view, and astounded.

Maestro Janáček pushes past him, planting his cane firmly in the freshly turned soil of his garden and gesturing with his other hand, which clutches his bound notebook. Other than the tree, the wild growth that had risen past his rooftop has been cast down and away, toppling the fence and opening up a view to the street. "Friend!" The Maestro tips back his head. "It is music that draws you!"

Not the notebook surely, but the stave flower that yet remains in the Maestro's study.

The tree rises, twice as tall as Paul remembers it, spearing into the starry sky.

"You are not a bashful one!"

Paul must take the Maestro's arm to help him past the roots and torn branches, for he wishes to approach the tree. Recalling how the branches had lunged for the stave flower, Paul holds firm on the Maestro's arm. "Please, Maestro, be careful."

"But it has come to see me!"

"Leoš!" Madame from inside, with Gideon at her side. "Away from me!" she says to the young man. "Leoš, we are leaving at once!"

"Quiet, woman!"

"Maestro. Come. Sit at the table."

Paul leads him to the white table beside the porch; the table now covered in dirt, as are the chairs sitting unevenly on the ground. The Maestro sits and, at least for a few seconds, abides.

Perhaps he's listening to his opera. Certainly, the silhouettes of guards atop the Conservatory seem to be dividing their attention between the music coming from distant streets and the crown of the tree rising past their vantage point.

Gideon emerges from the house, slouching past with hands in his pocket, staring up. He ducks—hoping no doubt that the Maestro will miss him and won't order him to return to Madame—and approaches the guards who have gathered near the gate. There, they murmur, light cigarettes, smoke.

"You too are a far traveler," says the Maestro. He sits in the gloom, looking not at the tree but at Paul.

"I am."

"*California* you once told me. Yet your voice betrays you."

Paul is slow to speak.

"Tell me, Mr. Arepo. What of our future? We Czechs."

We Czechs.

Paul sees Masaryk's body floating in solemn midnight blue. He hears the faint heartbeat; he feels it now, tingling on the backs of his hands, on his cheeks and chin.

In the street the guards step back. Gideon straightens, points.

"I was once told a prophecy." The Maestro opens his notebook. "Of the Jews of our Republic in dire trouble." He turns to an empty page then pats the pocket of his dusty suitcoat, locating his pen. "I have seen that prophecy materialize, sir. But not just for the Jews. For all peoples in our land."

"It will be difficult, Maestro." After watching Gideon, who steps back into the garden, his back to them, Paul adds, "Another *White Mountain*, certainly. But now, there is great hope."

On the street three young men pass by. They wear the uniforms of 9forces. They ignore the guards, ignore Gideon. They stare in wonder at the tree and before passing into the distance, they spy the Maestro seated at his little table beside the porch, amid the sundered garden. One nods. One touches two fingers to his forehead. One simply stares.

The Maestro nods, his pen poised on the paper, his eyes afire. "Yes! It will be bloody! But we are ready to fight!" With swift motions of his hand, he sketches three stave lines. "And now. You." The Maestro leans forward. "I know you."

Paul stiffens his shoulders.

Another group of young men walks by. These are not 9forces. Their hair is bright blond. They are silent, as though processing along a church nave.

"You are familiar to me. Beyond the Hukvaldy forest. Yet I cannot . . . "

Paul says nothing; and the Maestro is only briefly distracted by the young people passing by.

A woman with an SdP armband lays a garland on the ground before continuing.

"Tell me. Why did you do this?"

Why?

Plower, plow.

Sower, sow.

"Why?" Paul mutters.

"My mitzvah," he begins to say.

The Maestro's pen hovers over the paper.

He thinks of Sona in bed beside him. The rhomboid of lamplight from Delmonica drive. And—intensely—of Olinka and little William and the rock dredged up by the sea that now sits, unnoticed, in the Čapeks' garden. Sona, Olinka, Willie, all of them frozen in time, as surely as Masaryk's body. An instant that will be returned to. Held in check, by the mitzvah.

"I came to offer my service, sir. To help you, Maestro, and Gideon. For the fight."

At this, the pen scritches on the paper, dabbing notes and bar lines; and Janáček leans close to the *nápěvky mluvy*, shaping it with further addenda, then, after a pause, the Maestro's eyebrows lift in surprise.

Paul watches the procession on the sidewalk. The stream of passersby is now constant. Some pause, briefly, to lay wreaths or branches or rocks on the ground beside the fallen gate; some gaze up at the tree but most merely gaze toward the little cottage and the little man with the white hair, who sits at the table beside the porch.

On the breeze, audible over the ghostly *scasovani* and the radio broadcast, a flute lifts and fades.

The Maestro has not looked away from Paul. As his pen lifts from the paper he says, softly, "I know you."

His eyes twinkle.

The flute, lifting and falling.

"Yes, Maestro."

Wreath, branch, rock.

The young people, both SdP and 9forces among the locals. Some touch their foreheads. Some press their hands to their hearts.

My homeland, they whisper.

The Maestro tears off the notebook page, the breeze tries to catch it but his fingers hold it firmly. "*Pavel.*" And again, an incantation: "*You are Pavel Haas.*"

Paul takes the annotated page from the Maestro's extended hand.

Dr. Leoš Janáček smiles courteously, closes his notebook and sets his pen atop. "I *have you.*"

As the last of those who have come to pay homage walk past the great tree and the sundered garden, Magdalena's flute once more lifts the familiar twists and turns of a melismatic melody close-by. The Maestro straightens in his chair, leans forward.

His ears hear large.

She holds the flute, which flashes golden against her white hand, and the garden trembles, seeming to yearn for the red fire of her hair.

In her wake, shy petals lift above the cobblestones.

AFTER

ROTAS, OPERA, TENET, AREPO, SATOR

Outside, the weather has turned lousy. The curtains are drawn and he is happy to be in the warmth of the living room surrounded by his paintings, in Brentwood, in 1949.

Madame has made him Earl Grey tea which he sips while studying the latest meticulous score sheet.

"Arne," she says, from the window.

"Close the drapes." He wants to neither see nor hear the rain. Better to try to complete the day's work.

Madame Schoenberg turns from the window near the wet bar. "Arne, there's a man out there."

"What, my dear?"

"A man, walking out of our tennis court."

Schoenberg can only think of poor Gershwin and the pleasure of matches long past gone. He rises slowly, and walks slowly to join her. His bones are tired this day. But he feels renewed, true, by the warmth of her presence, and tries to ease her fears by laying his hand gently on her shoulder. By the time he looks through the window the tennis court, the path—indeed the entire property—is absent of any visitors. For an instant he follows the shimmering silver rain out and farther out to a hint of tangerine sunlight. "Whoever it was, my dear, they were merely passing through."

He pulls shut the drapes and leads her back to the warmth of the living room.

"Let Spring build green vaults over the pioneer work of Autumn. We underground forces have done our duty."

—*The Gardener's Year*
by Karel Čapek, 1929

ACKNOWLEDGMENTS

My thanks to Pete Crowther for publishing this trilogy; Nick Gevers for shepherding the project to completion; Jim Goddard for his thoughtful and meticulous editing of this present volume, and for his ever-present wit and cheerfulness, much needed. Hearty thanks also to Vlad Verano for the beautiful art (check out Vlad's other work at Mystery Monotreme.com), Robert Wexler for the lovely insides, and Brian Stableford for the introduction. Sandra Bennett did much to shape the project in its early stages. Therese Littleton met me regularly for coffee and made me feel like an actual cool author. Ted Chiang, Peter Orullian and Fleetwood Robbins helped to keep me somewhat sane in the world of publishing. Christopher Paul Carey was everpresent with friendship and support, and many late night conversations that somehow tended to triangulate around Bob Dylan, Doug McClure and Ignatius Donnelly.

John Tyrrell's two-volume masterwork, *Janáček: Years of a Life* was crucial to this book. Also *My Life with Janáček: the Memoirs of Zdenka Janácková*, edited and translated by John Tyrrell, *Arnold Schoenberg's Journey* by Allen Shawn, *The Coasts of Bohemia: A Czech History* by Derek Sayer, *A Double Life* by Miklós Rózsa, *Jewish Brno* by Jaroslav Klenovský, and *Toward the Radical Center: a Karel Capek Reader*, edited by Peter Kussi. My thanks to Robert Wechsler, publisher of Catbird Press, for his kind permission to quote from the *Reader*.

While Leos Janáček's life has been fully documented, there are few-to-none English-language resources on Pavel Haas save some insightful liner notes. By the time I began writing *One Who Disappeared* I managed to track down the Czech-language biography Pavel Haas by Lubomír Peduzzi, one of Haas's students; but this slim volume is more an appreciation of Haas's music paired with a very straight forward biographical essay. Thus, the Paul, Sona and Olga Haas in my book remain more my fantasy of them than a true portrait. I hope that everyone will forgive the artistic license.

Hugo Haas did indeed emigrate to Hollywood, where he wrote, starred and directed in a number of B pictures's, including *Pickup*, *Edge of Hell*, and *Lizzie*, an adaptation of Shirley Jackson's *The Bird's Nest*. He has yet to have his work properly represented on VHS, let alone DVD. A new look is needed, especially regarding his still-beloved Czech films, which I've had no luck obtaining. For those curious to see Hugo in action I would recommend the 1951 *King Solomon's Mines*, where he plays a sort of Colonel Kurtz type named Von Brunn. Hugo died in 1968. To the end of his days he refused to discuss his brother.

Karel Capek had always been in precarious health. After the signing of the Munich pact, his health deteriorated ('stabbed in the heart,' suggested some wag, 'by Neville Chamberlain's umbrella'). He died of double-pneumonia on Christmas day, 1938.

When the Nazis invaded the Czechoslovak Republic, they made Karel's arrest a top priority, unaware that he was no longer among the living. At the Capek's house they found Josef instead, and arrested him. He spent the war at Buchenwald, later moved to Sachsenhausen, and finally to Bergen-Belsen, where he died just weeks before the German surrender.

Unlike his brother, Josef's oeuvre is not well known outside the Czech world, which is a pity. His short stories, children's books (some translated into English), art books, stage designs are all wonderfully charming and unique. A biography was recently published in Czech; here's hoping for an English translation.

David Herter is a graduate of Clarion West 1990, where his instructors included Gene Wolfe. In 2004 he spent a month in the Czech Republic celebrating the 150th anniversary of Leoš Janácek's birth, an experience that led to his Czech trilogy *On the Overgrown Path*, *The Luminous Depths*, and *One Who Disappeared*. His other novels include the far-future *Ceres Storm*, the Vernian cheese fantasy *Evening's Empire*, and the Halloween horror *October Dark*. Forthcoming is epic planetary romance *The Cold Heavens*, inspired by C.L. Moore, Gustav Meyrink, and Weimar Berlin. He lives in Seattle, Washington. Visit his blog at www.davidherter.blogspot.com.